THE ANCHOR OF TIME

TINA CAPRICORN

LUPUS OBSIDIAN
PUBLISHING

For my mother, who never doubted and whose kindness must be from Aoer-Eterna or some other place beyond the stars.

---

*And for my moon and stars, the lights of my life, MALT house —
thank you.*
This book also belongs to you.

PREFACE

*"**Y**ou will mark Her return by the wolf and the*
warrior—and a mortal's reoccurring dream.
The Death Bringer, ever Binding and ever Bound,
will Anchor Time with the turn of the tide
On the shores of the Obsidian Sea..."

———

Elderaen Folklore and Myth Through the Ages Volume I. Vincent Lemair. publishing date unknown.

PROLOGUE

NEW-ASHEMORE, AMARANTHINE LOOP

Vincent's throat felt like gravel. But he couldn't stop speaking—couldn't stop repeating her last words to him. He inhaled, the air at dawn clawing against his exposed skin. The darkened windows of the closed storefronts lining the street reflected his image. He was naked. Daybreak and the sleeping streets of New-Ashemore his only witness.

He opened his eyes and held a trembling palm to his face. He noticed the stain of blood on his fingers.

Vincent felt her blood inside him, drowning him in a millennia-old sorrow he thought he accepted long ago. Her power raged inside him. He winced, attempting to subdue the excess of energy causing his fingertips to spark and sizzle, lighting the surface of his skin with a golden incandescence.

Glowing vapor swirled around him. His core Elder-spark, energy that had been endowed to him at almost the beginning of time, was a golden fog pluming behind his shoulders like a cape. The energy, free and delirious, flowed over him, like water being released to save a dam. It was the only way he could conceive to keep upright.

He felt tears prick his eyes, a small surprise.

Suddenly, as if appearing out of nothingness, a lone figure stood before Vincent. Backlit by the pink sky behind it, the figure was only discernible by its silhouette.

"A dream and a prayer, are they not the same for a goddess? At least, I think that's how the story goes. I admit, I haven't finished reading your Volumes on Elder folklore and mythology, but I do remember the story of the Eight Maidens. It was the first story Maman told me." The voice was decidedly male, raspy, with a soft accent.

Vincent stared in silence, struck by the sudden appearance of the mysterious figure.

"Like clockwork," the figure continued. "This is the only spot. I never find you at any other point."

Vincent growled. He lowered his hands, clenching them at his side.

"A strange duality that I can enter at this point," the figure spoke again, not acknowledging Vincent's wordless warning. "The moment after my darkest legacy. Ironic you might say." The figure paused, as if choosing the right words.

Vincent straightened his spine and narrowed his gaze. He calmed himself and felt the familiar tingle of energy buzzing and pricking against the surface of his skin. Whoever was before him was a common and unyielding adversary—a Tracker, a being rivaling only Elders in age.

Vincent's eyes glowed in anticipation, hovering over the figure still managing to be obscured by the timid light of the early morning.

"Salut Vincent, Ça va?" the figure said, and took a step forward, letting the light slowly illuminate its features. The Tracker had on a smart, dark-gray suit—the iron line of his gray office slacks pointing straight down to his black, polished shoes. His face was distinct. A large nose complemented his robust mustache. His eyes were framed with tangled and arguing eyebrows that snarled and sloped across the plane of his forehead. His hair was combed back and was so shiny it looked wet. His body was mortal and had aged probably sixty to seventy Earth years.

Vincent sputtered, disbelieving his senses. The energy signature was that of a Tracker but also human, and alive. Trackers usually inhabited human corpses, stealing them from death. The Tracker spark would emulate the human, like a wolf in sheep's clothing, but could not revive the being. The entity before him was more than a walking corpse—this Tracker had a heartbeat and vitality to its flesh.

"I come from another time," the Tracker began again. "I am not what I was before, what I was to you. We are no longer enemies then—in my time—which of course is also now—"

Vincent shook his head. He stared past the edifice of the Tracker's physical body and looked within, to the recesses of the cells, searching for the hidden spark of power that would reveal the Tracker's identity.

Vincent's eyes widened.

"Aldric!" he gasped. "Do not think to manipulate me—" he snarled. "You are changed, more alive than before—part *human.*"

"I am reborn," Aldric began. "I balance no Ledger, nor do I Track the Count of All Things." He paused, locking eyes with Vincent. "I come to you at the turn of the tide. You are lost in an unraveling Amaranthine loop."

Aldric's words began to penetrate Vincent's disbelief. He swallowed, observing the Tracker before him more closely. Aldric's eyes softened as he met Vincent's gaze.

"Too bad neither of you can remember the Future War," Aldric said, blinking a few times. "She is still lost in time, but the degradation of this temporal reality suggests she may find you here sometimes. Look at me, I'm living proof!" He chuckled, opening his palms.

"Impossible," Vincent said, still staring intently at Aldric with disbelief. "This cannot be. You were destroyed in Aeor-Eterna."

"Aeor-Eterna is a peculiar place with many secrets. A fragment of ancient and sentient power that even Elders during the Future War underestimated," he replied, sighing. He scanned Vincent's body, his eyes lingering on his blood-stained hands. "And *that* wouldn't have happened. I regret my part in it, I truly do—as much as one can regret the actions of their ancestors. I cannot change the past Vincent, but I am attempting to save your future."

Vincent stared, silent. Aldric removed his hand from the inside of his suit jacket, producing a slim metallic case.

"I explain this to you every time we meet. I don't know why I bother repeating myself." He smiled sadly, and opened the case, withdrawing a cigarette and lighting it with almost a sleight of hand.

"Renata—" Vincent said, grasping his head.

"There is power and truth in a name. She told me that once," Aldric said, blowing smoke into the morning air. He smiled, his eyes crinkling in the corners again.

For a split second, Vincent felt a vague awareness that Aldric's eyes had distinct similarities to hers... the paleness of the green, the slant of his brow.

"You don't remember what she is, do you?" He snorted, breaking free of Vincent's penetrating gaze. He took a long drag from the cigarette and slowly let out a cloud of smoke from his lips. "Mierde. This time loop is your prison. It is an Amaranthine, so the longer you stay, the more you forget. No wonder you wrote so many books of Elder history, you were trying to hold on to your memories!"

"My library?" Vincent said, squinting.

"Oui. At some point, you must have known you existed in an Amaranthine. I can imagine you also wanted to forget. For some, war never ends." His brows creased as he took another long pull off the cigarette.

"Amaranthine loop..." Vincent replied quietly, his blood burning anew. His eyes crackled with Elder light, his body levitating slightly. His blood stained hands contracted into fists. His inconceivable grief and rage had returned.

"Oui," Aldric said. He dropped the cigarette to the ground, mashing the cherry with his heel. "Keeping the last living Elder trapped in a time prison balanced the Ledger. That, and your sister's... commitment." He gave Vincent a knowing look. "Now that you've absorbed her spark, the Amaranthine has no power and is unraveling. If I let you remain, you will be destroyed." He paused, looking at the crushed cigarette butt on the ground and flicking some ash of the cigarette off his shoe. "Unravelling also an Anchor Point. The idea! It contradicts all the temporal laws I know of time and space! Impossible, oui? Just like someone else we both know." He winked.

"It is not possible to change an Anchor," Vincent mumbled.

"As you would say, tricky—"

"It is an *absolute*."

Aldric grinned. "Oui, but she has never let that stop her before." His expression grew serious, but he didn't pause. The words fell out of his mouth as if he'd said it a hundred times before. "Please, forgive me."

Suddenly, he clicked the metallic cigarette case closed, and a shrill sound pierced the air.

Vincent winced in agony, placing his hands over his ears. His body exploded into golden dust, coating the pavement like grains of sand.

"Would you believe me if I said it would hurt worse if I let you remain?"

Aldric clicked a smooth button on the end of the case. Every golden kernel and scrap that was once Vincent the Elder rose off the ground and spun like a cyclone into a hole the size of a pin, located on the bottom of the cigarette case.

"The funny part is, you would think the Amaranthine loop your penance," he mumbled. "I'm sure you're aware, at this moment, that you have yet to understand what penance is."

Once the last bit of golden grit was safely ensconced,

he opened the other side of the case and produced another cigarette. He lit it, squinting into the morning light, and exhaled.

"It's the only way to save you," he cursed at the sunrise, "Papa."

1

LUPUS OBSIDIAN, CERULEAN DIMENSION

A ldric pressed the smooth panel on a waist-high counter that served as the interface of the quantum computer Centius. The screen projected a hologram at eye level, its warm, burnt-umber light reflecting off his hollow cheeks.

He inserted the thin metallic case that also served as a niche cigarette wallet on his frequent outings to the Amaranthine loop. It was the only time he smoked and the only vice he allowed himself—the Quantum travel radiated and aged his body, weakened his bones, and sallowed his complexion. What harm was a cigarette after all?

His gnarled fingers brushed the slot by the interface, letting go of the unblemished metal square. Aldric looked up, observing the Time Lab's walls. Centius was a sprawling Quantum-Supercomputer encompassing the entire Time Lab with transparent panes. The golden sand behind the panes were essentially Centius' CPU.

The panes themselves were evenly spaced with metallic

frames interlocking them symmetrically, creating an entire hexagonal room. Behind the panes, golden sand spun shapes and patterns—acknowledging the disc and his contribution.

Aldric turned back to the holographic screen, observing the calculations that were speeding across it and gasped.

"Only one remains," he whispered. He unconsciously stroked his wide mustache that had more gray than brown in it these days.

"Papa!" a sprite, feminine voice said. In an eye-blink, a young woman appeared in the Lab. She had tight red-orange curls that fell well below her waist. Aldric couldn't help his smile when she bounded into the room.

She came to stand beside him, staring at the holographic screen. The subsequent results Centius displayed caused her next few words to tumble out in a flurry.

"The Amaranthine is unraveling!"

Aldric nodded, and leaned down to kiss her on the cheek. "Ça va, Peaches," he said.

"There is only one more loop, Papa!" she sputtered. "It is collapsing at last—"

"I would not believe it," he said, his voice quiet. He grasped his daughter by the shoulder, hugging her against him as he watched the numbers speed across the screen. "But Centius is never wrong." He kissed the crown of her head.

"These Quantum calculations are unassailable Papa," she replied, beaming up at him. "You've done it!"

"Almost," he said, relaxing his grip on her. "There is still one left."

"I could go," she said, disengaging from him. She looked up. He could feel her taking in his age—the creases on his forehead, his silver hair, and sloping posture. "Papa, I could go."

"Non, ma choupinette," he replied, looking down and locking eyes with her. Her blue eyes—they had the same vibrancy his mother's had, different color, but the same vibrancy.

He let his fingers glance down the side of his daughter's cheek, her unblemished ivory skin contrasting against his gnarled, withered fingers. Traveling to the Amaranthine loop had accelerated his aging, the human cost of the Quantum missions he had been conducting.

"I'm worried about you," she said, sliding in for another hug, her head snuggling beneath his chin. Her hair had a light floral scent.

"I know," he said, stroking her hair. "But we must finish. I made a promise, chérie."

Peaches let go, looking at her father.

"I didn't know your promise would cost this much," she said, reaching up to his face. Her fingers touched the silver in his temple.

"That is just vanity speaking," he said, brushing off her fingers. "I am like a fine wine, I just get better with age."

"Papa," she said, frowning. "When is the next opening in the Amaranthine?"

"Soon," he said, stepping down from the dais with the holographic screen and interface. His legs shook a little as he stepped down the short stair, and he gripped the railing for support. Peaches remained, observing him critically. "I will rest and take in a few liters of Quantum-fluerites. My strength will return—"

"The Quantum-fluerite drip isn't working as well as it used to," she said, following her father. "You've gone too many times. You haven't been able to properly recover. Another reason you should let me—it is only once more!"

"Non," Aldric said in French, his voice low and authoritative. "C'est pour moi—it is for me alone."

Peaches nodded, her expression resigned. They both knew when he used that tone there was no arguing.

"Will you see her?" she asked, following him down the stair.

"Her?" he replied, turning to look at his daughter. He knew who she referenced but wanted to hear her say it all the same. He had been bracing for this conversation.

"Grand-mère. Renata," she said, her voice hushed, as if afraid to utter the name.

"Ma pétite," he said, his eyes softening. He extended his hand, entreating her to walk with him to the medical suite. "She is lost in time. It was an accident, decades before you were born..." He smiled sadly, his eyes crinkling with the effort. "Peaches, mon coeur—there is always risk during these missions. Your grand-mère is an extraordinary being. She escaped the Amaranthine once already, this Lab as well as I are the product of that. She knew better than most the effect of tampering with time..." He trailed off, his dull eyes distant with memory. "I have Quantum circuits dedicated to finding the computation that will yield her relative time and location, I've been searching for centuries—"

"Centius has evidence of her existence—" she interrupted.

"That is not enough, I need a time lock and location lock before she can be accurately found. The technology in this Lab is limited to the technology when she and I built it. Your assistance updating the equipment promises that we are likely to find a more accurate space-time lock but, it is difficult to lock on an eighth dimensional being. I more often than not find out merely where she's been—"

"You know the Amaranthine unraveling cannot be mere coincidence," Peaches said, almost vibrating. "The Binder and the Bound, there is a thread she can follow back to us! It *must* be her."

Aldric stopped, turning to his daughter. He bracketed her shoulders with his hands, looking her square in the eye. He sighed. He knew how much she wanted the evidence of Renata's return to be true. Of all the things she wanted in this world, it was a family. It was a truth about her that defied space, time, and dimensions. He frowned at her with sympathy. It was just him and the Lupus Obsidian for Peaches—it was all she knew.

"Before my last excursion, I calculated Quantum-form axioms with Centius. I could not come up with a definitive probable event that could explain why the Amaranthine had begun to unravel," he said, looking at his daughter, feeling the weariness of his search through time. "Believe me, I wanted it to be her, but the math never came together." He pinched his fingers and shook his hand. "So, I am choosing to do what I have always done, retrieve as much of Vincent as I can. With the final loop upon us, I think that was the wisest choice." He looked at Peaches—her bright expression, her eyes hungry for knowledge, and an awareness that the knowledge she needed most was out of reach.

"But the radiation spikes—" she protested.

"Centius has been monitoring the radiation around the Gate. The levels are fluctuating, but not enough to cause the collapse of an Amaranthine," Aldric said, defending his position. "The fluctuations could just as easily be due to our entanglement with the Gate—"

"When she made the Gate during your escape—"

"You're giving me a lot of credit in this escape," he interrupted, winking at her. "Your grand-mère did not even realize she was pregnant with me when she left the Amaranthine loop the first time—"

"Fine, *her* escape," Peaches said, rolling her eyes. "The electrons entangled with the Time Lab's Gate are emitting a similar radiation to that of an Anchor *of Time*—"

"Oui," he said. He raised an eyebrow, waiting for her to continue.

"So we agree on that at least," she huffed, blowing an orange curl out of her face. "Then you must also agree that an Anchor of Time has slightly different mass, why did you and Centius exclude that in your most recent study—"

He sighed, weary. "Whatever mass you use, either Anchor Points or Anchors of Time, the results are still not definitive. The radiation confirms that time travel occurred. Is this *her* time travel? Perhaps. But it is likely due to mine—from my initial exit as well as subsequent returns."

Peaches crossed her arms, her enthusiasm deflating.

"The Gate's existence itself is a Quantum anomaly—"

Aldric droned on. "All of these could contribute to the Amaranthine's degradation. There is no irrefutable evidence to back up your hypothesis, chérie."

"And yet—" She rolled her shoulders back for another go at her father's logic. "Centius has also reported spikes in radiation that are consistent with active Quantum Gates when the Time Lab has *no scheduled trips*. That cannot be a coincidence!"

"Coincidence or chaos—they are the same," he said, clearing his throat. His hand swept over Peaches' forehead, moving an errant curl that had sprung in front of her face during their conversation.

"Her energetic presence has the density and mass of an Anchor *of Time*," she protested, her cheeks flushing, unable to relent. She rattled off several Quantum equations to support her statement. "Technically, her presence could unravel an Amaranthine loop. If it is the last loop, she is bound to be there. Literally, the Binder and the Bound is what Grand-père's Volumes describe!"

Aldric nodded, turning from his daughter to continue shuffling down the well-lit hall. She snaked her arm in his, leaning her head on his shoulder as they walked.

"Perhaps, ma pétite," Aldric finally admitted. "But I have never seen her there."

2

NEW-ASHEMORE, 3RD DIMENSION

Daylight vanished on ghost feet. The city stood, a twilight kingdom, as the sun retreated. On the north side of town, Renata Stone was finishing up with her last client. She was the only one in the salon this late on a Friday, the other stylists having gone home or gone out hours ago.

"Renata," Sara said, inspecting her hair one last time. "Ren—this looks great! As always. You wanna ride home?" Sara finished primping and turned from the mirror.

"Ah, no thanks, mija," Renata said, shaking her head as she leaned down to put her blow dryer away. "I've got some cleaning to do here. If it's raining really hard when I'm finished, I'll get a cab. Come on, I'll walk you downstairs."

"Fine," Sara said, pouting. Renata looked up to discover Sara still watching her.

"What?"

"You look tired."

"It's the end of the week, chica!" Renata grinned, but it

didn't reach her eyes. "I'm always this tired by Friday. Luck-ily, I can do great hair in my sleep!"

"That's not what I mean."

"I don't sleep much—" she mumbled. "Too busy."

"It's the dream, isn't it!" Sara said. "Renata Stone, it's been a year! You've been having the same nightmare since the accident! Don't you think it's time—" Her voice dropped to a whisper, even though they were alone at the salon, "—to seek professional help?"

Cansada. That's it, Renata thought. *I'm just tired. Not haunted. Not cursed.* Renata blinked, realizing she needed to respond. She shrugged.

"Have you even had another 'episode' thing since the accident?" Sara handed her cash.

"You mean a seizure?" she asked, holding the cash in her hands. "Want any change?"

"Keep it—" she said dismissively, before continuing her conversation about Renata's condition. "I know you don't think it's seizures. I've seen the same bottle of anti-seizure medication in your bathroom for months."

"Snooper." Renata pressed the screen of her tablet, bringing up her online calendar. "Same time in seven weeks?"

"Yes, to both," Sara nodded. "I can't help it! I'm worried about you! It's not my fault you keep it next to the antacids."

Renata frowned. "It's a medicine cabinet. That is where medication goes—*Sara*."

"Stop plying me with wine every time I come over, and I'll stop snooping in your medicine cabinet!"

"Plenty of wine and listening to your boring gossip is

among my top ten sleep aides." She winked, looking up from the tablet in her hand. A small, authentic smile finally breached her professional facade.

Sara huffed in response.

"And for the record, I haven't lost time since then," Renata said, returning the tablet to her workstation.

"Lost time," Sara shook her head. "Sounds like we're discussing an episode of the X-Files."

"I don't think it was aliens, but I haven't completely ruled it out..." Her smile was wider now.

"Ren! Don't tease me! I am genuinely concerned." Sara sniffed.

"Vamonos, mija. I'll walk you out—" She smiled again on reflex, hoping the conversation was over.

RENATA FUMBLED with the lock on the door, watching Sara's red taillights disappear into traffic. The city lights illuminated the dark, lending the urban landscape a false twilight well into night.

She trudged upstairs and began collecting the remnants of her day. She dumped a hamper full of used towels and capes in the washing machine, which was hidden in a closet at the end of the hall. Pressing 'start' on the laundry would be the first thing she did tomorrow morning when she returned to work—groggy, sleep-deprived, and with the strongest coffee she could find.

Thunder rumbled. Renata paused, looking out at the skyline. Low clouds had moved in. From her vantage point upstairs, she could see for several blocks. Suddenly, the lights flickered and went out.

"Mierda," she swore as she grasped her cell phone from the back pocket of her jeans. She shone it on the small pile of blonde hair she had been sweeping.

"Dammit, Jim, I'm a hairstylist not an electrician." Her voice echoed in the empty salon. Lightning replied, transforming everything in the room for a split second with a bone-pale hue.

She turned on her phone-light and gently propped the broom against the wall. Placing her phone on her cabinet to light the floor in front of her, she began to untie her apron, clenching her jaw against the anxiety clawing its way up her spine. Even the windows offered no light from the typical orange haze of light pollution common to cities—the blackout stretched as far as she could see.

She glanced up into her mirror. Something moved in the shadows.

Renata spouted a few garbled curse words in Spanish before explaining away the strange phenomenon.

"I'm here too late, I can't see a damn thing, and I'm exhausted." She closed her eyes and took a deep breath. Blinking, Renata shook her head and reached toward the mirror to clean it. It was a smudge she saw, nothing more.

But her arm met no resistance. It was as if she extended her arm through an open window or doorway. Her arm, having breached the threshold of the mirror frame, was in a room that felt cold. Renata looked up, surveying the mirror. It was suspended against a brick wall.

"Impossible," she whispered.

Stranger still, she was not alarmed. A small part of her

noted that she should jerk her arm from the frame and back away in fear and disbelief.

Instead, she leaned in deeper.

Sinking further into the mirror, her eyes rolled white, merging with a powerful force that existed beyond the here and now—a power that was simultaneously hers and not hers.

This felt familiar.

She knew this.

This was intrinsic, like breathing.

Breathing. She mustn't forget to breathe.

Renata exhaled. A quiet ecstasy enveloped her as her limbs stretched across the lip of the mirror frame. It should have been glass, but instead, she swayed, her body pressing beyond her reflection. The mirror swallowed her as if she were collapsing into a lover's embrace.

RENATA OPENED HER EYES.

Nada. No paso nada. There's nothing to see, it's only black, her mind thought distantly. *I was in the salon. I'm in the salon. That's where I am.*

Renata looked up from the floor. Her head throbbed.

She took a deep breath. Her mind was numb, her thoughts slow ships in a distant sea. Propping herself up with her arm, she felt a hot liquid slide down her forehead and drip onto her cheek. She breathed purposefully, attempting to ignore the blood she felt on her forehead and sat up.

The storm had passed, she noticed. All was silent.

Several blocks surrounding the salon remained in blackout, yet lights twinkled in the distance. Reaching up to the cabinet at her workstation, she found her cell phone and pressed the unlock button. She swiped through her contacts and tried to call the salon owner, Marcy. A recorded message played, indicating the number was disconnected. Renata frowned.

She pulled a tissue from the box on her workstation, holding it up to her forehead.

"Disconnected?" she said. "Did Marcy get a new number and forget to tell me? She always answers..."

She called three other stylists, and all of their numbers were disconnected, or her phone immediately dropped the call.

"I'll call Sara." Renata held her phone up to the window, wincing in pain. "Is it dumb to think holding it up will somehow help?" she wondered out loud, attempting to alleviate her anxiety. She scanned the screen of her phone, searching for service bars. None appeared.

"*Que suerte mia*," Renata sighed. "Must've been quite a storm if all the phone towers are out."

She pulled the tissue away—blood had completely soaked it while she was using her phone.

"Alright," she said to the empty salon. "Time to clean myself up, I guess."

A FIRST-AID KIT was essential at any salon, considering all the employees worked with scissors. Renata's was well-equipped to handle almost any cut.

When she felt positive she had slowed the flow of blood from the cut on her forehead, she pinched it with a butterfly bandage. She picked up her phone from her workstation again. She had propped it to cast enough light to accomplish mediocre first aid on herself. She froze.

She didn't remember hitting her head against the mirror.

"I walked Sara to the parking lot. I went upstairs. I cleaned up. The power went out," she listed all that she could recall. "I was looking in the mirror... and I woke up on the floor." She whispered, shuddering.

Unsure of what to do, she walked across the room, into the hall and opened the employee coat closet. She deposited her phone in her purse that was hanging on a hook next to her rain jacket. Numb, as if in a trance, she took her coat, purse, and house keys and slowly shuffled down the hall, clutching a thick piece of gauze on her forehead. It was then she noticed her breath in the air. *Que frío. When did it get so cold?*

She tried calling Marcy once more, but the disconnected recording just played again. Her hands shook as she put her phone back in her purse and put on her rain jacket. She walked down the hall to assess the damage to her workstation, using her cell phone light to observe the scene.

Like points of a star radiating out, the mirror was cracked on the left side, at about Renata's height. The cracks created a strange mandala, the broken pieces an intricate circular pattern with unnatural perfection. The shards pointed at the floor where she had been laying. The mirror frame itself seemed to shimmer in the darkness, its white lacquer somehow imitating the glow of the absent city lights.

"Weird," she said to the shadows and turned on her heel.

Renata hummed loudly—an attempt to dilute the ominous feeling the strange pattern on the glass had imposed. She kept humming, down the stairs and out the door. She didn't stop until the latch was shut to the building, the door locked.

She lead against it, her exhale coming out as a sob. She put her hand to her face, attempting to compose herself as rain misted drops of water on her exposed hair. Orbs of it beaded on her jacket, clinging with the promise of another storm.

3

NEW-ASHEMORE, AMARANTHINE LOOP

R ain turned the lights into misty halos dotting the streets. Renata was almost home.

Her neighborhood was in the historic district of New-Ashemore. It had wide, nostalgic streets and sidewalks of clacking brick—patterns worn smooth from the step of a generation across its back. The trees lining the streets made a quaint canopy, the promise of spring buds winking on their branches.

Renata slowed her steady stride as she approached the city's edge—something was off tonight. The normal end-of-work traffic was absent. There was no familiar sound of children playing or the sight of cars parked in driveways. Every house on the street was vacant and dark.

Her hands trembled. Her stiff fingers crept over her mouth, as if to silence a promised scream.

She continued walking. Disbelieving her eyes, she saw her apartment halfway down the block. Decades of neglect obscured its facade. Shingles from the side were missing.

Paint peeled as if the building were shedding. There was a sapling growing from the chimney. A large crack split the front dormer. The roof was sway-backed and sinking into the middle of the house.

Renata swore rapidly in Spanish, using words that would have made even her feisty abuela Noni blush. Then after a pause, she switched to English.

"Hello? Is anybody there?" she shouted to the empty street.

A few pigeons startled from their roost were her only reply. The houses stared vacantly back at her.

Renata stepped backward, her feet acting of their own accord. She stumbled off the brick sidewalk, shaking her head, her disbelief collapsing the hood of her rain jacket. There were no cars, no other pedestrians, no traffic.

"Weird doesn't sum up how this night is turning out," she whispered, her breath visible in the cold night air. She smeared the misted rain that had collected on her forehead, running her hands through her hair, attempting to convince her eyes of the truth before her.

"This can't be real," she croaked. Blood trickled down her forehead and mingled with the cold sweat on her face. She winced, vaguely aware of the pain through her panic as the stinging cut in her scalp bled anew.

Desperate, Renata clutched her purse and drew out her cell phone. Her hands shook. Her mind felt bleached by terror as she numbly thought of who to call. Her parents? They lived in Courier City, roughly four hours away. What would she say? *Hola, Mamá, I can't find my apartment? Hey, Dad, I came home to my apartment, but it's obviously been vacant for many years.*

She stifled a strained laugh. What would her over-educated parents say to that? Sara at least would somehow find humor in the situation.

"Get it together," Renata said, her teeth clenched, resolving to try and call Sara.

A voice resonated out of the darkness.

"I would not use your wireless short-range transmitter if I were you."

Renata dropped her phone in surprise. It clattered on the pavement, the screen flickered and died.

"Short wave transmitter?" Renata shook her head. She glanced up from the pavement and her broken phone. The rain had cleared away to reveal a full moon, casting a pale glamour on the night-slick pavement.

The municipal street lights were the only source of illu-mination. Frail fluorescent light penetrated the dark and otherwise forgotten neighborhood. The wet asphalt reflected a filmy imitation of the lights above, and he stood below them—with a brimmed hat like out of a black and white movie, his trench coat in chiaroscuro. His face was obscured by shadow.

"The Trackers will look for you." The words broke the silence of the neighborhood, a lone voice echoing in the emptiness. "You have Quantum Glass all over you. They can sense the imbalance, like a ripple in a pond. That wire-less transmitter—"

"My phone?" Renata interjected, nodding to the pave-ment where her lifeless phone lay.

"...phone you manifested only magnifies it," the figure finished.

Renata stared down at the broken phone on the pavement. She hated its absence. Her cellphone felt like a lifeline that had suddenly been cut. She looked back up at the mysterious stranger.

"Manifested? What the hell are you saying?"

"It is a complete Quantum Manifestation. It doesn't really exist in this dimension," the trench-coat figure replied.

She blinked several times, a disbelieving scoff bursting from her lips.

"Were you able to make any calls?"

Renata swore.

"There are Quantum remains all over you," the figure continued. Renata stared, uncomprehending. "And inside you. From your Quantum Gate," the figure said plainly, and then tilted its head to the side, as if muttering to itself. "You smell like fire. Is your Gate in the building that was burning?" A beat passed. She could only stare in shocked silence. "At any rate," the figure straightened its dark, faceless gaze. "I would abandon the clothes."

The figure took a few steps forward. Renata unconsciously drew her rain jacket closed, holding the lapels around her throat. Her eyes widened—her throat went dry.

"I forget, you humans—so quick to assume the worst intentions—" the figure began.

"You're the one in a trench coat talking about manifesting cell phones, and then some quantum shit," she yelled, hoping to stall for time. She slid her hand slowly into her purse, her fingers blindly feeling for the mace spray she usually carried. "Like I'm going to undress in the middle of the street, pendejo!"

"Oh, and your wit! Ah, I forget about humans, your

biology combined with emotions and desires that Elders—"

"What in the actual fuck is wrong with you?"

"Shh, pobrecita!" the figure moved fast. In between eye blinks, he was only inches from her face. Renata's eyes widened, she felt a chill bloom in her stomach and mushroom up her spine. "I will help you."

She sucked in a breath. He had uttered the phrase her abuela Noni used when things weren't going well. She swallowed and looked up. He was so close, and yet she still couldn't see his eyes. His face only a shadow.

"Help me?" she whispered, unsure. The figure pressed two fingers to her forehead and whispered indistinctly.

Renata felt a pillow softness envelope her mind, her vision clouded. She felt her body rise off the ground, suspended in an egg of pale light, each layer of clothing unstitched. Her sweater became rivulets of yarn, surrounding her body like the rings of Saturn. Her jeans were murky wads of denim, like muddy clusters of blue ink suspended in water.

It was the glass that glowed, creating the oval of light around her. Once the hat-brimmed figure was certain every last piece had been extracted from her skin—the rain had done a good job getting the last bit of dust—he released her.

Renata shivered violently. She lifted her head, wet tendrils of hair clung to her face, entwined in the weeping cut at the hairline above her eye. The wound bled anew, diffused by rain. Yarn and denim radiated around her bare feet, and as the light of the Quantum Glass dimmed, the remnants of her clothing faded away.

The cloaked figure removed his trench coat and wrapped it around her.

"I am Sid. We must go now. The rain will cover your scent for the moment," they said. "They will find you if we linger here."

"We?" Renata chanced a look up at the hat-brimmed figure. Without his trench coat, he was smartly dressed. Sid wore dark trousers, upturned above the ankles above classic leather boots of a midcentury gentlemen. He wore a waistcoat with a dull red scarf tucked into it. A wide brimmed hat was positioned low on his face, still obscuring it from view.

"Trust me," he said. "I can say no more, for now, no time remains." He put out his gloved hand.

Renata looked at it, pausing. *This is it. This decision, to take his hand, will decide the fate of the rest of my life.*

"We will not decide your fate now, little lamb. For now, we run. We must run."

Instinctively, Renata felt her hand reach for his. When she felt the sleek touch of his glove, her body jerked in sudden awareness.

Fully embraced, his arms pressed the lining of his coat against her bare skin. She felt movement, like wind passing by an open window. Objects and lights blurred. Her mind was numb, confused, out of time. She couldn't count. Her throat was parched, and her stomach seized, protesting its terrible hollowness. Her consciousness faded, the slow, meandering way it does when one realizes they are fainting and every second is an epoch.

4

PILLAR OF THE ELDER,
AMARANTHINE LOOP

I t was the stillness that woke her. And the dryness of her throat.

Sid began to disengage from their embrace and Renata emerged into wakefulness. Her eyes blinked in disbelief, while her thirst drove a weary pulsing into the base of her skull, dull and aching. She rubbed her face roughly, looking around.

It was twilight. Bittersweet light burned through the trees on a forgotten lane at the edge of the city. Thorny brambles had overgrown this street, reminiscent of some fairy tale briar that imprisoned an entire kingdom in a century of slumber. Writhing branches consumed distances between street signs and lampposts, a quiet triumph of nature.

The briars stretched across the road irreverently, up the trees, even eclipsing the street sign. The house was no different, except the front door and the large bay window seemed to be winning slightly against the winding foliage.

"Vincent will be here soon," Sid said, a dark gazeless face looked down at Renata. She was kneeling, her eyes wide and her mouth set firmly as she observed the house and surrounding forest. "He is a second generation Elder, but I do not think he has spoken to a human since the Future War, so it would be best if—"

"You bring a human here?"

A voice came from behind Renata. She gasped, clutching the trench coat tighter around her body and turned, searching for Sid's counterpart.

Vincent was tall. His muscled forearms were pushing through a bush with white blooms, grasping the branches out of the way until he stood before Sid and Renata in the clearing. Renata studied the features of his face, noting the planes and angles of his high cheekbones and square jawline, blurred by the stubble of a two-day old beard.

"Vincent!" Sid's voice smiled. "You are here early! You snuck up on me as never before in this millennium! Time moves strangely around this one." Sid's dark, blank face glanced down at Renata.

"I was curious," Vincent began. "I began to look for you. There are more Trackers out in the city than usual. I could only assume—"

"That you had finally gotten rid of me!" Sid interrupted, chuckling.

"Never," he paused, his blue eyes flashing with golden light. He had wide, powerful shoulders and a raw physicality that reverberated in the deep timbre of his voice. "I was going to say, you found some trouble of your own."

Renata felt his gaze. She felt his eyes burn into her like noon-time sun on bare skin—scorching, searching, deep.

"Stop—stop looking at me like that," she managed to whisper. She squeezed her eyes shut, and the feeling diminished.

"Well," Sid said after a pensive moment. "I did not expect that. Not only can she detect your Elder power, she can resist it too."

There was another pregnant silence.

"A mystery," Vincent said finally, nodding toward Renata. When he nodded, the wavy hair framing his face almost brushed his shoulders, the color impossible to discern in the waning light. "She smells human and something... else."

"I thought so too," Sid said. "She has traveled by Quantum Mirror, you can see it in some of the quarks of her—"

"Excuse me," Renata said, opening her eyes. "What do humans smell like? As in, you're not?"

When Vincent didn't answer immediately, she kept needling him with questions.

"Where am I? What is this place? And while we're at it, exactly what do my quarks smell like—" She snorted, looking over at Vincent again, but the rest of her questions fell silent in her mouth.

His complexion emitted a subtle glow, like a low banked ember existed beneath his skin. Renata didn't understand how, but she sensed time hidden in him—lifetimes bound up and unseen—like the dust that collects in the spine of an old book.

"Hyacinth in bloom," he said, his nostrils flaring. "On a clear crisp day—just the beginning of spring." He paused, returning her gaze. He carried his timelessness like a yoke —it stole joy and humanity from his eyes. Even so, if it were another circumstance, Renata would have admitted to herself that he was remarkably handsome. And sad. Handsome and sad...

"I knew the Pillar would be safe from prying eyes," Sid said to Vincent, interrupting his stare.

"She is weary," Vincent nodded toward Renata, who remained seated. "How long did you apparate with her?"

"What the actual—you know I can hear you!"

"Indeed, I have pushed time with the human, in a dimension not her own," Sid said, ignoring Renata's comment. "She is unique, certainly you can sense that."

"But mortal," Vincent said, owning the word. His eyes locked with Renata's. She felt herself unable to look away. His full force stare contained a power that made her want to tremble. It was only then she realized he was dressed almost identically to Sid—he wore a waistcoat with a button-down shirt underneath. He had a tweed jacket instead of a trench coat, but the same pants and classic boots. A vial of liquid hung around his neck. It looked like water, except it had a dull sheen to it—like pearls caught in candlelight.

Renata broke their stare when she felt the slow, warm trickle of blood on her forehead. Distracted at last from his gaze, she blotted the wound with the sleeve of the trench coat.

Vincent moved with predatory speed, like Sid had before, moving faster in a blink of an eye than seemed possible. He crouched before Renata, framing her face with his hands. His palms warmed her cheeks and directed her face towards his. His nostrils flared, like a predator sensing his prey.

Up close, Renata could clearly see his eyes. They were the darkest, deepest blue—his pupils only vaguely discernible.

She inhaled quietly, wrapping her hands around his wrists, his palms cupping her face. She closed her eyes. There was a scent to his presence, a scent she felt drawn to, as if it were reminding her of a dream she had not dreamt yet. In her mind, she tried to define it, the smell of him—

Roses, memory, salt, and prayer, she thought distantly. *Muchos sueños.*

"Dreams from an eon of dreaming," he said, finishing her thought.

Her eyes blinked open. She knew, as much as she knew anything, that this being, Vincent, was not human. She let go of his wrists.

"What are you?" they said to each other in unison. Renata's eyes were round with alarm.

"Well, that's a first," Sid said. "Shall we?"

The door of the cottage creaked open as the vines slowly moved and untangled themselves.

"The vines moved," she said, her mouth open in shock.

"And the door as well." Vincent stood up from his crouched position in front of her. He walked toward the cottage, his arms behind his back, and turned once he was in the doorway. "It's a quite safe, solid construction." He knocked the doorjamb with his knuckle.

"Is the house *alive*?"

"Alive?"

"I guess I'm asking if it is a who rather than a what," she said.

"Tricky." Vincent smiled.

"So, it is alive?" Renata cocked her head, her mouth still open.

"The house? No." Vincent shook his head. "Well, actually now that I think about it, yes. Or, perhaps maybe. The house is part of my pocket dimension—which is an illusion, just as everything here is."

"The house may be alive and may also not be here," she said, standing. "And here may not be here, because here isn't here at all—it's an illusion? Have I got that right?" She pushed her hair behind her ear before crossing her arms in front of her.

"Perhaps we should both agree that the house is here, in my Pillar," he replied evenly.

"Your what?"

"Dream dimension," Sid supplied, the voice coming from inside the cottage. Somehow, Renata had missed Sid entering the house altogether. Vincent still lingered, half turned in the doorway.

"Listen, we could chat about all of this inside over a nice cup of tea." Vincent cocked his head toward the interior of the house.

Renata eyed the doorway skeptically.

"Alright," she agreed, stepping forward. "It's not necessarily the weirdest thing I've heard today, I can tell you that much."

"**H**OW DO YOU TAKE YOUR TEA?" Vincent spoke with his back toward Sid's houseguest, shoulders drawn with tension as he gauged his own reaction to her.

"*At least there is never a dull moment,*" Sid said into his mind.

Vincent didn't reply to Sid, and turned to look at the human with a discerning gaze, probing her with his eyes.

"Tea?" The human seemed to mouth the word, dazed. She looked up at Vincent with wide eyes.

Clattering sounds came from the kitchen, a small room only a stone's throw from the front door. Vincent gestured for the human—her pulse distracting his train of thought—to follow him into the library.

She stared at where he gestured. He followed her gaze as she peered at the room that also encompassed the abrupt foyer they now stood in. The library, as he called it, was nothing more than an open room to the right of the front door, with a hearth and several overcrowded shelves on the other end. All were across the hall from the noisy kitchen.

The human paused in the doorway of the cottage, her breath and pulse hitched, clutching her hands to her chest. Sid appeared and gave her a glass of water.

"Where's Sid?" she said, after drinking with fervor, wide eyes assessing the room. "Do you live here with him?"

"I am Sid."

Sid locked eyes briefly with Vincent. "*She doesn't see me as you do,*" they said to Vincent alone.

Vincent examined Sid's appearance critically. He shrugged, nothing was amiss to him. Sid appeared as they always did. This version of Sid had golden-ochre skin, and lush ebony hair woven into intricate plaits with turquoise beadwork and golden thread. This Sid was also quite short, and had to look up to lock eyes with Renata. They smiled and shrugged before returning to the kitchen across the hall.

"What?" Renata said, her eyes round. "You can't be—"

"But I am," Sid's voice sang from the kitchen.

"Your name is Ren," Vincent interrupted, his head cocked to the side, listening to something. He let a small smile transform his face. "Renata," he said, his mouth savoring the word. "Why don't you follow me to the library, there are many places to sit."

Renata blanched, her mouth open in surprise.

"How did you—"

"Is it a common custom to repeat one's name? Over and over again?" Vincent kept his head bent slightly, not meeting her eyes.

"I didn't say anything—"

"You don't say anything." He squinted, biting his lip to suppress a smile. "You damn near shout it though—'*I am Renata Stone.*' Are you trying to convince yourself or me—"

"Vincent!" Sid yelled from the kitchen. The reprimand and admonition was communicated eloquently in Sid's single pronunciation of Vincent's name.

"Please," his pleasant smile returned as he gestured to the library's threshold.

A WELL-USED HEARTH held court in the open room that Vincent had referred to as 'the library'. There was a fireplace nestled in a hearth of river-stone on the farthest wall. Vincent knelt beside it and a tidy stack of firewood. Plucking a log from the stack, he added it to the crackling fire before turning back to Renata.

"If you will permit me, I believe I have some attire that you will find appropriate," he said, his gaze carefully fixed on Renata's face. Finished with tending to the fire, he now stood beside a honey colored butcher block table, which, combined with the three wooden chairs, created a makeshift dining area next to the hearth.

Why three chairs, she wondered. *Do they have a roommate?*

Vincent suppressed a smile, his eyes creasing with humor as if he had heard her thought about roommates. His eyes glanced down at the three wooden chairs, and he paused, in thought.

"Oh, that would be wonderful," she said, adjusting her grip on the collar of the trench coat. "Thank you."

Vincent nodded and left the room.

Renata walked slowly along the other wall of the open room, observing the ocean of books that had flooded over the shelves into stacks below. She spun a globe squatting on a desk adjacent to the middle shelf of books. Standing over it, Renata gazed at papers of varying sizes that peppered the top of the desk. Some were maps and some were more like a cartographer's fantasy—alien geopolitical maps, star charts of varying sizes. A lonely telescope leaned against the desk, pointing its upturned eye toward the large bay window. The window itself had a deep sill, home to half a dozen robust plants of assorted sizes, shapes, and colors.

Renata turned, surveying the layout of the house. Across the narrow hall, on the western side of the cottage was a small kitchen. Even from her limited vantage point from the library, Renata could see there was floral wallpaper, and it was stained and peeling near the edges where the wall met the ceiling.

Vincent appeared in the hallway that divided the kitchen from the library. He was holding a folded gray t-shirt and black stretch pants in his hands.

"I think these will fit," he said.

Stoic and silent, Renata nodded at the clothes in his hands but didn't approach him. On instinct, she remained still. Vincent surveyed her. His nostrils flared and his eyes suddenly flashed a bright gold. For several seconds, he remained transfixed on the open cut on her forehead. The air became stuffy in the cottage, and she felt sweat blossom on her skin.

Then, he cleared his throat and blinked. The temperature plummeted, and the air thinned. Renata exhaled, unaware she had been holding her breath. Vincent gave a small, polite smile.

"You know my name and you got just-happens-to-be my size yoga pants?" She said on a shaky exhale, attempting a grin. "This feels more and more like some reality TV new-age retreat. You gonna have me do goat-yoga next? Because the answer is no, amigo. No goats!" Her hands shook as she waved her finger in the air with mock concern.

"You are not making sense," Vincent said. "Perhaps if you sat—" He gestured to an armchair in the study.

"I'm okay," she sighed, rubbing her face and running her hands through her hair. "Whistling in the dark."

Vincent stared, serious and unblinking.

"It's not even worth explaining," she walked toward him, gesturing. "So, tell me, where am I?"

"Well," he said, extending the clothes toward her, "I am hopeful to clarify that after you explain how you arrived here—"

"By Sid," she replied, not attempting to quash the anxiety obvious in her voice. "With Sid, I mean, Sid found me. He... She?" Renata paused, waiting for Vincent to correct her pronouns. When he offered no critique, she continued. "Sid said we had to go, that 'they' would find me. I don't even know who they are, but I went with Sid—"

Vincent bent his head again slightly, his gaze softening.

"Describe to me how Sid appeared."

"Sid was—well, they dressed just like you—" she said, grasping the clothes in Vincent's hands.

Her fingers brushed his and their gazes locked. Time stood still.

Renata felt Vincent's thoughts—somehow, contact with him lifted a veil between their minds. She felt him stop himself from recoiling from her touch. She knew he enjoyed the sound of her heartbeat, the hum of humanity beneath her skin. To him, she was electric. And in the moment of her touch, he let time slow, moving like honey. He observed her pulse flutter in her throat, her eyes widen.

She trembled but did not break away from his gaze, unable to fight Vincent's influence over time with her eyes.

Hyacinth in bloom, his voice melted her thoughts. *On the first crisp, clear day of spring. But also fog, that banks low on the mountains, enshrouding tree limb and budded flower. Mortal—and yet also of time. Who are you, Renata Stone?*

What the actual—Renata managed to swear telepathically, before she leaned forward, vomited, and promptly fainted.

"**D**ID NOT SEE THAT COMING." Sid appeared in the hallway, holding a large ceramic mug full of hot water.

"Really?" Vincent said, clothes still clutched in his hands. He remained bent over Renata after catching her in a dead faint. "Your house guest vomits all over herself in our parlor this evening and you missed that, did you?"

"Surprised the trench coat lasted as long as it did, really." Sid plopped a round metal tea infuser into a ceramic mug, bobbing it up and down. "Your clashing psychic projections on my appearance were so completely different —that alone could have caused such a reaction. Humans aren't known for being adept at interpreting psychic phenomena."

"She has strong telepathy for a human," Vincent said, exasperated. He grumbled to himself, wiping his hand of vomit with the clean t-shirt, still staring at Renata's motionless body. He didn't want to admit that something stirred inside him when he looked at her.

After he cleaned his hands, he moved a few strands of hair that had fallen over her face.

"No doubt she felt you appraise her like meat on the slab," Sid added, bobbing the tea infuser with particular attention, the accusation simmering between them.

Vincent broke his study of Renata's unconscious form long enough to scowl at Sid. Sid continued, side stepping into the study to avoid Vincent and Renata.

"She is an empath of a kind—no control though. At any rate, I knew what you were thinking, all the way in the kitchen." Sid shrugged again. "You thought it really loud."

"What?"

"What?" Sid repeated Vincent's question, removing the tea infuser from the mug. "A mortal time travels into our dimension, has a natural resistance to your Elder power, and all you have to say is 'what'?"

Vincent stared at Sid for a beat, and then down at the motionless human on the floor. He looked up.

"Well, Sid—" Vincent raised an eyebrow. "You brought a mortal into the Pillar of an Elder. That is, historically speaking, a bad idea."

"You are not listening to me," Sid said. "Or, you are ignoring your own senses. She is *of time*."

"I am listening to you," Vincent said, rubbing his face with his hands. "I am also having trouble concentrating—"

"I found a mortal with inexplicable Quantum abilities," Sid sniffed defensively. "Not every day I stumble upon Elder folklore come to life, Vincent!"

"I did not know Tardigrades were so superstitious," he said, a sardonic smile breaching his serious facade. "The Forgotten Queen... that is a reach, quoting my own volumes at me to agree to your newest crazy idea." He ran his hands through his hair, glancing back down at Renata on the floor.

"There is power in belief, and in belief, there lies power," Sid said, waving the mug of tea enthusiastically.

"What do you look like to her?" Vincent said, still crouched. He began wiping her face and arm with the proffered t-shirt.

"A stranger," Sid said, putting the teacup down on the table. "Quite fantastic though. You and I had similar appearances to her perspective, before she met you. It is as if she anticipated your outdated clothing choices." Sid sniffed again, calming down.

Vincent's brow pinched, his gaze taking in Renata—her breathing had begun a steady rhythm. Her mind had taken refuge in the most profound depths of sleep. In this state, he could sense her calmness and feel what he thought of as her 'animal mind' take over—the automatic parts of her brain that regulated adrenaline, breath, sleep, and hunger.

"I admit I know little about the true dynamics," Vincent said. "But inter-dimensional Quantum Glass travel is... impossible for a human. That is exclusively a Tardigrade ability—that is to say, a power humans will never evolve to have, in any timeline." Vincent stood and fixed Sid with a stern gaze. "Tardigrades are the only ones who know the secret of Quantum Glass travel, and they suffer from extreme fatigue and weakness after such travel, do they not?"

Sid nodded.

Vincent continued, "I do not even know the effects of Quantum Gates on a mortal—how did she even survive?

How did she get here? Impossible." He crouched down again to inspect Renata.

"Too many questions," Sid said, picking up the mug of tea. "Let us clean her up, and then you can pick my Tardigrade brain about Quantum Gates. Very poor manners to leave her on the floor...although, she does seem to be sleeping quite well."

5

LUPUS OBSIDIAN, CERULEAN DIMENSION

"She is in the Amaranthine." Peaches leaned in the doorway of the medical suite.

Aldric was resting on a gurney, a bag of Quantum-fluerite suspended like an IV drip next to him. His hands were folded in his lap, his head leaned back against a pillow. He cracked open one eye at Peaches.

"What?" he said, his voice almost a whisper.

"Grand-mère," Peaches said. "I have proof. Centius double checked. It is her. She has found him."

Aldric opened both eyes, his deep gaze taking in his daughter.

"Her presence does not necessarily mean she has found him," Aldric said finally, not moving or sitting up. Peaches ignored her father's statement and pressed forward. She took a tentative step into the room.

"I have been testing a few probable axioms with Centius to see the most successful outcome—"

"What would you quantify as success?"

"Her return," Peaches replied. "Her return to the Time Lab that she created with you! Why are you being so obtuse?"

"Logical," he said. "I am being logical." He cleared his throat and let his hand drift to a button on the side of the bed. He pushed it, and the bed moved until he was sitting.

"I have more than logic to support this, I have the math." She handed him a glass tablet, its holographic interface open and projecting a long string of numbers and symbols. Aldric squinted at them for a brief moment before looking back at his daughter.

"Ma choupinette, these equations are based on the result you desire," he said, his voice soft. "An unbiased answer lies in these numbers, and I do agree, the spike in density and radiation within the Amaranthine could indicate her presence—"

"But, Papa—"

"It could also indicate that the Amaranthine's degradation is so severe that a black hole is forming in the center of the time loop, and the dimensional realities within the Amaranthine are close to collapse. One does not base scientific hypothesis and theory and eventually laws by starting with the outcome most desired and working backward to find data that supports it."

Peaches remained silent for several moments, her eyes glassy with emotion. Finally, she looked down at the tablet in her father's hands and reached for it, shoulders slumped in defeat.

"Pétite," Aldric said. "I am not saying you are incorrect. Further research—"

"I can feel her," Peaches said, her voice cracking. "I know I am right about this in my very bones!"

Aldric observed his daughter. Her orange-red hair almost glowed in the sterile, bright light of the medical suite. It was pulled back, but a few errant spirals had still escaped, framing her heart shaped face. Her skin was unblemished pale cream, spectacular in its consistency—there were no freckles or marks of any kind. Aldric knew this was not only from her lack of exposure to real sunlight, but also her more-than-human lineage.

"Your eyes are electric when you're this way," he said, staring at her. "Determined and on the brink of a new discovery. Hers were the same, except they were green." He smiled, but it didn't reach his eyes.

"This is our last chance, Papa," Peaches said, her voice low to hide the emotion she felt. "Once the Amaranthine is collapsed, the statistical probability of—"

Aldric held up a hand, and Peaches stopped talking.

"I have come to a decision. You will be making contact with Vincent on the final loop, cherie." Aldric looked pensively at his daughter. Fatigue engulfed him. He could feel the Quantum-fluerite dripping into his veins, and he could feel the battle of his body between repairing the Quantum damage while adjusting to the Time Lab's pocket dimension. He also knew there were other forces at work causing his diminished state.

"Papa," Peaches said, her voice shaking, her eyes searching him and confirming what he felt. "What's wrong? Why have you changed your mind?"

"The Quantum-fluerite cannot mend what is happening to me. I do not think my body can handle... another trip,"

Aldric said slowly, his breathing shallow, as if he struggled for breath. "There are thing that must come to pass... in the final loop of the Amaranthine." He chuckled, but it was a hollow sound. "I too feel things in my bones."

Peaches' eyes rounded. "What?"

"I know I have never told you explicitly," Aldric began, pausing. "But I am sure your calculations also show that a different version of me exists within the Amaranthine... This final loop will... finally destroy that version of me."

Peaches put her hands to her mouth, her eyes absently streaming with tears.

"The stories in our blood are undeniable—across space, time, and dimensions. That is what it means to be Aeorian —" He coughed before continuing. "Ma pétite, I have a dark legacy within the Amaranthine and it has played out as many times as I have gone to collect Vincent."

Peaches remained silent, her breath shuddering as he continued speaking.

"As well there are things about you that I must tell you, before the Amaranthine collapses," he said, wheezing. "But for now, I must rest. I know you and Centius will research what I've said—you will undoubtedly piece together some of what transpired in my past, but know this—we share blood, and blood will always out the truth. The truth is that I love you. Now go, let me rest."

"Papa?" she said, her hands dropping from her mouth.

"Go," Aldric said, his eyes at half-mast. "You need to prepare as much as you can, the Gate will be viable in seventy-two hours."

6

NEW-ASHEMORE, AMARANTHINE LOOP

"Quantum Gates affect weather patterns," a soft female voice said. Hard rain pummeled the roof of Aldric's car in the Amaranthine. It was parked in the historic district on a vacant street, still and silent in the lingering gloom of a late winter rainstorm.

Aldric, an ancient Tracker, squinted at his passenger's dark figure in the rearview mirror, his hands relaxed over the steering wheel. He knew as well, the weather was no mere front moving through.

"There are... forces at work," he agreed.

"It is Quantum Gate energy," the girl almost purred. "Are you certain Vincent is still captive in his own illusion?"

"This is not from the Elder." Aldric sniffed the air and exhaled. "The Ledger is certain."

"Elders can escape through Quantum Glass," the girl said, her voice careful. "The Chosen can. He is Chosen—"

"Trackers have to be creative to avoid these deficits in their pursuit of balancing the Ledger," he replied woodenly, hoping the conversation was concluded. *Was that curiosity? An echo of emotion from her deceased form?* Aldric could not see her reflection in the rearview mirror, her face obscured by darkness.

Instead, he gazed out at the historic district—a tomb of suburbia lingering at the city's edge. He opened his sunroof, allowing large droplets of rain to pelt his hair and face.

He tilted his head back, eyes gently opening despite the rain. His cheeks were hollow, dark circles shrouding his bloodshot eyes. He was weary with the Count of All Things for his Ledger—a constant script in his Tracker consciousness. The Count precluded the balance, a mathematical figure all Trackers aspired to, but few ever realized —such was the ever-shifting nature of the Universe. The unyielding nature of his duty created an ache between Aldric's dead eyes.

"Ever counting," the girl whispered from the back seat. A streetlamp next to the car flickered and died out again, momentarily highlighting her face. Her complexion was corpse-like, sallow skin cobwebbed by cuts and scrapes. Sunken, dark circles created pits around her eyes. Her haunted white irises gleamed with reflected streetlight. "Trackers always have too much time, and yet never quite enough," she said.

Aldric grimaced. He pulled up the lapels of his rain jacket and ran a well-manicured hand through his short, cropped hair. He stared at the street, looking for signs of what he knew he smelled.

Time.

He smelled time on this street. The crumbs of another dimension that a time traveler leaves upon entering this one.

Aldric snorted, not believing his reasoning.

"This dimension is stable," Aldric responded. "The Amaranthine is intact."

"Vincent," she whispered, savoring the name.

"Has been captive in this Amaranthine concluding the Future War." Aldric replied, giving her a knowing glance. "You saw to that."

"Your precious Ledger saw to that," she said. "I am just a well-placed variable in an equation, to keep the margins in your Ledger *spotless,* for your ineffable *balance* —"

"He has a Tardigrade," Aldric interrupted, putting up his hand to stop her from talking about the Future War. Aldric looked for her in his rearview mirror. Without the sputtering streetlight, all he saw was darkness, her form hidden among the lingering shadows of the desolate neighborhood. He continued, speaking to her in the dark. "The only way he is pure enough to even have a psychic symbiote is complete and absolute abstention. That is what it means to be Chosen. So, he gets to survive the Future War and starve, forever, in the Amaranthine Loop. If he deviates but a little—"

"He would bring imbalance," she ground out.

Aldric turned around from the front seat, his words final.

"Even though you are a 'well-placed variable' in my Ledger, know this," he said, his voice sharp and cutting— old anger seeping in. "If it would balance, he would already be dead—his atoms scattered among the star dust of his other destroyed ancestors. This was his only opportunity for reprieve."

His words were sharp, pin pricks in the dark. She didn't respond, and they both resumed watching the rain.

7

THE PILLAR, AMARANTHINE LOOP

Renata was clean now, her hair fanned out like a rumpled battle flag across the pillow. Her head slumped to the side, a pale sheet pulled to her chin. Vincent and Sid sat by her bedside in the back bedroom of the cottage. A large window ushered starlight into the room, and an oil lamp burned quietly in the corner.

"Do I look like Elaria now?" Sid asked.

Vincent gazed evenly at Sid who was pressing a damp cloth to Renata's forehead.

"Yes," he replied. "You look like you always do."

Sid, the Tardigrade, had a particular and habitual appearance with Vincent. Not a hat-brimmed figure without a face, Sid was currently, and usually, an ebony-haired girl—Elaria. Just a wisp of a thing, she had narrow, gray-green eyes like the sea after a storm. Sid emulated the memory of Vincent's deceased sister in an almost flawless fashion.

"Then your link has been re-established," Sid replied. "When the human wakes, she will see me as Elaria as well."

"Elaria," Vincent whispered, as he studied the mortal's sleeping profile. Though Sid had been emulating the memory of Elaria for time beyond measuring, Vincent never mistook Sid for anything but Sid—his Tardigrade, his Chosen.

He sighed. He was surprised he did not wince at her name, as he thought he would. There was just a hollowness instead.

Sid removed the damp cloth and submerged it in a steaming pot of water on the bedside table. The smell of lavender permeated the room.

"She had a psychic link with me, even if she did not know," Sid as Elaria said, nodding at Renata.

"Do you think some mortals are more sensitive than others?" Vincent asked.

"No." Sid frowned. "Few humans have any psychic ability of note. She reacted acutely, as if she saw clearly, and empathically—gifts that defy her human form." Sid's fingers—a psychic and physical emulation of Elaria's deft hands—wrung the washcloth out. "She is a miracle of a mortal, in this respect."

"Curious," Vincent said, pausing as he searched for the right words. "My link with you felt... interrupted."

"A-ha! Your psychic projection was conflicting with hers," Sid said. "A human psychically projecting! Impossible. I wonder why we cling to any laws of nature if the Universe insists on breaking them!"

Vincent smiled down at the vial of liquid around his neck, closing his fingers around the glimmering water. Sid, a creature as old as the Universe itself, was still appreciating the mysteries of existence.

Silence lingered between them as Sid continued to think about the inexplicable human sleeping before them.

"Her psychic ability is raw, to say the least." Sid's eyes— Elaria's eyes—flickered up to Vincent in the dim light of the bedroom. "She has no control but is very strong. She could probably understand anything you might have thought." Sid smiled. "You have lived alone with me too long, beloved. You do not shield your thoughts."

Vincent remembered his split-second thought to devour the mortal—his brief daydream of exsanguinating her body and irradiating her flesh until it was nothing but dust. He winced. The truth of what he was he could never escape.

"The human glimpsed only a truth of what you could be, but not what you are—"

"Which explains her sickness." Vincent broke his guilty silence. "I must remember not everything is as indestructible as a Tardigrade." He ran his fingers through his hair, grasping the necklace, clutching it against his chest again— the vial of liquid glowed in his hand.

"Well, keeling over sick every time you get confused would be quite unhelpful traveling in the vacuum of space, through dimensions—"

"Don't forget extreme temperatures," Vincent whispered, his eyes closed. He knew the virtues of his Tardigrade by heart, as Sid had been repeating them to him since he was Chosen, after the Future War.

"At any rate, Ren—Renata—had her own psychic link with me." Sid resumed patting the human's face with the damp washcloth. "We could not have interacted any other way."

"You've already mentioned this," Vincent said impatiently, letting go of the necklace.

"Human intelligence has not evolved at any point in the timelines I am aware of to have such strong psychic ability," Sid said sharply. "All of my knowledge accrued over the vast spans of time concur with this fact, and yet—"

"Before us is a human with a psychic link to a Tardigrade," Vincent interrupted.

"You are my Chosen, our link will always be superior. Yet, it was not so at first. And in your absence, she imagined my appearance remarkably similar to yours, without the face of course. As if we would ever dress alike—" Sid scoffed.

"Could be my psychic imprint on you," Vincent offered.

Sid shrugged. "In the end, the stronger link will adjust the perspective and both minds will see the Tardigrade from the stronger psychic perspective. Yours." Sid continued dabbing gently at the cut on Renata's forehead.

Vincent's gaze lingered on the jagged pink scar just at her hairline. The pungency of her mortality drew him closer. Renata's blood was magnetic and insistent. He felt his conversation with Sid fade away. In an eye-blink, his face lingered above Renata's. He inhaled.

Her blood sang to him.

It was a song of mortality, vibrant and temporary. He heard her emotions too as they hummed quietly under the veneer of sleep. But it was the siren song of her blood that transfixed him. He leaned in closer still, and the briefest hint of time eclipsed all other nuances of her blood. It was time that felt familiar.

Vincent pulled himself away.

He pressed away from the bed, his back to Renata and Sid. He shuddered, clenching his palms that itched to touch her. He stared ahead at the blank wall of the bedroom. He stared a thousand stares, hoping to keep buried the desires that still whispered to him in the dark.

Eventually, the hungry must eat.

8

NEW-ASHEMORE, AMARANTHINE LOOP

I t rained all night, stopping just at the edge of dawn's first light. The streets were cloaked in fog. Lingering drops of rain clung to the old oaks lining the brick sidewalks of the historic district of New-Ashemore.

Inside the only car on the street, the girl—Aldric's passenger—lay in the back seat of the dark sedan, her bruised arm slung over her face.

Aldric opened his car door and breathed deeply. The Tracker's eyes, whatever was human about them, only vaguely maintained. His wide gaze scanned the empty streets, looking for something.

Several abandoned houses dotted the old thoroughfare. Forgotten in time, many of the old genteel houses with their large breathing porches had been left to rot.

The Tracker palmed a silver cigarette case with his initial engraved on the front. Inside the case was a neat row of hand-rolled cigarettes, mirrored by a neat row of his business cards reading *A+ Real Estate*, Aldric's real estate firm.

Flipping the case closed, he ignited a match with an almost sleight of hand. He savored the first inhale. The cherry burned red-orange in the gray cloak of predawn light. He exhaled, and it was as if everything—every beaded raindrop, every second of the minute—paused with him for a lingering exhale.

Aldric thought of the apartment buildings A+ Real Estate Development had purchased. He smirked at the houses before him, the sallow and forgotten century-old architecture of the historic district, calculating the neighborhood's worth in a split-second glance.

He knocked a little cigarette ash on the ground, smoke curling from his lips into the still night air.

The numbers flew before his eyes like birds.

His dark gaze compared the bleak houses before him to his sprawling and gleaming apartments on the South Slope. A grunt passed through Aldric's lips. Smoke whispered into the air, imagining the details of his business strategy. He smiled. Business was good.

The ash of his cigarette hushed and scattered onto the rain-slick pavement.

This neighborhood was evidence of what Aldric already knew. New-Ashemore was changing. Real estate was sky rocketing, jobs were hard to come by, over half the households in the city lived in poverty, and the cost of living in New-Ashemore continued to rise.

For Aldric, these were ideal circumstances.

Money was the shackle. The humans imprisoned themselves—two jobs, three jobs, no matter. Money was the whip, the concubine, and the temple. It was uncanny, but humans served money like no other master, not even as they had served the Elders.

"Keep the humans busy," Aldric muttered, cigarette dangling from his lips. Greed was the base equation he used for the Count of All Things that were human.

He walked along the deserted sidewalk, cigarette pressed to his lips. He glanced down. Grass and weeds were thriving amongst the clay bricks. He exhaled, and the smoke encircled his head like a wreath. Looking up, he flicked the butt of the cigarette down and stamped on the glowing ember.

Even after a night of rain, he could smell new time on this street. New time, and Quantum Glass.

He would never forget the smell.

"The Future War," he muttered into the fog, his words searing the air. His mind swam with memories, a Quantum Gate was how they had escaped him then.

Aldric inhaled sharply, remembering.

Even now, he did not understand Elders, for truth did not always bring balance. Trackers were meant to balance the Ledger—balance, at all cost, was their only objective.

And then he spotted it. A broken thing— out of time, soaked and exhausted on the sidewalk.

Aldric appeared next to it, traveling half a block in less than a second. He took a handkerchief out of his pocket and lifted what appeared to be a cell phone from the worn bricks. It lay awkwardly, its screen cracked.

"New time," he growled into the hushed, dark morning.

He put the cell phone in his mouth.

He crunched on the keypad and the glass. His tongue

ran over the SIM card and the motherboard, as small as his pinky. The metal and glass cracked and tore into his mouth, the Quantum energy used to create it disintegrating onto his tongue. He felt her, the human woman who had once held it. The machine had traveled through time—was time. He could feel the current of Quantum energy, still echoing against its atoms, every neuron and proton that gave it substance.

He could feel her, the last microscopic vestige of her breath caught in the metal, plastic, and glass. Water-logged and abandoned, out of time, and in the wrong dimension— he could feel her still.

He spat onto the sidewalk. The rain began again, dark clouds veiling the morning sun.

"A Quantum manifestation," he exclaimed, looking back at the sedan. The girl opened the car door as if summoned and walked toward him.

"She has come for him," the girl said, finally standing next to him. He looked at her for a moment, framed by the gray-washed seam of daybreak. "As she promised she would."

"We must find her," Aldric agreed. "Or the Amaranthine could collapse."

She inclined her head, her brittle eyes downcast.

"Master," she whispered, and vanished.

9

THE PILLAR, AMARANTHINE LOOP

Renata felt soft sunlight easing through her half-open eyelids. She resisted opening them all the way. She had never felt a sleep this peaceful.

Stretching her legs, she felt the press of the small mattress, her toes feeling into the corners where the sheets were tucked.

She heard the dull sounds of movement from the other room. Her mind was listless, and she soon gave up any attempt at fully rousing from her slumber.

She dove back down into the hidden depths of a sweet, syrupy sleep.

She did not dream.

"When do you think she will stop sleeping?" Vincent asked, picking dead leaves out of a newly acquired peace lily. It had appeared behind a tall stack of books. Random plants sometimes appeared in the cottage, and Vincent felt obliged to care for them.

"She will sleep until she is done," Sid replied, sitting across from Vincent at the dining table that was now covered in leaves and other plant detritus.

"How much sleep does a human actually need?" Vincent dipped his finger into the soil of the pot, testing to see if it had recently been watered. "I have heard and seen conflicting information..." For two days, he had remained at Renata's bedside. There, he observed her body metabolize the Quantum energy it had absorbed traveling through the Gate. She slept deeply.

"Her cells are in shock and are adjusting to this dimension. Quantum Glass travel reduces many novice Tardigrades to a state of cryptobiosis," Sid said, elbows propped on the table, observing Vincent work.

He grunted in acknowledgment. "How long does 'cryptobiosis' last?"

"It depends," Sid paused to yawn. "Mmm, it can last indefinitely if the environmental situation calls for it."

"Indefinite *and* mortal? She cannot be both," he said, eyes glancing up briefly at Sid, who sat chin in hand. A log cracked in the fireplace, and the fire flared momentarily, casting sparks and ash into the air.

"Are you ever going to ask how I found her?" Sid said, nonplussed by the hearth's dramatics.

Vincent shrugged by way of reply and continued trimming the peace lily. Finally, after a moment, he spoke. "I am more curious why you thought bringing her to my Pillar was a good idea."

Sid leaned across the table. "She is a human who traveled through a Quantum Gate," Sid said, letting the statement hang in the air between them. "That in and of itself is terrifying and impossible. That got my attention."

"How ironic, your attention is both terrifying and impossible to keep—"

"She Quantum manifested the immediate objects around her," Sid said. "This is not easily done, even by one who is well versed in Quantum Gate mechanics."

"Quantum manifestation?" Vincent looked up. "That is... impossible. Only the Supreme Elders were ever able—"

"Precisely," Sid nodded. "It is a rare knowledge and has been forgotten since..." Sid paused, letting the rest of the sentence remain unsaid. Vincent's shoulders relaxed, grateful. Sid continued, "Combined with her dexterous use of the Gate—"

"You are hypothesizing she created the Quantum Gate? Impossible again." He frowned, working his hands into the soil of the pot, feeling for the roots of the plant.

"Yes... although Renata did not seem to understand what Quantum Glass was when I mentioned it..." Sid said, slumping back in the chair. A log cracked in the hearth again.

"Tricky," Vincent said in agreement. "Tell me more about how exactly you appeared to her."

"I believe she was remembering you."

Vincent felt an unease spike in his chest, withdrawing his hands from the soil.

"That *is* terrifying and impossible," he said, his hands covered in potting soil. "A mortal, from another dimension, and she remembers me?"

"The image she subconsciously chose supports this theory," Sid said, shrugging.

"And we have not encountered her before?"

"Time does not appear linear to me in our most mundane moments," Sid said, leaning back from the table, watching Vincent work with the plant.

"I do not remember her. I could consult my library..."

Sid nodded in agreement. "With her quarks still in a state of Quantum shock from the inter-dimensional travel, I cannot clearly define anything about her except where she is at the present—"

"How *did* you find her?" Vincent asked, looking up after a moment of pensive silence. "I lost you while I was interrogating those Trackers we had cornered on Saville Street. Remember?" He shook his head. "They said they were tourists from Florida. Typical."

"I felt her," Sid said quietly. "Like feeling the temperature drop when a window is opened in another room. Very subtle. I doubt any Tracker understood what they felt."

Vincent nodded for Sid to continue.

"This is where it gets curious. She lingered at the Quantum Gate she had created, tending her wounds. As if she were not aware—" Sid paused in mid-thought. "The building burned around her, but she psychically projected, like you do with the Pillar. Combined with her Quantum manifestations, all of this created a perfect, if temporary, biome—a shadow world. It protected her from the flames."

"That is an advanced Quantum skill, no mortal will ever..." Vincent paused, his eyes wide for a moment.

"She is an anomaly," Sid said, nodding.

"She did not know what she was doing or how she got here?"

Sid nodded again.

"Trackers may not sense 'a window opening in another room' but they could certainly sense a building burning downtown," Vincent grumbled, collecting the dead leaves from the peace lily and moving them to the table's edge. "I am surprised no other humans in New-Ashemore found her either."

"The building was empty, as was the entire street," Sid said. "I am inclined to think her dimension was similar to this one. She did not seem to indicate anything was amiss until she left the city."

The dead leaves turned green in Vincent's hand. A golden glow of Elder-light surrounded them as they floated to the the stems of the wilted peace lily.

"I am surprised no Trackers located her—the residual Gate energy alone attracts attention," he said. "It is likely as well many Ledgers have already marked her arrival—though they may not understand what they have included in their Count. Quantum phenomena is difficult to Count."

"Quite," Sid replied.

"I wonder, could amnesia be a side effect for humans who travel through Quantum Glass?"

"Humans cannot travel through Quantum Glass," Sid replied immediately. "Their biology cannot tolerate the physical forces associated with time travel. It is only for the ancient beings like Tardigrades or Elders."

"I suppose by that logic, even Trackers would fare better," Vincent said.

Sid nodded, leaning forward, palms flat on the table.

"You must discard this notion that she is merely mortal, Vincent. Though for all appearances, she is just that. Mortal and infinite. What mystery the Universe has brought us!" Sid clapped, eyes glowing with excitement.

The peace lily lifted its weary white bloom. The green stems adjusted their posture, flourishing with the assistance of the golden light from Vincent's palm.

"Do you have any initial calculations," Vincent asked, "about her home dimension and its relative time?"

"Yes," Sid replied. "And no... It is slow going. I need more time... to see." Sid squinted their gray-green eyes, as if trying to focus.

"Let's hope she has some time to spare then," Vincent replied, brushing his hands together.

"It will be easier once she is awake."

Vincent paused, looking at Sid.

"I know you know," he said. "But it bears repeating—I don't like the idea of Renata lingering in my Pillar. The Trackers will start to add it up in their Ledgers, an Elder and a mortal..." He gave Sid a knowing look.

"Beloved, she is an acceptable risk," Sid replied.

Vincent ran a hand through his hair.

"We should go back to New-Ashemore, third dimension, and inspect her Gate," he said.

He placed the peace lily on the bay window, into a healthy beam of sunlight that had penetrated through the leaves of the trees surrounding the cottage.

"That may give you an indication of her timeline and home dimension, will it not?" he asked, turning to Sid.

"Yes! That is the best idea you've had this morning!" Sid nodded, eyes twinkling with excitement.

Vincent unrolled his sleeves as Sid's image evaporated before his eyes. He shrugged into his tweed jacket that was hung on a row of wrought iron hooks by the front door.

The cottage door creaked open, and the vines receded from the doorway.

"Do not let her leave," he said to the vines. "Do not kill her either!" He added quickly, his head half turning over his shoulder to look back at them.

He kept walking, across the small front yard and into the brush, promptly vanishing into the foliage.

10

NEW-ASHEMORE, AMARANTHINE LOOP

Vincent stood next to Sid on the fourth floor of a parking garage in the heart of downtown New-Ashemore. A beast of cement and iron, the garage crouched on the spine of the city, overlooking several blocks in all directions. The street below was bustling with humans. Vincent stared at them, sensing the Trackers who hid among them.

"See those two? Down there," Sid said, nodding almost imperceptibly at the crowded street below. "They have been creeping around this building quite a bit since we got here."

Vincent looked at the charred brick building across the street—it stuck out like a sore thumb. From this height in the parking garage, they had an excellent vantage point to the crumbling building containing Renata's Quantum Gate.

Sid had mentioned the building had burned around the human, but her shadow world—much like a Pillar—had protected her. The tall brick facade of the store front was a testament to this, surviving a fire perhaps two or three years ago, Vincent estimated. Although time did not exist in his Pillar, sunrise to sunset at his cottage was often a year or more in the outside dimensions his Pillar branches extended to.

He paused over the cement ledge, his eyes glowing a deep blue, and his skin turning a translucent gold. With a subtle pop, the gold energy vanished. He was now adjusted to the time and space that governed this dimension.

"I see what you mean," he replied hollowly, distracted by the changes in the city since his last trip here.

"Vincent," Sid chided.

"Yes, yes," he said in acknowledgement and concentrated on the dilapidated building with Renata's Quantum Gate.

Using his Elder senses, he could taste the ash of the fire on his tongue. He could smell the decay from across the street. He noted that the roof was completely gone, and black soot still charred the building's walls. The elements had done little to wash away the evidence of the fire, but nature was persevering. Vines and other plants were beginning to take root, staking claims on the ruin. A thin undercurrent of rot and neglect was present in the air.

Vincent stared at the skyline and frowned. His old eyes, which had gazed on the progress of mankind in this branch for many centuries, took in the city before him. There was a different feel to the air now. It smelled strange—acrid and sweet at the same time.

He counted several new hotels. A crowded homeless

shelter sat across the street from a bustling construction site. The future hotel, emerging out of the bedrock of New-Ashemore, surveyed the city with an indifferent gaze. Work was almost completed, and this would soon be the newest addition to the downtown New-Ashemore skyline. He shook his head and looked at his hands, splayed over the cement ledge of the parking garage. Vincent had been in the world long enough to know human's savagery didn't become more civilized as a culture advanced—it became more cunning and pragmatic. Money was the tooth and claw of the predator in this age of man.

Not trusting the pace of change, Vincent had a nagging fear. Trackers could be altering the city in an attempt to find the human woman, Renata. He felt sure there were more Trackers in New-Ashemore since he last visited the city, before she had arrived.

The wind changed, and Vincent blinked, his attention caught with the shift of the breeze. He turned his head to take in more of the view. He surveyed the blocks surrounding and framing the historic district, north of downtown. Vincent leaned into the wind, listening deeply to the city and what it ached to say.

"They must be hungry to balance this after so many years," he whispered.

"Look," Sid said, nudging him and pointing at the sidewalk full of tourists. "They always pretend they are from Florida. Other states have tourists. Try being original—*for once*." Sid glared down at the street.

"Stereotypes fit into the Ledger easier. Simpler base equation," he replied. "Stuck perpetually in linear time without a trans-dimensional body, perhaps I would make the same choice. Although, I've always thought stereotypes communicated a lack of imagination—base equations of the third dimension not withstanding, of course."

"Touché," Sid replied.

The wind moved a strand of hair into Vincent's eyes. He smoothed the hair away from his face.

"They will have much to balance in the Ledger if they can Count a mortal from another dimension is here."

"The Ledger," Sid huffed.

"That is their purpose, to balance the Ledger with the Count of All Things. It is what they were created for, and they are unyielding in their commitment. That alone should inform you of the level of risk harboring a mortal in—"

"Weary with age, and a brain clouded with a mathematical computation so complex, there is room for nothing else." Sid interrupted, and frowned at Vincent. "I will choose an Elder over a Tracker any time. Less math. Now, *look*."

Vincent frowned back at Sid, who was leaning over the waist-high ledge of the parking garage, pointing at the building across the street.

Vincent followed Sid's gaze and leaned against the cement ledge as well. Together, they watched a group of Trackers-as-tourists congregate around the building containing the Quantum Gate. Vincent looked through them, searching for the kernel of Tracker spark hidden in the recesses of their cells—hidden in corpses pretending to be living flesh.

"It was the room upstairs. Do you see the broken

Mirror frame?" Sid's question broke Vincent's concentration.

"Yes." He nodded slowly, his hair still dancing in the wind. "Lots of them down there. They sense the imbalance."

He watched the Trackers in silence for several more minutes before looking at the broken frame, just visible through the shattered second floor window.

"I still see some energy waves, very vague, around the frame." He squinted, brushing his hair out of his eyes again. "Do you think they sense it is Quantum energy?"

"Maybe," Sid said, looking up at Vincent with grey-green eyes. Their hair was swept back severely, in tight, and intricate plaites whose length almost passed their lower back. Vincent noticed Sid's rendering of Elaria's appearance was not having any of the hair problems he seemed to be having on the parking deck. "They are less attuned to Quantum remnants. But our proximity is probably enhancing the sound. Quantum Glass always calls out to Quantum creatures." Sid smiled.

"The Glass is calling out to us?" Vincent raised an eyebrow.

"Metaphorically speaking, yes." Sid sniffed.

"Is Quantum Glass sentient?"

"Not like humans, but it does have a presence. It is alive like the stars are alive."

Vincent pinched his chin, staring across the street. "Is this Quantum Gateway still active? Perhaps we should shut it down—"

"Not without Renata," Sid interrupted. "Quantum Gates are very personal creations—the creator's life energy is imbued in it. I do not think we should tamper with anything until we know what she is."

Vincent straightened up from his stance over the ledge.

"Yes," he said, his eyes distant. "What she is, what she was, and what she may become."

11

NEW-ASHEMORE, AMARANTHINE LOOP

The neighborhood had a dark history. At least, that was Aldric's opinion. Surveying the dismal street and its shuttered store fronts only confirmed his thoughts about the real estate here on the north side of town.

The corpse of a building peered down at him as he got out of his car. Scorch marks were still visible while ash and dirt, crumbs of its edifice, littered the sidewalk.

Aldric sighed and looked down the left side of the street. The old garden boxes gaped at him like empty graves. He shook his head. In the early days of his real estate career, the historic neighborhood had just begun to earn its reputation.

Aldric produced some sunglasses, placing them over his eyes before palming his cigarette case. Opening it, he produced a hand-rolled cigarette. He lit it, exhaling a long cloud of smoke. The sunglasses obscured his dreary eyes, and the smoke kept humans from getting too close.

Just then, another car pulled up, and a nondescript man jauntily opened the door. His face was puckered, as if he was holding his breath, afraid to catch a scent of the rotting houses that sat just around the corner.

He looked up at the old building in front of him, his purpose for being on this desolate street today.

"Good afternoon," the real estate agent said.

Aldric had to admit, the building had a *vibe* about it. A Quantum vibe. For several years he had searched, looking for gaps in the Amaranthine loop where she could have entered. But her Gate only whispered, and few Trackers remained who knew what to listen for. Knew what it meant.

Aldric knew. He would know the sound anywhere, thanks to the Future War.

"I've got the keys if you want to go inside," the agent shook some keys happily at him.

Aldric dropped his cigarette to the ground and smashed it with his shoe, extinguishing the cherry. He checked his watch. "That won't be necessary."

"You sure—" the agent said, pocketing the keys before Aldric could respond. "Gotta foul history, whole neighborhood does. I gotta be honest, I thought it was a joke that you wanted to tour the place."

Aldric grinned, or rather, did an imitation of a grin, drawing his lips above his teeth and bending his mouth up like he had observed other humans do in social interactions. "I've already sent the appropriate paperwork to your office, in triplicate."

"Pardon?" the real-estate agent said, opening the file folder he had been holding in his hands. "Have you looked up the public records on it? We've been hired by the City of New-Ashemore to lease the property—"

"No lease," Aldric said, almost impatiently. He took a passing glance over the agent as if to size him up. "I am buying this building from the City."

"Oh!" The agent fumbled with the folder and thumbed through a few pieces of paper. "I mean, I did not anticipate this, so I've left that paperwork back at the—"

"No need." Aldric turned his full attention on the agent. "I had my lawyer transfer the closing costs already. All the necessary paperwork is back at your office, as I said. Your office admin didn't tell you?"

"Er—" The agent felt the pocket of his sports jacket and reached inside for his cell. "Oh, I did miss a call." He squinted at his phone.

"No problem," Aldric said, keeping his mouth upturned in a fake smile. "I would appreciate being able to use those keys."

"Of course! Thank you so much for your business," the agent nervously blurted, accidentally dropping the keys on the sidewalk. Picking them up, he recited the chain of events that would occur during the buying process for the property. "After due diligence, we can finalize the purchase—"

"No way to skip the due diligence is there? Fast track it maybe?"

"Uh..." The agent reshuffled the papers on his leg and placed them neatly back in the file folder. "I could look into that if you'd like, but I strongly encourage you to take the full thirty days to inspect the building—"

"I want to own it now," Aldric interrupted again. "I do

not require thirty days to know what I already know. I want that building."

"If it's construction you want to get started on, those permits from the city generally take a few weeks to acquire anyway—"

"No construction," Aldric said, abandoning his aggressive tactic. "I think I will go for a walk inside—"

"Of course." The agent smiled, relieved.

"Alone," he said, and turned back to the building. He took in a deep breath, as if enjoying the scent of a flower or the smell of a beautiful woman. "I can drop the keys by your office later this afternoon if you like?"

"Mr.— "

"Call me Aldric, please—" he interrupted, his voice pleasant but hard.

"I can't legally allow you to remain on premises," the agent said. "I do apologize, sir. The building has a lot of structural problems, if I can refer you to the—"

"Good lord, we got down to business so fast, I didn't even catch your name—as you know, I'm Aldric Enthenial, A+ Real Estate. I'm well aware of the laws, son, I'm in real estate myself." Aldric extended his hand out to the real estate agent. "Your name?"

"Ben Gelderson," the agent said, his expression bewildered.

"Ben, I just quadrupled your yearly take home pay. I'm going to pay an extra $10,000 upon closing if you leave me alone with this building right now."

Ben Gelderson didn't even blink as he extended his hand, placing the keys in Aldric's waiting palm.

"No need to stop by the office," Ben said, walking to his car. "We've got a second set."

"Excellent." Aldric's grin was no imitation this time.

Inside the dilapidated building, a broken Quantum Mirror covered in soot and grime quietly hummed a song only the Tracker could hear. It was all he could hear. The call of time, and the woman who had traveled through it. With her, Aldric could finally close his Ledger—his Tracker obligation since the beginning of time. He had been Counting with numb clarity for eons.

As Ben Gelderson drove away, Aldric remained. Alone on the street, staring at the building he had just purchased, he felt the crushing weight of his Ledger—his balance of the Count of All Things.

He had been adding and subtracting even in the early dark, as the stars were born. He was there, in the dark, as the solar system which eventually produced Earth was spun out of gas, dust and the encouragement of surrounding exploding supernovae.

Aldric was Counting as Earth came to life. He knew he would still be Counting when the yellow star that brought the planet to life billions of years prior died in the melodramatic way stars do.

He reached into his pocket for the cigarette case. Tears pricked his eyes, remembering the peace of the early Universe. He rolled a cigarette pensively between his fingers, his eyes distant.

"This is fucking exhausting," he muttered, lighting his cigarette. He inhaled, letting the cigarette burn, pale smoke curling around his hand. After a long moment, he ashed it on the sidewalk. The slant of his spine exuded the dispossession he felt over his body. His wan complexion proclaimed he was less than alive, but more than dead.

At first, Aldric had dreaded the Quantum incident that had interrupted his carefully balanced Amaranthine Loop. But now he had the Gate. Now, he had an opportunity.

He took a long drag off his cigarette, smoke curling and burning inside his dead lungs. With her he could do more than close his Ledger, more than balance. If he could find her — this world, every dimension, everything he had ever desired—would be his.

12

LUPUS OBSIDIAN, CERULEAN DIMENSION

P eaches slowly unwound the hand crank that had been synching the vice. It had been tightly clutching a book, made in the old ways—the few crafts and objects of Earth her father would allow on the Obsidian.

She held it, feeling the smoothness of the spine under her aching fingers. She ran her hand over the gold embossed cover, letting her fingertips glide into the creases she had made in her studious labor to reproduce a relic such as this.

She had ceased all research on the Amaranthine after the alarming admission by her father. Combined with his declining physical state, research that could somehow strain her relationship seemed inappropriate at best. She gave it up without a second thought.

"This is turning into a boot strap paradox," she muttered and glanced up, looking at the roughly hewn piece of metal that had been polished until its high shine was almost a mirror—almost. She observed herself curiously.

There were no mirrors in the Time Lab or anywhere else on the ship as a matter of safety. She had made this one in material impossible to be rendered as a Quantum Gate and would shatter instantly if exposed to Quantum energy.

"All the other books in Centius' library have a picture or two," she said, staring at herself as she spoke. Her fire-orange curls spiraled around her face and lay against her shoulders, the length just ending at her waist. She put the book down on the counter, grasping her hair in her reflection. "I'm just keeping up with tradition."

A clear pane of glass lit up, golden sand flowing and creating patterns as if communicating, interrupting part of the book studio's holographic appearance. The sand, and the unknown wind that blew and shifted it behind the pane, was Centius' secret language.

It had been a distinct moment in her otherwise confined life onboard the Lupus Obsidian when Peaches had realized she could decipher the patterns, understand the sand empathically. It was Aldric's bittersweet karma that he could not, even though the sand was the fruit of his dangerous incursions into the Amaranthine.

Peaches turned to the illuminated pane and let her gaze un-focus, concentrating on the sand. Her eyes dilated as she absorbed the information it was communicating.

"I've only done a small revision on the first volume of Elder history," she said, defending herself. She paused for a moment, staring at her reflection. "They read like fairy tales. Papa said Grand-mére read them to him, out of a red book with gold letters." Peaches paused again and sighed, putting her hands on her hips. "The book isn't in your library anymore. I can't find any record of it. As if you've forgotten it, so it doesn't exist. But I *remember* them—all of them. You must have written it in the earlier loop, before..." She averted her eyes from the pane, turning to stare at the mirror again. "I hypothesize you once knew the details of your reunion with Renata... Elders perceive time with a fluidity, and before the Amaranthine truly took hold... I think... I think you attempted to hide your truths in fictions, to outsmart the Amaranthine, to leave clues for us." Peaches nodded, assessing her reflection and hypothesis.

The sands shifted, the pattern undulating and scattering like stardust across the glass. She observed its communication in the mirror's reflection.

"I think the future was recorded in those first few volumes," she said, letting her statement hang in the air for a moment before she continued. "As far as the text, base equations were the most widely known written language among the Supreme Elders at the end of the Future War —" She paused, blinking. She studied her face, touching the dimples on either side of her mouth when she smiled, fingers probing her large eyes. Fascinated, her blonde eyebrows rose as she observed herself.

"I can only hypothesize what form of communication your library comprehends in the final loop... so, I have written it in several that pertain to your past and future! Base equations of the third dimension, Latin—"

The sand lit up, peppering the glass. Peaches nodded in understanding, moving her hair behind her ears.

"Yes, and the Pascal Computer language was a nice touch." She exhaled, continuing to stare at herself in the mirror, imagining Renata. Aldric had mentioned once that Peaches resembled her grandmother—except Renata had green eyes, not blue. And darker skin. *Like sand in sunset*, Peaches remembered him saying.

Peaches turned from the mirror to look at the sand behind the pane. It continued to make strange patterns, glowing with a golden light. She squinted but did not look away.

"The plan was to destroy the mirror once the illustrations are complete," Peaches said easily, before beginning her argument to keep it. She moved a cork-screw curl back from her face, pinching her chin as the sand blew more insistently. "But, it's not like it's a carbon-based mirror, all Quantum Gates have carbon—"

The sand blew with increased speed, the light increasing in intensity.

"I am no more vain than you are a pile of dirt!" Peaches responded, stomping her foot. "I'm not a child, and you don't get to tell me what to do!"

She stepped back, pointing her finger in the direction of the rough-hewn metal mirror. It compressed into a small, succinct wad of metal—making a haunting, abrupt sound as it shrank. Peaches withdrew her hand, startled by the ferocity of her effort. A tiny bead of blood appeared at one nostril and rolled down, meeting her lip.

"There," her voice croaked. "Happy now?" Peaches reached into her pocket, withdrawing a piece of synthesized chocolate wrapped in foil. She put it in her mouth, the sugar and fat immediately easing her telekinetic headache. "You and I decided to do this together, you know, which is technically accepting my father's advice of not coming to a conclusion and finding data that would support it. We are instead abandoning scientific method completely! So don't chide me about vanity. Now, let's get going. I'll meet you at Exports."

Peaches gathered up the book, holding it gingerly against her chest. She paused, feeling the weight of all the words and illustrations she had recreated, as precisely as she could, behind the leather-bound tome. She wondered if Renata would feel anything about this book. Would she feel the love and dedication Peaches had put into it? This was their family history—the key to returning home to the Time Lab, as well as Peaches and Aldric, and the primary mission, to reunite with Vincent.

Centius' sand made a gesture to Peaches to hurry.

"You're so bossy! I can't even get a minute, I've been working non-stop," she huffed, wiping her bloody nose on her knuckle before stomping out of the holographic book studio and entering the Time Lab. "Do you know my hands actually hurt from creating this?"

Centius' panel next to the dais with the primary interface lit up, beckoning Peaches.

"No, I said Exports. We're going to QG1, she's already Quantum manifested in the Amaranthine, I have the precise coordinates."

A panel by Exports lit up, the sand sifting in a garbled pattern that Peaches instantly understood.

"You know, you drop consonants in your French when you're in a hurry," she replied. "Fine, you're right, you should manifest it in your library."

Peaches hopped up the steps to the dais, her fingers grazing the smooth panel, initiating the holographic interface. The light of the holograph reflected against Peaches' creamy complexion. She approved the numbers on the projection with a flick of her wrist, and the metal slot that usually accepted Aldric's cigarette case widened until the book could be accommodated.

Peaches looked at the book in her hands, the hieroglyphics glittering and reflecting in her eyes. She smiled.

"A dream and a prayer, are they not the same?" she said wistfully, placing a light kiss on the cover. She pushed the book into the slot Centius' nano-technology had instantly constructed. Once behind the pane, the book glowed, the spine opening, and the pages rustling as if in a strong gust of wind. Golden particles consumed it until it was pure light and burst into nothing and everything.

13

THE PILLAR, AMARANTHINE LOOP

R enata opened her eyes. Her limbs felt like lead weights, as if still immersed in sleep. Her tongue was thick and dry, lips brittle with thirst. She could feel her pulse throbbing in her temples.

She squinted at soft sunlight beaming through the curtain-less bedroom window. Turning her head, she saw a tall glass of water waited for her on the bedside table.

Her arm, stiff and heavy from disuse, trembled as she forced the glass to her mouth. Small rivulets of water spilled out onto her chin as she drank, finishing the glass of water in one long, loud gulp. Dry lips glistening, Renata eased herself back onto the pillow.

The room was small. A large window with old glass, uneven and warped, gaped with late afternoon light. Almost the golden hour, the sunlight was a familiar amber color, contrasting against the shadows on the wall.

Outside, Renata spied trees and a thicket opening into a vast sloping field. The field was picturesque, with tall grass that swayed in a gentle breeze. The sun beamed with gentle assurance—it was late, and soon would disappear beyond the horizon.

The house was silent.

During her infrequent wakeful moments, she had sometimes heard muffled voices and soft footsteps from the other two beings who resided in the cottage. She pressed her hand gently to her head, closing her eyes.

They aren't men. Not human men.

A choking sob rumbled in her chest. She exhaled slowly, her hands grasping the twisted sheet of the bed. To begin crying now would unleash an overwhelming panic.

"Piensa, Renata," she whispered, remembering what her abuela Noni used to say when she was upset. The familiar phrase comforted her and slowed her breathing.

There were more clothes left out for her in a chair by the window—a soft, baggy, cable knit sweater, pale gray like a goose feather in fog. Underneath it, a black shirt and jeans.

"I guess some clothing items are universal," she said to herself, her voice hoarse from disuse. Her dark hair hung in clumps—large lazy curls cascading around her shoulders. She rubbed her eyes and noticed her fingers came away with eyeliner on them.

She slowly walked to a small square mirror on the wall by the door and touched the black smudges of liquid eyeliner on her eyes... *From last night or was it...more? ¿Cuantas noches? ¿Una semana?* Renata looked away from the mirror and scanned the room for clues on how long she'd been sleeping. There were none.

Carefully, she stepped over to the bedroom window,

eyeing the clothes on top of the chair. Getting dressed seemed like the next logical thing to do.

She leaned on the chair for support, her body feeling weak. She put on the shirt and sweater. She was amused to see the sweater was baggy and hung just above her knees.

"No underwear, no deal," Renata said to the jeans, limp in her hands. She refolded them after a brief inspection and left them on the chair. "I'm not wearing someone else's pants without underwear, because *gross*."

She looked down, and suddenly, a sealed package of cotton underwear and a sports bra were draped over the chair. Renata's eyes went wide, and she grasped the chair as not to fall back.

She looked around the room, confused.

"Okay," she said, her voice cracking. "Clearly not awake yet because I did not see that, at first..."

After she finished getting dressed, she spotted old leather boots and socks beneath the chair. She sat on the bed to try them on. They were exactly the right size but clearly broken in. They were a classic style, old leather high-tops with a thick sole. She puzzled over why there were boots here as well that fit... perfectly.

Renata grabbed the empty glass from the side table. She was still thirsty, and also uneasy sleeping any longer in the house without explanation.

"You're my weapon of choice if things get weird," she said, looking at the glass in her hand.

With a weakened grip, Renata put her hand on the doorknob. Careful not to alert her hosts, she leaned against the wooden door, listening. The house was quiet. She didn't know enough about the two beings' habits to know if that meant they were here or away. Bridling her anxiety and quieting her breath, she opened the door just a crack and peered through the slit.

Down a short hallway, she had an excellent view of a hushed, well-loved library. Crowded with books, it appeared as if someone was reading several different tomes and manuscripts at once. There was a honeycomb of coiled maps perched on top of each other. The rolled maps were fencing in several abandoned books that lay with their spines spread like castaways on a deserted shore. Behind all the clutter was an impressive homage to horticulture—a half-dozen spectacular and varied potted plants huddled on the sill of a wide bay window. The window was looking out into a brief break in the trees, a sunny yard surrounded by dense vines.

Renata glanced quickly to double-check the window behind her in the bedroom. The thicket at the back of the cottage seemed to be the edge of the foliage surrounding the house from the front.

"The house must be surrounded by trees," she whispered to herself. "Which is why I've never seen it walking home from the city—if I'm still in the city—or anywhere near the historic district."

She blinked, realizing she had no way of telling where she was.

Rolling her shoulders back, conviction straightening her spine, she swallowed her fear once more.

"Ahora, Stone," she whispered, looking down at the empty water glass in her hand, summoning her courage.

She gripped the glass tight and slowly opened the door.

RENATA CREPT AROUND THE COTTAGE, looking for signs of Sid and Vincent. When she realized they were not present, she began taking more liberties with her surroundings.

She prowled through the library, gently touching the spines of the books.

Some of these are ancient, she thought. Her fingertips followed the undulating pattern of the books lining the shelves. She observed her hand splayed across the book spines, noticing her blue nail polish. *I remember picking this color*, she thought. *Why does that seem so long ago?* She pushed her hair behind her ears, crossing her arms.

Stepping over to the large bay window, she surveyed the odd assortment of potted plants. She absently touched the leaves of a peace lily that looked freshly repotted. Renata stared out of the window at the vines. She could have sworn the vines stared back.

A book from one of the over-burdened library shelves thudded to the floor. She jumped, startled by the abrupt sound in the otherwise quiet house.

She tilted her head to read the title of the book splayed face down. The edges of its red-wine cover sloped at its dulled corners like overly long fingernails. The gold embossed text was indecipherable but glittered with what could only be explained as an inner light. She bent down to get a closer look at the cover.

Realizing the text was more like hieroglyphics than words, she gave up trying to read it and instead picked up the book. She turned it over, smoothing the crumpled pages. The book had fallen open to an ornately illustrated page. The text inside seemed to be hieroglyphics as well.

She squinted at the image on the opened page and an icy terror enveloped her chest.

"Un sueño," she sputtered. "It's just a dream!"

The book was open to a page depicting a woman, chained to a rock. A distant crescent moon hung over her, against the background of a pitch black sky—

She stared until her eyes burned, afraid to blink. She was holding in her hands an illustration of the same woman from her reoccurring nightmare.

Trembling, she dropped the book. It landed on the floor with a heavy thud, the pages clumping under the weight of its bulky cover.

She backed away, her feet heavy and weightless at the same time. Her right hand stretched out, blindly reaching for the doorknob behind her. Desperation flushed her cheeks as she grasped the knob—it turned, but the door didn't move. She backed into it, in shock, still staring at the book. Frantic, she pushed with all her weight against the door. Still it didn't budge.

It's the front door Stone!

She sputtered a stream of incoherent curse words at her own stupidity before she finally yanked the door open. It ricocheted, crumbling some of the plaster where the knob bashed against the wall.

Vines covered the doorway. Thorny, winding branches crisscrossed the threshold to the front doorway of the cottage.

"You've got to be kidding me!" she exclaimed, her eyes wide with panic. She stepped into and through the vines, hoping to avoid the branches. As if they anticipated her movements, the vines wound themselves around her wrists and waist. She screamed. Her legs kicked into the air as her body was suspended awkwardly above the ground.

She continued to scream, allowing her panic to take complete control. The more she struggled, the tighter the vines' grip became.

Tears began to blur her vision, and her screams subsided. She continued to kick, gritting her teeth in desperation. She could feel the blood being choked out of her hands—they felt cold and prickly. The vines around her waist tightened, immobilizing her. As they wound their way up her torso she felt something snap.

"Let her go!"

Vincent appeared at the forest's edge, in a clearing of the briars. The young girl with golden-ochre skin and long, plaited hair stood beside him. Renata recognized her from before, when she first came to the cottage.

"You are hurting the mortal," the girl said, as if speaking to the plants themselves.

The vines immediately loosened, dropping Renata to the ground. She sat trembling, her breath coming in short wet gasps.

"You directed the vines to stop her?" The young girl next to Vincent was looking at the vines with a worried expression.

"You were there, I merely indicated they should not allow her to leave." Vincent sighed.

"Hmm—" The girl looked from Vincent to Renata. "Plants are very literal creatures. They would have killed her to stop her from leaving, and it would have still been following your orders."

"I was explicit," Vincent growled. "I asked them *not* to kill her!"

The girl rolled her eyes and sighed. She walked over to where Renata was hunched on the ground.

"I am sorry about that." The girl glared at Vincent. "Please, may I see your wrist?"

Renata offered her wrist up, her mind numb. She inhaled sharply when her right arm became fully extended.

The girl's expression soured. "Your rib as well?" She glanced quickly over to Vincent and then back to Renata. "Can you show me?" The girl bent down to lift Renata's sweater.

"No," Renata said through gritted teeth, deflecting the girl's hand. She stood up to her full height, winced and clutched her side before continuing. "Tell me what is going on. Now."

"I think you are injured—again." The young girl glanced meaningfully at Vincent this time. "And very tired from your long journey through your Quantum Gate—"

"Why do you all keep saying that?" Renata snarled. "I don't know what the hell a Quantum Gate is, I don't know where I am, and I don't know who you are."

Renata was clenching and unclenching her fists. One wrist began to seep from a broad but shallow cut. Blood dripped onto the ground. Vincent turned his head from the sight, as if in pain.

The girl looked at Renata's bleeding hand, frowning. She glanced between Renata and Vincent, her image flickering in and out of focus. Renata felt a strange tugging in her mind as the image of the girl standing before her faded into thin air.

Renata gasped and stepped back. Her skin became drenched in a cold sweat, a lightheaded sensation overcoming her panic. She glanced over at the remaining figure of Vincent. His head was turned down and away, not meeting her gaze.

"Please, calm yourself." The vanished girl's voice echoed in the empty air. The girl reappeared, slowly coming into focus. She was frowning. "Your wound is making Vincent anxious, and your emotional energy is obstructing the psychic link that allows you both to see me. Very curious," she finished, almost to herself.

"I'm curious?" Renata shouted. "Where's Sid? Sid brought me here, and Sid can take me home."

"Sid is before you," Vincent said, still looking at the ground.

Renata frowned at the girl and shoved her out of the way, approaching Vincent.

"Do I look like an idiot?" Renata demanded. He did not answer her, his eyes deliberately fixed to the ground and away from her. In frustration, she struck him across the cheek.

Vincent glared into the ground, a low growl emanating from the back of his throat. Like a lead weight, he lifted his gaze.

She shuddered. She felt the eyes of a lonely hunter, finally finding its prey. His blue eyes had gone very dark, his brows drawn down. A muscle in his cheek twitched, but his expression remained blank.

As his gaze fully encompassed her, the temperature

around her body spiked a few degrees. Renata swiped her hand across her face, blood and dirt mingling with her sweat, her eyes wide. She blinked, her fear taking control. She bolted suddenly, running to the side of the cottage, hoping to cut across the field she'd spotted earlier from the bedroom window.

THERE WAS no sound in the brush.

It was eerily quiet except for Renata's own rushed footfalls. Outstretched tree limbs and vine-covered branches attempted to seize her by her hair, sweater, and bootlace. She struggled, stumbled, and drew more blood when she landed briefly on her hands and knees.

Every chamber in her heart urged her to run, panic propelling her up from the ground.

She burst into a thicket that lay before the grassy, sloping field. More forest lay beyond, beckoning from the crest of a steep hill.

The sun was bright, turning pink-orange as it dipped closer to the top of the mountains. Long grass tickled her knees and obscured any rocks or clumps of soil underfoot. She stumbled and fell a few more times as she scrambled up the gentle incline.

Getting back up was pure agony. A pain, clear and bright, blazed in her side. She felt cold but was sweating as painful shivers seized her chest. Her breath felt choked— as if she were breathing through a straw. Determined, she managed some rapid, shallow breaths and continued climbing the hill.

The third time she fell, she remained on the ground. The desire to get up vanished. Laying on her side, she felt a stillness amongst the tall grass rippling in the wind. She brought her knees to her chest and stifled a moan. The world became small and quiet as she realized—she was alone.

Renata closed her eyes, attempting to think clearly.

Suddenly, the wind stopped. Even with her eyes closed, she could sense Vincent sitting next to her in the field. His proximity had a warmth to it, pungent in the stagnant air.

"I paused the sunset for you," he said, his voice velvet and warm. "You are not facing it. Truly beautiful, and I estimate only about seven billion more Earth years to enjoy it."

Renata opened her eyes and looked at his long shadow. Stretched against the sunlight, it was like a dark blanket cast across the ground.

"I do not make promises lightly," Vincent said from behind her. "When you live as long as I do, you tend only to make the ones you can keep. Integrity is everything. We carry it with us, always."

His shadow shrank as he drew closer.

She could feel the heat of his gaze on her back. Her animal instincts stirred, clawing at her with the refrain, *Nothing about this man should be trusted.*

"I promise," Vincent said, defying her fear, "I will not hurt you. I will protect you from harm."

Renata turned from her side and lay on her back, her breath now slow, managed gasps.

"This is my promise, but I can only keep it if I know

who you are." Vincent locked eyes with her, and she felt her heart slow, her body relax.

She noticed she could breathe easier when he looked at her with his strange, blue eyes. They bore into her—brimming with lifetimes of desire and regret. They were mesmerizing—glittering, it seemed, with distant pinpricks of starlight.

She sensed the age and weight of his power. It manifested as a searing, blazing heat that punctuated the air. She exhaled in surprise—he was *terrifying*.

Nevertheless, his promise hung in the still air between them.

She knew with clarity that he really had paused time. She glanced beyond him, to the sun lingering in the sky, a photograph of itself. The tall grass lay at awkward angles, frozen in place, restrained by a suspended breeze coming out of the west.

Finally, she extended her hand out to him, a silent offer of trust. He held her hand in his. The sun resumed setting, like a gold coin descending into a pocket of mountains. The sky faded to orange and periwinkle before she spoke.

"I have had the same dream since the..." she began slowly but didn't finish. Renata cleared her throat and then winced, holding her side tenderly. "I saw a picture of my dream. It was in a book, in your house."

Vincent looked at her with concern. "Perhaps we should start with names again."

Her eyes squinted at him in the twilight, daring him to question her last statement. Finally, she spoke, her voice only a hair above a whisper. "You know my name."

"Renata Stone. I am called Vincent." He gently stroked

her palm with his thumb. "Please, let me lessen your pain. You are wounded. I can heal you." He placed his finger on his opposite wrist and drew downward. As he did, golden energy pooled like blood and spilled over the line traced by his finger, as if it were a blade piercing his flesh.

Renata snatched her hand away, eyes widening.

Vincent whispered hushed, quiet words of comfort and slowly took Renata's hand again. "I am an Elder, I can heal mortal wounds with my life essence, what you would call blood."

Her brows furrowed. "Will it hurt?"

"No," he said, his body framed by the waning light of the evening.

"How do you... do it?"

"Show me where you are wounded," he said, his voice strong but distant. "I will do the rest."

She held her right palm up and saw his wrist hover over hers. She watched bright drops of golden energy seep into her skin. Her entire wound glowed with an amber light. His golden energy felt warm and pleasant, like a long nap in the sun. The feeling faded with the light and only smooth skin remained. She didn't even have a scar. Renata silently produced her other wrist and Vincent healed it as well.

"Your rib—you must remove this." He gently indicated the sweater.

Renata drew her arms up defensively.

"As you know by now, your nudity will not affect me," Vincent said evenly.

Renata's face was pained. "What?"

"You were unclothed when we first met."

"What?" She coughed, wincing with the effort.

"Sid's appearance and clothing are merely psychic projections, one that I was not sharing when we initially—" he said over her cough. He stopped, putting his hand on her chest, lessening her pain. She inhaled slowly, looking at him with grateful eyes. Finally, she spoke.

"You saw me?" she croaked. "I had Sid's trench coat—" she paused in confusion. "Sid is a projection of what—what did you say?"

Vincent frowned.

"Perhaps I said too much, too quickly." He paused, considering his words. "The fact remains that I must be in close contact to heal you properly. You have no need to fear me."

"I'm not afraid," she said contritely. "It's just not every day I meet an Elder-vampire-being-thing that wants to put his hands in my shirt." She faltered, feeling embarrassed.

"I will be the perfect gentleman."

Renata muttered some choice curses in Spanish while tentatively lifting the long sweater up. She winced with pain as she guided his hand chastely to her rib.

"Just do it," she whispered.

The sweater stretched and draped over Vincent's arm. She relaxed her head against the grass, looking up at the night sky. Stars were starting to twinkle and glow like distant beacons.

"It's there," she said, wincing.

He went to work quickly. His palm, fully illuminated by his Elder essence, pressed firmly under her breast and into the intercostal space of nerve, muscle, and sinew between her ribs.

After the pain diminished she felt the fever of his touch, searing and intimate. She also felt her bone warm and reset itself.

When he touched her, she caught glimpses of his age, sensed her lifespan was merely a shudder of breath in his throat, the life-age of humanity thus far barely an afternoon to him. His blood told stories. She felt them, like snowflakes collecting and melting on her tongue. She immersed herself in them as best she could. Although, being so foreign to her concept of time, the story of his life was muffled. She caught only distinct snippets, like a song playing in the background of a crowded room. An eerie sense of Deja-vu whispered under the current of energy pooling inside her from Vincent's touch.

She continued to look at the stars, his warm hand lingering on her body, and time began to have no meaning. It was only at the end, when he moved his hand away, she realized she had been looking not at the night sky, but his eyes.

"Rest a moment," he said, withdrawing his hand.

Vincent rolled his shoulders back, stretching his arms. Finally, he stilled and looked up at the horizon full of stars, a lazy smile spreading across his face. It did not meet his eyes. Instead, his gaze seemed to linger, out of time, staring at a moment just out of reach. He blinked several times, and the look faded away.

"Do you see them? Up there. Your neighborhood constellations. There is the Big Dipper," he spoke at last, pointing into the sky. "And Orion's Belt. And there are the Seven Sisters." He pointed to a cluster of stars. "They will be close to one another for at least 250 million more years."

"Pleiades," Renata breathed, finally finding her voice.

"Yes, Pleiades," he agreed. "The seven divine daughters of Pleione, according to the Greeks. Many Earth cultures have adopted them into legend. Because of our time spent on Earth, Elder culture has done the same." He smiled up at the sky.

"What is the Elder story of them?" she whispered, not yet ready to move.

"This is the Forgotten Queen's constellation, and the stars are the Seven Maidens of Time," Vincent began. "The legend goes that there is an eighth star, or eighth maiden—the Dark star. She is the Queen of the Dark, the Aeor, the Origin from which all they all emerged."

"Why can't we see her?"

"She fractured herself into seven stars, scattering herself across the night sky, to watch over the Universe. The remaining part of the Forgotten Queen exists as only as *time*."

"Wow," she whispered. "How is she a 'Forgotten Queen' if she controls time? Seems like it would be important to remember her name at least—"

Vincent smiled. "These are all metaphors of course, but she is also called the One of Many Names, the Great Mystery, Light-Breaker, the Binder and the Bound. Elders mainly call her the Forgotten Queen or the Queen of the Dark, because she knew time before it began, before this Universe." He waved his hand dramatically.

"Time before it began?" she said, frowning. "Sounds... lonely."

"The divine daughters of Atlas did not fare much better. Zeus turned them into stars as a mercy."

"Only because Orion was a stalker!" she retorted.

"The Seven Maidens of Time is a sad story too," he relented. "But also a noble one. The Forgotten Queen fractured herself into the Seven Stars, and scattered herself across distant galaxies and nebulas to watch over and protect this Universe." Renata quirked a brow, still not convinced. Vincent continued, "One of the seven, Aeor-Eterna, sacrificed herself as a gift to the Supreme Elders, and her blood created the Henge of Time... Or so Elderaen folklore and mythology would tell you." Vincent winked, but Renata was silent.

Her fear once again found purchase and quivered like a caged animal in her chest. She felt a tug in the hollow between her collarbones, and warmth cocooned her body. She felt herself calming—it was the effect of sharing his Elder-light, she realized. She gently touched her chest, her eyes watering. His essence moved in her, and she knew Vincent could feel her fear as well.

He crouched next to her, cupping her face with his hand, eyes scanning for injury.

"What causes this fear?"

"—the sacrifice...is she in the dark? Alone in the dark?"

"So the legend goes—"

"Like my dream," she said, sitting up, her eyes wet with silent tears. "There is a woman, bleeding, chained to a slab of rock, in the *dark*. She doesn't speak, she only stares at the night sky. She is afraid. She is angry. She always knows I am there, staring at her. I never quite see her face." Vincent's eyes widened at that last admission. "Her image —it was in your book, and now you're telling me Elder folklore that's—" she blinked a few times, exhaling. "I've

dreamt it repeatedly, the same dream since the accident—"
she trailed off, remembering the night she woke up in a
field, her car wrecked on the side of the road.

Vincent stared at her, reading her thoughts. "With your
car. Tell me more."

"That's it," she said, sniffling. "That's all of my dream. I
don't remember the accident."

"Tell me about right before the accident," he said,
brushing a few stalks of grass off the back of her sweater.

"I was driving back from my parents in Courier City. It
was late, and I was on some back roads... It's fuzzy."

"Fuzzy?"

"The memory. I don't remember exactly what
happened. I was driving one moment, and the next—I
woke up in a field by the road. My car was destroyed, I
mean *crushed*. Beyond recognition, burnt to a crisp—no
way I could have made it..." She inhaled sharply, dismissing
the grim thought. "There were large gouge marks on the
side of the road, the fire was so hot it even melted the
asphalt. But there was no other vehicle. I was alone before
I... lost time. I remember... before the accident... there was
no one."

"They did not believe you," he said, his eyes looking
through her, seeing into her and to the memory itself.

"No," she shook her head. "No one did. I lost my
license because of a 'medical inability' to drive. But a
seizure sure as hell didn't throw me from my car and crush
it like a soda can."

"Humans are not fond of that which they do not understand, historically."

"The dreams started after that." She shrugged. "The

woman in the dark. I've never told anyone about them. Not completely." She looked down at her hands, remembering the last time she saw Sara.

"Is that why you came here? To learn the meaning of your dream?"

"First of all, I don't know where 'here' is!" She wrapped her arms around her knees. "Second of all, I didn't try to come here. I just did. Suddenly, I was here... I think I lost time again..." She finished on a whisper.

"No, that's not possible," Vincent said, easing back on his knees in the tall grass. "Not unless you have some latent ability as a mortal to time travel—which is unheard of. Please, tell me of the night you met Sid. Spare no detail."

"Well, it was a normal night until the storm started—" Renata told Vincent as best as she could remember what happened before and after she'd locked the salon up for the night.

"You were cut by Quantum Glass?" Vincent asked after she finished.

"You mean the mirror?" She shivered and absently touched her head. Vincent nodded, and removed his tweed jacket, placing it over her shoulders.

"I must confess, I do not know how that will affect you," he began after a pensive moment. "Quantum Glass came into contact with your blood. That is like dipping your hand into the stream of time itself."

"Huh. Well, I wish I could say I feel the same," she looked down at her hands, "but I am different. Even though I know my hands look the same, I know they're different... it's hard to explain. I just feel different, but I can't tell you what it is. It's as if I know the answer to a question that hasn't been asked yet."

"Well, give me some time to rectify that," he said, smiling. "I have many questions. You are a very curious mortal, Renata."

She smiled uncertainly. "You keep saying I'm in another dimension. I don't know much about any of this, but it looks pretty much the same. Except for my entire neighborhood being abandoned. That was weird. Then Sid found me, which was even weirder."

Vincent was nodding slowly, his brows pinched for a moment before he spoke. "I am almost certain you are from a mirror dimension, similar in many ways to this one. When you woke up on the other side of the Mirror, did everything appear as if you were still at your place of employment?"

"The salon?"

He nodded.

"Yes," she said. "It was all exactly the same as the salon..." She paused. Talking about her life in New-Ashemore still felt strange, like an old memory. She ran her hands through her hair. "So, can you tell me what exactly happened to me? And what exactly you and Sid are? And why was I *naked* when we first met?"

"One question at a time." Vincent put up his hands. "But I am happy to answer all." He picked up a long stalk of grass. "You traveled here by a Quantum Gate, which I know we have discussed briefly before. Quantum Gates come in many forms, most have a carbon structure and a highly reflective surface—it is why they are also often referred to as Quantum Mirrors... A Gate is a powerful object, bound with the energy of their creators. You created yours in your salon, its strength bolstered perhaps by the other mirrors there, if I were to guess."

Renata's eyes were wide. "Well don't stop there, Vincent! I mean what the actual f—"

"Indeed," he interrupted, nodding. "Quantum Glass is the substrate, the means of travel through different realities, dimensions, and time. It is created by a being who can understand multidimensional realities and how time and physics interact with them." He paused, waiting for Renata to catch up. She was quiet, contemplative, and pinching her lower lip in thought.

"Basically, what you're saying is that someone much smarter than me can travel by Quantum Glass," she said.

"Not smarter." Vincent shook his head. His neck was regal, complementing his symmetrical jaw. "Someone versed in this knowledge which is both ancient and vast. Renata, you are young and finite, by which I mean— mortal," he clarified, twirling the stalk of grass in his hand. He paused a moment before beginning again. "What I'm saying is, it is not outside the realm of possibility you could learn Quantum Glass travel. But as a mortal, you have not yet been alive long enough to study that process with any great mastery. Nor will you live long enough for that study to ever bear fruit."

"My lifetime is that brief to you," she said, mostly to herself, a note of grief in her voice. She was not accustomed to her mortality being laid so bare. She felt it keenly against the timelessness of Vincent's perception and comparative lifespan. "So, there's that. Obviously a third party involved in this whole 'Quantum Gate' thing."

"A logical conclusion," he agreed. "The thunderstorm you experienced, the power outage around the city, these are inexplicable clues—for what I am not sure of, yet." He paused, thinking. "You were cut with Quantum Glass. As a mortal, I do not understand how it will affect you. One who travels by Quantum Glass puts a great deal of their physical and psychic matter into its creation. The Quantum Gate created in your salon mirror was done by someone or something with a deft and accurate knowledge of time, space, and *you*."

Renata stared at Vincent, the night settling around them like a shroud. She let several moments pass while she mulled over what his last statement could mean. Who had made her a Quantum Gate? And why? Vincent's Elder essence kept her from feeling alarmed by this information, but it was a shadow cast across her mind.

"Do you think I still have a connection or whatever to the Quantum Gate?" She stumbled over the right words to choose.

"Yes, absolutely."

They both sat in silence for several moments looking across the field. The cottage windows glittered in the post-twilight landscape.

"Where are we right now?" she said, indicating the vast sloping field.

"My cottage, this field, and the surrounding forest are all part of my Pillar. The Pillar of an Elder is like a pocket of air inside the current of time."

"So... how long have I been here?" she asked, puzzled.

"Time and paradoxes are not the rule of law here," he replied.

"Is that an answer?"

"I control the Pillar absolutely," he continued. "It is on a cycle of a single day from my memory. You've been here three of those cycles."

"What about whoever Sid said were after me—"

"Trackers. They may not enter a Pillar of the Elder," Vincent said quickly. "You will always be safe here. Were you to leave, I could not guarantee that."

"What about the Quantum Gate thingy?"

"In here, your link to the Quantum Gate and any remaining energy from the Quantum Glass cannot find you," he said, his spine straightening as he spoke.

"It's like Switzerland," she replied. "Are there any more of these Pillar places?"

Vincent smiled sadly, his posture deflating. "There are not any Pillars left—" He was about to begin explaining more when her stomach growled.

"Sorry," she said, rubbing her abdomen. "It's been a while."

"Sid is making dinner as we speak."

"Which one?" she asked.

"The only one," Vincent began. "Sid is a Tardigrade."

"A what?"

"The Tardigrades exist across the cosmos, even on your Earth."

"Have I seen one and not noticed before or—"

He shrugged. "They are quite small. Unseen perhaps to your human eyes. Tardigrades are beings who can exist indefinitely, with or without food and water and in the vacuum of space."

"Alright," she nodded slowly. "I'll accept that, since I

time-traveled through a Quantum Mirror and now I'm in a dream dimension and all that."

"Sid is Chosen and therefore has the most advanced psychic power of any other being or Tardigrade. Sid's physical body is here," he grasped the small, glass vial that hung from a cord at his neck. A tiny cork acted as a stopper for the top.

"Sid is here, but not... here?" Renata struggled to understand.

"Here with me, but as you can see, Sid is not psychically present with us. It is possible for me to say that Sid is also in the cottage, just as I would say any three-dimensional object like a book or a cup is also in the cottage."

"Okay..." she squinted, attempting to wrap her head around the concept. Her brows were drawn together, her green eyes focusing intently on Vincent's face in the soft evening light.

"Sid's psychic ability creates physical form, at least in a way to satisfy the senses of the being it has a psychic link with." Vincent paused, observing her.

She felt his gaze. A warm current of air fluttered over her face, the heat of his eyes emanating their warmth and subtle predatory power. The heat lingered on her for a beat and then evaporated altogether, like a shade drawn over a bright window.

"Have you and Sid always... been this way?" she asked, blinking. The echo of his glance still warming her despite the chill in the air.

"Sid Chose me after the Future War," Vincent said. "We became one. We are forever connected, two embers that burn as one light."

Renata stared at Vincent, her eyes absorbed in his story. This man, or creature—Elder, whatever that was—was older than she could comprehend. He was connected to an immortal psychic being that seemingly was and was not present with them at the moment. *This shit is crazy*, Renata swore in her mind.

Vincent's eyebrows rose with amusement, but he remained silent.

"So, Sid is... kind of like a shared daydream?" she ventured. "Or an astral projection?"

"In a way, for us," he agreed, indicating Renata and himself.

"I don't think I dreamed Sid the same way that you do," she said softly. "At least, not at first. Was Sid that girl who was with you in the forest? Because there aren't two Sids..."

"Yes, the girl you saw earlier was also Sid," Vincent replied. "But you made no mistake, your first encounter with Sid was what your subconscious wanted to see. You wanted Sid's trench coat to be real, and so it was, to you."

"But not for you," she said. Vincent shook his head.

"When we both projected what we thought Sid was, you became quite sick. It can be an uncomfortable experience if you are not used to using your mind in such a way."

"I couldn't ever see his face," Renata said, almost to herself. "Or hers, or whatever..."

"I have imagined Sid as my younger sister longer than you have been alive. It is why you have also assumed that projection."

"You picture Sid as your sister?" Renata asked carefully.

"She perished at the end of the Future War," he said, his voice gliding over the words.

"I'm sorry for your loss," she said, meaning it, but also feeling the limited human empathy behind the words—not enough to comfort an ancient creature such as Vincent. Tentatively, she reached toward him and grabbed his hand. It was brief, and she awkwardly withdrew. She felt sympathy, but also trepidation. Vincent was a tremendous being. Renata was not entirely convinced the form he presented to her now was necessarily his only form, or true form. After absorbing his Elder essence she understood more about him... combined with a tacit knowledge she possessed before they met. *Is the Quantum Gate why he feels so... familiar? This is all fucked up.*

Renata swallowed, anxious bravery bullying her next words out of her mouth.

"But, Vincent, I saw something else, besides Sid's appearance change. I saw you—"

"My apologies." He reached and grasped her hand back, which had retreated inside his tweed jacket. Well-worn and cozy, his jacket slumped roomily over her shoulders and arms. "I am not accustomed to an empath and did not attempt to hide my thoughts."

"I'm not an empath," Renata snorted. "I just saw it, y-you wanted to eat me, I think? It's kind of hazy but I know it terrified me..."

"Renata," he said. "Look into my eyes, I will never hurt you."

She felt her heart wince. She had formed, almost immediately, a connection to this being, Vincent. But she was also fearful—there was danger in feeling any kind of bond to a creature she may never completely understand.

Vincent interrupted her thoughts.

"We have had a great conversation, but I think now, it is enough. We have many more things to discuss, but there is plenty of time. Please, let me escort you to the cottage. Sid is probably done preparing dinner."

"A psychic Tardigrade that can survive the vacuum of space—and cook?"

Vincent laughed as he stood up and held out his hand. She took it without hesitation.

There was a part of him in her now, she could feel it. His blood, his life essence, whispered in her veins. She felt connected—acutely aware of all the bonds of energy interconnected in the Pillar.

She looped her arm around his and was reminded of his touch. It was electric and balmy, like a soft blanket left out in the sun. She felt where his hand had been on her chest.

It was still warm.

14

THE PILLAR, AMARANTHINE LOOP

The table was set. Renata leaned over the three small place settings, surveying her handiwork. Folded cloth napkins sat like fat doves nestled between the fork, spoon, and knife. A small smile crept over her face at the sight of them, perched in a frame of cutlery. She was reminded of her abuela Noni and the Sunday evening dinners her family used to have. It was an excuse to get all of the extended family together again— never mind that the grandchildren lived so close, and abuela Noni saw them for dinner after church every Wednesday. Sunday dinner was sacred. Abuela Noni always used her best silver for family dinners, a wedding gift from her husband Archie's family. She was house proud.

Vincent and Sid did not have fine silver. Their ceramic plates had a dark blue glaze—blue like the night sky lit by a crescent moon, Renata decided as she placed them on the table. The blue contrasted against the honey colored wood of the table, and paired well with the small copper cups she had discovered.

She frowned. Their cutlery didn't glisten like abuela Noni's either, but it would have to do.

Renata walked to the kitchen, filling the copper cups with water.

"My apologies," Vincent said behind her. "If the silverware is not to your liking."

She startled at the kitchen sink, putting a hand on her chest.

"It's fine," she assured him, a little breathless. "You snuck up on me there—" she said, turning to look at him. She smoothed a strand of hair behind her ear.

"What did she make?"

"Pardon?" Renata asked, blinking. She turned the faucet off to look at him fully. His eyes were a vacuum, round blue orbs that swallowed everything—the whole room, every thought, every movement. She decided to look at his forehead instead of his eyes.

"Your grandmother." He squinted, listening to something. "Abuela Noni."

"How did you—" she said. He cut her off with a wave of his hands.

"You have some of my..." He paused searching for the right term. "When I healed you—afterward, it makes your thoughts easy to read." He gave her a reassuring smile before continuing, "You have warm memories of her."

"You would too, if you ever met." She crossed her arms. She glanced along the hairline of Vincent's temple, to the ear pinning back some of his hair. She felt uneasy about his ability to guess—no, *read* her thoughts. She decided not to agonize over it, since that was the least weird thing that had happened to her recently.

"Who is to say I never will."

"She died several years ago," she said, her smile sad.

"She lives here," he replied, and pointed to her head, and then to her heart. "Your memories of her are treasured. What did she cook?"

"Tamales, and sopa de pan on special occasions." Renata's expression brightened, remembering. Her eyes scanned down his jawline, strong and angular and shaved clean. *Had he shaved for dinner?*

"I did." Vincent smiled. "Where was abuela Noni from on your Earth?"

Renata blinked in surprise, quickly shifting her gaze away from his face. She busied herself with putting the copper cups on a tray to take back to the dining table. Afterward, she leaned back against the counter, her posture relaxing as she spoke.

"Mexico. She and abuelo Archie moved so he could finish writing his doctorate thesis on the Entomology of Southern Mexico and Central America. They married in Chiapas first, and then in Lyon, France—because abuelo Archie grew up there. It was afterwards they moved to the States—he got a prominent position as a professor at a university. After they had my mom they applied for citizenship."

"They sound like an unusual couple," he said, smiling.

Renata nodded, returning his smile. "Abuela Noni said she loved having two weddings because it meant two anniversaries." She laughed, and covered her mouth with her hand, remembering. "The farm was her idea. When they moved to the States, she convinced abuelo Archie to buy a house with large pastures and a river alongside it. She raised sheep, just like her parents had. She had a garden like she did as a girl. She grew corn. Fresh greens, I can see fresh greens and dark soil in my hands," Renata finished, her gaze soft.

"You loved to cook with her."

She nodded. "She had a special soup pot. My mamá got it when abuela Noni died." She paused, inhaling as if she could catch a whiff of abuela Noni's Sunday dinner. "The tamales always got perfectly steamed in that pot. She would wrap them in corn husks first, the tamales I mean, and arrange them around the pot in a small wire basket above the water. But the pot was special."

"What was so special about it?"

Renata shrugged. "It was magical. Plain and simple. Nothing to look at. The under part was black, but nothing ever burned or singed or tasted less than amazing—we all called it '*La Olla*.'" Renata lifted her hands up in mock exaltation.

"'*The Pot*'," Vincent translated. "Perhaps it was magical because she cooked for you in it every Sunday."

"Maybe," Renata said, suspicious of his knowledge. Her gaze settled on his mouth instead of his eyes. She felt uncomfortable with how much she liked looking at his mouth and instead hazarded a glance back up at his eyes. "But '*La Olla*' was older than me. I think it was a wedding present. I know it came with her to the States, I think it was a wedding gift..." Renata paused, her gaze distant. "She always cooked for the family with that pot. She never returned to Chiapas, so I think in some way, *'La Olla'* made her feel closer to home."

Vincent stared at Renata, their conversation lulled for a moment. She felt his eyes on her—felt herself being deeply seen. She locked eyes with him, and for several lush seconds, she felt his emotion too, as if she were turning the radio dial and suddenly stumbled upon his frequency.

It was warm. She felt her muscles relax and her blood thicken to honey. Even her heartbeat slowed in his uncompromising stare. Renata felt air burning in her chest as she paused in the heat, forgetting to breathe. She fought against closing her eyes, to give in to the lethargy the warmth of his attention produced. She saw his thoughts—or maybe just a fragment of a fragment of his thoughts, vast and ancient as they were. She couldn't focus enough to understand his intent and was instead hypnotized by the heat of his Elder power.

"You have abilities you should be more careful to control," he muttered, his voice almost a guttural sound.

"But that wasn't me—" She managed to reply in a wheezing exhale.

The heat disappeared. It was like a door slammed, and she was in a dark, cold room—except she was in Vincent's well-lit cottage. A log cracked from the blazing fire in the hearth in the other room. Renata flinched.

The duality did not make sense. The light remained the same, but the feeling, the warmth was gone.

Humans mistook them for vampires... Could they have mistaken them for angels as well? She thought, scrubbing her face with her hands. Feeling his power, the heat and the energy, was almost an ecstatic experience.

"I think it a grave mistake for a human to think we are any more than what we are," Vincent said to Renata, answering her unspoken thoughts once more.

She looked up at him then and saw him for the predator that he was—his bewitching gaze, his lithe and ethereal body. The muscles in his arms and broad shoulders strained against his white button-down shirt. He didn't visibly breathe, and his blue eyes never blinked. How anyone could mistake him for human was unimaginable to her now.

"In time, you may come to understand what an Elder is. Angels we are not. Devils neither," he finished quietly.

"Dinner is ready!" Sid walked into the kitchen with a steaming pan of soda bread. "Bread is done, stew is piping hot! Shall we eat?"

Renata blinked a few times and took a deep breath.

"Table is set," she said, half-smiling. She glanced quickly away from Sid and to the floor, refusing to look at Vincent. "Excuse me, I need to wash up," she said, turning.

In a small, almost primal way, it felt unsafe to turn her back on either of them. Vincent and Sid left the kitchen as she stood at the sink and twisted the faucet. Renata felt the water flow over her hands. She rested them under the tap for several long seconds.

She needed a moment to compose herself, the interaction with Vincent had needled something inside her. The nagging familiarity of him. *That's what it is. He can't be familiar. He shouldn't even be real.*

She squeezed her eyes shut, attempting to banish the thought. The feeling persisted, however. *Weird. Super weird.*

She dried her hand on a towel hanging on a hook in the

kitchen window, collected the tray she had placed the copper cups of water on, and walked back to the make-shift dining area next to the hearth.

She attempted a convincing smile. "Let's eat!"

"**T**HIS IS AMAZING," Renata said through mouthfuls of bread.

Sid had two more skillets of bread cooling on a rack in front of the roaring hearth. A large pot of stew sat on the table, the ladle resting beside the pot.

"It is my favorite new specialty!" Sid exclaimed. "Mortals need food, and I have always wanted to excel at cooking."

Renata tore a piece of bread and sopped up her last spoonful of stew with it.

"I can't believe I ate so much." She stifled a belch and covered her mouth with her hand, smiling. Vincent raised an eyebrow. "Sorry. Food is so...great," she said with an apologetic sigh.

"Please, have more!" Sid scooted a plate of bread toward Renata.

"I'll need to wait a moment." She pushed back from the table and sighed again, rubbing her belly. She closed her eyes, smiling.

"*Is this normal?*" Vincent said telepathically to Sid.

"I think my life is beyond the definition of normal at this point," Renata said, eyes still closed.

"You heard my communication with Sid?" Vincent said audibly.

"Yeah—" she cracked one eye open. "When you speak out loud, even us puny mortals can hear." She adjusted in her seat, drawing her knees up in front of her.

"It was not 'out loud'—you heard us through our telepathy. Vincent fails to shield his mind as he should," Sid said, giving Vincent an accusatory shake of their head.

Vincent rolled his eyes at Sid's small rebuke.

"Clearly, you have some latent abilities of a kind. You can see me, first of all, and now you can communicate telepathically. Remarkable," Sid finished, looking at Vincent with wide eyes.

Renata grasped her hair. "Well, we're all dreaming the same thing here, Sid, so it doesn't seem so weird that I'm in on the conversation."

"Humans will never evolve enough to communicate with Tardigrades or Elders telepathically," Vincent said, dipping his finger into the copper cup until the water became wine. Renata's eyes almost inflated out of their sockets. "It is impossible on many levels."

Sid nodded.

"Right, if it's going to be another one of those conversations—" Renata pushed her copper cup toward Vincent, inclining her head. "I'll need a little bit o' the magic touch I saw you give your glass of water, please and thank you." Renata cleared her throat as Vincent let his finger graze the surface of the water. It swirled with an inky purple, the smell of fermented grapes and sunshine wafting to her nose. She let out a little gasp.

"The Tardigrade will contact human mortal life in about 250 billion years or so, but the means of that communication has not even occurred to us yet," Sid added, watching Renata's reaction to Vincent. "Let alone the fact that a human's current ability to hear any psychic phenomenon is inferior at best. Your psychic link with me defies the timeline we have for mortals in this dimension." Sid stopped talking and frowned as Renata was staring, slack jawed at them. "Sorry, I do not often speak to anyone but Vincent, so I do not know when to stop and only say it... in my mind... " Sid trailed off. Renata stared for several seconds at Sid, and then to Vincent, pensive.

"Well, boys—" she sighed, breaking the awkward silence. She leaned forward in her chair, plucking a piece of bread from the table. "Sorry Sid, and girls—"

"I do not identify with either sex," Sid said genuinely.

"Noted," Renata said, nonplussed. "I think I'm going to have seconds." She stood up, draining the cup of wine before filling her bowl with more stew. Sitting back down, she also grabbed another slice of bread. Sid moved the butter dish toward her.

"Oh," she said absently, reaching for the butter. "Where's the knife—" As she said 'knife,' the buttery blade slid of its own accord toward her across the table. It stopped at the threshold of her hand, which was now gripping the table ledge. She looked up, eyes wide with shock.

"How did you accomplish that?" Sid said immediately.

"No! I thought you—" Renata looked around helplessly. "I didn't! No, no, no." She buried her face in her hands, her elbow shoving the knife off the table. It clattered unceremoniously on the floor.

"Can you... try again," Vincent said, standing beside her chair suddenly, his voice calm. He looked at her in silence while she tried to gather herself.

"I don't know how I did it," she whispered, fighting back tears.

"Renata," he said, bending down. "Do not fear what you can do. Please, try again."

She sighed and leaned over the side of the chair, looking at the knife on the floor. It was surrounded by breadcrumbs, leaving a swipe of grease on the scuffed, wooden floorboards.

"Knife," she said, opening her palm on the table. She repeated the word. The knife flickered in movement.

Renata looked at Vincent. He was standing back now, hands clasped behind his back, his expression unreadable, blue eyes keen and observant.

"Again," he whispered, his gaze flaring.

"Cuchillo," she tried calling it in Spanish, closing her eyes. It flipped over on the floor but did not rise to her hand.

"Think what you were thinking when you called it before," Vincent suggested helpfully.

"I was thinking about how delicious buttered bread is," she snapped.

Vincent nodded toward her and shrugged.

She sighed, exasperated. "*Knife*," she said out loud. It rose slowly and plopped itself into her outstretched palm.

"Curiouser and curiouser, to borrow a phrase." Sid looked meaningfully at Vincent.

Renata looked at Sid as she spoke. Her eyes brimming with unshed tears, her gaze piercing and emotional. The Tardigrade didn't appear to notice. Renata turned her head to the other room and looked at Vincent's library. She stomped toward the bookshelves and scanned their spines.

"*Libro*," she said forcefully. A plant on top of the bookshelf shuddered as the red-wine colored book with gold hieroglyphics sank into her grasp.

She stalked back across the room to the dinner table, shoving her dinner plate aside. She placed the heavy tome down.

The book landed with a thud. She flipped it open to the illustration of the woman in the dark she had seen before.

"What is this?" Renata pointed angrily with her blue manicured finger. "And more importantly, what am I?" Her jaw flexed in a grim line as hot tears dribbled down her cheeks. She smeared them off with a shaking hand. "This isn't *just* my dream."

Vincent leaned over the table, brow furrowed, squinting at the book. His fingers touched the page with the woman's illustration. She was chained, her face upturned to a distant moon.

"This is... not a book I recognize," he said at last. He gave Sid a sharp look.

"It was in your library," Renata exclaimed.

"That it was." Vincent nodded, turning the page.

"What does it say?" she asked, her voice getting desperate.

"This is not—" he paused, squinting at the text. "This is not a language I know..."

Renata's hands collapsed at her side in defeat. She turned, exasperated, and walked to the hearth. There, she slumped in Vincent's waiting armchair, putting her hands over her face.

"To everything there is a season," Sid said to the room.

"Perhaps we should all settle in by the fire. I will make coffee."

VINCENT DIDN'T RESPOND. His gaze was on Renata who sat in silence, wiping her tear-streaked face.

"*This book is about the Future War,*" Vincent said telepathically to Sid. He watched Renata in his armchair, her figure backlit by the fire. He looked down at the book, thumbing through some of the illustrations.

"*A book about the Future War mysteriously appears in your library?*" Sid replied, peering over the book as well.

"Strange that I can't read it," Vincent replied, audibly. It was the truth, and he wanted Renata to hear it.

"*You often have potted plants appear in your library as well,*" Sid said inaudibly, shielding their communication from Renata.

"*Those are plants,*" Vincent said privately to Sid. "*This book is a... memory of mine.*"

"*What is her dream doing in your memories?*" Sid glanced up at Vincent.

Vincent's eyes remained on the book, his expression closed.

"*This is a large book. It may not be all about her,*" he said, unable to answer Sid's question.

15

THE PILLAR, AMARANTHINE LOOP

S id insisted they all have a cup of coffee by the fire and continue their conversation about the book.

Vincent brought in cups of steaming black coffee, while Sid followed behind him holding a tray.

The tray was lacquered wood with a delicate painting of a summer landscape on its sleek surface. The tray held a small ceramic cow filled with cream, whose upturned head served as its generous spout. Next to it was a small silver chalice overflowing with sugar cubes. She smiled, thinking of her late grandfather, Archie, who had enjoyed after-dinner coffee and making her listen to jazz on his old record player.

As she looked between Sid and Vincent, she realized they were doing this for her. They had no need for food or drink—or audible conversation, for that matter.

She sighed, stirring milk into her cup and enjoying the white cloud of cream swirl and lighten the depths of her mug. The familiarity of these rituals around food—dining at a table, having after-dinner coffee—did have a grounding effect. She put one lump of sugar in and stirred. She took a tentative sip of coffee, testing the heat.

"The best answers are given to the best questions," Sid began.

Renata set her mug down between two star charts sprawled on the library desk. She inhaled deeply, her eyes downcast and unfocused on the steaming coffee.

The trio were silent for several moments.

She wrung her hands. They were beginning to sweat. She exhaled, realizing that she had been holding her breath. The nagging feeling persisted. She shivered and reached for her mug. *Café? Sí, I used to drink this in New-Ashemore. My favorite coffee shop was just up the street, I stopped there almost every morning...*

She sipped in silence, trying to solidify the memories of her former life in her mind. More and more, that world seemed like an echo, the fine details becoming hard to remember.

"I must be somehow tied to all of this," she said, finding her voice. She turned to Vincent and Sid, who had been observing her in silence. She lowered the mug from her lips. "How else can any of this be explained? Me being here, now, with you—I have a sort of connection. That much we know, right?"

"A mortal with a Quantum Gate, found by a Tardigrade and brought to a Pillar of the Elder," Vincent said. "Were I not witnessing it now, I would tell you this is impossible."

"I'm in the company of two beings who are... I can't even—" she stopped speaking, looking defeated. She cradled the mug in her hands.

"The image here is a divine one—" Vincent picked up the book Sid had retrieved from the dining room table. "Ah —like the Christ in Christian mythology. The crucifixion is a divine symbol of Christ, correct?"

Renata nodded, her brow furrowed.

"Just as the Christians from Earth depict Christ on the cross, Elders depict Divine Death. Essentially, it is an image of the Forgotten Queen chained to the Stone of Time. The chain is meant to represent the Universe she is Bound to, the Stone represents the void she fragmented herself from, turning into the Seven Stars," he said.

"The Queen?" she said.

"Remember the story I told you, about the Pleiades cluster?" Vincent replied. Renata stiffened, sucking in a breath.

"But you said those were just stories—"

"That's correct," Sid interjected, cutting their eyes at Vincent. "This is all Elder folk-lore. Mythology, religion, call it what you want—"

"How could I be dreaming of *her*?" she whispered, pressing her hand against her chest.

Vincent looked sharply at Sid before speaking. Renata leaned in, frowning.

"What are you saying to each other? Spill it!" She barked, pressing her hands over the book. The hieroglyphics glittered and moved in response.

"Look!" Sid pointed at the book. "It changed."

"It did?" she said, looking down. She moved her hand. The gold lettering rotated in and out of different symbols, but every third or fourth rotation there were actual phonetical letters Renata knew she recognized.

"I can read English and Spanish, maybe a little French if you pressed me—*merci Grand-père Archie*—but some of those words looks like Latin... sometimes. Sometimes it looks like absolute numbers, just a long string of them..." Renata said, moving her hair behind her ears. She crossed her arms, letting her gaze leave the book and travel to Vincent, who remained silent and transfixed.

"I do not know," he finally said. "The hieroglyphics, if they can even be called that, seem to have a pattern... but I can't read it, I almost can, but it's not quite..." He grew very still, his hand paused over the book.

"The story of the Queen is also a metaphor about the beginning of time," Sid said, filling the silence. "You Earth mortals have stories about the stars and the beginning of time, do you not?"

"Yes. But why have I been having dreams of *Elder* folk-lore? And it's the same dream—over and over!"

"You are here because you must be," Vincent said, closing the book. "There are forces at work with you that I do not completely understand, yet. But you are here for a reason."

"As for what you are, there are more unknowns in the vastness of creation than knowns. You number among the unknowns," Sid supplied.

"Is that supposed to be comforting?" Renata asked, her voice cracking. She rubbed the back of her neck, frowning.

"The Arbiters of Nihil," Vincent suggested, his gaze dark and serious. "They might have knowledge regarding this—"

"That is a bit pre-mature, Vincent," Sid interrupted. "We must first calculate their current location in the

Breaking of the Light, and that is after we determine if it is even *appropriate* to contact them..." Sid pinned Vincent with a measured look, Renata could not read the intent.

"Who are the Arbiters of Nihil?"

"The Arbiters of Nihil are a council of Supreme Elders who are locked in the Breaking of the Light as penance for the Future War," Sid replied.

"What—" she sputtered. "What does that even mean?"

"The Arbiters know a great deal of the history and future of the Universe," Vincent said. "Their knowledge is vast."

Sid interrupted, their tone sharp. "The Arbiters are indeed destined to know all of the history and the future of the Universe, to be shorn of their bloodlust and past transgressions from the Future War—to be instead a wealth of knowledge. But the Breaking of the Light makes an estimate nearly impossible to know their current... disposition—"

"What is the 'Breaking of the Light' exactly?" Renata asked.

"I believe you would refer to it as a black hole," Sid said.

"Oh," she nodded, biting her lip.

"The Supreme Elders who escaped the Future War remain forever in the Breaking of the Light. They are undying and unyielding—destined never to interact with the Universe they must bear witness to," Vincent clarified.

"Sounds... harsh," Renata replied, making a face.

"But because of their unique position in space-time it is likely they have knowledge about who and what you are..." Vincent looked at Sid, his jaw set.

"They may have great knowledge," Sid said, pausing to choose their next words wisely. "But to inquire with them is not without danger."

A silent pause was shared by the three of them.

Renata sipped her coffee. She stole a glance at a star chart spread on the library table—hoping, conveniently, that it would have a big bright dot exclaiming 'Arbiters of Nihil' so she might better understand where they were. Distances and time aside, this was all strange new geography. Her idea of the world and the Universe as a whole was growing exponentially at the moment. She wished for a map suddenly to reference it all.

"If you did all your calculations, and sent the ANs your version of an inter-galactic e-mail, how long will it take to, you know, hear back?" she asked, breaking the silence.

"The 'ANs'?" Sid asked.

"We gotta shorten that name."

"Oh! Like a nickname?" Sid exclaimed.

"Yeah," she replied. "Like a nickname."

"I do not know how long it will take to hear from them," Vincent said, widening his stance. He crossed his arms. "The Arbiters live cyclically in the Breaking of the Light—"

"Breaking of the what again?"

"Black hole," Sid said. "Time does not adhere to any laws near them, making an estimate... difficult."

Renata nodded.

"Actually, depending on the result of our calculations on their spacetime—" Vincent stopped as Renata held up her hand.

"Speak human to me," Renata interrupted. "None of that means anything."

"The Arbiters of Nihil exist on what Earth scientists would describe as the 'event horizon' of a supermassive black hole—the rim of the Breaking of the Light. There, they exist indefinitely," Sid replied.

"Gosh, Sid—" Renata sighed heavily, rolling her eyes. "Thanks for the clarity."

"You are welcome." Sid smiled.

"You do not know that the center of what you call the Milky Way Galaxy is a super massive black hole?" Vincent asked.

"Ugh," Renata said, flipping her hair behind her shoulders and shrugging. "I guess."

"At the center of your galaxy, as it is with most galaxies across the Universe, there is a supermassive black hole. Time moves strangely and very slowly in these environments. There, the Supreme Elders remain forever in timelessness. As the eons pass, they have become the Arbiters of Nihil, as they are now, will be, have become, beings with the most knowledge about this Universe."

"So, it's going to take a while to hear back?" Renata grasped her mug, listening. Holding it under her chin, enjoying the warmth, she felt a momentary sense of security and nostalgia.

"At the rim of the Breaking of the Light—or black hole as you call it—time is very hard to decipher. That is why before we contact the Arbiters, there is some research Vincent and I must complete..." Sid said in a serious tone.

"Can't I just—go home? I mean, until you guys, er—sorry, Sid—until you both hear from them, can't I just return to my dimension thingy? I don't have my phone to check, but I'm pretty sure I have a full book of appointments next week. I'll receive a few choice comments from my clients if I take an unexpected vacation... And there are some bills I need to get on top of, and this music festival—I have tickets, and it's at the end of the month... It's been a few days, but you know, there's stuff I need to get back to." Renata shrugged, taking a big swig of her coffee.

Both Vincent and Sid stilled, the steam of their coffee whispering casually up into the air. A beat passed.

"Yes, of course," Vincent blurted. "We will research those calculations as well—"

"—I think you should stay here for just a few more days," Sid said at the same time. They exchanged glances and Sid continued. "Your Quantum Gate is of great interest to the Trackers in New-Ashemore. The longer you stay away from it, the more the energy goes dormant. They will soon be unable to Track it."

"Dormant? But I don't want it to go dormant, I need it active, so I can get back, right? To my home dimension-thingy."

"For you, it will always exist," Sid said. "Your life energy is tied to it."

"Kind of like the Pillar is to Vincent?"

"Kind of." Sid nodded and glanced meaningfully at Vincent.

"Renata—" Vincent put his mug down and looked, full force at her. "Is there anything else you can tell us about your life in the other dimension? Your accident, your job—any detail that you think may give us more clues to just what is going on here, what you are?"

"What I am?" Renata scoffed. "I'm human. I was born, I grew up, I got a job. The end. The craziest thing to happen in my whole life, besides the car accident last year, *is this*!" She put her arms up, gesticulating. "Landing here, in another dimension!"

"That is a synopsis of your life," Vincent's eyes narrowed. "Think deeper."

She thought of her home, New-Ashemore. She thought about her job at the salon. It seemed like a dream more than a memory. This cottage and the two beings who stood before her were seeming like the most real part of her life yet.

Renata looked down at her hands. She thought of the knife, coming toward her across the table at dinner—as if she had thrown a fishing line out to it, the lure her thought to butter bread with it. The knife had obeyed her thought, following her energy like a receding tide to her hand.

She had done it before.

She shook her head, her hair spilling over her face. She pushed her hair behind her ears, remembering. It had been her scissors back then. She hadn't been the same after the accident. Afterward, she had moved scissors to her hand like that—like the knife. She'd only done it once, before she began a haircut on her first day back. She had blamed it on the anti-seizure meds at the time, clouding her judgement. *It was nerves*, she'd told herself later. *I imagined it.*

"I'm sure being an empath has helped you with your job —" Vincent broke the silence. Renata looked up from the pensive study of her hands, meeting his probing blue eyes. "What about the telekinesis?"

"Teleki-what?"

"When you moved the knife, and the book," he said helpfully.

"I've never done that before." She lifted her chin. "And I've told you, I'm not an empath."

"So, these powers manifested on this side of the Gate?" Sid said.

"Yeah, I guess." She glanced away to the corner of the library, anywhere but at the two beings before her.

She didn't want 'powers,' didn't want to go down the path of what all this could mean. She'd felt cursed by some dark destiny since the accident and didn't want to admit that some of this present situation seemed inevitable, or almost achingly familiar—Deja-vu, as lame as it sounded. She thought about what Vincent had said about the Quantum Glass. She had been cut by the Glass as she traveled through it... "*Like dipping your hand into the stream of time itself.*" Had it poisoned her? Was it mutating her genes? If she were to leave the Pillar, would she mutate? Her eyes widened at the thought of growing a second head and the arguments she would have with her other head. Awful.

"Listen," she said, putting up her hands. "My life before was pretty humdrum. No teleki-whosee-whats-its, no empath mind-reading stuff." She paused. "I cut hair, and I'm pretty sure I cut hair in linear time. All of this is new to me. I'm sorry, I don't have any helpful details."

She shrugged and smoothed her hair over to one shoulder. She could feel Vincent assessing her words, her body language, her attitude. His gaze was intent, as if he were listening, could almost hear her heartbeat.

"You must be tired, Renata," Sid said. "Quantum travel

is exhausting for Tardigrades, so I imagine it is even more acutely tiring for a mortal."

"Please," Vincent said, approaching her. In less than an eye blink, he was face to face with her, his gaze ensnaring her. "You want to sleep now." Renata nodded mutely, her eyes closing as she dropped her coffee cup.

It shattered on the floor.

THE ROOM WAS DIMLY ILLUMINATED from the starlight bleeding through the windows. Vincent put Renata in the bed, pulling the covers up to her chin.

He paused, watching her. Her pulse spoke clearly to him. He was getting used to the reliable rhythm of it, strumming like a constant chord.

He knew by her pulse alone she was holding back about her past—he'd felt it in the library.

Her strange heartbeat was a familiar song to him too. *Had it always been familiar?* Her heart skipped a beat whenever she locked eyes with him. He'd noticed it when they first met, again in the field, and finally in the kitchen where she had stumbled into the slip stream of Elder energy that was also an entrance to his psychic mind, the depths of which manifested all that she saw and experienced in the Pillar.

What does that missing heartbeat say?

He stared at her as she slept, mulling over the mystery that was Renata Stone. She had powers, that was undeniable now. They were strong and unrestrained. That much he knew was true.

He turned, leaving his mystery of a mortal to sleep for now. The question of her being would wait.

He closed the door behind him with an audible click.

BACK IN THE LIBRARY, Sid was standing, looking at the shelves of books, as if to pick on out. Sid enjoyed Vincent's penchant to store much of his knowledge in an imagined library, full of imagined books.

Sid's pleasure aside, Vincent had long ago decided to imprint his thoughts, memories, and comprehension of the Universe into tomes, atlases, literary prose, star charts, and cosmological maps. Vincent manifested all of it, placing the books onto shelves and closing their spines. The maps were rolled up and delicately stacked on each other in a small cubby next to the bookshelf. He condensed his culture and heritage into volumes, creating the only ency-clopedia of the Elders in existence. The irony was, he no longer remembered the precise reason he'd started the library—only that it was very important for him to always maintain it.

Vincent noticed Sid's gaze was faraway.

"It could take some time to hear back from the Arbiters," Sid said, not turning from the books lined neatly across the shelf. "The ANs."

Vincent felt the ghost of a smile in Sid's voice.

The Elder stood over the broken coffee cup and the puddle of liquid on the floor of his study.

Backward, he thought.

From his commandment, the pieces lifted and fused

to form the cup they once were. The cup retreated back to its original position—held just about at arm's height, full of coffee. Suspended in mid-air, Vincent grasped the mug by its sloping ceramic handle. He placed it on the desk.

"Mortals do not have time like we do."

"Yes, I know," he replied to Sid. "But we are in the Pillar, in an alternate dimension from her own. Time is different in this pocket dimension. Her body will not age here, though she may mark the passage of days."

"Renata has been here for only three days, but back in her home world, she is long forgotten," Sid said, turning finally to look at Vincent.

"I had wondered," he said, his eyes breaking from Sid's and looking at the coffee cup on his desk. His dark blue eyes, large and shadowed, held a passing moment of grief in their gaze. He exhaled, preparing for what he was about to hear.

"I estimate that every day spent in your Pillar is at least a decade, perhaps more, back in her home dimension of New-Ashemore. The branch of your Pillar leading to our dimension of New-Ashemore moves at quite a clip anyway—"

Sid turned away from the library shelf and faced Vincent.

"You are suggesting she has no home to return to?" Vincent met Sid's gaze.

"It is usually an entire Earth year in our branch of New-Ashemore for a single day here in the Pillar," Sid said pensively.

"Do you think the distance between her original

dimension and ours will likely accelerate the passage of time there?" he asked.

"Yes," Sid's eyes flashed, their brows pinched in concern. "The farther she remains from her home dimension, the faster time will pass there. We are suspended in time here due to the nature of your Pillar, but outside—it moves on."

Vincent moved his hand over the coffee cups on the desk, and they vanished. He sat down in his favorite brown chair in front of the hearth by a large stack of books. He stroked his chin, looking at the floor.

"Extraordinary circumstances aside, she is our ward now by virtue that she is in fact homeless—a stowaway of time," Sid said after a moment.

"Would it be difficult to return her to the exact moment she left? Once we re-establish the connection to her Quantum Gate, I assume?"

"There is no 'we' in this equation," Sid said. "Quantum Gates, as I said before, are very personal entities. They can only be instructed and controlled by their creator and traveler."

"The Gate is intrinsically tied to her, but where is the creator—"

"If I had not seen the clear evidence, I would not believe it myself, but Vincent—*she* built that Gate. She may not know it, but it is *her* creation." Sid paused.

"I cannot deny that her power, her essence, is tied to it..." Vincent said in acknowledgement.

"As it always must be, as long as the Gate survives." Sid came to stand in front of Vincent, since the Elder was seated they were both at the same eye-level. Sid stared at

Vincent with the emulated gray-green eyes of Elaria for a moment. "She has forgotten how to work her Gate, for reasons that are not clear yet. But without that knowledge, she may never return home."

Vincent frowned. "You could deduce what dimension she is from, surely? Reopen it using her life force and send her back. That could be done—"

Sid scoffed. "That solution has many hazards, most too cruel to contemplate." Sid turned to pace along the shelves of books, hands behind their back as they spoke. "No, beloved, she is with us now. We must discover for what purpose this mortal has found her way into our presence."

"What of the Arbiters' knowledge," Vincent said. "Perhaps they may instruct us on what to do with her." He put his arms behind his head and leaned back in the chair.

"You trust them," Sid said, still pacing the library. "I have already begun my calculations. For better or for worse, they will define themselves by their answer."

"I trust their knowledge," Vincent said. "Many of the Supreme Elders who survived the Future War were friend and more to my father. They are almost as old as time. If not the Arbiters, then ask the Tardigrades in their approximate spacetime—"

Sid stopped pacing and looked directly at Vincent.

"Vincent, you are very closely related to a Supreme Elder, you have the strength and discipline to conduct Sanguis—"

Vincent apparated, standing whisper close to Sid in less than a second.

"I admit that outcome has crossed my mind." He swallowed, almost growling his next words. "Extraordinary circumstances aside, Sanguis with a mortal is categorically *forbidden*—in case you have completely forgotten the Future War—not to mention your daily reminders of the last few millennia to *abstain*." He finished with gritted teeth.

"I am aware what a blood bond between Elder and mortal risks—" Sid began, but Vincent interrupted.

"The Universe, for starters," he snarled. "And *you*."

"If the ceremony were done under my discretion—"

"You are the worst Tardigrade I have ever met," he said, stomping to the other side of the library.

"I am the only Tardigrade you have ever met," Sid argued. "Think of it, Vincent. Sanguis, here in the pocket dimension of your Pillar, would be a harmless way to answer all of our questions."

"Harmless?" Vincent seethed, turning to face Sid.

"Can you see another way?"

"Perhaps with the Arbiters of Nihil as a fourth dimensional guide in the ceremony... She would not be tied to me alone," he said, pained by even the suggestion.

Sid sighed. "In Sanguis with them, she and her power would be at the mercy of an entire council of Supreme Elders. *That* is a repeat of the Future War. I stand by my recommendation of you alone conducting Sanguis."

"I would never let her come to harm," he growled.

"I do not doubt that." Sid smiled at Vincent.

He blinked, broken out of his momentary posturing for Renata's safety.

"I am merely—"

"Enjoying the company of a sentient being," Sid said, eyes alight.

"Yes," he agreed. "What are your intentions then, since you disagree with my plan to contact the Arbiters."

"To train her," Sid said simply. "She has significant power that she does not understand or comprehend."

"She was dishonest earlier."

"Oh?" Sid said, perplexed. "Oh... yes... She had moved an object before, like the knife."

"It terrified her," he said. "So, she suppressed her powers. We terrify her. Has it occurred to you that the truth might be more than her human mind can comprehend?"

"Perhaps her powers increased in strength when she traveled through the Gate. Perhaps these powers were merely dormant, sleeping in her physical body until the right conduit came along. She has time in her blood, I know you can smell it. I have many theories..." Sid paused, deep in thought. "Regardless, she should be instructed on how to control and use her abilities."

Vincent frowned at Sid. "And once she knows how to use these abilities you are so graciously going to instruct her in, then what?"

"Well, first," Sid began. "*You* will instruct her. Then, she will reopen the Gate."

"What?"

"What do you mean 'what'?"

"You are unbelievable! We court the destruction of the Universe with your plans, just as we court Tracker involvement by merely harboring her." Vincent ran his hands through his hair in exasperation.

"I considered all of this the moment I saw her," Sid said. "I found her an acceptable risk—"

"An acceptable risk?" Vincent pinched the bridge of his nose, his brow creased in frustration. "You bring a mortal to my Pillar, then you suggest Sanguis, now you are asking me to work closely with her—"

"I could be wrong," Sid sniffed. "But that rarely happens."

Vincent snorted, rolling his eyes as he leaned against the shelf.

"Beloved, have you considered what would have happened if we did not intervene?" Sid retorted.

"Your point?"

"She should be instructed, and she should be protected. From herself and Trackers, at the very least."

"Thank you for the illuminating clarification, Sid," he said, shaking his head. "Will you then protect her from me, or have you forgotten your entire role here?"

"The book is an inexplicable clue," Sid continued, ignoring Vincent.

"The book is a psychic projection," he said, pausing next to the desk covered in star charts. His hand touched the cover of the book, his fingertips pressing the golden hieroglyphics as if to know their silent meaning.

"The book is *your* psychic projection," Sid reminded Vincent. "Not hers."

Vincent's face grew solemn, his body stiff and subdued. He looked up at Sid, dumbstruck.

"Only you can decipher the text," Sid said.

"The illustration depicts Divine Death," he said, his voice a harsh whisper. "That was outlawed before the Future War, before my time..."

"Do you not think it strange," Sid began, "that this

mortal's dream suddenly appeared in a particular book, in this particular library, at the same time she did?"

"She does not know what her dream means—"

"Many of these facts are pointing to a conclusion you find... uncomfortable. There is an inevitable bend in her timeline. I cannot tell if it is her future or her past that is—"

"Enough—"

"*Vincent*," Sid implored.

"I do not wish to revisit any more legacies from the Future War tonight," he snapped. "I will train her, as you have asked. I will do whatever it takes to expedite the process of returning her to her original timeline. That is all I can offer."

"What if *this* is her original timeline?" Sid said derisively.

"Impossible," Vincent said, and disappeared from the library.

16

NEW-ASHEMORE, AMARANTHINE LOOP

Aldric sank to his knees before the Mirror, surrounded by a silent audience of ash and debris. He felt keenly the decomposition of the building, felt it lean and ache as year by year it toiled to dust.

He slipped the building key in the pocket of his slacks. He had been advised by Ben Gelderson—the jaunty and malleable real estate agent Aldric had easily bribed—to avoid the second floor due to structural integrity problems within the building.

It was advice Aldric had immediately ignored.

He could hear the Quantum energy. It sang softly, its frail voice almost covered by the night noise of the city. His large hands sifted through the rubble and soot before him.

Quantum energy had a peculiar smell. In the Future War, it had burned his nostrils as the Supreme Elders were battled through the last Quantum Gate at the Time

Henge, to rot in their prison of inescapable time. Guilty of imbalance and an insatiable hunger for power, the Supreme Elders were condemned to exist forever where time bends in on itself, is compressed, and finally destroyed—the Breaking of the Light. Trackers calculated the radiation would burn away their hunger, shear from them their visceral all-consuming greed and lust for domination. It was a purification. Calculations indicated the Breaking of the Light would leave only the Elders' vast knowledge behind, producing some additional balance to the Universe after the Future War. Still, Aldric's Ledger remained slightly uneven from that time forward, no matter how many times he checked the math.

This Quantum Gate smelled different. This smelled older than any Quantum energy Aldric was familiar with, and yet younger at the same time. Sweet and somber, of granite and water, starlight and spring breeze. How could it have this duality?

"Human." Aldric inhaled again, his chest expanding. "*Mortal*."

He looked deep into the Mirror, hoping to see a sign, a glimmer. There were broken shards, angled and collapsed in on themselves. His wide face and white eyes were all that stared back.

The Mirror was not burned. Surrounding it were the cobwebbed pieces of what the building once was. With wide strokes of his muscled arms, he cleared the rubble strewn before the frame.

He found more glass in front of the Mirror frame, in a perfect semi-circle, with one shard capsized and pointing back at the Mirror itself. Gently, almost tenderly, Aldric picked up the pieces.

They thrummed in his hands, like a bee caught in a budded flower. The Tracker began to arrange them back in the broken frame itself. Small tendrils of light started streaming into the cracks, seaming the glass back together. He stared in shock as the pieces of glass fused themselves inside the frame. The Quantum song was stronger now, a scream as soft as a whisper. There was no mistaking it.

Potential grazed his fingertips. He gently caressed the glass. He pressed his face intimately to it, hoping to break the threshold.

But it was still glass. Without finding the creator, the Gate would never open.

He whispered to it. Galvanizing his courage, he licked its frame, his tongue collecting ash and residue from the Mirror's facade.

"You'll be mine, you'll be Bound to me, and you'll be mine," he said, promising the Mirror.

A cord, a single tendril of power, erupted from the glass surface and struck him like a whip to the face. It flung him backward across the room and into a sooty pile of rubbish. As jarring as the experience was to be flung by white-hot Gate energy, he didn't miss the sound that accompanied it.

The Mirror screamed.

17

LUPUS OBSIDIAN, CERULEAN DIMENSION

A shrill alarm woke Peaches. She put an aching hand to her head, her fingers still sore from the endless hours in the holographic book-making studio.

"What now," she grumbled, pressing a button next to her bed and bringing up a holographic screen. The display lit up, its warm light illuminating her features in the otherwise darkened room. She didn't even bother sitting up, reading the screen lying down.

Her eyes grew round as she read the spike in energy coming from the Time Lab.

"Centius," she said. "Protocol 8133, radiation in the Time Lab has exceeded safe—"

A glowing pane in the room lit up, the sand behind it sifting in a blurry pattern. Peaches ran her hand through her hair, her curls springing up and poofing with the attention.

"If you've already enacted Protocol 8133 what do you

need me for?" she said, annoyed. "And the Gate just started leaking power on its own? What a complete mess. I can't even go back in there until it's quarantined! You'll have to do a neutralizing bio-sweep of the second and third—"

The sand shifted again, and this time, Peaches sat bolt upright.

"This *didn't* come from the Gate?"

The sand shimmered, and a new holographic display showed an array of numbers. Peaches practically fell out of bed. She scrambled to the doorway, pressing a hidden panel in the wall. Storage in a facility such as this was at a premium, but radiation suits were embedded in a small enclosure within every domicile and lab with radiation neutralizing metal surrounding it to prevent contamination.

Peaches dressed quickly, shoving the helmet over her head but cursed when her hair got in the way.

"Mierde," she said, taking the helmet off and sweeping her mass of orange curls into a tight bun at the base of her neck. "Close off the medical suite, I don't want any radiation getting—"

The sand in the panel rotated and changed direction, glowing and pummeling the pane with its frenetic effort.

"Way to bury the lede," Peaches snapped and ran out of the room, heading for the medical suite.

18

THE PILLAR, AMARANTHINE LOOP

L ight from the edge of dawn was whispering through the windows when Vincent returned to the cottage.

He stood over Renata, entranced by the cadence of her steady breathing. Vincent could sense her mortality, it was the same feeling for all finite and fragile things. Her pulse was steady and inevitable, he could hear its subtle and regular announcement even in the farthest reaches of his Pillar. Despite all this, in sleep, she appeared timeless.

He moved a strand of hair covering her eyes and whispered her name. Her eyes slowly fluttered open.

"Come with me," he said.

"Now?" she whispered, not quite awake.

"Now." He pulled her out of bed and braced her by the elbow.

"I can't," she said and yawned.

He brushed her hair out the way, smoothing it behind her ears.

"Yes, you can. Put your boots on." He let her go, and she sank quickly onto the bed. He realized then her boots were still on from the day before.

"Still on," she said numbly, head slumped on her chest.

"So I see," Vincent said. "Follow me."

The half-dark bedroom of the cottage disappeared, and instead, they stood in the sloping field behind the house. The sun was beginning to ink the horizon with bold colors, imbuing the morning sky with a fiery hue that bled into the landscape.

Renata's head snapped up in alarm.

"What the—" she began.

RENATA SHIFTED INELEGANTLY and found herself sitting not on the bed but on long stalks of dewy grass in the field behind the cottage.

Vincent apparated, appearing at the crest of the hill, in a small field at the forest's threshold. Renata stumbled instead of standing, and stumbled a second time before she began to walk, taking long strides through the field.

Vincent waited for her as she scrambled up the final embankment, panting. She knelt beside him, attempting to catch her breath.

"*We go into the forest now,*" he said into her mind and turned to face her.

"Wait," she said. "My boot, I think I'm getting a blister."

"*Are you?*" He looked at her, an eyebrow raised.

"What, is that how Elders deal with blisters? Imagining they're not real?" she said, unlacing her boot.

"*I would not imagine them at all,*" he replied.

"If I didn't want a blister, I would imagine these boots slightly bigger, or my socks slightly smaller," she retorted. "And while I'm at it, I would imagine something besides this—" Renata pulled at the thick cable knit sweater that came down to her knees.

"*It can be so.*"

"Is this a trick?" she squinted at him. "Are you secretly going to be seeing me naked, *again?*"

"*You are in my Pillar. I can see what you see. And you see very little, but you are human, so I understand. See more, and it will do more than clothe you.*"

Renata realized she was staring at Vincent's eyes. She blinked, attempting to look away. It was then she realized he was not talking.

She gasped.

Vincent smiled down at her and spoke. "I can see why abuela Noni calls you little lamb. Harness your powers, use your mind. Innocence, like most mortal things, will not last. Knowledge does, mija."

She glared at him.

"Suit yourself," he said, turning and disappearing into the woods.

"Wait!" She stood up. "Ugh!" She shouted at the entrance of the forest.

Renata huffed, crossing her arms. Closing her eyes, she took a deep breath, calming herself. She tried to remember what she wore the last time she went jogging on the greenway back in her dimension of New-Ashemore.

Her memories were like dying embers. Dimly, Renata recalled she liked to collect t-shirts from the live concerts she attended. They usually ended up as work-out attire because she rarely wore t-shirts to work. She thought of her oldest t-shirt, so worn out the flaming skull on it was barely visible. It was from the first concert she had ever been to in New-Ashemore.

She opened her eyes, tears threatening as she wondered if she would ever hear that music again or go jogging on the greenway next to her neighborhood.

"It's far away," she said quietly to the tall pines in front of her. "All of it. Far away."

She wiped her eyes and glanced down to see she was dressed differently. She jumped, holding the old shirt out from her body to stare down at it.

It was an exact replica, complete with all the holes and threadbare parts—just as she remembered.

"Vincent! I did it!" Renata shouted, following his trail into the forest.

19

LUPUS OBSIDIAN, CERULEAN DIMENSION

Peaches scrambled down the hall, her helmet fogging with the effort.

"Status report," she yelled, stumbling. The radiation sirens were blaring, and the red emergency lights flickered to life as the main power to the Time Lab shut off —a part of the radiation containment and power conservation protocols.

The screen within her helmet spewed a series of symbols and numbers that caused Peaches to go cold inside.

"Papa," she said. She ran down the hall, ignoring the emergency lights and booming sounds of the Time Lab straining under the Quantum forces that were being unleashed.

"Protocol LD-2130 activated," a robotic voice blared, and another radioactive siren wailed.

Peaches was running, but somehow the hallway felt like

it was longer, and she couldn't run fast enough. It felt like forever before she came to the doorway of the medical suite. Inside, she saw the crystalline forcefield surrounding her father's body. It was opaque, blurring his features until he was only a dim mass behind it. Peaches heard screaming, but as she approached his bedside, she realized it was her own voice that had called out in terror.

"Status report," she choked, tears blurring her eyes. The information displaying itself inside her screen caused Peaches to yell again in anguish. "Papa, no," she wheezed, her helmet almost completely fogging with her exhale.

Strong arms came up behind her, moving her away from the bed.

"The radiation levels around Patient 001 are higher than your suit can withstand," said a voice. "Please stand back."

Peaches felt as if she were watching the scene outside her body. She felt herself being moved from her father's bedside, out of arms reach.

"No," she screamed, straining against whoever was removing her from the room.

"The radiation levels in the medical suite are exceeding your suit's recommended limit," the voice repeated.

"No!" Peaches screamed again, her voice rough and angry. Her arms flailed from her side, gripping the doorway. "Papa!"

"Centius, 10cc tranquil-elite in helmet 002," the voice said.

Peaches felt a puff of air on her face, and the temperature in her helmet fell by a few degrees. Her eyes became heavy, and the terror that had just gripped her seemed distant.

"Papa," she said, her voice only a whisper. "Come back to me."

20

NEW-ASHEMORE, AMARANTHINE LOOP

ldric searched for the human trespasser who had entered the Amaranthine. He searched by watching the energy trickling from the Quantum Gate—the tendril of energy grew strong, once flinging him out of the building itself.

As the weeks passed, the coil of Gate energy became almost as thick as a rope. It cracked and spasmed at him like a whip. The season changed, spring transforming finally to summer, and Aldric found he could no longer get within an arms span of the Mirror.

No longer able to approach the Mirror, he paced around the squalid building, wringing his hands, as summer slowly gave way to autumn.

The first tortuous year ended, and he still could not even lay a finger on his prize. It was almost painful, to be so close to the Gate the trespasser had used and be unable to harness its power. Sometimes, on dark winter nights, Aldric sat in silence across the room from it, closing his eyes. The Gate's Quantum song was hypnotizing and maddening.

His need to control the Mirror's power became an obsession, which at least eased the burden of days that turned into a year. Time was irreverently passing, with no luck of finding the mortal woman who had created the Quantum Gate.

The second year, Aldric noticed the Gate energy became heavier, denser. If before it was a like trickle of water, now it was a stream. The energy poured forth from the Mirror, winding its way through the rubble and trash, racing down the stairs and onto the street where it pooled and ended. Water always knows where to go, not so with Quantum Gate energy. It searched for her, too, and like Aldric, could not find her.

As the second year passed into the third, the stream busted its banks. The Gate energy flowed over the threshold of the door and out onto the sidewalk. It wound down the street and out into the city.

Aldric, who looked every day a man who had lived in a derelict and condemned building for three years, ambled after it. Like a castaway searching for fresh water, he followed the Gate energy, almost delirious. The energy flowed down the street, winding its way into the dilapidated historic district. Finally, the stream of power turned into a little lane Aldric had never thought to go down before—had never even walked by. As if before seeing it this particular moment, it did not exist.

Vines and thick shrubbery obscured his path, but the tide of energy continued on. Like a river whose current was buoyed by a flash flood, the Gate energy rushed forth, disappearing into the bushes.

For a moment, Aldric thought perhaps she was dead. *Mortals do that, you know,* he thought. But then, if she were dead, the Gate would be as well. The energy would disperse and evaporate into the ether.

The Gate energy was not dispersing. It was racing. Toward a destination. Toward her.

Aldric attempted to enter the bramble but was blocked. His hand passed through the vine like a mirage. Images of leaves were like a fine mist coating his hand. His fingers attempted to grope the thorny bramble and vine. Instead, their image dispersed like smoke, and a force, invisible but insistent, denied his forward progression.

The vines were hiding his quarry—his Gatekeeper. It had concealed the human to such an extent that even her life force, bound to the Quantum Gate, could not find her. Until now.

A dark smile plied Aldric's lips. He reached into the old office slacks he had donned three years ago—on the day he purchased a burnt-out shell of a building on the outskirts of New-Ashemore. He produced a cell phone and dialed a single number. The other end picked up, but no one greeted his call, merely waited for instruction.

"I have found his Pillar. She is with him," Aldric began. "Get here." He hung up.

It had been many centuries since Aldric had encountered his Pillar. In truth, he believed there were no other Elders outside the Amaranthine, and certainly no others existed in the mirror dimension of the Amaranthine—this time loop was for Vincent alone.

"Vincent," Aldric spoke into the vines. "As if staying could change the past."

There would always be a score to settle between Trackers and Elders. Always a balance to exact, a Ledger to fill.

Finally, Aldric could balance his Ledger. Vincent harbored the human, Aldric was certain of it. That alone was all he needed to destroy him, taking the human quarry as his own...

He smiled.

21

THE PILLAR, AMARANTHINE LOOP

The forest in Vincent's Pillar was carpeted with pine needles, silencing Renata's footfalls. A cathedral of evergreens surrounded her, nimble and narrow pines created not just a forest, but a hallowed space. She could feel their presence, similar to the vines around the cottage—it was as if the trees were watching her. They seemed ancient and alive—conscious, in a way.

Renata kept running, it could have been the entire morning, or maybe three quarters of the day, or perhaps only a few minutes. The pines stole any sense of time, obscuring the sun and cooling the air. She barely perspired and yet could feel her body tiring, as if she had run for miles. Finally, she slowed her pace and walked. The forest had become like a meditation, and her mind was quieting too.

Abruptly, the tree line broke.

There was a clearing that had not been there a moment before. There, the forest ceded to rock. Beyond the rocky outcropping, a small stream bed intersected a thicket with tall spindly bushes with wide green leaves and pink, pungent blooms. Vincent stood on a boulder, his back to her, gazing down at the stream. He turned at her approach.

His eyes widened a little at her appearance. He nodded in silent recognition. She had successfully imagined different clothes.

"What is this place?" she said, panting.

"A shrine," he said, looking down at her from his stance atop the boulder. "For all we lost."

"Lost?"

"The Future War exacted a heavy price," he replied, extending his arms. "This forest, these trees, contain a fraction of their essence."

"You don't say death or died. You say lost?" she said, partly to herself.

"Matter can neither be created nor destroyed," he said, letting his arms fall. "More like a ceaseless change of form."

"I guess I don't think about death the same way you do." She frowned, pushing some of the hair that had popped out of her ponytail during her run through the forest behind her ear.

"Death is a term you should discard, the finality of it is a mortal notion."

"Well, I *am* mortal, so I get a pass on all my mortal notions. Besides, I don't think lost is quite appropriate either," she began, tossing her head. "I can feel them here. They're not lost, not completely."

There was no mistaking it this time, Vincent's eyes did widen. He jumped off the boulder to stand before her.

"You can feel them?" he asked, his blue eyes locked on her.

"All around me," she replied, shrinking back from his interest a little. She crossed her arms. "What *is* this place?"

"A holy place. So that I may never forget the cost of the Future War."

"The vines at the house feel the same way," she said, pausing. "It's like—they're *watching* me."

"That is because I asked them to." He nodded at her startled expression. "But the trees, each have a part of a Blood Orphan who was lost in the Future War. I carried their essence here and contain them in the pines. Their memory helps sustain the Pillar."

"Blood Orphans?"

"Like you, they were stowaways of time," he said. His gaze became introspective, his eyes faraway. "They were humans once, saved from their moment of death, plucked from their original timeline by an Elder that found them... worthy. The Orphans were brought to live in Aeor-Eterna by my father and the other Supreme Elders. It was they who first brought mortals to the Undying Lands... There, the humans evolved... they became *more*..." His words trailed off as he stared beyond her, into the pines.

"What is Aeor-Eterna?" she asked after a beat, inter-rupting his reverie.

"My home," he replied, glancing into her eyes. "Before I created this Pillar."

"These pines are taller than any I've ever seen," she said, looking up. His gaze followed her own. "Are they like this in Aeor-Eterna?"

"Similar," he said, offering no further explanation.

Renata shivered. The forest, which at first felt meditative, almost nurturing, now felt foreboding and full of a quiet but relentless sorrow.

"Come," Vincent said. "There is much to teach you."

"TRY AGAIN," Vincent coaxed.

"I am *trying* right now," Renata said, blowing a strand of hair from her face. The back of her neck was sticky with sweat. It was mid-day and had become quite humid in the forest.

Vincent turned his attention back to her palms, which were not giving out the spark of energy they had a moment ago.

"Yes, but you are being impatient," he said. "Relax your mind." He had been demonstrating a few Elder abilities, one of which was concentrating power into a wall or curtain of light and energy—his power, so concentrated and intense, made the air stuffy, almost sweltering. Meanwhile, Renata hadn't even warmed her hands.

"You relax your mind!" she squealed in frustration. "Have you given any thought that this is an ability I *don't* have?"

Vincent looked down, closing his eyes and pinching his brow. After a moment he looked up. "Take a break. Perhaps I have been pushing you too hard."

"Perhaps?" she scoffed and put her hands down.

He looked at Renata, her human scent of sweat and irritation a subtle fragrance rising above the acrid, crackling ozone of his Elder power. Warm afternoon sunlight trickled between the branches and leaves of the forest canopy. Vincent knew what he had seen—white sparks of energy erupting from her hands. There was no doubt in his mind this was a power she possessed. However, he remained uncertain how to compel her to manifest it.

"You are stubborn," he said finally, rubbing his face.

"I am not stubborn!"

"Only a stubborn person would say that."

"Gimme a break—" she said, before trailing off in Spanish.

"I am giving you a break! If you were not so stubborn, you would not even need one," he replied. "You have created Quantum Glass. This is much easier, yet you resist—"

"Resist?" she interrupted, her mouth agape. "I'm a human, if you haven't noticed. I don't *have* magical powers!"

Vincent sighed. He noticed her anger, combined with the heat, flushed her cheeks. He also detected her heartbeat quicken when she was particularly obstinate. She stood before him with her hands fisted at her side, legs braced, resisting with all her being the truth of her potential. He shook his head, his hair fluttering with the movement.

"It is not *magic*. It is intelligence, an ability or dexterity like any others you have."

"Maybe I'm dumb," she said, frowning, her mouth a thin line.

"No, you speak quite well and quite loud—in and out of my mind."

She rolled her eyes. "Not *literally* dumb, and I don't

'speak in your mind'—and for the last time, I am *not* an empath!"

"Technically that would be more of a telepathic ability—"

"You know what I mean!" she said, her voice rising.

Vincent put his hands up, sighing. "Calm," he said, her heart rate baiting his inner hunger to stir into awareness. "Calm. Let's try apparating again, you almost had it—"

She rolled her eyes again, exasperated. "I'm just a fast runner."

"It is more than running or walking. It is condensing yourself, the matter that makes up your being, and traveling at the speed of light through time and space."

"Is this you trying to make it sound easier?" She scoffed, crossing her arms. "Because that isn't helping."

"Catch me," he challenged, and in an eyeblink disappeared, reappearing at a tree several yards away. "If you catch me, we can go back to the cottage for lunch."

"You're on," Renata said and began to run toward Vincent, but he had already disappeared.

RENATA SAT at the edge of the forest after a long morning —that had bled into the afternoon and finally evening— exhausted. They had not returned to the cottage for lunch. She watched the sun as it dipped below the spine of the mountains, not turning when she heard Vincent appear behind her in the tree line.

"You beat me," he said, an edge of surprise in his voice.

"Only because you let me," she hedged. She was backlit

by the setting sun, the grass of the field rippling in the wind. She gazed back at Vincent from the clearing—and held her breath.

Framed by trees, the evening sun lent a hazy, golden glow to his face. His white button-down shirt was only half tucked in, his sleeves lazily rolled up to his elbows. The collar was unbuttoned to the top of his waistcoat to accommodate the heat of their work this afternoon. His hair, haphazardly pinned behind his ears, grazed the top of his wide shoulders. Renata gazed down his forearms to his stout hands. They were well formed, he had large knuckles, and a few callouses. They were workmen's hands, not a student's, she decided.

She remembered a moment when his fingers had glanced against her own and thought how strange that he chose *those* hands. She felt herself staring a beat too long at him, the late evening sun somehow highlighting his other-worldly appearance even more. His blue eyes pierced the distance between them. He observed her with the same curiosity. Renata snapped her head away.

"You do not apparate, but you are faster than I antici-pated," he admitted, his voice carrying from the tree-line.

"I thought you beat me," she confessed. "I assumed you were already back at the cottage. Had to stop," she paused, pointing at the sunset. "Can't beat the view."

Vincent smiled and apparated, sitting down next to her. She was leaning back with her legs crossed, the grass tick-ling her knees as it waved in the wind.

"Yes," he nodded. "It is a good view."

"It's a memory, isn't it? I can sense that. Or feel it. I'm not sure."

"It is a memory," he agreed. *"Empath."* Vincent looked at her, one eyebrow raised.

"Must've been a really good day, if it's that day every day," she said, smiling. She sat forward and threw a stalk of grass into the field. "Not an empath." She looked at Vincent, her expression resolute.

"I believe it was a good day," he said and plucked a piece of grass, twining it between his thumb and forefinger.

"What? You *believe*? You don't know?" She said, mouth agape. "How can you use a memory you can't remember?"

"It was a beautiful day. Bittersweet that I can't quite remember why, but I held on to this image at least."

"Bittersweet," she repeated, her voice becoming soft. "A beautiful day, but you don't know exactly why. You remember the sunset with such clarity..."

"The sunrise not so well," he said. "Mornings go by fast here if you haven't noticed."

"Yeah, I have." Renata looked back at the horizon. "Which is too bad. Mornings are my favorite time of day. Especially rainy mornings. When I don't have to go to work." She smiled.

"You were good at your work?"

"Yeah." She nodded. "But it was hard work. Not like this, you realize—" Renata nodded back at the forest and their day running through the brush.

"Do you miss it?"

"Strangely, no—" she said, and laughed. "Don't get me wrong, I had moments I enjoyed, and moments I didn't mind, and other moments I wished I could just walk out on my client in the middle of their—" Renata caught herself before the cursing began. "Anyway, it was never my long-term thing."

"What was your long-term 'thing'?" Vincent stared at her, she felt his gaze hot upon her check and tingling on her neck. She turned, her eyes intent.

I guess I can't deny it anymore, she thought.

"What does it matter? You're currently looking at my long-term thing," she said, instead.

"You cannot deny what?" Vincent replied, blatantly reading her thoughts. Renata frowned, still not comfortable that he could read her thoughts so easily. She needed to pay attention to that, somehow.

"I can't deny that I've felt different my whole life, but more so since the accident," she began, plucking another stalk of grass. "And that everything I've felt, everything I've *dreamed,* makes sense here, in your Pillar. A place that I've never been to before, and you—a person-Elder-whatever —*you* make sense, *you* seem familiar..." she trailed off. "The longer I'm gone, the more it seems like my other life was the dream."

Vincent's face was unreadable. He placed his hand on her shoulder. Renata's breath caught in her chest.

"Your life, in whatever dimension, is real," he said, letting the statement hang in the air for a moment. "And precious. Sid and I will get you home. I promised, remember?"

Renata nodded, pensive. She refused to meet his eyes, concentrating on the stalk of grass in her hand.

"Good to know a promise is a promise," she said, sighing.

"An inter-dimensional promise at that." Vincent smiled, turning Renata's face gently up towards his.

"You're all I have," she whispered when she faced him. "I'm counting on you and Sid." He nodded imperceptibly. They locked eyes for a brief moment before Renata looked away.

She threw a stalk of grass into the wind and stood up.

"Race you to dinner?" she said, turning and looking down at him, hands on her hips. Vincent was still sitting, long legs stretched out in the grass.

Before he could answer, she vanished—apparating for the first time.

THAT NIGHT, Renata insisted on helping Sid with dinner.

"Trust me," she said. "This is the easiest way to cook the chicken."

Sid nodded.

"Burrito bowls are by far the most cost effective and delicious way to eat on a budget," she continued, chatting absently while Sid looked on. She placed the chicken inside the pressure cooker with several generous dollops of verde salsa.

"Money is not something I have considered," Sid admitted.

"Well," Renata said, putting an extra spoonful of salsa in the pot. "I guess it's comforting that adulting can't reach *all* dimensions."

"Adulting?"

"Never mind." She smiled, and closed the lid. She

pressed several buttons on the front of the pressure cooker. "Super handy you have this thing."

"I do not think we have such a device," Sid said, staring at the pressure cooker like it might sprout a second head at any moment. "Seems you are taking to Vincent's tutoring."

Renata's mouth hung open at Sid's revelation.

"So, I imagined this?" She looked at the pressure cooker.

"Along with all the groceries." Sid nodded to the other pots simmering on the stove. One had pinto beans with diced chilis and onions, the other had brown rice almost bubbling over.

"Oh!" Renata noticed and turned the burner down. She turned back to Sid. "I don't think that's possible. They were here already when Vincent and I got back from the forest. I assumed you went to the store..."

"No, I did not," Sid said. "This is all you, Renata."

She blinked, still not quite convinced, and wiped her hands on a dish towel.

"Right, well, dinner will be ready in twenty minutes. Wanna set the table?"

DESPITE SID'S wariness of the pressure cooker, they ate two entire burrito bowls. Sid gushed about the salsa verde and sour cream between mouthfuls of beans and rice. Renata thought it was probably the only victory she was pleased with today.

"Sometime, we'll have to make crepes," Renata winked

at Sid. "Since you're such a fan of cooking. I'll teach you all my family recipes!"

"Yes, please," Sid said. "This was delicious."

"Sí," she said, wiping her mouth with a napkin. "I'm surprised Vincent didn't join us."

"Ah, well," Sid said. "More for me."

"Where did he go? I haven't seen him since I started making dinner."

"He has things to do," Sid said vaguely.

"Ah yes—intrepid Elder stuff. Fate of the galaxy and all the dimensions at stake, I'm sure."

"Never thought of it quite so dramatically," Sid admitted.

"Well, I'm cleaning up," Renata said, standing. She reached for Sid's plate. "May I?"

She walked the dishes into the kitchen and deposited them into the sink. It was a large farmhouse sink, and she already had the pots from dinner soaking in soapy water. She turned on the faucet, setting the handle to the left and placed her hand under the running water, feeling for warmth.

"Oh, I'll make coffee," she said to herself. She reached to the stove top, which was separated from the sink by only a small countertop. She picked up the kettle and filled it, placing it back on the stove, turning the burner to high in almost one solid movement. With the water still running over the dirty dishes, Renata peeked in the fridge for creamer.

"*Gross*," she said. "Sid, have you *ever* cleaned your fridge?"

"We do not have such a device," Sid said, appearing

suddenly behind Renata.

Renata looked blankly at Sid. "Well, I didn't imagine a fridge full of science experiments and dust. Honestly, this is like a fridge from Cronenberg world or something."

Sid peaked around Renata, to see what she was referencing. There were large clots of black mold spread over the interior of the appliance. There were sinewy mounds of what was once food splayed on the shelves. Sid's eyes grew large with concern.

"What?" Renata noticed the change in expression. "What?"

"Renata, step away," Sid said quietly. "Let go of the handle."

Renata looked down, her hand still grasping the refrigerator door. She let go, and the entire appliance disappeared, like her clothing had the first night she met Sid. She swore several garbled curses in Spanish as the last bits of Quantum dust fell from her hand.

"You Quantum manifested inside Vincent's Pillar," Sid said, mouthing the words.

"Ugh, gross." She brushed her hands together, the dust pluming.

"Run your hands under the water," Sid said, looking at her. Renata had a thousand questions swimming behind her eyes, causing her to pause. "Do it now!" Sid barked.

Renata rushed to the sink, shoving her hands under the scalding water. She submerged them into the pots soaking in the sink. She rubbed her palms, feeling the grit dissolve.

"You must never do that here, Renata," Sid said gently.

"I didn't mean to—" she protested into the sink, not meeting Sid's face.

"You must not Quantum manifest in the Pillar. Trackers can sense the energy, they would attempt to find you and destroy Vincent's Pillar in the process."

"How can I control what I don't understand?" Her voice broke.

"We will help you understand," Vincent's voice boomed. He was suddenly in the kitchen doorway. "But you must accept first that you are gifted in ways other mortals are not."

"But—"

"I will not entertain any more denials, Renata," he said, his voice held a quiet threat like a distant storm. "Please wait for Sid and I in the library. We will join you in a moment."

Renata finally looked away from the dish laden sink and toward Vincent. His blue eyes were dilated, his nostrils flared. The look on his face was unnatural calm hiding unnatural wildness. She felt the temperature rise, the kitchen becoming stuffy and sweltering.

Renata broke eye contact, withdrawing her hands from the sink. She wiped them roughly on her sweater and began to apparate to the library. Vincent stopped her in the kitchen doorway, his grip a hot circle around her arm.

"Walk, please," he growled. "Like the mortal you claim to be."

Vincent withdrew his hand as quickly as he'd placed it upon her. Renata shuddered, shrinking from his touch. His eyes were alive, his body starting to glimmer with golden waves.

Her tears flowed freely as she walked to the library.

22

NEW-ASHEMORE, AMARANTHINE LOOP

Aldric crouched in front of Renata's Quantum Mirror, holding a shard of glass.

The girl, his servant, walked up behind him, surveying the dilapidated room. The old building, his home these past three years, shuddered quietly—as if the structure itself was trying to shrink away from its two occupants.

"So, this is where you've come to die," the girl said out of the darkness, the distant city lights illuminating only segments of her face.

"You're showing your age," Aldric replied, his voice raspy. "Still clinging to the idea of death."

"I've known for a millennia when my time with you would end," the girl replied. "I've counted the days. I've wished for *death*."

"The end is just the beginning," Aldric said, turning to her.

His white eyes, clouded and aged, squinted at her from

his human face. The face itself was now more mask than anything else. He held up the glass shard, its pointed edge leering at the girl.

"Now that the Gate has found its Gatekeeper—" Aldric said, and stuck the point of the shard in his mouth and drew downward across his tongue. Syrupy, dark hemoglobin erupted from the cut and coated the glass. He withdrew the glass fragment from his mouth and held it away from his face. A writhing, dark smoke encircled his hand. The black smoke meandered around the tip of the shard, where his blood still dripped, coating his hand and stippling the ground below.

"What would you have of me," the girl asked, her wide white eyes never leaving his hand, clutching the fragment of Quantum Glass.

"You are still what you once were," Aldric said, observing her. "Even though you are shorn from your Elder spark—part of you is still a Blood Orphan, even after all this time."

The girl nodded. "Despite this, I have served you well."

Aldric nodded and handed her the shard. "Only two services remain that I require of you. After you are done here," he paused, indicating the Quantum Glass fragment he had just handed to her, and then pointed to his chest. "Go to the entrance of the Pillar. Wait for him. I wonder if he will be driven mad when he sees you still live? Or at least, this portion of you. Remarkable that he has forgotten! You are the reason he followed me into the Amaranthine in the first place." Aldric gave her a weak smile, blood covering his chin. "And they say Elders have the best memory."

She put out her hands. They had a certain grace about them, attached to thin and delicate forearms. She wore her destruction like fine jewelry, her beauty still recognizable beneath the veneer of abuse and self-inflicted wounds. Aldric placed the Quantum Glass shard in her outstretched hand, nodding.

She held the glass and locked eyes with him.

"Master," she said, her voice delicate among the rubble.

His shirt was in tatters but he removed it anyway, wiping the soot and grime from his chest with it. He addressed her, indifferent of the blood flowing out of his mouth.

"I only seek balance," he said with a mouthful of blood.

"As he starves, alone, losing a little more of himself—" she growled. "While he remains in the Amaranthine, your margins clear a fraction more. It is why you kept us both here. Do not think to hide behind your quotations of balance—I know vengeance sleeps between the margins of your Ledger. Because you could not Count him as you did the Supreme Elders, you have an unbalanced Ledger, a true embarrassment for a Tracker—"

"Perhaps," Aldric said, cutting her off. Wiping the blood off his chin with his old shirt. He stood before her, his palms out, shoulders back—inviting her. "You know me best, after all."

"Perhaps," the girl said, and like a cobra struck him quickly—plunging the glass shard into his chest. "You didn't anticipate the Amaranthine helping *Her* return."

Aldric did not cry out. His face turned red. The blood vessels at his temple throbbed with life as his heart hammered in his chest once again. Aldric's blood-slick hands gripped hers as she braced them against his chest. He felt the gravel-like friction of the glass abrading his rib cage. He tightened his hold on her hands, helping her push the shard further still until it was swallowed by his flesh and she could grasp it no longer. The shard was hot in his chest as he felt the power course through him.

Aldric fell to his knees, dark smoke and blood billowing out of the wound. She put her hands around his throat. With inhuman strength, she lifted his crumpled body, black smoke serpentine around them.

"For what it's worth, I hope you find the human," she snarled.

"Finish it," Aldric said, but not from his body—from all around the room, in the shadows and beneath the rubble. "Cast me into the Gate."

The girl complied and threw Aldric across the room, his body buckling like a rag doll. She saw it fall toward the broken Mirror in the corner of the room, its jagged Cheshire smile more of a snaggle toothed grimace.

Her eyes widened as she saw his body bridge the threshold and disappear behind the glass.

23

LUPUS OBSIDIAN, CERULEAN DIMENSION

Peaches' eyes fluttered open. She was staring at the ceiling of her quarters, in bed.

"Papa," she said hoarsely. Her throat was dry—probably from the yelling. She placed a hand on her head, trying to gather her thoughts.

"Dry mouth is a side effect of tranquil-elite," a voice said. It was coming from the comms panel by the door. "I have left two doses of bio-fluid beside you. Once you have consumed those, please join me in the Time Lab." The panel switched off.

"What?" Peaches said, almost wheezing. She turned her head to see two bags of a water-electrolyte-vitamin compound stacked symmetrically on the small cube that served as a bedside table.

She gripped the tab covering the straw on the first bag and proceeded to consume it with one long gulp. The second bag she took her time with, almost sipping it toward the end. Her mind lingered on who the voice could be.

"Must be an A.I. Safety Unit," Peaches mumbled to herself. "Activated only when one of us—" She couldn't finish the sentence. Her grief emboldened her curiosity and she sat up. She sat at the edge of the bed, gripping the mattress pad, attempting to get her bearings. She looked down, realizing she was in a radioactive extraction suit. Her eyes rounded. "Meirde."

She bounded up from her bed with preternatural speed and left her room, rounding the hallway to the Time Lab. She wanted answers, now.

Peaches didn't know what to expect when she entered the Time Lab. It was certainly not a human man with over-grown dark blonde hair. The beard, speckled with orange and red, also threw her off. He was over six feet tall, with wide shoulders and muscular arms that strained against the radioactive extraction suit he was also wearing. How had there been a man hidden on the ship without her knowing it?

"I was in suspended-hibernation in the cryptobiosis chamber," the man said, unprompted. He turned from the glass panes he had been staring at, a blizzard of golden sand suddenly ceasing as Peaches entered the room.

Her voice caught in her throat. She could only stare, her blue eyes round as marbles.

"Hello, Peaches. I am a contingency your Father predicted this Lab would require," the man continued. He turned fully toward her then and locked eyes with her. His gaze lingered a beat. Though he had a kindness in his dark brown eyes, Peaches knew immediately he was more than just human. Her eyes traveled over him. His sleeves were rolled up enough to see his forearms. He had pale skin. It had a fawn tinge to it, like his skin had been under the light of a star once on a planet somewhere. Various scars crisscrossed his forearms, she guessed from armed combat long ago. Each wrist had a nanite cuff encircling it.

Peaches looked back into his eyes. Thin nanite bands around each of his pupils shimmered in time with the wider bands that encircled each of his wrists. In the stark light of the Time Lab, she could tell too that his eyes held a density and awareness that was too keen to be genetically human alone.

"You're the only other human I've ever met besides my father," she said, baiting him for information.

"Alas," he replied. In that one word, she caught a slight accent, but as he kept talking, it became buried again. "I am not human. I am genetic material once gifted to the—"

"Genetic material? You were once human at the very least," Peaches interrupted and then crinkled her nose at how plebeian her comment was. "That is to say, your original genetic material was likely human."

"Correct," the man nodded, the nanite bands in his irises widening as he spoke. "However, my original genome has been altered several times. My skeletal and muscular structures has been further enhanced with Numerean nanite."

"You're a Numerean! Numerean pirate ships are renowned for their genetically enhanced crew members. I've read stories that Numereans could fly into the center of a dying star—explains your high tolerance to radiation —" Peaches bit her lip, aware she had been babbling.

"Sorry, I haven't had a lot of social interaction besides Centius..."

It was his turn to be silent. He looked at her, never letting his gaze leave her eyes.

"I was once called Lachlan Dark," he said finally, bowing. "To the Numereans I was LD-2130."

Peaches approached him, her scientific fascination winning over her wariness and grief.

"May I?" she asked, before she put her hands on his arm. He nodded slightly, his gaze pinned to her. Peaches put her hands on his forearm, sliding it over his skin. He shivered, his skin turning to gooseflesh as she touched him.

"Sorry," she said, pausing. "Am I making you uncomfortable?" He blinked, shaking his head.

"Aye, but it is only because it has been so long..." he paused, deciding what to say. "Since I've been touched."

Peaches paused, her frown deepening. She let her hand linger on his forearm as she returned his gaze. "Me too."

"This is what you're after," Lachlan offered, turning his wrist over in her hand, offering her a look at the nanite band. She touched it, and a holographic display came up, stating his name, rank, date of creation, and the ship he served.

"You served on the Vellinor?" Peaches said. The man's expression darkened, and he released his arm from her hold. He took a step back.

"I serve the Time Lab now, mistress," Lachlan said, putting his large hands behind his back. "Aldric saved me from certain death, and by the laws of my ancestors, my life is now his. He placed me in the cryptobiosis chamber until a time arose when my services would be required. Because of the high levels of radiation, that time is now."

"When?" Peaches said, her voice cracking. She felt her eyes getting wet again. "When did he save you?"

"Time is relative," Lachlan said, his brown eyes searching hers. "But his instructions were clear. If anything ever happened to him, I was to take his place in the Time Lab and complete the mission."

"Oh," she said, her chin trembling. "Do you know then... what happened to him?"

"The destruction of an Amaranthine loop is never pretty," Lachlan replied. "A past version of Aldric became exposed to the Quantum forces in your grandmother's Gate. The Quantum energy affected his entire time stream as well as his physical body and the Time Lab..." Lachlan quit speaking as he watched Peaches absorb his words.

"He's gone then," Peaches managed to whisper.

"The medical suite has a forcefield around the particulates and energy that make up his being in this reality. That is all that can be done for now. Your role in the last loop of the Amaranthine may enable his return."

"Okay," Peaches nodded, folding her arms across her chest. "Okay." She nodded again, looking down at the floor.

"For now, you should rest," Lachlan said. "Centius and I will complete the equations for the last trip to the Amaranthine. Continue to wear the suit, it will draw out the last of the radiation you were exposed to while in the medical suite."

Peaches nodded, looking at Lachlan. She hicupped, smearing tears across her cheek with her palm.

"Tears," Lachlan said, his voice low. His deep brown

183

eyes gazed at Peaches, he reached out and wiped them from her cheek. "Rest will help," he said after a thoughtful moment.

"Okay," Peaches said, turning slowly for the exit, her arms still crossed. "Rest will help."

24

THE PILLAR, AMARANTHINE LOOP

Vincent woke Renata before dawn, just as he had the previous morning. They walked up the hillside behind the cottage in silence, Renata's sleepiness making her quiet. She listened for the familiar sounds of morning, like bird song, but heard nothing. The morning was more of a poorly disguised dress-rehearsal for the afternoon and evening. Even late morning and early afternoon were detailed and nuanced in a way that almost fooled her into believing this was a real place and not a dream dimension.

"We begin by creating a conduit for your power," Vincent said as they reached the perimeter of trees.

"As if I know what that is," Renata thought and then blushed as she realized she'd responded to Vincent telepathically.

"Energy is not an unknown variable in your world. Humans use energy to power many things."

"And your point is?" She quipped, uncomfortable with the mind to mind communication.

"You are made of energy," he replied bluntly. "Now more than ever before."

"Okay." She looked at him skeptically. He returned her stare until she looked away.

"This would be easier if you had coffee." Vincent extended his hand, golden light emanating from his palm. The light coalesced into an insulated coffee bottle with a plaid pattern around its base and a rickety metal handle.

"That's my dad's travel mug! How did you even—"

"All matter is energy," he said. "Of a sort."

"Are we talking about nuclear physics before coffee?" She reached for the container. He let it go as her fingers encircled it like a precious object. She twisted off the top, which also served as a mug, and turned the inner top, gently pouring the dark liquid into the makeshift mug.

"Humans were just starting to understand energy when you left Earth." Vincent nodded, observing Renata drinking coffee. "In the beginning, pure energy created all of the mass of the Universe."

"Uh-huh, like the Big Bang Theory?" she said, filling the mug and handing the insulated container back to him. He nodded and twisted the top closed before letting the golden light that created it break apart.

"Hey!" she chirped as it faded away. "What if I wanted a second cup?"

Vincent raised an eyebrow at Renata before continuing.

"The energy we both wield is more than our forms can manifest or contain," he continued, serious. "That is why you need a conduit."

"Lost me already," she said, sipping coffee.

"Consider the tree." Vincent placed his palm against the trunk of the closest tree. "There is a constant process of photosynthesizing light energy with the leaves into chemical energy—which creates food, nourishes, sustains and expands the plant's form. The tree uses this light energy or food from photosynthesis to create its structure, that of a tree."

"But we're not trees," she responded.

"No," he said. "Not at the moment."

"So, what am I photosynthesizing? What do I absorb to create form?"

"Energy," he replied. "And your photosynthetic process is your mind. Whatever you can conceive you can create, you can be."

"Or destroy?"

He shook his head. "That is a conversation for another time. Conduits, remember?"

"But we're talking about trees!"

"Yes," he nodded. "As I said, conduits."

"So, the trees are conduits?"

"For me," Vincent said, touching his chest.

"What is my conduit?" she asked, curious.

"At the moment, nothing—" Vincent nodded at her, jutting his chin out. "And that is not working well—for either of us. Your abilities have evolved a great deal since you arrived in this dimension. It is time for you to create a conduit of your own."

Renata's eyes grew round. "Create my own? I just figured out how to create groceries for dinner, I think creating a forest is a bit of a leap—"

Vincent sighed, pinching the bridge of his nose.

"Let's re-frame this equation," he said. "Perhaps a different perspective will help."

She stared blankly at him and continued to sip coffee.

"Are you familiar with human folklore and witchcraft?" he asked.

She groaned. "Oh, here we go—you said all of this was *not* magic and now we're talking about witchcraft? Pick a lane, Vincent."

He grinned at her barb. "Have you heard the term 'witch's familiar'?"

Renata nodded, hesitant.

"Perhaps instead of thinking of your abilities in terms of physics and energy transfer, you would be better served imagining your abilities as a companion," he said. "Another being, that is a conduit of your energy—is of your energy, is of *you*. This being is innate to you. Pull its creation deep from within yourself. You are imagining an energetic confidant."

Renata nodded and closed her eyes, hands still around her coffee as the steam wafted over her face. Vincent smiled again, seeing that his suggestion had an immediate audience in her.

"Pick whatever form feels right," he said, his voice soothing. "Something you strongly identify with."

Renata's eyes remained closed, her brow pinched in concentration.

"This form is only a suggestion," he said. "Whatever form you choose is an illusion. An illusion made flesh."

Renata exhaled slowly, centering herself.

"Whatever you imagine, this being, your companion or

familiar, is strong. As strong as you, for it is made of you. This entity holds and neutralizes your power. This entity is always with you, seen or unseen, it is your energy housed in another—"

A lone wolf howl broke the silence of the forest. Vincent's next word died on his tongue as he listened, eyes wide.

"It worked!" Renata said, clapping her hands. Her eyes flashed open, crackling with golden energy, the proof of her accomplishment easy for Vincent to hear. He nodded in silence.

"I mean, I couldn't think of anything, and then this wolf popped into my head—" Renata babbled, out of breath.

"Very good," he replied, his voice subdued.

"What else do I need to do?" she said, reforming the coffee container in her hands. "Like, the conduit is carrying some of my energy, and then what?" She twisted the lid, golden light pouring into her cup.

"Calm," Vincent said, noticing the streak of golden light pouring into the cup where there should have been black coffee. "Concentrate. Your human mind likes to flit about like a seed in the wind. Your mind must be a river, the flow of your energy constant."

"Alright, okay—" she said, her voice wavering with enthusiasm. "It's just, Vincent, I can feel it! I made a conduit!"

"The lamb that beckons the wolf," he said, scanning the forest. "And a lone wolf at that. You couldn't have imagined a pack? It would disperse the energy better."

"No," she said, pausing. "The one is fine."

Vincent's eyes danced, but a shadow passed across his expression.

"Then we go to the Pool," he said after a beat, clearing his throat.

"Wait—" she said, standing in Vincent's path. "Shouldn't I meet her?"

"Your conduit is you. You are the wolf," he retorted. "Would you wait around to meet your own hand?"

Renata frowned, but said nothing.

"Follow me then, *ma louloutte*," he declared, apparating.

VINCENT LED Renata to a cliffside within the forest, one that they had somehow not come across the day before. She was sure they had run through every inch of the forest, explored every plot of underbrush.

"So, this is in another dimension?" Renata tested the ground, rubbing her heel in the dirt. "Feels the same."

Vincent turned to look at Renata, he shook his head. "We are still in my Pillar. The entrance to the Pool of Verite is over this cliff. The Pool is in another dimension. The cliff to the surface of water is the precipice between dimensions. I call that a twilight dimension. Come, look."

Renata walked slowly toward the edge of the jutting rock. A long drop stared back at her. At the bottom, a small sapphire pond beckoned. The sun, which was high overhead, reflected across the surface.

"Looks like a pond."

"Come." He pointed over the cliff's edge. "The Pool of Verite awaits."

"It doesn't look very deep." She shook her head.

"It is deep enough," he said. "You can always slow your descent if it makes you more comfortable."

"What?" Renata snorted.

Demonstrating, Vincent walked off the cliff's edge. He stood, suspended on air—like he still had ground beneath him.

"See?" he said, smiling at her.

"Nope," she said, shaking her head again. "Can't do that."

"Your old denials of who and what you are have grown tiresome." Vincent tilted his head to one side. "You have just created a conduit for your power, as an Elder would."

"I can't just break the laws of gravity—"

"Just like you cannot move a knife or book when you call to it? Just like you cannot travel through time to come all this way, to another dimension?"

"I don't know how I got here!"

"Follow me." Vincent stretched out his hand, feet standing on air. His gaze was insistent.

"Fine!" Renata sized him up, and the drop below. She stepped back a few feet, and ran, vaulting off the cliff's edge.

RENATA TREMBLED in Vincent's arms, shuddering as she floated high above the Pool.

"Ah, little lamb," Vincent whispered in her ear. "Remember, never let your attention slip."

"What?" Renata leaned back, looking at his face.

He cleared his throat and blinked. He kept his eyes politely trained to her hairline and the top of her head. After a beat, his hand squeezed her waist, his warm fingertips pressing into the flesh of her hip.

"I forgot my clothes!" She didn't have time to blush as she and Vincent began to fall immediately. "No!" she shouted.

They slowed, the scenery passing by at an almost imperceptible pace.

"Clever," he said. He plucked the gray sweater from her shoulders, inspecting it between two fingers. "This is more familiar to you, so you imagined it first. What else could you be wearing?"

"What?" she said, her voice light and panicked.

"Dream with me," he said. "Relax your mind. Think of other clothing. Use a memory if you want. Imagine every detail. The color, the feel of the fabric against your skin."

They floated, like a dandelion puff on the wind, meandering slowly to the base of the cliff where the Pool beckoned like a sapphire sun. Vincent kept his hold around Renata's waist, watching her manifest a power she could not possibly possess.

While he maintained the tweed jacket and dark pants he usually wore, Renata transformed. Blurry white light eclipsed her body until the energy coalesced into a silver and white gown, the color contrasting beautifully against her ochre complexion. The gown had large puffed sleeves that sat on her shoulders like meringues. Silver fabric fluttered over mounds of tulle fabric, creating a cartoonishly large bell-shaped skirt. Renata smiled, her eyes glowing with memory.

"Your quinceañera dress. A vivid memory, that's a good one. Let us stop completely," he suggested, glancing down to measure the distance. "Can you do that?"

"Mmm-hmm." She was biting her lip, squeezing her eyes shut as her fingers dug into Vincent's forearms. Their descent slowed, then stopped. They floated, two dancers paused in midair.

"This has been the weirdest morning ever," she said, her eyes still closed.

"Why not go for that swim now?" he said, scanning the gown she had imagined. "Afterwards, we can go home for some breakfast. You've mentioned you like breakfast."

"Breakfast? More like lunch," she said, finally opening her eyes. "We've been out here for hours."

"So we have," he chuckled and met her gaze. He watched the dappled forest light turn strands of her dark hair gold. Enraptured, he noted the constellation of freckles over the bridge of her nose, only slightly contrasted against her golden-ochre skin. His gaze roamed further, over her full lips the color of dusty rose. His eyes, empty of a loving look for more than a thousand years, consumed her.

A savage and irresistible hunger threatened to overwhelm him. Vincent's hands tightened their grip on her waist. He blinked and froze in alarm.

He hadn't realized they'd drawn so close to the water. He groaned, chastising himself for being distracted as the dimensional forces of the Pool ensnared them both. He clenched his jaw, willing his Elder strength to prevent him from exposing his truths to Renata. The Pool slowed time when it drew out the truth, making the present almost a euphoria.

Renata inhaled sharply, pulling away from him, and avoiding his mesmerizing gaze. His nostrils flared, his predatory Elder consciousness detecting a trace of fear. He clenched his jaw and withdrew his hands. They floated, independent of each other for the first time.

"I feel like I've known you longer than a week," she said after a few moments, her gaze distant and lost in the trees surrounding the pond. "It feels like I've been here forever," she whispered. She looked down at the water below.

"Do you know what forever feels like?" Vincent half smiled.

"No." Renata smiled shyly back. "But time here is weird. I know we're standing still but... a part of me is outside this Pillar. Outside, in the dimension Sid found me in. And to the dimension before that, my home dimension, you might say. I can feel it. I'm tied to those places, some-how. It's this heaviness I feel, here—" she rubbed her chest, indicating her heart. "I guess it's nostalgia, I don't know. It just... it *feels*." She paused, struggling for words. "I wish I could say more. There is no word in Spanish, English, any language I know—"

Without warning, Renata pressed her hand to Vincent's chest, as if to cast her emotion into him, so he could understand all the context behind *to feel*.

She succeeded.

Vincent gasped. To feel. It was a weight, like a stone. To feel was like a stone, warmed by the sun, projecting radiant energy. Her life energy. To feel was her connection to the Gate, which throbbed with an aching emptiness. He could feel the cords of her—the smallest, nimblest stretches of energy—connecting her back through time, through dimensions. A web of missed opportunities and potential destinies. To feel was the snarls of time reverberating and moving, bound to an Anchor in the present, straining against the past and the future.

"*You are a mortal Anchor,*" Vincent exclaimed.

"*¿Qué?*" Renata replied.

"*It is quite impossible, but you are a mortal Anchor of Time.*"

Vincent was almost sure of it. What she felt was the wrenching of all of her timelines through the Gate. Even in the Pillar, this feeling was palpable, he realized. The Pool with its strange power enhanced this feeling, and she managed to cast the emotion into him. She probably didn't understand what she was feeling, much less the empathetic casting—another ability no mortal could possess.

He was almost sure Renata was feeling time itself.

"*Impossible,*" he repeated.

"*You keep saying that, but I'm not really sure what you're referring to.*"

"*Impossible that you cast your emotion, impossible that you are a mortal Anchor, that you can feel time, everything...*"

"*Oh, just all that.*" She smiled, her eyes sad. "*Do Elders not er—catch a feeling sometimes?*"

"*It's quite an advanced psychic ability to cast an emotion. Empathy or empathetic casting, I cannot even do it with Sid.*" Vincent's smile didn't reach his eyes either.

"*Any luck with other Elders?*"

"*I can with other Elders, but not Tardigrades. They do not really have emotion, not like we would define it.*"

"*What about with me?*" she asked, shivering. Vincent

noticed the acute effects of her abilities on her physical body. Her internal temperature was decreasing as an innate power within her unfurled.

"*Impossible,*" he said again, disbelieving what he was witnessing, what he was about to do. He had no other choice but to transmute his true emotion and his unguarded feelings for her this close to the Pool of Verite —despite that he was wrong for having them, and could never act upon them. She was human, and thus forbidden. He spared another glance at the sunlight bending and refracting in the atoms of her hair.

"Not impossible," she said, her voice a whisper. Her eyes widened and her expression softened as his emotions rolled over her like the tide. Vincent shuddered, vulnerable with desire. His eyes tore at her with unmistakable need.

"Vincent," she whispered.

His nostrils flared, and he gritted his teeth. He felt desire blooming inside her blood, responding to his need. *She is an animal, a human, after all—they are creatures made to desire,* he thought privately. He had smelled desire in her blood before. Desire mixed with fear—the opposite forces tugging and arguing with each other for dominance.

He knew which dominated her blood now. He placed one hand at the small of her back, the other clutching her dark hair, mahogany curls surrendered in his fist.

"The warmth," she said dreamily. "It's your hunger, and your power..."

"I do have an appetite for you, this I cannot deny," he said through clenched teeth, his long canines breaching past his lips with the effort.

"Yes," she said, the yes more of a hiss in her throat.

"I was not made for love, Renata," he warned, resisting the influence of the Pool over his thoughts, his actions. He attempted to break away from her arms. He let her hair slip through his fingers, but she clung to him. It was like electricity pulsed through their bodies, and the Universe shrank to the wound of his eternal, aching loneliness and the precious, fleeting balm of pressing her warm body against his.

He grabbed her waist and clutched her against him. He felt her readiness, an instinctual relaxing of her hips, as she melted into their embrace. He felt his expression change, becoming feral, almost predatory. He nuzzled her head back, nipping her earlobe. His insistent mouth planted a trail of ravenous kisses down her throat. She wrapped her legs around him then, and he felt the warmth of her core, her excited pulse playing like a melody in his mind.

He grasped her roughly, letting her sex rest against his response. She mewed with surprise, and they kissed again. He dipped his tongue past her lips, tasting her. He dominated her with his desire, let his power tease her senses in ways no mortal man ever could.

In the background, the fragile cadence of her heartbeat taunted him. If he wanted, he could destroy her, down to the last atom. He gripped her tighter, resisting his predatory urges. Her physical fragility only increased his desire for her, to protect her as his tongue dipped past her lips once more.

Suddenly, a haunting Quantum song pierced the obliterating heat of his lust. It was the sound of timelessness, booming in his ears. The ancient, familiar tone echoed in every cell of her body, urging him to remember something—

What is her dream doing in your memories? Sid's words echoed in his mind.

Vincent's eyes shot open, his embrace disintegrating. He felt something stir inside him and shift as he ended their kiss.

He released Renata from his intimate hold. When his eyes met hers, he felt an ancient awareness of him staring back.

"What's wrong?" she said, looking up at him, her lips pink and ravished.

He shook his head, his mind silent. Something ancient and inexplicable existed within her—most troubling of all, it was familiar.

"Who are you?" He spoke into her mind, the Quantum knowledge her body shared still lingering in his thoughts. She stared at him, her brow pinched with confusion.

He shook his head, and his Elder warmth extinguished with a pop, like a glamour evaporating in the air around them. Withdrawing from her, Vincent ached with a familiar loneliness that he had somehow forgotten he felt.

Renata's body stiffened. Tiny ice-crystals appeared across her skin as his Elder power faded. Her skin turned beige-blue in the noontime sun, her psychic abilities betraying her physical form.

Numb with cold, Renata's frozen body splashed into the water only a few feet below.

RENATA IMAGINED Ophelia as her dress ballooned up and around her in the water. Her rigid body became entangled, the water-logged fabric weighing her down. In a matter of seconds, she slipped below the surface of the pond.

Emoting psychically into Vincent had caused all of her extremities to fall asleep, all together—an effect she had been unaware of, surrounded by his Elder essence.

Her fingers crackled with blood, attempting to fill her empty capillaries. Vincent's essence, or warmth, or hunger —Renata wasn't sure which—was a slip stream of warm air that was hidden around him like some migratory weather pattern. She had felt it in the kitchen too, but this... this had been different.

"*Atención, Stone,*" Renata thought. She tried to condense all of her thoughts on getting her limbs to move. They were creeping back to life, but she continued to sink. Dimly, behind the bubbling panic and adrenaline, Renata also remembered the finer details of *Hamlet*. Specifically, she recalled that Ophelia was quite mad—which was not completely unlike how she felt, at the moment.

Renata thawed and forced her eyes open. She gazed into the water, expecting the depths to be clear and illuminated by daylight. Instead, it was dark. She gasped, water crowding her mouth and eclipsing her breath. Long water weeds swayed in the murky blue water, crowding her against the cliff side.

Moving her sluggish, frozen joints required all of her will. She lifted her neck in increments, while her body floated down to the base of the pond. She could not struggle, her body betrayed.

The cliffside met the pond bed, several dark feet below

the water. A story abuela Noni used to tell, about when she was young and almost drowned in a cenote, popped into Renata's mind. It was a story Renata knew well, almost tattooed in her memory, she had asked her abuela to repeat it so much.

"*Nunca debes nadar sola, mi querida,*" abuela Noni would finish the story, reminding Renata never to swim alone.

But Renata was not alone.

She faced a woman—who was chained to a throne of rock—the woman from her nightmares. She seemed to be gasping for air as blood gushed from a terrible wound at her neck.

Renata attempted to scream, to swim up and away, but she couldn't. She looked down at her hands. They too were chained with large shackles.

She let out a scream, water rushing into her mouth. A large Quantum Mirror was at the bottom of the pond, situated at the navel of the cliff. It was built into the rock, emerging from the rubble. In it, Renata saw herself brace against the chains, her shoulders and arms flexing against her bonds. She stared at the image of herself, seeing her own eyes burning back at her with recognition through the water. It was her and not her, a version of herself that did not yet exist and also existed long ago. A crown of glass and bone fell from the woman's head to the blood-soaked ground at the base of the stone. Renata recognized the fear and despair in her expression. Renata stared, enraptured, as she felt blood bubble and slither with whisper-soft tendrils from her neck, and the reflection became her reality.

She screamed for Vincent as best she could under the water. The woman screamed with her, but she made no audible sound. Water muffled Renata's voice as it burned into her lungs.

Like Ophelia, she was drowning.

As her consciousness faded, she noted vaguely that her reflection did not mimic her, but stared silently as Renata began to fade away.

RENATA SPUTTERED, vomiting water on the muddy bank. A large wolf stood at the shoreline, golden eyes glowing and teeth bared at Vincent in a silent growl.

Vincent stood above both Renata and the wolf, bare-foot and shirtless at the edge of the pond. His hair was wet and hanging in rivulets around his face. His long eyelashes dappled drops of water onto his bare chest. He put his hand tentatively on the wolf's neck, stroking the fur. The dark wolf looked up at him before vanishing into thin air.

Renata coughed and sobbed into the beach, clawing for purchase on the shore. She sat up, sputtering and glaring.

"*¡Pendejo!*" she barked hoarsely between violent coughs.

"Renata—" Vincent began, pushing his wet hair back from his face.

"What the hell is wrong with you?!" She erupted, her voice now only allowing a hoarse whisper.

Vincent winced as she spoke, raking his hand through his wet hair again.

"How long do you have?" he responded after a moment, holding up a large towel. He produced it out of nowhere, without even a flourish or pop of power. Renata swore a string of rapid-fire curses into Vincent's mind. She continued to cough but managed to get to her feet. Water beaded off her skin. She looked down at her body. Mud was caked on her feet, knees, hands, and elbows. Her hair, sopping wet, clung to her form like a river serpent, a crown of glass and bone atop her head.

Vincent's eyes widened, taking in the crown.

Renata saw him staring. She followed his eyes, and gingerly reached above her head. Touching the crown, she gasped. With trembling, mud encrusted fingers, she tugged on it and threw it to the ground. Her eyes, round with disbelief, blinked several times as her chest heaved with heavy, troubled breaths.

Vincent could hear her heart, its rapid staccato rhythm racing faster than her terrified thoughts, which he also felt simmering between them.

He picked up the crown and gently turned it over in his hand.

"I don't know what that is." Renata shuddered. She shook her head, her wet hair clinging to her face and neck. She folded her mud smeared arms over her chest.

"You do." He looked up impatiently from the crown to her face. "It is your truth."

"I'm telling you, it's *not*."

"Why do you deny the truth to yourself?" Vincent's eyes flashed in frustration.

"I could ask you the same question." Renata stuck her chin out at Vincent, eyes daring him.

He frowned at her accusation but said nothing.

She swore again and snapped the towel from his hands, covering herself with it. "I knew you were emotionally unavailable, but you don't have to be such a dick about it."

"Renata..." Vincent began, attempting to explain himself. "You are a mortal, it is—"

She was using the towel to squeeze the water out of her hair. "Forbidden? Save it, Vincent. Unfortunately for you, I know whatever you're saying to me *isn't true*. Your self-control isn't the problem."

"Renata—"

"I scare you," she said, her jaw trembling and eyes inflating with angry, unshed tears. She was in a baby-blue bathrobe now, with fluffy pink slippers. Vincent's proffered towel was wound around her head like a turban, her face clean. "I'm going back to the cottage, eating lunch, and taking the rest of the afternoon *off*."

Vincent watched Renata apparate, leaving him and the crown discarded by the shoreline of the Pool.

25

THE PILLAR, AMARANTHINE LOOP

Renata's silence hung like a pendulum. She wrung out a washcloth, staring through the kitchen window above the sink, her eyes gazing beyond the glass. She lowered her limp hands until they were submerged with the ceramic plates under the hot water.

¿Qué vi? What did I see?

A dish shifted in the sink and broke her stare. Her hands wound into the washcloth again, gray water dripping off her chapped fingertips.

She wiped her wet hands on her sweater, shivering. She didn't acknowledge Vincent who lingered in the doorway, observing her. The red book with golden hieroglyphics was open in his hands.

She hadn't spoken to him after they left the Pool of Verite. She had eaten dinner in silence with Sid, moving her food around the plate until it was unrecognizable.

She squeezed her eyes shut, her hands still submerged

in the steaming water. She bit her lip, attempting to suppress a sob.

Without warning, she broke away from the sink and disappeared through the threshold of the kitchen, passing Vincent like a cold wind. She sped past Sid, who looked up in surprise from a large tome of star charts in the library.

She made it to her bedroom and slammed the door. Her back slumped against it. She choked back a howl, her shoulders shaking with restrained panic.

This place isn't real, and yet it exists.

She ran her hands roughly over her face, thinking to rouse herself awake. Her thoughts felt blurry and detached.

Un sueño. Maybe this is a dream.

Her head throbbed, as if her brain was bursting.

I saw what was true in the water.

All of her senses confirmed it, as much as she wanted to deny it. She knew it was true like she knew how to breathe.

Renata's glassy eyes looked at the floor, late afternoon light sprawled across the wooden floorboards. She looked up at the sun as it leaned into the bosom of the mountains. Hot tears threatened her eyes, and the late afternoon light became a blur.

That was how I died.

Renata collapsed onto the bed and began to weep in earnest, using the mattress to smother her cries.

AFTER A FEW MINUTES, Vincent quietly appeared in the back bedroom. A room that, in the course of a few short days, he thought of as distinctly Renata's. It was the one he had placed her in when Sid first brought the mortal to the Pillar.

The window was large for a bedroom, but with the spectacular view through the field and the mountains beyond, understandable. Through the window, Vincent could see the sun sinking behind the mountains, producing an autumn gold—rich with orange and tinged with pink—coloring the evening sky.

Renata was quaking with hacking sobs, illuminated by the ethereal glow of the sunset pouring through the window. It was the golden hour.

Vincent could taste her fear. It was like a noxious cloud, flavoring the air of the room. Her animal mind, her instinct, was taking over. Instinct ran on fear, it was the life source of fear itself.

"Renata," he said.

He crossed the threshold and sat on the bed next to her. She shrank away from him, wounded.

"Renata," he said again. Compassion stirred Vincent, and he gently placed his fingers on her shoulder. He mouthed a few indistinguishable words. Her panic subsided, and he felt her body relax, though her diaphragm still spasmed in distress. Finally, her breathing slowed and deepened. She looked up at him.

"*Ma louloutte,*" he said telepathically. He moved her hair from her tear stained face and drew the bedsheet over her. He sat quietly next to her on the bed before speaking.

"I'm sorry," he said out loud. He paused, searching for the right words. He glanced at Renata. Her eyes were distant, glazed, and bloodshot from crying. "I was not made for love, and—"

"What were you made for, Vincent?" She interrupted, her voice hoarse.

"Truth," Vincent said. "Elders were beings of truth and benevolence, before the Future War."

"How old are you?"

He shrugged. "How old are you?"

Renata paused. "I don't know anymore, actually."

"We have that in common at least," he said, chuckling. Several minutes passed in silence. Vincent watched her out of the corner of his eye. She stared ahead as the last tendril of sunlight stretched across the room before she finally spoke.

"I saw how I died."

Vincent's eyebrows went up. "In the Pool?"

Renata nodded. "It's my dream."

"You saw your dream in the Pool?"

Renata nodded again. "It was in a mirror... I think I've been dreaming of my death. In a past life, I guess."

Vincent leaned his head back against the headboard of the bed, his hands clasped.

"Did you see anything else?"

"No," she said. "But she saw me."

"Who?"

"The woman. Me. Whatever. I saw myself in the mirror and the me in the mirror saw *me*. Get it?"

It was Vincent's turn to nod.

"And as trippy as all that is—" Renata began. "My mystery is not really solved. I still don't know how to work a Quantum Gate."

"But you made Quantum Glass," Vincent said, turning to Renata in bed.

"No," she said.

"The crown—it was made of Quantum Glass."

"Was it?" Renata looked at Vincent, her eyes bulging with tears. "Vincent, I don't know how it got on my head." Her voice broke. "I don't know if I'm making anything or how to not make them. How can I control what I don't even know—" she sobbed.

Vincent turned to her without thinking, embracing her. She wept in his arms. He held her as the sun finished setting, and the room finally darkened. He felt every ounce his innumerable age, holding her this way. Renata kept her face buried in his chest, hot tears rolling down her cheeks.

"I don't normally cry," she said between sobs.

"Not a lot of normal going around."

"What if I never remember?" she said into his chest. He stroked her back as she choked on another sob.

"Never is a long time. You will remember."

Renata hicupped, and Vincent loosened his arms. They looked into each other's eyes. He felt a pang of the desire he'd felt earlier.

"You are safe with me," Vincent said, reminding himself as well. "Always."

He wiped the tears from her cheek. Her eyes were electric and seemed to beckon him. Whatever Renata was, he wanted her—with a familiar, damning ache.

"But are you safe with me?" Renata said, unraveling into tears once more.

26

THE PILLAR, AMARANTHINE LOOP

"*I*t is a good theory, and she said it herself—prior to creating a crown of Quantum Glass," Vincent muttered telepathically to Sid.

Vincent trudged up the hill behind the cottage, a lone figure walking in the moonlight. He left Renata sleeping at the cottage, hoping a walk outside would help him think.

"*Manifesting Quantum Glass!*" Sid exclaimed into Vincent's mind. The Tardigrade had retreated back into the corked glass vial of water swinging from Vincent's neck. "*If it had not occurred in the Pool of Verite's dimension—*"

"*She is evolving,*" Vincent said. "*Whatever buffer the Pillar would be for another mortal is not effective with her.*"

"*We could not know what effect a Quantum Gate would have on a mortal.*"

"*Do the math, Sid. If she is the creator of that Gate, and her mortal energy tied to it while the Gate is suspended through time and different dimensions...*" Vincent shook his head, stuffing his hands in his pockets. He began a slow walk up the hill.

He could see his breath in the air, the night crisp and clear. *"This confluence of inter-dimensional events has caused her to evolve somehow—even though she remains in the Pillar where time is suspended. She has become a mortal Anchor of Time. I am convinced of it."*

"That... cannot be," Sid said.

"Another broken law of the Universe as we know it. How many is that now?" Vincent paused on the hillside. He looked back, marking his progress while taking in the night landscape.

"Pillars were not made for mortals. Perhaps this is an effect of the Pool—"

"The Pool revealed this to me." Vincent shut his eyes, suppressing the memory of kissing Renata, which had seared itself into his mind. He shook his head in frustration.

"The branch of your Pillar in this dimension of New-Ashemore has a space-time that equals one year there to our one day in the Pillar. I am still making my initial calculations, but in Renata's home dimension many, many years have passed," Sid said in awe. *"The distance between these dimensions is vast, and the longer she is apart from her home dimension, the faster time passes there. I calculate many hundreds of years to every sunrise in the Pillar..."*

"Enough time for even a mortal to understand Quantum Glass?" Vincent said, moving his hair back from his forehead.

"Perhaps. Until then, there is no other place for her. She must remember who she is, or was, or may become," Sid said. *"With her Quantum Gate open in two dimensions, I hypothesize the development of her abilities has accelerated."*

"She will break," Vincent said, frowning at the thought.

"I know of no creature or being able to harness and hold the energy of an Anchor. It is why they are irrevocable points in history."

"They are a Quantum constant." Sid agreed.

"There is no equation to change time. An Anchor of Time is an immortal, unyielding, cosmic constant."

"A mortal Anchor!" Sid said. *"She is a paradox within a paradox."*

"She emoted into my mind today, Sid. Impossible."

"Take me to the crown."

Vincent apparated to the Pool of Verite and stood on the shoreline. A bleak darkness surrounded the Pool, as if the Quantum Glass were somehow absorbing some of the light wavelengths around it. The crown lay discarded in the water. Vincent gingerly picked it up.

"It is Quantum Glass," Sid exclaimed telepathically.

"She is firm in her belief that she cannot do this," Vincent replied. *"I assume it took on the form of a crown because of her nightmare?"*

"Perhaps it is a memory."

Vincent looked at the crown in his hands. *"A memory from her original timeline?"*

"Before the Future War, it was called Divine Death, was it not?"

"You are suggesting the impossible," Vincent said. *"That, at least, is consistent."*

"The Future War was long ago, the practice of Divine Death older still," Sid said. *"Perhaps her dream is a memory of her mistreatment. The details of Divine Death are lost, but it is a powerful ceremony, and only Supreme Elders could participate. Perhaps Divine Death was when she made the Gate—to escape, or alter her timeline?"*

"Divine Death? Sid, she's human!"

"Is she?"

Vincent scoffed. Of course she was. Never mind that she had accidentally time-traveled, had amateur telekinesis, and could, as of today, psychically cast emotion too. Renata breathed. She had a heartbeat. She was mortal. Sort of.

"I see no other alternative but to travel to the Henge of Time," Vincent frowned. *"There are Quantum Gates in the Henge powerful enough to contact the Arbiters. If she continues to gain energy, even the Pillar will not be enough to conceal her from the Trackers. She could split the dimension outside the Pillar apart."*

Sid's psychic energy emerged from the small vial of water around Vincent's neck. Small clouds of misted light whispered to the ground like fog as the Tardigrade took psychic form. Outside of their previous psychic conflict with Renata, Sid always manifested for Vincent as Elaria. Her image lingered before him as Sid finally solidified. A curtain of sable hair fluttered around Sid-as-Elaria's small frame, the psychic projection a perfect imitation of Vincent's deceased sibling.

Vincent blinked and stared at his companion. Freshly re-imagined, Sid bent down to more closely inspect the crown.

Sid clutched the crown; slender, delicate imagined fingertips grazing over the glass. Touch was information, touch was a story. Sid sat silent, and after a few minutes looked up at Vincent.

"It has Gate energy, but something more... Radiation from the Cerulean dimension..."

Vincent's expression froze. *"What are you saying?"*

"This crown is a Quantum Manifestation. She drew it from another part of her timeline."

"Another part of her timeline?" Vincent's eyes were wide, almost vibrating. Sid looked at Vincent, the moonlight creating dull shadows on the ground.

"You already know what I'm going to say," Sid said.

Vincent turned away.

"Aeor-Eterna," he shuddered. *"The Future War is calling me back."*

RENATA OPENED HER EYES. Moonlight crept around the curtain-less windows. She sat up, moving the sheet Vincent had pulled to her chin when she finally fell asleep. She looked out the window as a wolf's howl shattered the preternatural silence of the Pillar.

Slowly, the corners and strong lines of the walls and windows of her bedroom bled into the forest until she was half in the cottage and half out. The floor turned to dirt, dotted with leaves, brush, and bramble. Renata spotted two yellow eyes watching her.

Without hesitation, she held out her hand, though her human mind shouted that wasn't a good idea. A different mind was in control now—an older part of Renata, a part of her that had aged beyond the Pillar, beyond her Gate. A consciousness both smooth and cool like river stone drew her hand forward with a tacit trust of the creature before her.

A wolf, its coat dark as midnight in a moonless sky, approached her. Its large head nuzzled her arm, pricking her palm with its wet nose. The wolf looked at Renata, golden eyes peering straight through her to the timelessness she held within.

"I'll follow," she said. She stood up from the bed.

The dark wolf turned, disappearing into the brush. Renata put her feet forward, felt herself following the wolf into the woods as if she was in a dream. Though she could not see the creature, she felt its presence.

She emerged into a clearing in an unknown part of the forest. Fog blanketed the ground and obscured any trail, but Renata walked forward. She knew the way, as if this were from a memory.

"Not my memory," she mumbled. "This must be Vincent's."

The fog opened to a steep and winding path, crowded on either side by ancient trees with fat trunks and gesturing branches. She ascended the trail, its peak revealing an open vista of a sandy shoreline and the ocean beyond.

The moon was almost full, its dim light dousing everything in a pale wash from the sandy beach to the dark, writhing ocean. In the distance, a craggy cliffside perched on the shore. A glittering circle of boulders stood on its crest.

Her wolf had already descended the path—two glowing eyes peered up from the beach.

Renata launched herself, bounding down the path with a buoyancy that defied gravity but was not quite flying.

Her feet sank into the beach sand, silver and gray in the moonlight. She looked across the beach, the tide making glistening imprints on the shore.

"Why hasn't Vincent ever shown me this place?" she asked her wolf. Her hand grasped for its fur, and the wolf manifested below her hand. Touching her conduit enflamed her senses, colored the landscape in more shades of gray and moonlight than she thought possible. Her eyes crackled with energy and her feet levitated off the ground, buoyed by the influx of power.

Renata withdrew her hand in fear. She fell in an ungraceful tangle of limbs onto the sand.

"So that's a thing," she muttered, sitting up and dusting herself off.

The wolf stared back at her, golden-yellow eyes in the dark.

"Is this where you meant to take me?"

The wolf sniffed the air, turning its head away and growling. Suddenly, it bolted from Renata and began to run along the coastline.

"Wait for me!" Renata exclaimed. She stumbled to her feet and began to pursue the wolf as fast as her limbs would take her.

Suddenly, her wolf stopped along the shoreline, growling. Before she could ask, a dark mist emerged from the sand, writhing and falling over itself like smoke. It attempted to create a form resembling a man. Despite this effort, it was no more than a misty specter—with small beady holes for eyes and a vaporous, trembling chin for a mouth.

"Renata," it managed to whisper. Renata stared, eyes round. She grasped for her wolf, and it stood, resolute and still in front of her but made no sound.

"What... What are you?" she finally managed to ask.

"I do not have much time," the specter said. "This form is consuming me, transforming me to what I once was."

"Will that be an improvement, or—?" Renata said, squinting to take in its form more critically.

"At the turn of the tide, we will begin to Anchor Time," the specter said.

"What?"

"I come from the future—to tell you—"

"Hello, from the future," she said, giving a small wave of her hand.

"There is a version of me in what you are experiencing as the present."

"Okay..."

"Please," the specter said. "We will meet again , here—" He indicated the coast.

Renata nodded, the wind lashing her hair against her face and neck.

"I am Aldric," the specter said. "You must take your place in the Order of Things, you must get to the—"

A din of screams, layered over each other in a chaotic symphony, rolled over Renata. She covered her ears, falling to her knees. Her wolf growled, the hair on its back rising. The specter, Aldric, lost its form and regained it. But the dark energy was different—frenetic, angry.

"Renataaaah," the black fog whined.

"Aldric from the future?" she said.

"Alllll-driiiic," it hissed.

"Oof," Renata said, getting up. "Well, I was trying to have a little night hike on the ocean with my companion here." Renata looked down at her wolf, which was still growling—its hackles were up, as it attempted to intimi-date the billowy form.

"You... abide with... the Destroyer... the Death Bringer —" the mist hissed.

"Whoa, whoa, whoa," she said, putting her hands up.

"He... cheated... balance," the mist replied. "The Future War—"

"Balance? Are you a Tracker?" Renata said, backing away. "Sounds personal, I'm uh—I don't think I have any business getting involved—"

The mist lunged for her then, wrapping her in its dark vapor. She panicked, her wolf snapping and snarling. When she touched her wolf's fur, a perfect clarity settled over her mind, smothering her panic. Renata felt an ancient power uncoil itself from within her and surge out of her body—flinging the mist into the oncoming tide with a brilliant spark of light.

The mist retaliated, reaching out for her, tendrils grasping her arms and dragging her with it toward the dark waves.

Renata screamed.

VINCENT SNARLED and turned back to Sid on the shoreline of the Pool of Verite.

"The Future War. It's impossible," he said to Sid telepathi-cally, letting his breath out slowly, almost sadly. The night was getting colder, and he could discern the barest hint of his breath in the air. *"None escaped the Future War."*

"You did," Sid said simply, tossing the crown back into the Pool. It disappeared beneath the water.

"I am Chosen," Vincent replied. *"You Chose me. I was given reprieve."*

"That is also true," Sid said. *"But for Trackers, your survival is a not a reprieve. To them you escaped balance, escaped justice, which contradicts your baser purpose as a being of truth and justice. You also have the possibility of redemption, a Count so rare that I doubt it has shown up in any Ledger."*

"The Trackers would seek to destroy me were I not Chosen," Vincent said, frowning. *"I'll grant you that. What does this have to do with Renata?"*

"Renata's mortal body is not accustomed to the forces she commands," Sid said. *"It is possible that is because in her other timeline, she was not."*

"Not mortal? Are you also suggesting that she is an Elder? From the Future War?" Vincent turned back to Sid, who was still crouched on the shoreline of the Pool.

"I'm only suggesting she was not mortal in the Future War," Sid said. *"What precisely she was, or could be, or currently is, remains a mystery."*

Vincent turned from Sid again, facing the pine forest containing all that remained of the Blood Orphans of the Future War. He stared deeply, gazing at the shred of their spark still contained within the trees.

"Beloved," Sid said, suddenly appearing next to Vincent.

Vincent averted his eyes, brushing a leaf off his boot. Sid looked up, gazing at the night sky. The stars dusted the horizon, and a pale moon smiled above the tree line in the west.

"There are more questions than answers with regard to our

new companion Renata," Sid began. "Sanguis could ascertain her true identity, inform us of her entire past. I'm not asking you to tether your life-force to her, take only what you need to determine the truth. Afterward, we could move the Pillar to another dimension, to another galaxy to avoid the Trackers."

"You cannot ask this of me," Vincent growled. A flicker of anger crossed his face like a passing shadow.

"You would rather journey to the Arbiters," Sid said.

Vincent nodded.

"The Henge of Time... is in a dead branch of the Pillar. It was so before I Chose you. Your future there is veiled to me..." Sid said, gazing up at the night sky. A thin cloud passed over the face of the moon, darkening the forest even further.

"I admit, it is starting to feel like there is some dark destiny pulling us both there," Vincent admitted.

"Do you not find this a remarkable coincidence?" Sid chuckled. "A difficult journey lies ahead in a land from both of your pasts."

A breeze moved Vincent's hair off his neck, he angled his chin up, closing his eyes and letting the wind press past him.

"The winds of change arrived with her," he replied. "I must accept that, as she must accept that she is special. It is forbidden to keep a human in my Pillar," he paused, letting the rumbling of his hunger—his desire for her simmer and cool in his chest before continuing. "But Trackers would certainly destroy her if I let her leave. I am in quite the impossible situation. Taking her to the Arbiters is perhaps my only choice."

Sid nodded. "Renata will continue to evolve, which could be more dangerous for her outside of the Pillar. In Aeor-Eterna, Sanguis may be necessary—"

The cloud unveiled the moon slowly, the brightness of its lunar face illuminating the forest in the night. Vincent's hands were fisted at his sides, his eyes glaring at the sky.

"What you ask of me it is to break my discipline. To risk what civilizes me from the others of my kind. It would disgrace me. It would disgrace Elaria, whom you resemble even now, after all this time. And my father—whose name is so old even time has forgotten its syllables—he too would be disgraced. It is forbidden for a reason. I cannot be trusted with a human."

"I no longer believe she is human," Sid said. *"Not entirely. Not anymore."*

"She is human," Vincent replied. *"And my Elder appetites threaten to consume her every day."*

"You must trust yourself," Sid said. *"You are capable of more than destruction."*

Vincent turned to Sid for the first time during their tense conversation, brows twisted in anger and disgust when a blistering scream echoed in the distance.

It came from the cottage.

THE PILLAR, AMARANTHINE LOOP

Vincent apparated back to the cottage. Renata's bedroom door ricocheted off the wall, the hinges protesting as he stormed into the room. His energy glimmered around his body, creating patterns of light on the wall.

Renata writhed in the bed, white hot electricity emanating from her hands that sizzled and burnt her flesh.

Vincent approached her, wary of what lay before him. Sweat beaded on Renata's forehead, her face a mask of agony. She wasn't awake—she was dreaming. The energy gathering in her hands was a form of defense, like she was warding herself from... something.

He ground his teeth in aggravation. Careful of Renata and her bristling power, he leaned down and attempted to place his fingers on her forehead. With tenderness, his fingers pressed the space between her eyes, attempting to wake her.

White energy erupted from her hands, singeing her

palms. It arched spectacularly—looking and pawing to find the source of its disturbance. It quickly found Vincent, and in a blinding crack of energy flung him across the room.

The bedroom smelled of burning flesh.

It was a pungent odor, not easily dismissed. Renata screamed in a blistering voice. Her body seized, her breaths short, rapid gasps.

Vincent closed his eyes and tried to enter her mind telepathically. He saw her mind was like a rushing river. He couldn't quite catch a coherent thought before it rushed by —half formed, trembling and detached. Energy, a wild and powerful rage, excised him from her mind and left a bitter metallic taste on his tongue. He knew the flavor of that energy. Trackers.

Vincent acted with haste. He bit his forearm, opening a vein of his core Elder light. A bright, piercing gold dripped like syrup from his arm. His essence drizzled over her hands, which were singed with radiation burns.

Renata's tissue began to restore itself. But the stains of blood, struggle, and fire remained on the sheets. She whimpered in her sleep, turning her head away from the dawn whispering through the window. Vincent relaxed his gaze and urged time to slow, her sleep to linger a little longer. He grunted as she resisted and tried to wake. All the while, he was compelling, with renewed effort, his life essence onto her wounds, into her body—to heal her and purge her of the Tracker spark grappling for control.

Once her hands were healed, Vincent shook Renata's shoulders. Her eyes, swollen from crying, slowly flickered open.

"Speak to me," Vincent said, his voice strained.

"Speaking to you," she said, sleep thick on her tongue.

"Get up." Vincent stood, his face expressionless. "Come with me to the library."

Renata sat up in the bed, rubbing her eyes. She looked at the singed bedsheets and blood.

"What the—"

"You had a nightmare," he said, sitting next to her on the bed. "You are okay now."

"Did I—" She pointed to the sheets. Vincent nodded slowly.

"Okay now," he repeated, gently brushing her hair from her face.

"Who's Aldric?" Renata said, locking eyes with Vincent, her voice hoarse.

His hand cupped her chin. "What did you say?"

"Aldric," she said, moving his hand so she could rub her eyes again. Afterward, she kicked the sheets off and moved to sit next to Vincent, her feet hanging over the edge of the bed. "I was running along the beach with my wolf, and then he appeared—"

"Library. Now." Vincent said and apparated.

"Good morning to you too," he heard her grumble as he left.

RENATA SAT down in her favorite wingback chair next to the fireplace. Sid appeared, offering a cup of coffee and a warm bagel.

"Just the way you like it," Sid said.

"Oh," she said, peering down at the coffee. "Thanks, Sid."

"You are welcome," Sid said before turning to look at Vincent.

He was at the other end of the library, thumbing through different maps, mumbling under his breath.

"Anything I can do to help?" Sid asked.

Vincent held up his hand, still mumbling and leafing through his map collection. With a flourish, he unrolled a map and looked at its contents. Satisfied it was the right one, he walked over to Sid and Renata. He spread it out on the long dining room table near the hearth, motioning for Sid and Renata to join him.

"Is today's lesson in cartography?" Renata said before biting down on her bagel.

"We have to leave," Vincent said. "This explains where we are going."

Renata made a muffled yet concerned noise, her mouth full.

"The Pool did not give satisfactory answers," Vincent said, running his hands through his hair, staring at the map. "And you dream-walked with a Tracker. Aldric is attempting to gain control of you because he has likely found your Quantum Gate. It is also probable Trackers have found the Pillar."

Renata put her coffee and bagel down. "Aldric *is* a Tracker, I was right!"

Vincent nodded thoughtfully, his eyes still fixed to the map. "Indeed. A very old and experienced Tracker..."

"I'm sorry," she said, looking down, her eyes becoming glassy with guilt.

Vincent put his hand under her chin, turning her face up to his.

"A promise is a promise," he said, looking in her eyes. "I will keep you safe."

"But, Vincent, what if I just left, or I don't know, what if we both did—"

A rogue tear slid down her cheek. Vincent wiped it away with his thumb.

"No," he said. "I cannot close the branch in New-Ashemore before you close your Gate." Vincent gently let go of her, his attention back on the map. "The answers we seek can be found at the Henge of Time. The Henge has Quantum Gates created by the Supreme Elders before the Future War. They are doorways to anywhere in space and time. We can contact the Arbiters."

Renata nodded, gobsmacked.

"The Arbiters can deduce your time origin from ingesting some of your molecular structure," he continued, staring at the map. "If we know your molecular time-origin, it will put us that much closer to getting you home." He looked up, glancing at both Sid and Renata.

"Vincent," Sid spoke up. "You could—"

Vincent gave Sid a dark, unreadable look which silenced his companion.

"It is a long journey, Renata," he said, his hand braced against a corner of the map so it would not roll up. "The effects of the Gate you feel now will increase. Additionally, we will travel beyond the bounds of my Pillar—"

"What does that mean?" she asked, her voice quiet.

"I do not know," he said. "We are beyond the bounds of what I know. It is likely you will begin to feel the physical effects of your power more keenly. In the Pillar, your phys-ical body does not age."

Renata's eyes were wide. "Am I gonna turn into the mummy as soon as I leave the Pillar?"

"No," Sid said. "But you will no longer be in a dream dimension suspended in time. Out of this dimension, you will be physically affected by your powers."

"Like last night?" she said.

Vincent's brow furrowed at that. "You must have dream-walked with Aldric outside of the Pillar. Perhaps the Trackers have not found it. But how did Aldric find *you*?" He stroked his chin pensively.

"What route will you take?" Sid leaned over the map, delicate fingers tracing the lettering of the named loca-tions. Curious, Renata stood next to Sid and looked down at the map as well.

Pictured on the map was a land mass the shape of an oblong kidney bean. The Henge of Time was labeled with gold letters that seemed to glimmer independent of the light. Surrounding the entire map was churning, dark water labeled '*The Obsidian Sea.*' A path wound from one end of the landmass to the other, stopping at the Henge of Time. Renata's finger traced it, winding along the coast and toward a densely forested region labeled '*The Night Forest.*'

"The road you are touching is called '*The Narrows*'," Vincent said. "It is the safest, most direct route to the Henge of Time."

Renata glanced up at Vincent, her brow piqued. "Doesn't look direct."

"Not direct as in direction," he said. "I mean in terms of time."

"Time?" she said, looking back down at the map. "How much time will it take to get from here to here?" She leaned over Sid, her finger tracing The Narrows and its switch-back path along the Obsidian coast and next to the Night Forest.

"Three hundred Earth years," Vincent said. "Give or take a decade."

Renata gasped, her hand covering her mouth.

"It will feel shorter," Sid said. "You will not mark 300 years. It is more likely to feel like a few days. Time is relative to your perception, after all."

"It is substantially shorter than taking the Time Road," Vincent said, tracing a straighter, as-the-crow-flies route from his conduit's portal and the Henge. "I still haven't come up with a number. Time blows like the wind there, and freezes like ice, depending on what part of the Road you are on. Its temporal inconsistencies make it dangerous, especially for a mortal."

"Still," Renata said. "Three hundred years is a *long* trip."

"Time is relative," Vincent said, echoing Sid's earlier assertion.

"This is crazy AF," Renata said, shaking her head.

"What?" Vincent said.

"This is just—*really* crazy." Renata cleared her throat and pointed to the land mass on the map. "Where is this? Or is this more of a what question?"

"Both," Vincent said. "It is in the Cerulean dimension. The land itself once bore the name Aeor-Eterna, although it hasn't been called that in..."

"A really, really, really long time?" Renata supplied.

"Yes," Vincent said. "Billions of what you would call

years. The Elders renamed it in their mother tongue—which, ancient Elderaen, I should mention, is very practical in its naming. They do not name out of sentiment, but out of purpose. And so Aeor-Eterna became the Future War, a location to store and allocate humans to accommodate the Supreme Elder's needs—that of conquest and consumption. This land, like me, is all that remains of the Future War."

Renata's expression blanched.

"The Future War is both a time and a place," Sid added. "Aeor-Eterna became the Future War the day Elders discovered it."

"Not enough coffee to understand that one," Renata said, putting her mug to her lips.

"The Future War was Aoer-Eterna's destiny," Vincent replied, his expression darkening. "After the Elders were given the Time Henge."

She scoffed, and then lowered her mug. "So they kept humans...?"

Vincent nodded his head. "The Supreme Elders kept the Sanguin-Laeth there, the beloved—and those chosen mortals changed, became something... else," he continued.

"Blood Orphans?" Renata guessed.

Vincent nodded again, his expression relaxing. He sighed. "Yes. Named so because they were never able to return to their original timelines due to the Supreme Elder's... interference."

Renata's eyes were wide. "This place sounds dangerous."

Vincent rubbed his jaw, staring at the map. "It is also dangerous to stay. I am concerned your powers may no longer be contained by the Pillar. Aldric's presence in your dream is an undeniable clue that the Trackers are aware of your existence."

"Oh, Vincent—" she said, covering her mouth.

He put up his hand, blocking another round of apologies. "The answers we seek are worth the risk. You are in my care. I will protect you."

"Meanwhile," Sid said, looking at Vincent. "I will remain here. No Tracker may breach the Pillar in Vincent's absence if the Chosen's Tardigrade is present. I will maintain the dream dimension, awaiting your return."

Vincent nodded in agreement.

"We must leave immediately," he said, rolling up the map. He produced a satchel and began placing books, maps, a compass, and other items from the library in the bag. It never looked full, no matter how many items he placed in it.

"Alright, Mary Poppins," Renata said, flabbergasted.

Vincent looked up from the satchel, confused.

"Oh, well she's a fictional character and she has a bag like—" Renata started and then stopped, seeing Vincent's expression of confusion remain. "I wonder what pop culture references survive dimensional shifts?"

"Get ready," Vincent said, closing the bag.

"I was born ready," Renata teased.

Vincent paused, looking at Renata as if for the first time.

"I believe that is possible," he said.

Vincent and Renata walked through the pines, early morning light beaming through the branches. Renata was quiet, contemplative. Vincent was quiet too, they both had been since they left the cottage.

He knew Renata's thoughts still lingered on the vision from the Pool. She worried her lip as she walked, her hands gripping a hiking pack that had appeared on her back as they climbed the hill.

The pines whispered to Vincent. A cemetery of Blood Orphans whose kernels of life essence thrived inside the trees were welcome company as Vincent started out on his return to Aeor-Eterna. He caged any trepidation about his and Renata's passage through the Pillar and into what remained of the Future War. Instead, he concentrated on the hush of the morning, the smell of star dust, pine sap, and memory emanating through the forest. Their names, unspoken in an epoch, the trees whispered as he walked by. In the distance, his cottage lights twinkled farewell. He looked at Renata, the impossible human, miracle of a mortal. She was still frowning, remembering yesterday.

"*Sanguis,*" Sid intoned. Though the Tardigrade's physical body was in a glass orb on the mantle in the cottage—and would remain there as Vincent left for another dimension —Vincent kept the same glass vial around his neck. Made partly of Quantum Glass, it afforded him a connection to Sid even as he traveled to Aeor-Eterna in the dimension beyond.

"*You are relentless,*" Vincent grumbled back at Sid.

"*Mortals were not meant to travel through time, into alternate dimensions,*" Sid said. "*And Aeor-Eterna is not the land it once was, the Future War poisoned it. You may have to break your vow before she reaches the Henge."*

"She is safer without being Bound to me," Vincent said, rebuking Sid's assertion.

"There are more dangerous things than you in the Night Forest," Sid replied.

Vincent turned and looked at Renata who had paused and was sipping steaming coffee out of a mug. Sid was right, mortal bodies were not meant to travel inter-dimensionally. Their mortality alone barred them from time travel. Vincent's Pillar had been integral to Renata's survival thus far.

"Keep up," he barked.

Renata gulped the coffee, putting the lid back on the thermos.

"Someone put their bossy pants on this morning." She trotted toward him, jumping over a log.

Vincent looked down at his pants. "These are the same pants I always imagine."

Renata winked, pausing to stand in front of him. "That's because you always have your bossy pants on." She sipped her coffee.

Vincent rolled his eyes. "When we leave the Pillar, you must stay close," he said in warning. "My Pillar is safe, but the Cerulean dimension is a different story."

"Cerulean dimension, stay close, got it," she said.

Vincent nodded. "And if you could please leave your stubbornness here, in this dimension—"

"I am not stubborn!"

"Only a stubborn person would say that."

Renata huffed.

"Come," he said, extending his hand. "I will take you to my conduit. It is also the nexus by which I travel to other dimensions."

Renata gripped Vincent's hand, and he drew her forward.

"Oh!" Renata exclaimed. Enclosing her in his arms, they apparated to the Tree of Aimer.

AEOR-ETERNA, AMARANTHINE LOOP

Aldric had never existed in pure form within the Amaranthine.

The Tracker had always maintained a golem —shaping a corpse to his specifications and using it to pass among humans as one of them. Even the transfer between golems had never felt this way. There was a freedom, a liberation in no longer requiring physical form to exist.

His entrance to the Gate had been a painful one. The radiation and energy burned the flesh of his golem away, leaving only his pure Tracker spark. Merging with the Quantum energy—her energy—had evolved him. He understood non-linear time, for one. And he understood to fully complete his destiny, he must find the human.

Aldric had been sure he would not be able to enter the Pillar, even understanding non-linear time, he could not violate the laws of pocket dimensionality. But he was connected to her Quantum energy—her life energy—in a tacit way now. He felt the energy shift and leave the Elder's Pillar.

Cerulean dimension, Aldric realized. *The Amaranthine is shifting dimensions.*

Being only energy, Aldric had little free will when it came to the flow of his essence. He was linked to her, like a parasite. He would seek her, in any dimension that her energy could enter, and with her power, finally balance his Ledger.

He thought it poetic that he would balance his Ledger in the same place it had been unevenly compromised.

The Future War, Aldric thought.

He felt his form penetrate the skin between worlds, the veil between dimensions, and enter Aeor-Eterna.

It had been more than a thousand life ages of man since Aldric had returned. He felt himself wind and burrow through the dense foliage of the Night Forest. The energetic forces the trees maintained grabbed at his spark, attempting to seize him, and the power that bled through him from the dimensions beyond.

Aldric writhed and resisted, but the Night Forest was relentless. And hungry. It absorbed him, changing him further, adding its volatile essence to his cause. Aeor-Eterna had been corrupted by the events of the Future War, and the source of the corruption had also recently returned. The Night Forest wanted vengeance or redemption, whatever the cost, it would pay—and Aldric was the perfect instrument to exact its terrible price.

29

LUPUS OBSIDIAN, CERULEAN DIMENSION

L achlan Dark flicked the switch on the comms panel, a lone figure in the Time Lab. He was taller than this Lab had intended. After an hour of stooping, Lachlan cursed the Lab for the pain in his back.

"This has been constructed with a smaller—" Lachlan winced, stretching his lower back. "—Quantum scientist in mind. Och." He grimaced. All of the physical computer interfaces he had been using, on the dais in particular, required him to stoop.

A small light began blinking in the corner of the dais, indicating to a small port on the left. In short order, Lachlan located a more direct interface method, bypassing the human interface he had been using.

The nanite bands on his wrist shimmered, interacting holographically with the port. The nanite bands in Lachlan's eyes glowed an artificial green as he began to interact with Centius' neural net. This was a faster and more comprehensive experience with the Time Lab, and what the hybrid technology surgically implanted into Lachlan was designed for.

He massaged his lower back while he processed the information download. Stiff from suspended hibernation in the cryptobiosis chamber of the ship, he shifted his weight onto his heels, whistling absently. He had not done the protocol of stretches and muscular injections after he'd emerged from crypto sleep—there just hadn't been time.

"Ever since I woke up, it's just been one damn thing after another," he said to the empty Time Lab.

Once the Quantum emergency had been handled—with Peaches sequestered in her quarters with an extraction suit—Lachlan had gone back to the Lab to determine the damages of Aldric's radiation spike. Indeed, the radiation spike, although short, had managed to degrade some of the Obsidian's hull integrity. Lachlan had been busy with minor repairs ever since.

"Aldric, mate, you should've woken me up long before this. Centius, you've been in need of a crew long before—"

The panes of glass lit up with Centius' golden sand, replying to Lachlan.

"Auch, no," he said, his eyes glowing green as he translated Centius' sand language. "I would have been fine. I'm adjusting to her now, aren't I? Centius, be advised after this next download, I need to get myself to the medical suite for post-hibernation protocol."

Lachlan had actually completed the Quantum equations for the next Time Mission several hours ago, shortly after he had left Peaches in her quarters, sleeping off the tranquil-elite injection. His request to see Peaches in the Time Lab had been for other reasons...

He stood alone on the dais in the center of the Time Lab. Centius displayed a long series of numbers and symbols, completing a third check of Lachlan's math on the Quantum superposition of Renata's Gate in the Amaranthine, as well as axioms to generate probable Quantum wavelengths to match it. He nodded, the nanite band in his left eye dilating and glowing green as he communicated with Centius.

"Assess all the variables," Lachlan said under his breath. "Strategize an approach. Complete the mission. Forget the past."

Aldric had left specific instructions in case of his demise. Lachlan would become the captain of Lupus Obsidian, and complete the mission. He would also become the guardian to the ship's only other crew member —Aldric's daughter, Peaches, a Quantum being who had only known the Obisidian, and her work on the Time Lab.

Lachlan frowned, feeling his sentimentality get the better of him.

Centius, bring up the files on L.O. crew member 002, Lachlan squinted, both eyes glowing green with the data flooding into his mind. *Pause. Bring up birth date.* Lachlan blinked, grasping the dais.

"Centius, mate," Lachlan said, his voice echoing of the Time Lab's walls. "Is that date an error?"

The sands behind the glass shifted in an erratic pattern. Lachlan's eyes glittered green in response, the nanite bands absorbing the information downloaded from Centius neural network.

It's her. Not a clone, not an A.I. unit. Aldric, what did you do?

His eyes dimmed, turning their normal golden brown. Lachlan pushed his thoughts to the side, leaning on the technological implants to distance and suppress his emotions—allowing him to concentrate on the task at hand.

"Centius," Lachlan said. "Bring up the star chart for the quadrant labeled Home Alpha 1."

"Are we really going home?" Peaches said.

Lachlan turned, almost startled. So absorbed in his thoughts, he had not heard her approach.

"It will eliminate some time inconsistencies—" he began, unable to look away from her.

"If you wanted to know about me you could just... ask," she said shyly.

Lachlan frowned. "I'm sorry, I always review the files of my fellow crew members. I meant no offense."

"It's okay," she said, pausing. Her blue eyes were round, inquisitive. He thought they almost glittered. "I haven't ever met her," she blurted, and it was only then Lachlan realized he had been staring intensely at her in silence. She leaned against the doorway of the Time Lab, arms crossed over her chest. Her fire-orange curls swept away from her face in a long braid down her back. "I don't even know what she looks like," she whispered.

"There are several images on file from her past," he replied, ignoring the glow of the nanite bands on his wrists in favor of staring at the corn-flower blue of her eyes. "Aldric... never showed you?"

Peaches shook her head. "He had his reasons. I never questioned them."

"Her current appearance is unknown," he said, concluding his perusal of Centius' data on the subject. His eyes and wrists dimmed. "A concern, and that may add some difficulty to the mission. Peaches I want you to know, I agree with your hypothesis—I believe Renata has found Vincent in the Amaranthine."

Peaches' eyes rounded, and she gripped the doorway to the Time Lab.

"You really think so?"

Lachlan nodded, allowing himself a small smile at her excitement. "Aye. There is evidence supporting this hypothesis. The density and radiation levels Centius has been observing is—"

Suddenly, a glass panel lit up, the sand contained behind it pummeling the pane.

Lachlan and Peaches looked at each other.

"The Amaranthine!" she exclaimed. "It is in dimensional shift."

Lachlan turned fully to the interface beside him on the dais. He felt his face become slack as he engaged fully with Centius. Both eyes were bright green, the glow reflecting off the Time Lab's walls.

"Indeed," he said after only a few seconds. He turned to Peaches. "Irrefutable proof of your equations. She *has* returned."

"The Amaranthine has also begun to collapse," Peaches said, her voice subdued. "Look at the numbers, the degradation in the first variable."

"This was anticipated," he said, turning back to the dais. He rattled off several computations, his fingers splayed out on the smooth paned interface.

"So, you're buffering the Gate," she said, hands on her hips. "Keeping the doorway open as long as..." She didn't finish.

"I am giving them every chance of escape," he said. "Before the mission deems it necessary to extract them."

Peaches nodded in silence and crossed her arms. She squeezed her eyes shut, attempting to fend off more tears.

"It's all on a knife's edge," she whispered, biting her lip.

"There's time yet," Lachlan said. "We should be in range within 0800 light-hours. In the meantime, are you available to monitor the Gate while I attend to myself in the medical suite?"

Peaches nodded. "Of course."

30

AEOR-ETERNA, AMARANTHINE LOOP

Renata's eyes opened slowly. Still in Vincent's Pillar, she was curled against a giant root jutting out at the base of an even larger tree. She could feel Vincent's power saturating the air. It was misty, and there was a sweet smell, akin to honeysuckle.

She looked up into the blinding canopy. The tree itself was massive, with a trunk easily five or more arm spans wide. The bark was white, almost glowing. Light billowed between its branches like vapor. The environment was saturated with this light, the glowing vapor a physical manifestation of Vincent's power.

She turned her head to find Vincent lying beside her. Light glanced off his features and also emitted from his skin. *He seems younger*, she thought. Time had not worn him so severely in this place, wherever it was.

"It's beautiful," she said.

Vincent stood up, offering Renata his hand.

"When we pass through the tree, we will leave the

Pillar," he said, pulling her to her feet. "Do not let go, whatever you feel."

"We're going through the tree?"

"Yes," he said.

"Whoa," she said, standing next to him. The tree branches stretched high above her with leaves that were iridescent—changing from pink to purple to blue to green to yellow to orange and then back to pink again. Renata stared, mesmerized.

"Renata," Vincent said.

She glanced up at Vincent. The color shift in the leaves was now an iridescent bubble of power that shimmered over his form like a second skin.

"You're glowing like the leaves!"

"This is my conduit," Vincent said. "The leaves are glowing like me."

Renata stared, mouth open. His rainbow of light-energy was hypnotic.

"Never let go," Vincent said, bringing Renata's clasped hand up to his chest. He kissed her knuckles and looked into her eyes. The spectrum of light-energy began traveling down Renata's arm—she flinched away. His blue eyes took hold of her, attempting to ensnare her with his gaze. "Stay with me."

The light-energy was at her shoulder now. The sensation was odd, as if something were stretching and pulling her skin.

"I don't like it," Renata said through gritted teeth. She flinched again, closing her eyes.

"Look at me," Vincent's voice commanded, but she was

cringing, the sensation becoming painful. "Open your eyes and look at me."

"It hurts," she said, her eyes shut firmly now, brow furrowed.

Vincent put his unclasped hand on Renata's face, turning her chin up toward him.

"Renata Stone," he began, his voice velvet. "I can lessen your pain, just look into my eyes."

Renata was shaking now, the pain acute and sharp everywhere the light touched. It was across her shoulders and traveling down her back.

"I can't—" her voice shook.

"*Ma louloutte*," he said, his voice soft, almost seductive. "*Ouvre tes yeux.*"

Renata still resisted opening her eyes, the pain so acute she couldn't think or move. Vincent pulled her face toward his and kissed her mouth. He parted her lips with his tongue, and her eyes shot open. His Elder light spilled between their mouths like a long exhale. She felt his warmth eclipse her pain, her body relaxing against him.

"*You speak French,*" she thought dreamily.

"*I speak all the mortal languages,*" he replied, his kiss deepening as he tilted her head back. The light was fully cloaking her now. "*Grand-pére Archie spoke to you in French, did he not?*"

Vincent wound his unclasped hand in her hair, his kiss ravishing her mouth as his Elder energy saturated her cells.

"*What are you doing to me?*" she thought.

"*Distracting you.*"

"*From what?*"

"*This.*" Vincent broke from their kiss and clasped

Renata to him. Holding her against him, rainbow light eclipsed their bodies. He pressed his back against the trunk of the tree, and they both oozed into its center. The bark of the tree encapsulated them with a stagnating heat and pressure that she had not been expecting.

Renata thought she knew what warmth was, but this was a heat beyond what she had ever experienced. Vincent's Elder essence moved in her, shielding her body from pain as the blinding white light of the tree saturated them—until the only thing that existed was light and heat.

Renata's heart hammered in her ears as Vincent's arms encircled her, protecting her from what she could only explain was oblivion. Well-lit oblivion.

RENATA FELT Vincent's lips brush her ear.

"We have arrived," he whispered, his arms still around her, pressing her against him.

Renata leaned into him, weak.

"I just need a minute," she murmured, certain that if she let go, her legs would give way.

"Take all the time you need," he said, moving his face away from her ear to look around.

"We're in... another dimension?" she mumbled. "We made it?"

"Yes," he said. "Welcome to the Cerulean dimension. Welcome to... Aeor-Eterna."

Renata opened her eyes, adjusting to the dim light in a subdued and ancient forest. She turned to see Vincent's conduit.

Instead of an immense tree that was blindingly white, there was a twisted gnarled trunk, wide and dark and glistening with oily black sap. Like a weeping willow, it had long tendrils for branches that hung almost to the ground. The conduit had dark blue leaves that shimmered and swayed in an absent breeze.

"Whoa," Renata said in alarm. Vincent turned his head to see her staring at the tree they came through.

"Sid said Aeor-Eterna was poisoned by the Future War," he said, surprised. "And with the branch of my Pillar closed, the dark energy here must have... I had not thought it could influence my conduit."

"I would say it's more than an influence," she said, biting her lip.

"Can you stand on your own?" Vincent asked, drawing Renata out of his embrace.

"I think so," she said, bracing her legs. Her muscles shook, her knees buckling slightly. Vincent stared in concern.

"We will rest here," he said, producing his satchel. "I anticipated this, based on your last experience with interdimensional travel." He drew a large canvas sheet out of the satchel and a large metal hook. He hung the hook in the air and attached the canvas. "Lean on this." He handed her a long walking stick from his bag. She smiled.

"Just like Mary Poppins," she said, laughing weakly.

Vincent went to work, staking each corner of the suspended canvas, turning it into a makeshift tent.

"Inventive," she said, watching.

Vincent pulled the tent flap to the side.

"Come," he said. "We have all the comforts of home in

here." He held out his hand to her. She walked to him, leaning heavily on the walking stick. Her legs shook with the effort, every step exhausting. She only took three steps before she grasped his outstretched hand, pausing at the doorway, out of breath.

"May I?" Vincent said with open arms. Renata nodded, her eyes heavy. He picked her up as she collapsed into his arms.

FRACTURED PATCHES of sunlight were scattered on the ceiling of the tent. The light had a desperate tone, as if it were relieved it had managed to penetrate the dense canopy of the forest at all.

The interior of the tent was larger than it appeared on the outside. It had an oblong rectangular shape, with open living areas divided by a stone chiminea in the center. The wing back chairs from the cottage bracketed the chiminea, with a soft blanket thrown over Renata's chair. Trunks, with overflowing stacks of books next to them, were sequestered in each corner of the tent. An odd assortment of mismatched lamps perched on the empty trunks, creating a dim ambience.

Vincent worked at a low desk near the entrance, an antique chandelier the only light above his workspace. The desk was littered with unrolled maps, various books from his cottage library holding the corners flat. He slumped back in his chair, chin resting in his hand, and surveyed the books strewn about his desk, their spines spread, various cloth bookmarks indexing their pages. In front of him, Renata's book, with the red-wine cover and gold hieroglyphics, remained closed. He touched it briefly and slid his chair back.

Standing up from the desk, he paused, eyes pinned to the tome that had mysteriously appeared in his library as soon as Renata arrived. His hand reached out to it again, his fingers lingering on the indentations of the hieroglyphs embossed on the leather-bound cover.

"*I wish to know your meaning,*" he said to the book, splaying his hand upon the cover.

The book did not respond.

Vincent raked his hand through his hair in frustration. He made a swift gesture, the lamps and the chandelier blinked off. He stretched, rolling his shoulders back and pinning his arms behind his head. After stretching for a few seconds, he relaxed, his arms falling to his side. He walked to the rear of the tent.

He slumped into the taupe loveseat beside Renata's bed. A small table faced the couch. It had a pitcher of water and a plate of soda bread and hard cheese on it. A knife lay on the plate next to it. Vincent picked it up, studying it in his palm. It was the same knife Renata had summoned on her first night in the Pillar. Vincent's eyes glowed a little, realizing how little he understood Renata's power, then and now.

"*Ma louloutte,*" he thought. "*You are no less mysterious than the day I met you.*"

"*I feel the same about you,*" Renata interjected into Vincent's thoughts. He looked over at her. She was sound asleep in bed.

"*Renata,*" he thought. "*Rest your mind. You are in Quantum shock.*"

"*How long have I been sleeping?*"

"*Not long enough,*" he said.

"*This tent is a pocket dimension,*" she said matter-of-factly.

"*Yes,*" he replied.

"*Something calls for me outside.*"

Vincent rubbed his face with his hands. "*You are feeling the Night Forest's power,*" he said. "*The tent is a pocket dimension, as you say, and you and I are the only ones able to enter. You are safe. Rest.*"

"*Rest. That sounds good. I'll go to sleep.*"

"*You are asleep. Try being more asleep,*" he chided her.

"*Oh...More asleep, then.*"

"*Out of my head please,*" he said. "*I'm tired enough as it is.*"

"*I'm not in your head,*" she replied. "*You're in mine.*"

Vincent looked over at Renata. Her body was still except for the steady rise and fall of her chest. Her eyes were shut, her face expressionless. He *was* in her head. He rubbed his face and ran his hand through his hair.

"*Apologies,*" he replied. "*I must not have realized...*"

"*Take your own advice and go to sleep.*"

Vincent nodded, punching the throw pillows on the loveseat. He propped one behind his head, long legs draped over one of the arm rests. He slung his elbow over his brow, covering his eyes. Uncomfortable, he began to shift on the loveseat, banishing one of the throw pillows to the floor in the process.

"*How often do you sleep?*" she asked.

"*Not often,*" he admitted.

"*Explains why you're so bad at it.*"

"*Excuse me —*"

"*Not enough practice,*" she continued. "*Maybe put a little more effort into doing nothing but laying around, and you would be a champion sleeper, like me.*"

Vincent laughed, sitting up from his awkward position on the loveseat to observe Renata's sleeping form once more. No mistaking it, she was completely asleep.

"*The loveseat was your first mistake,*" she continued.

"*Really?*"

"*Yeah,*" Renata said. "*Get a loveseat that reclines or don't get one at all.*"

"*Noted, for the next fully furnished pocket dimension I create.*"

"*You can sleep next to me...*"

Vincent's humor vanished, his complexion paling.

"*Don't get weird. I said sleeping. As in what you are histori-cally bad at. I'm sure you could be much better if you just put your mind to it.*"

Vincent couldn't resist smiling.

"*Or imagine a reclining loveseat,*" she said. "*The choice is yours.*"

"*I will not be imagining a reclining loveseat. I need to conserve my energy,*" he said.

"*So, sleep in the bed.*"

"*Renata—*"

"*Save your sanctimonious 'It's forbidden' crap for when I'm awake—it's hilarious.*"

He felt her mind soften, and like a door closing on an already lightless room, she withdrew into the hidden depths of her mind. He sat alone. Whatever psychic connection they had was lost to sleep.

Vincent bent down and took off his boots. Woven wool

rugs were laid asymmetrically on the floor, making a criss-cross pattern that stopped within a few feet of the brazier. He pressed his feet on the rug, his toes grasping into soft wool. He unbuttoned his shirt, revealing his bare chest, the light playing with angles and hollows of his smooth skin over taught muscles.

He folded the shirt, placing it next to him on the loveseat. He tiptoed to the bed, easing in beside Renata who rested on her back, her lips slightly open as she breathed.

He lay on his side, watching her breathing, the steadi-ness of it like an eternal tide. He watched her, hypnotized, until his eyes became heavy and finally shut, and he slept for the first time in a thousand years.

AEOR-ETERNA, AMARANTHINE LOOP

"*Of course it's changed,*" Vincent thought, staring at his maps again.

The lone chandelier shook overhead, reacting to his frustration. He frowned and slumped back into his chair, resting his chin in his hand. He hadn't anticipated his conduit would place them this deep in the Night Forest... and the forest had expanded quite a bit since the last time he had been in Aeor-Eterna.

Vincent heard the covers of the bed rustling and turned to look at Renata, who was sitting up in bed, tangled hair framing her face.

"Why am I still so tired?" she said, putting her hand to her head.

He got up from the table at the front of the tent, apparating to Renata's bedside.

"It is the Quantum shock," he said, kneeling at her bedside. "Your atoms are still in flux."

Renata breathed slowly, her legs shifting to the side of the bed to get up.

"If you say so," she said. "I don't remember feeling like a truck hit me last time."

"You only slept for three days in the Pillar last time..." he said, pinching his chin.

"And this time?"

"It's been about three weeks," he shrugged, shaking his head. "But time is relative so don't—"

"Three weeks?" Renata's mouth hung open.

"Could be a month." He massaged the back of his neck in an absent gesture. "Again, I wouldn't attach yourself to any perceived passage of time in Aeor-Eterna— "

"A *month*—" she sputtered, and shook her head. "I just —" she looked at him. "You must have been bored out of your mind!"

"I slept for a while as well," he admitted, dropping his hand from the back of his neck.

"You got tired too?"

His eyebrows rose. "Yes, inter-dimensional travel affects me too. Also, I hadn't slept in about a thousand years—"

"A thousand years!" she exclaimed. "You haven't slept in a thousand years, you don't eat—no wonder you're such a grump."

Vincent's hand waved away Renata's insult. "Do not think to lure me into an argument about my disposition."

"So, you're admitting I'm right. Ah, you see? You've grown so much these last three weeks." She stretched, yawning as her arms reached above her head.

"Would you like breakfast?" He asked, arching an eyebrow at her last comment.

She nodded. He produced a plate of food, his usual penchant for creating food and other physical items seemingly out of thin air still intact inside the tent's pocket dimension. He handed her a plate of scrambled eggs, bacon, toast, and a side of fruit salad with pungent strawberries, blueberries, and apricots.

"I forgot about fruit," she said, plucking a strawberry from the plate.

"Can you sit at the couch?" he asked. "There is a table there."

She nodded. "Is there coffee?"

Vincent gave Renata a look. "I like to think I know that about you, if I know nothing else."

She smiled.

RENATA SNAPPED a piece of bacon in half and put one piece up to her mouth. Chewing slowly, she sat cross legged on the couch, a blanket wrapped around her shoulders.

Vincent sat opposite her in his wing-backed chair, legs crossed, and hands clasped. He had been silent, watching Renata eat. She had consumed the entire plate of eggs, toast, and fruit, starting with the latter and working clockwise around the plate. The bacon, at 11 o'clock, was the last of her breakfast.

Vincent poured more coffee from an insulated carafe on the table.

"Better?" he asked.

"Better," she confirmed, pausing to drink. "So, what have you been doing while I was sleeping and you weren't?"

"Studying," he said. "We did not enter Aeor-Eterna where I anticipated."

"Oh?" she said between a mouthful of bacon. She leaned back into the couch, adjusting the blanket.

"We are in the Night Forest. And will be for the majority of our journey to the Henge."

Renata shrugged.

"The Night Forest has... peculiar powers," he continued. "The Forest is an entity in and of itself. It will attempt to trick you to step into the trees."

Her expression paled.

"The trees steal memory. And once you are an empty shell, and do not remember how to exist, they assimilate your energy too," he finished.

Renata swore.

"Never step off the path, and you will be fine," he said, dismissing her reaction.

She rolled her eyes at his cavalier attitude. "Is the path clearly marked at least?"

Vincent shrugged. Renata scoffed into her mug.

"I have not returned to Aeor-Eterna in... a great span of time," he said, pausing. "My maps are not entirely accurate."

She put down her mug. "Well, is there any good news?"

"Yes," he said. "I think we are closer to the Henge of Time than I originally estimated."

"Oh," she replied, adjusting the blanket around her shoulders. "That's good, right?"

"Yes, if my maps can be trusted. They change slightly every day, adjusting to this reality."

"Too bad the Cerulean dimension doesn't have GPS," she said, putting the last piece of bacon in her mouth. "By the way, why can't we just, I don't know—apparate to the Henge of Time?"

Vincent stood up from the table, his blue eyes distant and observant.

"There are a few things we must discuss before our journey."

She looked up at him, chewing in silence, her expression puzzled.

"The energy here is bad," she said after swallowing. "Is that what you're going to tell me?"

Vincent was quiet, and finally nodded. "Yes," he said. "It happened at the end of the Future War. It ended the Future War, really. Elders could not keep humans here eternally if the land was poisoned."

Renata's eyebrows went up. "Poisoned?"

"Poisoned is not quite right...There must have been a Quantum event at the end of the Future War. Only that could explain why Aeor-Eterna is... dimensionally corroding," he said, averting his eyes for a moment. "Dimensional corrosion affects temporal reality, it is why time is inconsistent here."

"You did this?"

He nodded slowly. "I do not remember the details in clarity, but my catalogue of Elder history has an entire volume on it. Additionally, the Night Forest does not forget."

"Wait," she said. "I just need to take a moment to wrap

my head around this. How could you forget—" she cut herself off, her eyes growing wide. "Wait, do you think the trees caused you to forget?"

He shrugged. "Perhaps. Once they have a memory, it is kept forever. This is a sort of photosynthetic exchange for the Night Forest. In a way, the Forest is living memory."

She blinked, listening intently to Vincent, but her expression was dazed.

"However, I need not listen to the trees of the Forest calling for me. The evidence of my power is quite easy to see if you know how to look for that sort of thing," he finished.

"Seems kind of extreme to poison an entire world, Vincent."

"They were extreme times."

She looked at him critically, her brow furrowed. "You can't draw energy from Aeor-Eterna," she said after a moment. "The energy would poison you too. It is... of the Dark." She put her fingers on her forehead, in pain.

"Do not engage with the Forest!" he barked. "Even telepathically. It is too dangerous. The Forest will manipulate you."

She opened her eyes, her pupils slightly dilated. "But, Vincent, your conduit and the energy here is... Bad isn't the right term for it. Tortured? In pain? Dying?" she stopped, searching for words.

"Dying is not an applicable term. But this place will slowly weaken me, and you, for that matter. No being of energetic manipulation can survive in the Undying Lands anymore." he said, waving her words away. He walked around the table and sat next to her on the small couch.

He put his hand on her shoulder. "What this means is I do not have an infinite resource of power as I do in the Pillar. Neither do you."

"That is a kink in the plan," she replied, her eyes wide.

Vincent got up, striding over to an armoire that was unremarkable, save for a small golden keyhole below generic, iron handles for the doors. He produced a key from his pocket and unlocked it.

Opening the armoire revealed three shelves with five rotund glass bottles resting on each shelf. Large glowing crystals sat between the bottles, flickering with a silvery-pearl iridescence. The bottles glowed too, with a white and unmistakable light.

"These Elder Glass contain pure energy from the Pillar," Vincent said, picking up one of the bottles. "We should consume them sparingly."

"We?" she said.

Vincent turned to Renata.

"Yes," he said. "We. We are both creatures of energetic manipulation and will require a vast amount to reach the Henge." He reached into the armoire and took a second bottle. He nodded at the armoire, and it obediently shut its doors, the key rising from his pocket to lock it.

He walked over to her with the Elder Glass. It was bright, illuminating his hands. He handed one to her, taking the cork stopper off the top and doing the same for himself.

"Cheers," he said, clinking his with Renata's. She stared, a little dumbstruck. "Drink this, and rest. We leave at sundown."

3 2

AEOR-ETERNA, AMARANTHINE LOOP

Renata adjusted her pack, watching the electric pink of the sunset fade from the scraps of skyline she could see through the trees. The Night Forest was an old forest. All the trees were large, sprawling affairs with gnarled roots and moss covering everything. Even the thick vines curled between the branches and trees like a web. The brush was practically impenetrable, save for the narrow muddy path she and Vincent were currently standing on.

"You don't need that," Vincent said, emerging from the tent a final time. He looked at the pack on Renata's back. "It will just require more energy to imagine it and carry it."

"But I like it," Renata said, turning to Vincent.

"This is why I packed clothes in the tent. You needn't imagine anything."

He gave her a measured look, his eyes holding the unarticulated words about being stubborn in this dimension clear for her to see.

"Fine." She relented. She took the pack off and handed it to him. He tossed it inside the tent.

"It will remain in the tent's pocket dimension," he said. "You can have it back when we return to the Pillar."

"Fine," she said again, sighing.

She stood in the Night Forest for several minutes of companionable silence while Vincent put the tent away in the satchel he brought with him from the Pillar. The satchel contained the tent as well as provisions for their journey.

"Need any help?" Renata asked after a few moments.

Vincent shook his head. "The tent is a pocket dimension. It takes a certain delicacy—and might I say panache —to properly store something like this..." his words drifted off as he concentrated. Once he finished putting the tent in the bag slung around his shoulder he closed the distance between them on the trail.

"Where is 'The Narrows', anyway?" she asked.

"There is a signpost," he said, nodding up ahead.

Renata squinted in the direction he had nodded. There was something in the brush along The Narrows that may have once resembled a signpost. Vegetation had overgrown its face, rendering it unreadable.

"Not improving my confidence."

"You are safe with me." He reassured her, and reached down, grasping the dirt from the mud path they both stood upon. He whispered a few indistinguishable words, and the soil started to glitter with golden light. Suddenly the entire path was illuminated. Renata watched the light unfurl in front of her like a thread that had wound its way along the small path.

Vincent stood and watched. Confident that The Narrows was well lit, he turned back to her.

"You must trust me, Renata," he said.

"I have this far, haven't I?" she replied, rolling her shoulders back.

"The Forest will test you. It will test us both. I need you to trust me absolutely."

"I do," she locked eyes with him. He paused.

"Then put this on." He produced a narrow strip of cloth. "Over your eyes."

"Is that a blind fold?" she scoffed.

"No," he said. "Think of it more as blinders. I want to limit what you can see, not blind you."

"Why?" She sputtered and then held up her hand. "Wait, do I want to know why?"

"I want you to concentrate on the trail," he said, his voice becoming honey. "Concentrate on the light, keep your eyes on the trail."

"Are you saying I have problems concentrating?" She crossed her arms.

"I am saying trust me, and wear this over your eyes. You can tie it so you can still see at the bottom of your vision. To watch the trail."

Renata looked at Vincent for a long moment, and finally uncrossed her arms.

"Alright, fine," she said.

"I like these little teachable moments we're having," Vincent tutted, and turned Renata around. He moved her hair behind her ears so he could tie the cloth more securely.

"You mean where I just do as you ask?" she said as he

placed the cloth over her eyebrows and eyes. He kept the cloth high enough that she could squint and would still be able to see her feet and the glowing trail below.

"Your compliance is appreciated," he said, cinching the blindfold tight. "You learn so much better when you obey." He flipped her hair over her shoulders.

Fuming, Renata spun around, her hand pointing in the air.

"*Pendejo*—"

"Thank you for turning around, I needed to do one more thing—" Vincent reached around Renata, tying a glittering golden rope around her midsection.

"What the hell," she swore.

"Step into it," he said, twisting the rope into a golden circle.

"This would have been easier before the blind fold," she grumbled.

"You can see to step into it," Vincent replied. "Think of this as practice. Keep your eyes on your feet."

Renata put one leg in a golden length of rope and then another as Vincent twisted the rope again. He tied all of it into an ornate knot right below her navel, whispering some Elderaen words, connecting it with the first length he had wound around her proper waist. He had created a make-shift harness, and attached the rest of the rope, sparing some length between them, to his own torso.

"Are we hiking or climbing?" she said, putting a thumb between the rope and herself.

"Walking, ma louloutte."

"I can follow a well-lit path—" she complained.

"You can also wander off a well-lit path," he interjected. "Think of it as insurance."

"Insurance? Insurance for what?"

"In case you bolt."

"I'm not actually a dog—"

"No, but you are prey," Vincent said into Renata's mind. *"Follow my footsteps on the trail, look down at our feet and copy me. Do as I say, and the Night Forest cannot harm you."*

Renata bent down, grasping the rope attached to her and Vincent. She stood, both hands grasping the length.

"Lead the way," she said, nodding.

RENATA AND VINCENT had been walking for what felt like hours. She walked close behind him, copying his footsteps and sometimes practically stepping on his heels.

"You don't have to walk *on me,*" he growled.

"Maybe, if I could actually *look* where I was going—instead of squinting at glowing mud—I wouldn't need to step on your heels!" she snapped back.

"Try squinting *harder—*"

"Squint this!" She stepped back as Vincent continued walking, allowing a buzz of power past her fingertips—instantly blistering them.

Her power crackled down the length of rope between them to the span circling Vincent's waist. He twitched when her power found him, pausing in mid-stride. Renata felt the rope tighten as Vincent turned around. Still mostly blinded, she couldn't see his face—but she could feel his ire from several feet away.

"*Renata.*" Vincent branded her name into her mind, his anger a palpable heat in the air. He gripped the glowing rope that connected them on the trail and yanked her forward. Her face bumped into his chest, and he grabbed the back of her neck in his palm, keeping her face tilted down. His thumb skimmed her lip hungrily, his hand splayed over her neck, sensing her pulse. She could feel his proximity—his tell-tale Elder heat warming her. It was only then she realized what a mistake she had made taunting him with a spark of her power.

He was hungry.

"*Renata,*" Vincent said again, releasing his grip from the back of her neck. He let his fingers run down the length of her hair, the heat subsided.

"*I'm sorry, Vincent,*" she sputtered quickly into his mind. "*I don't know what I was thinking—*"

"*You were not thinking,*" Vincent snarled. "*You were reacting. I realize you are young for a mortal, but there is no reason to behave like a petulant child—*"

"*You're right,*" Renata said. "*I'm sorry, I—*"

Vincent interrupted Renata's apology. "*This is not a game, it is dangerous here—*" Vincent cut himself off, gripping Renata's shoulders to confirm she were still in front of him. "*Something comes. Look to the light. Empty your mind. It cannot harm you.*"

"*What?*" Open-mouthed, Renata attempted to look up at Vincent. Anticipating her movements, Vincent gripped her neck again and pointed her head down.

"*Look to the light. Empty your mind.*"

A density, a smothering all-consuming stuffiness, prickled Renata's senses. It didn't seem to have a body at first, instead was an element of the atmosphere. Contradicting her first impression, the entity made noises in the brush akin to a jack hammer—a deep, repetitive sound she imagined was its jaws, its teeth clacking as it searched the Forest for its next meal.

"Empty your mind, Renata," Vincent said. *"It cannot harm you if you think nothing of it."*

"What is it?"

"A Dream-Catcher," he replied. *"It only has the power you give it. Relax."*

Renata resisted the urge to run, though her body twitched with adrenaline. Vincent confirmed his grip on her neck, his other hand running down the length of her arm and finding her hand. Their fingers interlaced, and they stood, facing each other with their heads down, the trail still glowing beneath their feet. It was only then she realized Vincent had a blindfold on too.

She shook with fear, her eyes peering down at the glowing trail. She started to count down from one hundred inside her head. She jolted involuntarily as she felt the Dream Catcher's breath on her neck.

"Nothing is there, Renata," Vincent's voice soothed. *"Look at the light."*

She sobbed out-loud as the creature ran its claws through her hair.

"There is nothing there," he said again.

She felt a tug at the rope and harness around her waist. She felt the knots untying, the golden lasso attaching her to Vincent fall away. She let go of Vincent's hand, grabbing the harness.

"No, no, no," her voice quaked. A grating and haunting

sound called her name deep in the Forest. She fumbled with the rope, attempting to re-tie it, but the rope kept slipping through her blistered fingers.

"*Renata,*" Vincent said, attempting to penetrate her fear. "*Let go of the rope.*"

"It's coming untied!" she said, tears running down her face.

"*No, it's not—*"

"It's coming to take me, Vincent!" she screamed.

"*Keep your voice down,*" he said. "*Nothing is coming to take you. I promised to protect you, remember? Now, let go of the rope, Renata.*"

"I can't," Renata choked on her tears.

"*You are safe with me,*" he said, grabbing both of Renata's hands. Her blistered fingers left blood streaks on his knuckles. Vincent inhaled sharply.

The Dream Catcher sensed an opportunity and writhed around them, skirting the trail. It dared not step on The Narrows—Vincent's power illuminating the path prevented that. But Renata could feel the Dream Catcher's tremendous presence. She felt it's hot breath, heard the mysterious clacking sound as it paced next to her. A cold sweat enveloped her body, and she exhaled in short rapid gasps.

"*Renata,*" Vincent said, his voice strained. "*You need to calm down.*"

Unable to respond, Renata felt her biology—thousands of years of fight or flight imprinted and evolved into her brain—make decisions for her. She yanked her hands from Vincent's, grabbing the blindfold and shoving it below her chin.

Time stood still. Renata looked at Vincent, whose eyes

were glowing behind his blind fold. His normally golden spark was instead a crimson vapor. The thin cloth barely obscured the red light of an ancient force he kept deep inside him—he was visibly glowing with hunger. Frozen in time, his nostrils flared, his predatory senses ignited.

"Destroyer of Worlds, Death Bringer," the Dream Catcher whispered. Renata instinctively covered her ears, even as the Dream Catcher spoke into her mind.

The forest moved, vines and willowy branches of the trees stretching out toward the trail. Renata noticed human skulls, rib bones and other decomposing detritus bound within the brush. She opened her mouth to scream, but no sound came out.

The vegetation gathered and rose next to the illuminated trail, coiling and spooling a large object within its clutches. Renata stared, frozen with fear. The Forest receded, revealing a corpse, dark hair covering its features —even obscured this body was well known to her—it *was* her.

"You think you have returned, but you never left," the Dream Catcher whispered.

"You lie," Renata snarled, bullying her courage. She felt her power coiling inside her, a heaviness in the pit of her stomach that promised to deepen—and hurt. *"I've seen my death. I don't end here."*

The vines responded by rolling back to the trail like a tide, heads in different states of decomposition caught in its clutches.

"You're not real!" Renata yelled, her momentary courage splintering.

One of the dead faces bound in the vines, teetered over

to Renata. It was her face, but different—with a waxy, white complexion, black eyes and a rotten mouth.

"This land is drenched in your blood," it spoke, its voice gravel and strained. Renata was mute, her eyes wide with panic. "You know this to be true. You have felt it since you came here."

Renata shook her head, still dumbstruck.

"Look into our mind," the Dream Catcher said through the severed head. "We do not lie." The corpse's mouth stuck on the word 'lie', its voice becoming shrill and hypnotizing.

Renata's face relaxed, her psychic mind reaching out. She felt her power extend into the stuffy void that was the Dream Catcher's presence.

"Renata!" she heard Vincent yell.

"You travel with the Death Bringer," the Dream Catcher's voice said into Renata's mind, the dark tendrils of its power exploring her.

Renata was still on the trail, looking out into the forest and beyond. She felt her foot lift as she prepared to step off the trail.

"RENATA!" Vincent's voice was louder, more insistent.

"He is the Destroyer of Worlds," the Dream Catcher said, seducing her. *"He destroyed you."*

"RENATA!" This time Vincent's voice boomed in her ears. She felt a tug, as he gripped the golden harness, attempting to hold her back.

Suddenly, a streak of red light burst through the trees. The corpse-head Renata had been staring at shriveled to dust, the light a potent antidote to the Dream Catcher's power.

The Dream Catcher snarled—the dank, corpse-laden vines and vegetation giving it form receded into darkness, unable to tolerate the glowing red entity that had emerged through the trees.

Renata blinked, and looked around, confused. She was standing on one leg, precariously balanced in mid-step.

Vincent gave her another tug, and she stumbled backward. He caught her in his arms as she began to scream and kick away from him. She rolled onto the well-lit path, shaking and still screaming, her hands in front of her to block Vincent.

"Renata," Vincent said, his voice sounding weary.

Renata couldn't think, her brain overwhelmed by fear.

"Renata, purge it from your mind," Vincent said psychically. *"It cannot control you. Only you give it the power."*

She was inconsolable, her face a blank mask of panic. The red light brightened from something beside the trail, the energy breaching the path and encircling her.

She rolled over on her side, shaking but finally quiet. Vincent bent over her, his fingers touching her forehead. She felt a calm roll over her, squeezing the fear from her like water from a sponge.

She began to sweat, feverish. She trembled, her body in shock. She felt Vincent's hands on her as he moved her hair back from her face.

"Let it go," Vincent coaxed. *"Release it."*

She flinched in pain, gripping her abdomen. She dry-heaved, and a black sludge emerged from her mouth, surrounded by the mysterious red light that had chased the Dream Catcher away. The black sludge had a long serpent body, but it shriveled and sparked as it touched the trail,

Vincent's Elder-light destroying it. The red light receded from Renata and Vincent, disappearing into the Night Forest.

Weak, Renata looked up from the ground.

"Vincent," she said, her voice thin. He grabbed her hand in response and felt her fade away into unconsciousness.

33

AEOR-ETERNA, AMARANTHINE LOOP

fter Renata had collapsed on the trail, Vincent quickly produced the hook and canvas from his satchel, setting up the tent and its pocket dimension on The Narrows. He whispered to the tent as he set it up, giving it instruction.

In a flurry of work and energy expenditure, the pocket dimension was finally formed. Vincent burst into the tent, the flaps waving behind him. As he stormed through the entrance, he was greeted by a copper tub with steaming water. It was next to the brazier in the center of the tent. A linen cloth was draped inside it, buffering the heat of copper from the bather's skin.

Vincent removed Renata's clothing, tossing it into the fire, destroying them. He observed Renata—she was unconscious but shivering, her skin like ice and growing colder, the mortal cost of using any psychic ability. Vincent had noted this reaction at the Pool of Verite and had planned accordingly.

He lowered Renata into the tub, the warm water opening her eyes. He held a bottle of Elder Glass to her lips.

"Drink," he commanded.

Weak, Renata opened her mouth, and Vincent trickled the glowing liquid onto her purple lips. She sipped it slowly at first and then tilted her head back, tipping the Elder Glass with her chin. After that, she drank fervently until she had consumed the entire contents of the Elder Glass. With faster than light speed, she yanked Vincent's arm. The empty Elder Glass fell into the tub, and so did Vincent, almost.

Off balance and surprised, Renata's teeth tore through Vincent's forearm, finding the vein of Elder energy running like blood under his skin. She drank him, his Elder light and energy glowing around her mouth. The bathwater began to steam as Vincent's raw power exuded a heat in the atmosphere around them.

"Warm," she said.

"That's enough," Vincent shuddered, but Renata didn't acknowledge him. *"That's enough,"* he repeated.

"Warm," she said again, and continued to drain him. Vincent was already weakened from their travel that day— the Night Forest had demanded his constant vigilance. As well, the Dream Catcher had cost him a great deal of energy. He had been caught off guard by Renata's power and ability to communicate with such an advanced psychic creature as the Dream Catcher. More surprising still, the Blood Light, the energy and memory of a Blood Orphan, came to their aid and drove the Dream Catcher away.

Vincent thought he had taken all the remaining spirits of the Blood Orphans with him, to the Pillar...

"That's enough, Renata," Vincent said audibly, his mind circling back to his present predicament. He put his other hand on the back of her head. Now she was consuming his rawest, deepest power—his core spark. Vincent felt his knees buckle. The white-hot energy of his core spark seared her lips, but still she drank, ravenous for his warmth.

Vincent grabbed Renata by the hair and yanked her head back. With a pop of golden sparks, she released her hold on his arm, splashing back into the tub.

She blinked up at him, shock on her face. Her body glistened, her skin dewy with Elder light and condensation from the bath. Her long, dark hair spiraled in the humidity of the tub, cascading over her breasts and into the water. Her green eyes were neon with power, her lips rosy from their latch on Vincent's arm. He observed her for a second, astonished by her beauty and her actions. She would have drained him completely, without realizing, had he not stopped her.

Vincent swayed, and collapsed onto the floor.

"Vincent!" Renata screamed, as his eyes fluttered shut.

HE AWOKE IN BED.

A white vapor surrounded him, encapsulating his body and barring any view of the rest of the tent.

Not moving, Vincent scanned his body. At his feet he spied an Elder crystal—from the armoire of Elder Glass—

emitting wisps of the same vapor that surrounded him. At his head was a similar crystal, adding to the plume of vapor hovering over him in bed, the crystal cast a pearly, warm, white light.

Vincent rubbed his eyes, still weary. He had fallen asleep for the second time in a thousand years.

"Technically, I wouldn't call it sleeping as much as passing out —" Renata barged into his thoughts.

Vincent growled at her. She receded from his mind, leaving him alone. He stretched, and yawned, enjoying the feeling of moving his limbs.

"I made breakfast," Renata said from outside the mist. "Pancakes and fruit!"

Vincent didn't rise, his head still on his pillow, attempting to squint through the barrier of fog.

"Coffee?" Renata appeared next to the bed, her hand penetrating the vapor. Vincent accepted the mug and sipped. "I made it with some of that liquid from the Elder Glass. Tastes good in the coffee. Better'n whiskey, I say."

"Renata—"

"He lives!" She teased, but Vincent could hear the undercurrent of guilt and concern in her voice.

"I am fine," he responded.

"You are not fine, you are definitely not fine. I know apologies mean nothing to you, but I am so sorry, Vincent— " Renata replied, almost frantic.

"As you say, I live." He sat up in bed, drinking from mug she had brought him.

"But I almost killed you!"

"You did not, and would not..." he paused, taking another

sip. He was surprised by how much he enjoyed drinking it this way.

"Dammit Vincent, would you please acknowledge that I am not an idiot?"

"What?" He put the mug down for a moment.

"We share thoughts, I know that I almost killed you. I had to contact Sid to figure out how to revive you."

Vincent could see the shadow of her profile, as she sat next to the bed. He took a sip of coffee, the smell doing nothing to diminish her familiar scent. Vincent tried to remember how he described it to her... *Hyacinth in bloom on the first clear, crisp day of spring...*

He paused, thinking, the mug halfway to his lips.

"Vincent?" Renata said. *"Earth to Vincent, do you copy?"*

"Earth to Vincent?"

"Well, that used to make sense. You okay? You went somewhere —I couldn't see."

"I said, I am fine. So, you contacted Sid?"

"Yes!" she said, practically jumping up from her seat.

"How did you contact Sid?"

"They left me psychic paper in case of emergency. And very specific directions." Renata sniffed, shifting again in her seat next to the bed.

"I see." Vincent drained the mug of coffee and she reached through the fog surrounding the bed to take it. He moved to get up.

"What are you doing?" She stood up as well, blocking him.

"I have work to do." He frowned at her through the fog.

"No," she said, widening her stance, coffee mugs in each hand on her hip. *"Sid said to keep you here for two days. I guess we're both in luck that you slept for the first one."*

"I slept for an entire day?" Vincent's eyebrows rose.

"Yeah. But..." she paused, and he could see her posture soften. *"Vincent, I know we're on a time crunch, if you don't want to stay in bed, you could just take some juice from me. I don't mind. It's my fault we're in this predicament—"*

"What are you saying to me?" His tone darkened.

"Sid said that was the quickest way to get you back to full strength—" she said, defending herself.

"Sanguis."

"Well, they didn't put it that way," she said, arms falling to her side. *"But Sid did mention me returning some of your spark could help—"*

"That is Sanguis by definition," he snarled, cutting into her words. *"To almost drain one completely and then return their power with some of yours."*

"Oh..." Renata said. *"But what if we didn't call it Sanguis? And what if it's not an energy exchange but a necessary medical transfusion—"*

"Do not offer yourself to me again," Vincent snapped.

"I was only trying to help!"

"Do you not understand what I am to you?" He sat up, gripping the edge of the bed. *"I am a predator! Elders consumed humans in the Future War, Renata! And did much worse things to your kind—the Sanguin-laeth, Sanguin-Aeor are outlawed for a reason."*

"Then call it something else!" Renata protestesd. *"Vincent—"*

"What you offer me is forbidden!" He sagged. His grip eased, and he slouched back onto the headboard.

"This isn't the Future War. It's just you and me. Besides, how

can you protect me if I have weakened you?" she countered quietly.

"My desire for you weakens me every minute I am around you, and yet I have kept my promise this far." He eased back onto the pillows, laying down.

"Vincent—" she gasped, her inflection sorrowful.

"An energy exchange would be Sanguis—we would become Sanguin-Aeor—"

"Sanguin-Aeor? What does that—"

"It is ancient Aeorian. It means 'blood-eternal'. It means we are Blood Bound, forever. My feelings for you only complicate this —we would be Sanguin-laeth and that coupling is outlawed across the galaxies," Vincent said, his eyes becoming heavy.

"Sid mentioned the Sanguin-laeth before," she said.

"The Sanguin-laeth are the beloved..." Vincent began, but then paused, unsure what to say. "It is a name, like any other, given to any in a relationship... but the Future War changed that— the Sanguin-laeth are considered an abomination now. I cannot risk you, Renata—my hunger, it is too dangerous."

Renata sat in stunned silence for several seconds, mulling over what Vincent had revealed.

"I want you, too," she said finally.

"Never offer yourself to me—to any Elder," Vincent repeated, weary. "Be compliant in this one area between you and I, Renata. Please."

She stilled, his words hanging and stagnating between them for a moment. She got up.

"Get some sleep," she said, before turning away.

VINCENT'S EYES OPENED. He sat up, stretching stealthily. He didn't know how long he'd been asleep. The fog had disappeared, he must have slept beyond the requisite two days. Yawning, he noticed his hair was past his shoulders now, and a sorrel chestnut color. He examined it between his thumb and forefinger, curious.

Vincent looked around. The light in the tent was dim. Renata had only a few lamps on in the farthest corner from the bed, as a courtesy. He turned his head, searching for her. She was on the couch. She had moved it, and subsequently, her back was to him, with the couch now bracketing the brazier with the wingback chairs. She was hunched over, a blanket over her shoulders. She used a bottle of Elder Glass for light, and had several books stacked on the table next to her.

He didn't want to disturb her but felt compelled to go to his study and consult his maps. He needed distraction, a moment to compartmentalize and distance himself from what had occurred between them. He was also vaguely curious how much progress they had made on The Narrows before their encounter with the Dream Catcher. He focused on that, not how Renata's mouth had felt, latched onto his forearm, her nude body glistening with water and his Elder light...

"Mornin'," she said, her voice softly disrupting his reverie. He blinked, eyes still locked on her and her dark hair spilling over the blanket wrapped at her throat. Though she spoke, she hadn't looked up from her book.

Vincent looked away and attempted to stand up from the bed. So much for stealth.

"Hello," he said awkwardly. He pushed up with the support of the knob on the headboard.

Renata remained on the couch but looked up from her book, turning her head toward him.

"Hello," she said back, studying him briefly. "Need help?"

Vincent shook his head.

"No. Thank you. I need the exercise. I was just going to study the maps, I need to find out where we are on The Narrows—"

Renata shrugged and looked back at her book. "Do as you must."

Vincent looked down, feeling what was said and unsaid between them. He knew only that as much as he wanted her, ached for her, what he felt was dangerous.

He squeezed his eyes shut, warding off the deep desire to approach her, put his arms around her, inhale the scent of her hair, and take her—her blood, her power, her body, all of her, to her last limit. In truth, he felt vulnerable, she having had so much of his raw energy from the Elder Glass and more personally from the energy he carried within him—the core spark of his Elder Light.

He shuddered. If he repaid her in kind—and more— she would be *his* and no other's. Sanguin-laeth, like the Blood Bound Elders of the Future War. They were only one misstep away.

Distract yourself from these impossible desires, he chastised himself.

Vincent winced, the denial of being with her was like irritating an old wound. He opened his eyes, thinking of the shape of Aeor-Eterna, and attempting to estimate where he thought they were on The Narrows.

Vincent walked to the front of the tent, the iron chandelier brightening above the table of maps and books that contained the memories and knowledge of his past. The red tome—Renata's tome—beckoned him, the golden hieroglyphics moving in an unmistakable pattern.

"*Are you ready to reveal your secrets to me?*" he asked, his hand outstretched to the book. The leather bound red-wine cover opened, splaying itself on the table. The pages turned, flipping open until it stopped on a chapter with an illustration that Vincent couldn't dismiss.

VINCENT STUDIED the book with such an intensity that Renata managed to sneak up on him several hours later.

"I brought you lunch," she said, appearing next to the table. Vincent jumped, leaning back in his seat, rubbing his hands over his eyes.

"You surprised me," he muttered. Renata placed a bottle of Elder Glass and a turkey sandwich on the table.

"You should eat," she said. Vincent nodded, rubbing his face with his hands.

"What, are you able to read my book now?" Renata peered over the tome, perplexed.

"Maybe," Vincent said, exhaling slowly. "I stare at the text and I can almost comprehend it..."

"Well, at least there's a picture," she said and then pointed to the image displayed on the page, eyes wide. "Is that a wolf?"

Vincent nodded again.

"Looks just like my conduit," she whispered.

"And that looks like me, if I'm not mistaken." He pointed to the man in the same image, who had long brown hair.

Renata nodded in agreement.

"Yeah, especially with the hair. What is that, a result of the crystals or what?" She looked at him. His hair was quite a bit longer than it had been yesterday.

He shrugged.

"I mean, your hair grew four inches, that would take—" Renata paused, squinting. "Hair grows half an inch to a quarter of an inch a month so eight months to over a year give or take."

"If I were human."

"You look human," Renata reminded him. "Ish."

Vincent gave a half-smile and picked up the turkey sandwich she had placed on the table.

"And you choose the human meal over the Elder Glass," she pointed out. "So maybe there's more than hair that's human about you."

"The crystals compress time and intensify energy," he said between mouthfuls of turkey.

"It's gonna be tough selling that line on the side of a shampoo bottle." She paused, looking back at his desk. "Have you figured out where we are on The Narrows yet?"

Vincent shook his head. "No, your book has been too engrossing."

"Oh." She thumbed through some of the pages experimentally. "But you still can't read it?"

"Not yet. The text is written in a language that is based on numbers..." he said, stroking his chin.

"Huh," she said, letting go of the pages. "Like a computer. Too bad you don't know HTML5 or we could be in business."

Vincent's eyes were wide. "A computer?"

"Yeah, don't computers use numbers as language? It's a code, right? Or am I confusing everything with *The Matrix*?"

Vincent's eyes almost vibrated in his head. "That must be—this book was written using some sort of mathematical code to communicate!"

Renata put her hand up. "So, my book is just a bunch of math homework. Great."

"Yes!" he stood up, running his hands through his hair, round eyes glowing.

Renata backed away from the table, her hands up.

"Okay, Sherlock. I'm just gonna leave you to it..."

"I wonder if the text is from the Universal base equations, or if I should start with two-dimensional..." he mumbled, pacing around the table.

"THE WOLF AND THE WARRIOR," Vincent mumbled, looking at the text he had deciphered.

Much later, when even the Night Forest had darkened and no light was visible outside the tent, Vincent had managed to decipher every third word on the page next to the illustration. That the book had opened to this page and this image was noteworthy to Vincent—his similarity of appearance to the figure depicted undeniable.

"I think that's all the words using the base equation of the Universe," he whispered to the text. The other computations he tried created words as well but combining words from other deciphered computations made only jumbled phrases that made no sense.

"Forgotten, Bound, War-den..." Vincent stumbled on the last word. "Or is that warrior again? No, it's *wander-er*. Yes, wanderer. Wanderer." Vincent finished, satisfied with his translation.

"How's it going?" Renata said, appearing at the side of the table.

"I thought I was on to something," he said, pinching his chin. "But my first instinct was not entirely correct. It is not a language solely constructed from the base equation of the Universe, but I have still managed to translate a few words."

"Are there other common... equations?" Renata hazarded a guess.

He nodded slowly. "Without Sid here it would take me an extraordinary amount of time to go through them all."

"Psychic paper?" she suggested.

Vincent shook his head. "The math is complicated enough, let's not translate it through the inter-dimensional equivalent of Tardigrade email."

"I see," she said, nodding down at the maps and star charts. "Well, why don't you take a break for dinner. I can help you with the maps of The Narrows for dessert."

Vincent was slumped in his chair, his hand over his

forehead. "I am fine, let me keep working at this. I am close, I have almost a phrase translated—"

"Nope," she shook her head. "You need a break. Get up, away from the table. Give it fresh eyes later." Renata took Vincent's arm, pulling him up. He was surprised that he was still a little weak and momentarily used her and the table to balance himself.

"I guess I did need a break," he muttered.

"Oh yeah?" she replied, bracing his arm over her shoulder and walking him to the back of the tent. "What's the score then, Renata 1 and Vincent 5,000?"

"Sounds about right," he said, his chin rising. She rolled her eyes.

Vincent enjoyed this proximity to her. He could smell her hair, it was sweet, floral. *My hyacinth in bloom*, he thought, letting himself feel the buzz of her pulse beneath his touch. He could sense all traces of the Dream Catcher were gone.

"Let's get a move on Methuselah, dinner is getting cold."

"Methuselah?"

"You know, because you're *old*," she said, adjusting his arm around her shoulder.

"Are you not supposed to respect your elders?"

"Are you not supposed to be so grumpy?"

Vincent grunted in response.

"It's good that we have life goals for each other."

Vincent braced on the couch for support and gingerly sat down. Renata sat across from him, a bottle of Elder Glass illuminating the table.

"You didn't drink any for lunch," she said, indicating the Elder Glass.

"It bothers you?"

"It bothers me. What I did. It's still affecting you," she said. She leaned forward in her wingback chair, hands in her lap, her expression concerned.

"It is not only that—" He copied her, using language to dance around exactly what transpired between them. "I do not have a conduit in this dimension. I cannot replenish my power."

"I wish I could understand why I did it. I just couldn't stop," she said, her voice dropping to almost a whisper at the end.

He remained silent, looking at her, not just at her but within her. Her mortality was still there, her heartbeat a steady rhythm. Her very human genome was intact but... changing. Into what, he could not guess. Her cells were still in flux, their electrons and gluons shifting in and out of this dimension and then reappearing.

"You psychically communicated with a very advanced being," Vincent said after a moment. "From what I have observed of you, whenever you use any psychic ability of note, you become hypothermic."

Renata sat up, listening.

"I had prepared for this," he continued. "However, you have only psychically communicated with me before. The effects were not so... acute, last time."

"I should avoid doing that here," she whispered, smoothing the blanket on her lap.

He nodded. "It would be for the best."

Renata was silent for several minutes, looking at her

hands. Vincent could feel she was examining the memory of what happened to her in the Night Forest, he could tell by the spike in her pulse.

"Vincent, I—" she started and then stopped, her eyes downcast. She pushed her long hair behind her ear. Vincent was silent, allowing her to collect her thoughts. "I saw *Sid* out in the Night Forest. When I was about to step off the trail, Sid appeared."

Vincent blanched.

"It was not Sid you saw then," he replied finally, dwelling on each word.

"It was who Sid... emulates?" she said, searching for the right word. "Elaria?"

Vincent didn't blink. He only stared at Renata. He had not seen Elaria. He had only seen the red light. Finally, he nodded, unable to speak.

"What happened?" Renata whispered. "Why is she here?"

Vincent's shoulders slumped, his face drawn in sadness.

"I cannot..." he paused, his voice hesitating. "All I can remember is how I feel."

She nodded, her turn to be silent.

"What you saw was her Blood Light," Vincent said finally, his voice low so it wouldn't shake. "The last of her spark, that which was Elderaen when she... Her human form is long gone, but this part somehow survives here still. She was a Blood Orphan, a human changeling given the gift of Elder Blood, a drop of their core spark... My father gave her this—making her my sister, my Sanguin-Aeor... The other Blood Orphans from the Future War are in the Pillar."

"The pines."

"Yes... after Aeor-Eterna was compromised—" his eyes cut to hers. "Some chose to ascend and exist among the stars, some chose to stay with me, in the Pillar," he explained. "They would be corrupted and poisoned just as the rest of Aeor-Eterna if they remained..."

"I wonder why she remains then," Renata said, adjusting the blanket around herself. "It must be important, for her to remain here if it so dangerous."

"Not everything has a reason," he said, shuddering. "Some things have no reason, they only *hurt*."

"Says the man who can't remember—"

"I am no man," Vincent growled.

"You look like a man," she said, indifferent to his reaction. "You're this tremendous being, and yet this is the form you chose. I find myself asking that more and more. Is it possible you were once human too? Like me? Like Elaria?"

Vincent furrowed his brow. This had never been a consideration of his. He was what he was.

"I am an Elder," he said. "I... I have always been an Elder."

"Yeah, but for all intents and purposes so am I," she countered. "I mean, all my new abilities are Elder abilities, right?"

"Elders cannot create Quantum Glass. That is a Tardigrade ability. Elders travel trans-dimensionally through their conduit, as we did to get here."

"So, I have all the abilities of a Tardigrade and an Elder?"

"I am not sure where this conversation is going."

"I'm just talking," Renata said. "I haven't had anyone to talk to for a while."

Vincent peered over at her.

"How long did I sleep?" he said, changing the subject.

"About three days," she said. "Lot of it going around though. After I contacted Sid and set up your crystals, I think I dozed off for at least a day. Aeor-Eterna feels like a leaky faucet, and it's slowly draining me dry."

Vincent nodded. "The sooner we complete our task the better."

VINCENT AND RENATA scoured the maps during dessert, as promised. It mainly involved Renata leaning over Vincent eating ice cream, asking about different landmarks on the map.

"Do not drip any of that on this," Vincent warned her. "It's older than you and I—combined."

"Oh, *an antique*, pardon me," she retorted, licking the back of her spoon. "How old are we again?"

"You know what I mean—"

Renata let out a small, sharp laugh. "So, have you figured out how much longer we have?"

"Because time is in flux all over Aeor-Eterna, there is no reliable estimate," he said. "But the good news is, we made quite a bit of progress on our trek the other day."

"Oh yeah?"

"Yes," he said and locked eyes with her. "Do you think you are ready to travel?"

Renata swallowed her ice cream, returning Vincent's gaze.

"Yes," she said. "As much as I can be." He noticed her pulse had already quickened.

"You have to keep your mind clear," he said. "Focus on the trail."

"Easier said than done."

"You can do this, Renata," he said. "We both can. We must."

Renata nodded, silent.

"We leave at sundown."

34

AEOR-ETERNA, AMARANTHINE LOOP

Renata insisted the harness be put on first, inside the tent.

"Admit it, this makes much more sense," she said, stepping into the golden lasso of rope. Vincent remained silent as he cinched her other leg in, attaching that free length to her waist. He drew the rope between them before finally tying it around himself.

"Turn around," Vincent said, not admitting anything. When her back was to him, he placed the blindfold high on her forehead so she could still see the illuminated Narrows at her feet. Vincent pulled the blindfold snug and tied a knot, his fingers absently grazing her hair when he was through. "Ready?" he asked.

"I was born ready," she said, convincing herself.

Still standing behind her, Vincent grasped her hand, squeezing it for a moment. She exhaled. He guided her in front of him by his hand on her shoulder. They stepped through the tent flaps together. He walked her only a few steps out of the tent before pausing.

"Stop here," he said, letting go of her shoulder.

Renata stood alone on The Narrows. Only a few feet behind her, she could feel Vincent from the slight tug on the rope connecting them as he deconstructed the tent and put it back in his satchel.

He had not yet illuminated the trail. It was dark, only the dimmest tendrils of a recently passed twilight lingered in the slim gaps of the forest canopy. As her eyes adjusted, Renata could make out parts of the trail at her feet. There was nothing remarkable about The Narrows—it was comprised of soil, dead leaves, sticks, and a fairly consistent time stream.

A consistent time stream is pretty useful, she thought. *Still looks like dirt though.*

Her head turned when she heard rustling in the brush, originating somewhere behind the tent. She tried lifting her head, attempting to get a better look beneath the blindfold.

"Vincent?" she whispered, squinting. She could barely see him, he was un-staking the last corner of the tent. He did not appear to notice the sound or Renata saying his name. Her hands grasped the rope at her waist. The knot was secure, and she could feel the tug of the rope connecting them. "Vincent?" she said a little louder.

Renata heard the mysterious sound once more—this time it was coupled with a distinct electric crackling. Tree branches whined and broke against something within the Night Forest. Vincent was still busy with the tent as if he had not heard the sound.

"Renata," the Night Forest whispered, its voice deep and melancholy.

Renata put her hands over her ears to silence the Forest.

"Renata," it said again.

She closed her eyes, tears spilling down her face. *"You're not real,"* she thought.

"We are very real, Forgotten Queen," the Night Forest replied.

"Renata?" she finally heard Vincent's voice, but the rope remained slack between them.

"It thinks it knows me —" She shook as she spoke.

"The Night Forest is speaking to you?" Vincent said.

Renata nodded, her tears coming in earnest now.

"The Night Forest speaks to only a few." Renata thought she could feel Vincent's lips brush her ear as he spoke. She thought she felt him remove the blindfold, his fingers grazing her eyes.

Another tug of the rope indicated Vincent was still in fact behind her, and the Forest was manipulating her senses. Renata trembled, keeping her eyes shut, holding her breath. Vines wound around her legs, circling her waist but cringed at the golden rope. The rope singed and burned the vegetation, impeding its progress up her torso.

"You're not real, you're not real, you're not real," Renata kept repeating, flinging the vines off her hands.

"Look, Renata," the Forest bade her. *"LOOK."*

This time, it was a command that she could not refuse —her eyes shot open.

Corpses surrounded her. The bodies stacked symmetrically, one on top of the other, only the crown of their heads visible. Too many to count, they towered over her, bracketing her in with their height.

"You return with the Death Bringer," the Night Forest said.

Renata screamed, the sound shaking the trees and the symmetrically stacked bodies. Some tumbled down from their perch at the top.

Renata froze, looking at the faces of what she could only assume were the remains of Blood Orphans who died in the Future War. A discernible dead face stared back at her on one corpse, its wide white eyes staring into nothing, another's head was so wounded it was impossible to recognize the face.

"And you, Renata, you are like us. You are of the Dark," the Night Forest said.

"Not! Real!" Renata covered her eyes with her hands again.

"Anchor of Time, Light Breaker, descendant of the Forgotten Queen, Wanderer of the Undying Lands, the Dream and the Prayer of Eterna—" the Night Forest said, its words sharp, accusatory.

Renata swore, her arms flailing and resisting the vines as it tried to subdue her and bring her to her knees.

"You are us," the Forest boomed. *"You are the Binder and the Bound."*

Renata collapsed onto the ground, holding her head in her hands. She felt like her head was splitting, her body breaking from whatever power the Night Forest was exerting on her physical form. In a cold sweat, she vomited, her hands braced on the ground as the reservoir of her innate power stirred from a depth she was not even aware she contained.

Renata screamed, the pain so intense, a blurry thought that her back might be breaking fluttered across her mind. Her limbs seized and extended awkwardly as her skin itched and almost burned. Her power felt hot and suffocating, and her human mind fell asleep as another, older awareness—but also equally a part of Renata—took control, encapsulating her fragile human form.

Renata became a wolf.

VINCENT TURNED FOR A MOMENT, packing the tent. When he heard Renata's startled cries, it was already too late.

The branches and vines wound around her on the trail. She buckled, kneeling on the ground, her head in her hands. Vincent bent down where he stood, saying a few words, and The Narrows ignited with his power. The Night Forest receded, but the damage had already been done.

"Renata!" Vincent said, jogging toward her crumpled form. The sun had set, and light in the forest was dim. Vincent could only see the golden harness wound in dark hair. He lifted the golden rope only to realize she was no longer human.

Renata was a large, black she-wolf. She raised her head, groggy, and looked up at Vincent.

"Do not change back," he said quickly. *"Remain in this form."* Vincent's mind raced—he couldn't believe she was alive. He feared changing back to human would be fatal.

Renata whined a little, tilting her head at Vincent.

"Can you walk?" Vincent asked.

Responding, Renata stood on all fours. She stretched, putting her back end up in the air and tilting her shoulders. After a good stretch, she shook, snorted, and looked back up at Vincent. She locked eyes with him, and Vincent could feel her—the mind of Renata. She was intact, but her human psyche buried deep in her conduit's form.

"Your conduit is containing you," Vincent said, astonished.

Renata groaned at Vincent.

"You are right, I should not be surprised," he said, still in shock. He checked the harness around Renata, adjusting it so that it was around her neck and shoulders and she could move with ease.

The Night Forest made a tremendous, haunting noise. Vincent winced, feeling its dark power leer at him. There was something else within the Night Forest that searched for Renata... And him, he realized. She had been telling him since they arrived, but he'd assumed it was the memory-laden trees surrounding them, tempting them to stray from the trail. But this was different. This power hunted retribution.

"I did not believe my own senses before," Vincent thought, running his hands through his hair and looking down at Renata.

The ground shook, and power swelled, a dark mist flooding through the trees.

Vincent's Elder light sparked from his hands in defense. *"Run!"*

RENATA BOLTED DOWN THE TRAIL—PRACTICALLY apparating—Vincent close at her heels. The mist pursued them,
billowing through the Night Forest, the trees and bramble
were propelling it forward. Vincent could feel the black
mist had a sentience—it contained an acidic hatred of him.

The writhing, angry mist attempted to grab hold of
Vincent but it missed, losing cohesion as it breached the
glowing trail. It screamed, the piercing sound siphoning
some of Vincent's power, even as he covered his ears.
Renata whined in pain, her keen lupine senses assaulted by
the dark vapor's screeching cacophony.

Vincent winced as the sound called forth more of his
energy, his stolen Elder spark appeared as smudges of light
blooming from his flesh. His leeched Elder light crackled
with white sparks as the mist consumed it, adding to its
own strength. Vincent shuddered, feeling the bright,
piercing sickness of fear prick his mind—it was an unfa-
miliar feeling for him.

The black mist taunted him, painfully siphoning his
power with its screams. It couldn't reach him on the
glowing Narrows—but, like a parasite, it could steal his
energy until he was too weak to keep his glowing ward
along the trail active.

The mist was unrelenting, he could feel the Night
Forest goading it and propelling it forward.

Renata snarled, the sound creating a bubble of golden
light around them. The dark mist singed itself on the
precipice of the shimmering vapor that had encapsulated
them.

"*Thank you,*" he said.

Renata howled, bounding down the trail at break-neck speed. The golden bubble of light bounding with them.

Despite this small victory, Vincent felt his legs seizing. They were going at a hyper-speed pace, and it was draining him quickly of energy.

Still, the mist pursued them.

Vincent kept running, feeling the enemy at his back. His limbs felt like they were made of lead. He concentrated on keeping his legs moving.

Their pace was beyond apparating, and yet the Night Forest seemed to lengthen, never allowing a break in the tree-line to establish any of the horizon.

"We should be beyond the Forest by now," Vincent thought. *"The Night Forest stretches to keep us within its grasp."*

Renata's furry, black ears perked up slightly, though they stayed pivoted backward, her entire body like a black arrow pointing down the trail. He could sense she was listening to him, assessing her surroundings, in an effort to make a decision.

Suddenly her head turned, though her legs were still in motion. She yanked the golden rope strung between them in her jaws, causing Vincent to fall forward and collapse in a heap on her back.

He made an undignified sound as he fell onto her. Renata's wolf-form seemed to increase in size to accommodate his entire body. He squinted into her fur, his hands wound in the golden harness.

"Just run," Vincent murmured in her mind. *"Stay on The Narrows."* He felt his power, like a light, grow dim with the effort he had made to outrun the shadows—the vengeful darkness that was intent on destroying him.

Renata lifted her head and let out a small howl, her legs making powerful strides across The Narrows. She didn't slow down.

VINCENT WOKE SURROUNDED by tall grass. The light was fragile, he could sense that it was only moments after dawn.

Renata—still a wolf—sat on her haunches, panting and observing the Night Forest. The black mist swirled and frothed at its edge but did not trespass into the clearing.

He lifted his head slightly and felt his whole body throb. Drained once more of power, Vincent felt his physical form. His head ached. His lips were dry. He thirsted.

Renata turned, her bright eyes piercing and observant. She was much larger than she had been initially—her paws alone the size of dinner plates. She had a hulking profile for a wolf, her shoulders wide enough to carry a full-grown man. As the morning's light became stronger, he could discern the black of her coat was not quite true black, its depth had an almost blue tone. The darkness of her fur made her eyes even more noticeable—they were a color he could not name.

"My bag," he said to Renata. He gingerly removed it from his shoulders. *"The tent is within my bag."*

Renata, the wolf, cocked her head to one side, listening.

"Just suspend the hook," he said. *"It is enough to enter the tent."*

Renata continued to stare at him. The little power he used to manifest the satchel and speak to Renata had weakened him further. He felt thin, and weak— like a piece of dry straw that could blow away with the wind.

Renata finally stood up. On all fours, she was even more menacing. She stood over Vincent. He looked up at her, weary and ashen. She lowered her large head and licked his face.

"Renata—" he protested weakly. As he finished mumbling her name, he felt the heat of her jaws at his throat. He felt the circle of her teeth around his neck, the exhale of her breath across his jugular. He didn't move, didn't protest, merely remained still and subservient to the creature that held his only hope for continued survival in her teeth. He was unsure whether it was an attempt to save him or savage him.

"If my last look is the dawn in your eyes... I am content, ma louloutte." Vincent thought. His gaze fluttered up to hers, and he stared into her unnamable eyes. The sun finally peaked over the horizon, illuminating the vast grasslands. *"I would gladly break... in your jaws."*

Vincent felt himself slide into darkness, the wolf still grasping his throat.

VINCENT WOKE UP BLOODY.

He immediately felt his neck, assuming the wound was there. He found the skin smooth and unblemished. Still a little weak, he let his arms fall back to his side.

He was on his back, just barely in the tent. He turned his head to see the underside of the table he used as a desk in his makeshift library. It towered above him, his solitary chair still pushed neatly underneath it, the ornately carved wooden legs only a few inches from his temple.

He heard Renata whine behind him. He rolled over, bracing himself weakly on his elbows to face her.

She was still a wolf, her black coat almost a void in the low light of the tent. Her eyes glowed, their color bright and ensnaring.

"I need a Time Crystal and Elder Glass," he said to the wolf, leveling his gaze at her.

After a moment, she got up. She padded down the length of the tent to the armoire. She barked at it, and the small doors flung themselves open, no need for a key. Renata was still quite large and didn't even have to stand on her hind legs to reach the Elder Glass. She clutched it gingerly in her jaws, bringing it to Vincent at the front of the tent. She returned once more to the armoire for the Elder Crystal.

"My bag," he said weakly. Renata exited the tent, her large paws padding quietly across the threshold and into the grassy field beyond. The light streaming in from the open tent flap had an ashy tone to it, as if it were still early morning. Vincent frowned, certainly he had been asleep for most of the day?

Renata emerged through the tent flaps, Vincent's bag in her mouth.

"Thank you," he said, sitting up. As Renata placed the satchel in his waiting lap, Vincent noticed a dark slickness covering her chest. Blood matted the fur at her neck and right shoulder as well. He recognized too late the scent of her blood, not sensing it before as it also coated the front of his shirt and chest. His senses dulled with weariness, he had thought the blood was his own. "Renata," he whispered.

The wolf cocked her head to one side, staring at him. When he said nothing further, she nuzzled the bag in his lap.

"Yes," he said, in shock. "Thank you for getting that." His eyes unfocused, either with denial or weariness or both. He had no time to consider the implications of the damning evidence before him. He'd lived a hundred thousand lifetimes of man, and suddenly he felt pressed for time.

His hands reached into the bag, searching. After a few moments, he produced a mortar and pestle.

He went to work, crushing up the remaining crystal. When he had ground the delicate crystals to a fine powder, he uncorked a bottle of Elder Glass. He wrapped his thumb and forefinger around the lip of the bottle, his other hand delicately tapping the powder from the bowl. Once all the grit was ensconced within the bottle, he deftly brushed the remaining crumbs of crystal from his fingers and over the rim. He replaced the stopper and turned the bottle over once, and then twice, and shook it from side to side.

Satisfied that his cocktail of Elder Glass and crushed Elder Crystal were thoroughly mixed, Vincent brought the bottle upright and uncorked it once more.

"I estimate we are a day's travel from the Time Henge," he said, his shoulders slack with weariness. Renata sat like a sphinx across from him on the floor, her unnamable eyes taking him in. "I say we leave the tent, take the remaining Elder Glass, your book, and set out for the coast. We travel light and fast. I bet we will see the shores of the Obsidian Sea by nightfall. We can climb the cliffs of the Henge by moonlight. This route, and time willing, we will be at the the top before tomorrow's dawn. At the Henge you can contact the Arbiters. Hopefully." Vincent looked critically at the wolf across from him. His brow furrowed—for a moment, he had forgotten Renata had ever been human. Strange.

Renata lay her head on her paws, looking innocently up at Vincent.

"Out in the open grassland, I don't think the mist can follow us," he said, taking a tentative swing of the Elder Glass. He belched a white vapor, his skin glowing with Elder energy. "But that's just a theory. I don't know why we are not being pursued now."

Renata let out a long exhale with a deep rumbling whine.

"Please, tell me your brilliant plan *louloutte*—" Vincent said, taking another swig, this one longer. He winced as his skin glowed, his eyes crackling with electricity. He belched again, white vapor bursting past his lips.

Renata lifted her head and barked once.

"It is not pleasant for me either," he said, putting his hand to his mouth to cover another belch. White vapor escaped his palm as he drew his hand away. "But I need the energy, I need it as fast as possible."

Renata groaned and got up, walking outside the tent.

"Right," Vincent said, standing up. He scurried about the tent for a few minutes, gathering the few supplies he needed. "We leave at once."

35

LUPUS OBSIDIAN, CERULEAN DIMENSION

Peaches stood on the dais of the Time Lab, watching the sand behind the glass. She was so enraptured by the spinning patterns, she didn't hear Lachlan enter.

"I've just come from the medical suite," he said by way of greeting.

"Oh!" she yelped, putting her hand on her chest.

"Apologies," Lachlan said, nodding his head slightly. He was silent for a moment before continuing. "Peaches. I am sorry, but... your father's residual dimensional energy has... disappeared. He's gone."

Peaches stared at Lachlan, silent. She tucked an errant curl behind her ear. Her blue eyes flickered back up to the glass, the sand still spinning and glowing behind the pane.

"He could never read Centius," she said at last, her chin pointing at the pane. "It always bothered him. He could use the interface Grand-mére created, but... so much gets lost in translation."

"They built this together," Lachlan said, indicating the Time Lab. His eyes remained on Peaches.

"Yes," she said, looking up at the ceiling, her gaze wandering the room. "Before I was born."

"In all that time, there is no record of you entering the Amaranthine," he said, keeping his tone conversational and light. "As well, you were not born or conceived in the Amaranthine."

"I was born on Earth, originally," she said. Lachlan's eyes locked with hers, and he held his breath. "Charing Cross, 2122.08 to Aldric and Eva." She paused, tears pricking the corner of her eyes. "It was after the Climate Wars, and Charing Cross was a remote and independent settlement, separate from the other Corporate Republics." Peaches wiped a rogue tear that slid down her cheek, thinking of her deceased mother. "She died a few days after I was born. After a few Earth centuries, Aldric moved me permanently aboard the Obsidian and we have been completing temporal missions ever since. But you don't need me to tell you that. What are you *really* asking?"

"If you are up for the challenge ahead," Lachlan said, blinking away his momentary hope that Peaches could recall anything of her life on Earth. She had only repeated exactly what was in her file in Centius' databanks. He looked down at the interface, and cleared his throat, focusing. "I am here to execute a mission of your father's. What he saved my life for and dedicated his to." Lachlan looked up, scanning the Lab. "The purpose of the Time Lab he created is to travel to the Amaranthine and collect—"

"Yes!" Peaches said before she could contain her enthusiasm. "I'll go. Absolutely. This is what I have been waiting for my entire life!"

"My concern," Lachlan began and then paused, searching for the right words. "My concern is the Quantum forces and the effect of the Amaranthine on you—"

"—Never affected my father permanently," Peaches responded, interrupting. "I can take a Quantum-fluerite drip to remove all of that timeline's Quantum energy from my quarks and sub-quark particulates as well—"

"Incorrect," Lachlan said. "These missions to the Amaranthine aged him and disrupted his cellular cohesion, in addition to the paradox of being entangled within the same time loop of his past self. The Quantum-fluerite drip bought him a few centuries, got him almost to the completion of the mission. But the incident here on the Obsidian—"

"Has nothing to do with him traveling back and forth in the Amaranthine loop," she snapped, interrupting again. "My father was conceived in the Amaranthine. It makes his energetic destabilization..." Her blue eyes trembled with unshed tears, but she didn't blink or look away from Lachlan even as the word that came next remained stuck in her throat.

"Inevitable," he said for her, nodding slowly. "For the mission to succeed. As the Amaranthine degrades, so does he. That much at least is consistent with the variables we are observing. I'm sorry he did not warn you of this."

Peaches let out a single sob, covering her mouth. Lachlan was silent for a moment, studying her. She cried silently into her hand, watching the sand spin in a pane behind his head, tears streaking down her cheeks. After a moment, she quieted, hiccuped a few times, and met his gaze.

"The past version of my father in the Amaranthine..." She said it without inflection, her lips drawn in a thin line.

"Centius indicated that not only was it likely, he was also involved in an Anchor Point..." Lachlan confirmed, his eyes glancing up behind Peaches' head as the sand behind the glass sifted in a cylindrical pattern. Lachlan glanced back at her, as if holding her stare could will the truth from her.

"I——" Peaches began when his imposing attention was back on her. "He... was going to tell me. He said before the Amaranthine collapsed there were things I needed to know. Something about his legacy...and something else... about me..."

Lachlan nodded, feeling the hope bubble up anew in his chest. "But he never had the chance to relate this knowledge to you?"

Peaches shook her head. "No," she said. "But the numbers don't lie. I could analyze the former loops, compress the variables. I could find out. I chose not to. I chose to remember my father as he was——my father, the only other being I have known in this life, besides you."

"Centius has completed the research on the Amaranthine you described," Lachlan said, his tone even. He blinked, letting his hope that she would recall her life in Charing Cross fade. The nanite bands in his eyes and wrist shimmered, as he let his mechanical processor take over, squelching any feelings of disappointment. Lachlan was a soldier, and he had a mission to complete. "You need to be debriefed on Aldric's Anchor Point before the final mission."

"I don't want to know what happened," she said through gritted teeth. Silent tears spilled down her face, and she smeared them across her cheeks with her palm. "I don't need to know." Her voice trembled.

Lachlan shook his head, his voice quiet. "If you want to remain ignorant of this knowledge, that is your choice. Without it, I cannot let you travel to the Amaranthine. It would jeopardize the mission."

Peaches' chin trembled, crossing her arms, she gave in. "Fine," she whispered. "Fine."

Lachlan straightened his spine, unaware he had been bending to lock eyes with her.

"Centius will debrief you in your quarters," he said. "Time is of the essence. Return to the Lab ready to enter the Gate."

36

AEOR-ETERNA, AMARANTHINE LOOP

Time was on their side, Vincent decided. The day had paused, time caught in the moment just after dawn. The cobwebs of night had only just vanished, and the light still held a hushed quality.

Vincent scanned the rolling hills of grassland before him. A glowing bank of fuchsia-toned wildflowers shimmered in the quiet light of dawn, the petals scattering on a soft breeze winding through the valley. The call of an owl came from the Night Forest, though Vincent hadn't remembered seeing any living creatures in the woods during his time recently spent there.

He shivered.

Though he and Renata made quick progress, and the Night Forest receded in the distance, it never fell completely out of sight—as if the Forest still gave pursuit.

And then the breeze changed, the Forest disappearing for good as they crested the final hill before the grassland gave way to the stony seashore. The land here seemed peaceful, almost welcoming to the two travelers. The wind blew gently at their backs as the promise of daybreak bled onto the frothing ocean. The rest of the sky was still a pungent periwinkle, a full moon ripe and high in the sky.

As they approached the rocky outcropping that delineated grassland from seashore, Vincent saw it. A speck in the distance, the Henge glittered like a diamond. It sat upon on a cliff jutting out into the shore of the Obsidian Sea.

"Do you see it?" he said, turning to Renata. She was trotting behind him, her tongue hanging out of her mouth in exertion. "Time is on our side." Vincent allowed himself a deep breath, smelling the sea air. He looked at the horizon, the sun had fully emerged to meet the dawn.

Renata's wolf growled and then yipped.

Vincent turned to discover the Night Forest loomed only a few feet behind him. Startled, Renata's dark wolf held a defensive position between him and the towering trees.

"How?" Vincent yelled. "It isn't possible!"

Renata's wolf snarled as a tree branch and exposed root slithered toward them. She backed up toward Vincent until his fingers were brushing the fur on her back. She let out a piercing howl. Vincent could feel the power rolling up through the sound and out into the air like an electric current. He fought against wincing as her howl caused his eyes to water and his hair to stand on end.

A blinding flash of light, followed by a thunderous crack, obscured the Night Forest. Vincent's palm grabbed Renata's wolf fur as he felt the ground disappear beneath his feet.

THE OCEAN WAS DARK. Even in the dawn, the water was almost black.

Vincent woke on the shore with an unencumbered view of the shoreline. Renata's wolf whimpered. She was splayed next to him, her fur wet with ocean spray. Her normally black coat had specks of white around the muzzle and chest— the last bit of energy use had aged her somehow.

"Renata," Vincent said, his voice hoarse. "We're almost there."

The wolf whimpered again, attempting to rise. Her stiff legs shook with effort, sinking into the wet sand. Finally, she stood and shook unceremoniously, water splattering across Vincent's face.

"Thanks for that," he said, wiping his brow and chin. He stood as well, looking back at the rocky outcropping they'd been standing beside only moments ago. It was now a speck in the distance.

Renata's wolf made a high-pitched whine, her nose upturned in the ocean breeze. Vincent broke his stare and turned to see what she was concerned about.

The Time Henge and the cliff it stood upon were only a few hundred yards away. In front of the steep cliff, a man stood, waiting for them.

"Mark her return by the wolf and the warrior, and a mortal's reoccurring dream," the man spoke, nodding to each of them, as if he were quoting a well-rehearsed line. "It is as you wrote Papa, an Anchor of Time on the shores of the Obsidian Sea." The man paused, his eyes twinkling. "I've had some time to catch up on my reading."

Vincent remained silent, taking in the stranger's appearance on the deserted beach. He had a white mustache and odd clothing. He seemed *thin*—not malnourished but *translucent*—as if he might blow away all together if the wind picked up. Vincent guessed he was an energetic projection of some sort.

"How have you had the opportunity to read from my library?" Vincent said. "Did Sid send you?"

"What is the future doing in your historical text?" the man responded. "A better question."

"You speak of prophecy, and mythological figures," Vincent said. "The Forgotten Queen is one of the oldest stories—"

"One of *your* oldest stories," the man said. "This is the final chapter in Elder history, and the first." He winked.

Vincent's eyes rounded, but he was at a loss for words. The man continued.

"The Amaranthine was my idea. Well, my predecessor—"

"Amaranthine?" Vincent said interrupting, scanning the coast. "This is a time loop?"

"Time prison," the man replied. "At least, that's how I described it mathematically. My Ledger teetered a little more toward balance if I tweaked a definition here and there. Not too much—numbers are implacable, but words... can be manipulated."

"Ledger," Vincent ground out. "So, you *are* a Tracker—"

"—Was a Tracker," the man interrupted. "Now I am more. Or I was." His expression changed. "There isn't much time left, *please* listen—"

Vincent cut in, anger powering his words. "Why should

I listen? You have freely admitted you were a Tracker and you somehow duped me into an Amaranthine." The wind swept Vincent's hair back from his face, his expression severe. "I should consume your power and destroy what little remains of you—"

Renata whined again, the sound turning into more of a grunt. Vincent stopped speaking and glanced back at her. She was shifting—her legs lengthening and her fur disappearing. When she stood upright, in the semblance of a human form, Vincent locked eyes with her.

This was more than the Renata he knew.

This was also the ancient part he could sense buried deep, the shadow of time in her blood. Her eyes had also changed—onyx and bottomless, save for purple irises, and pupils that glowed like blue fire. Her hair billowed leisurely over her shoulders and around her expressionless face. She was unclothed, but equal parts light and shadow shimmered across her skin, obscuring most of her body.

"I've come to you at the turn of the tide," the man said, squinting into the wind. "The Amaranthine is collapsing, and a sickness chases you across Aeor-Eterna, a sickness of your own making..."

The wind picked up, and the ocean began moving in with every wave that met the shore.

"Who are you?" Vincent barked, his eyes glowing a threatening Elder blue.

"I am Aldric—"

"He is our *son*," Renata replied at the same time, a hint of surprise in her voice as if she had only just deduced that fact.

Vincent looked between the two, dumbstruck.

"We have met so many times, Papa. You never remember. But that is the nature of an Amaranthine," Aldric said, his eyes crinkling in the corners, the wind whipping his almost transparent white hair.

Renata, her eyes crackling with blue flame, tilted her head. She studied Aldric but remained silent.

"Impossible," Vincent said after a moment. "Elders cannot be controlled by an Amaranthine, and Aldric is a *Tracker*, I couldn't—"

"The Aldric in the Amaranthine is a Tracker," he said. "And he has sacrificed everything to find you. And her." Aldric inclined his head, indicating Renata. "To wield a descendant of the Forgotten Queen's birthright—to hold the power of time in his hands. He has been combined by the toxic energy remaining in Aeor-Eterna, left over from the Future War. This Aldric has only one purpose, to take Renata's mortal body as his golem and be *reborn*—"

"You will not touch her," Vincent ground out. He stood, braced against the wind with his palms facing the ghostly visage of Aldric, his hands spasmed with light as power and rage burst past his careful control. "You will never be reborn *Tracker*—"

"But I was," Aldric interrupted. "And I am. Not in the way I planned of course. Renata absorbed my spark. She transforms me..." Aldric paused, looking at Renata. Her eyes gave nothing away, but she stared deeply at him, hanging on every word. "I have a daughter, your granddaughter, Peaches, who will come for you at the next Anchor Point—"

"Peaches," Renata mouthed the word, her expression

neutral. "She need not come. This is the Time Henge. Vincent and I can exit the Amaranthine here."

"No, you must listen, there isn't much time. I come for you even now..." Black smoke started to leak out of Aldric's mouth, his eyes weeping black oily tears. "You must go with her at the next Anchor Point, or you will be destroyed —" Aldric's words were momentarily choked by the mist as it attempted to silence him.

"Fight it," Renata commanded, walking toward him. The density of her power was palpable in the air—there was a heavy, smothering essence as the sand blew away under her feet. "Do not let it control you." A whisper of gray blue smoke billowed off her body, turquoise and magenta sparks igniting within the smoke, as if she walked in a cloud of muffled starlight.

"I cannot fight... destiny," Aldric said. "This too... is an... Anchor Point." He practically choked on his words, the mist flooding from his mouth and nose. The waves crashed even closer to them on the beach.

"How will we know it's the next Anchor Point?" Vincent shouted into the wind. Aldric's fading form glimmered for a moment, as if resisting the influence of the corrupt power attempting to overtake him.

"Elaria," Renata whispered, staring at Aldric. Vincent blanched, his mouth clenching in a feral hiss. Then, the semblance of Aldric's form was taken over, the black mist using it as a puppet.

"No!" Renata shouted. She flung her hand out, as if inviting the mist to attack her instead.

The mist reacted, arching toward her.

"*This was an inevitability,*" the mist intoned, billowing

within inches of Renata's fingers. The Aldric that had been speaking before was no longer present. Only the noxious black smoke of his Tracker essence, fused with the tainted power of Aeor-Eterna, remained inside the visage of his body.

Renata became distracted as the tide ceased lapping at their feet, and the ocean became still. She only noticed the water wasn't moving when the wind stopped as well. She glanced up—a glowing red sphere emerged from the depths of the Obsidian Sea. She heard Vincent gasp beside her, falling to his knees.

The Blood Light of Elaria hung like a blood red sun, several handspans wide, above the still water. It radiated warmth and smelled of iron.

The black mist audibly whined in agony. The Blood Light floated toward Renata and Aldric, its reflection giving the impression another orb hung below it in the still, dark ocean.

Renata spared a glance at the mist as it moved Aldric's form in jerky, unnatural postures back from the seashore.

"Elaria?" Vincent whispered. He walked into the water as if to greet the orb, but it floated past him, unresponsive. He turned, following it, tears staining his cheeks.

Renata stepped toward Aldric's crumpled body. She bent on one knee next to him, her purple irises glowing and giving even the sand beneath her feet a lavender hue.

"The end is just the beginning," she said, her voice steeped in power. She put her palm to his face. Aldric sat motionless, propped against a boulder that spanned the base of the cliffside. When Renata touched him, the dark vapor shimmered across her skin as well—blistering her with its dark essence. Her skin boiled and sizzled, but she did not let go.

The Blood Light reached the shore and hovered over Renata and Aldric. The atmosphere around the pair glowed with a faint red hue, and the dark mist began to wind and evaporate over Renata's entire body. Aldric's form finally collapsed into vapor, caught like smoke in glass inside the orb.

The Blood Light began funneling its power over Renata's entire body, disrupting the blistering touch of the dark mist. Her eyes were closed with a pained expression as the red light lifted her off the ground. Fully ensconced in the Blood Light, she levitated, suspended in a cocoon, her eyes glowing red and her body spasming with a volatile current of energy.

As the last wisp of Aldric was absorbed, every blood vessel lit up beneath her skin, exposing the crisscross of capillaries and veins that pumped furiously with blood and a spark of energy it was never meant to contain. As her mortal body struggled to keep cohesion with the tremendous power it was consuming, she tilted her head back and screamed.

"Renata!" Vincent jogged out of the water. Without hesitation, he entered the orb's red atmosphere. He felt himself rise, the orb channeling some of the energy through him as well. His palms itched and sparked with electricity.

"Renata," he said, grasping for her. She had stopped screaming, but her face was stony and unreadable. Vincent touched her hand, winding his fingers with hers. "Renata, look at me." His other hand grasped her neck, rolling her head forward to make eye contact with him.

Her expression still frozen, the ancient power within her stared back with black eyes, purple surrounding blue flame. Despite this, he felt a connection immediately with her when he grasped her palm. They had an ancient connection, Bound by blood, and Binding their destinies together—Sanguin-Aeor. He gasped, understanding for the first time since he met her that she was—

"Sanguin-laeth," she said to Vincent, her voice echoing. Her face remained stony, her eyes glowing with the blue flame of her most ancient self.

"Ma louloutte," Vincent whispered, hand stroking her face. Vincent felt his eyes grow wet with tears as he looked at her. "Come back to me."

"We must take our places in the Order of Things," Renata said, her eyes still glowing.

Vincent closed the distance between their faces and kissed her. He surrendered himself to the desire he had tried to deny. A tremendous energy surged between them, and he felt their Blood Bond even more—newly refreshed by their journey through Aeor-Eterna.

The Blood Light lifted them. Vincent held Renata protectively against him. He bit her lip seductively, drawing her deeper into their kiss. She melted into him, in a quiet ecstasy, as they ascended the cliffs of the Time Henge— enraptured with each other for the first time in thousands of years.

ALL TOO SOON, Vincent felt the ground beneath his feet. The Blood Light set them down at the entrance to the Time Henge. He broke their kiss as their heels touched the earth but kept his hand entwined with hers, his other palm cupping the back of her neck, keeping her lips close to his.

"I would love you in a thousand other lifetimes," he whispered, kissing her forehead.

Renata blinked, her entire body trembling. A shimmer of light erupted through her skin. With a spasm and a loud thunk, a blinding pop of energy surged out of her and into the orb.

The orb of Light lifted off the ground—without them, holding instead the energy that had just left Renata's body. In a few seconds, it disappeared completely into the white mists of the Time Henge.

"Vincent," Renata whispered hoarsely, grasping him back. Her arms circled around him desperately as she drew him against her. "Vincent." She said again, as if confirming it to herself.

Vincent held her to him, stroking her hair. "We've made it."

"We have?" she said. "Where are we?"

"You don't remember?" he asked, drawing her away from his shoulder so that he could look into her eyes.

"Yes... and no. Bits and pieces. We were in the Night Forest," she said, squinting. "I was a wolf?"

"You shifted," he nodded, searching her eyes for a reaction. This was the Renata he was familiar with, and he worried for her. This was beyond the scope for most humans. "You became a black wolf—"

"Just like the book!" she interrupted, nonplussed.

Vincent nodded, quirking his brow. This was his Renata alright.

"I am always your Renata," she said, her eyes glittering.

"Snooping in my head?"

"You don't conceal your thoughts well around me—ever."

Vincent laughed, touching her face. "Renata," he whispered.

"And the beach just now," she said. "Aldric, I remember Aldric."

Vincent nodded mutely, not yet prepared with words about the news of Aldric.

"And nothing else?" he asked after a silent moment. "Not helping me in the tent after the Night Forest? Or the grasslands? Teleporting us to the cliff?"

She shrugged her shoulders. "Guess I needed a nap?"

He chuckled, pressing her to his chest.

"I don't have much time," she said into his shoulder.

Vincent's brows furrowed, pulling her out of his embrace to look at her. "What do you mean?"

"The other me," Renata began. "Or the rest of me? Anyway, the me that just left in the orb of Blood Light is waiting in the Henge."

"Okay," he said, unsure.

"I am giving myself time to say goodbye." She shrugged. "I think."

"Goodbye?" Vincent scoffed, grasping her by the waist. "I think *not*."

"Not goodbye exactly, just—" she paused, looking up into Vincent's eyes as if she could find the right words there. "I am going in there to die."

"No," Vincent snarled, shaking his head.

"It's the reoccurring dream," she said. "We're here...
aren't we?"

"Renata," Vincent whispered. "I can't—I can't let you
do this."

"I can't let you stay in the Amaranthine any longer!
This is the way out."

"Explain to me why Divine Death is the only way out of
the Amaranthine?" he said, frowning at her, his expression
feral. "You would *butcher* yourself to stop time!"

"Vincent," she said, cupping his face. "I am in Divine
Death right now. I am a fragment of power, lost in time. I
was given this mortal life in an attempt to return here."

"My hyacinth in bloom." He touched her face.

She nodded, blinking back tears.

Vincent let go of her then, and walked away, wringing
his hands.

"Sanguin-laeth," he said, feeling the word on his lips
without shame in a millennia. He turned, his expression
pained. "What you ask of me is terrible."

"I am the last fragment to return," Renata said, her
eyes flashing with the innate power she still contained.
"Only once before have I come here with you, thinking we
would both leave the Amaranthine. I was not complete,
but I was strong. Not strong enough to change destiny, it
would seem."

"And what of the Arbiters," he said, pausing. He
grasped Renata's hand. "We set out on this journey to
speak to them. Will you ask them nothing? I would be
curious to know their opinion of your sacrifice."

It was Renata's turn to let go and walk a step away from Vincent. Finally, she spoke.

"I think they... put me there."

Vincent gasped and then began to pace.

"Why can I not remember on my own?" he said through gritted teeth.

"It is the Amaranthine," Renata said, reaching for him in his pacing. She grasped his hands and looked up into his eyes. "It seeks to keep you here—forever. That is why I must go and take my place in the Order of Things. I think once I do that, I can destroy it—"

"Renata," he said, holding her face with his hands. His blue eyes glimmered. "We set out on this journey together. I promised to protect you. I'm going into the Time Henge with you—"

She nodded, a breeze off the Obsidian Sea moving a few strands hair across her face.

"Okay," she said. "But we must go—*now*."

LUPUS OBSIDIAN, CERULEAN DIMENSION

P eaches braced the wall, her palms flat against the cool metal.

"Screen off," she whispered, swallowing hard. Tears pricked her eyes, but she blinked them back, staring up at the ceiling lights in her quarters. Peaches stepped away from the wall, wiping her face with her hands. She turned, pressing a small panel. Her closet opened, and she reached inside for a transparent glass band that she slid over her wrist. She ran her fingers through her hair, retying the length in a long, tight braid.

A light flickered on the comms panel by the door. Lachlan was summoning her back to the Time Lab.

"On my way," Peaches said. She wiped another errant tear from her cheek and got dressed.

Rounding the corner from the hallway connecting her quarters to the Time Lab, she ran straight into Lachlan. He enveloped her in his arms. They were strong, and didn't smell of the cold, dark of space. That's all it ever smelled like here, that or stale cigarettes when Aldric returned from the Amaranthine missions. Lachlan smelled of salt and sweat—the light of a distant star still evident in the glint of his hair and the freckles marking his skin. The human part of him was from Earth for sure.

"Ooph," Peaches said, stepping back a half second later than she planned. She missed being embraced. She looked up, her cheeks flushed. "The last Anchor Point," she whispered, swallowing hard. "How could my father do *that*?"

"He was not your father then. Think of him as an... ancestor of your father. I know this is difficult," Lachlan said, locking eyes with her. His gaze was warm with concern, the softness of his eyes at war with the firm set of his jaw. "But the equations are complete, and the Gate in the Amaranthine is starting to entangle with ours. I need your help in the Lab."

"Of course," she said, nodding and wiping her unshed tears roughly across her cheeks with her palms. "I'm ready."

Peaches and Lachlan busied themselves in the Time Lab, adjusting the energy streams feeding the temporal portal that accessed Renata's Gate in the Amaranthine Loop. Centius needed to channel the same Quantum wave function of power that Renata did on the other side. This created not only a Quantum entanglement that resulted in a portal through space and time, but a beacon to call her forth.

As Peaches worked, curls popped out of her braid, framing her heart shaped face. She used a collection of thin tools she kept on the inside of her Time Lab jumpsuit; each had their own pocket on an inside flap of her uniform. She worked quickly and methodically, almost in a trance.

Suddenly a strange sensation came over her, as if a presence was watching her through the Gateway. She looked at the energy readout, measuring the superposition Centius was dictating. The golden sand behind the panel shimmered, flowing erratically and pinging the Glass.

"We've matched her," Peaches said, exhaling. "I can... feel it." Peaches looked at the energy sparking and coiling within the Gate. She could have sworn the Gate peered back at her, aware.

Lachlan stretched his back. He was sitting on the dais, connected to a port underneath the interface. He kept his connection to Centius but stood up next to Peaches and looked over her shoulder at the Quantum circuit readings.

"Aye," he said, nodding. "That we have. Are you ready to go?"

"Almost," she said, placing her last tool in the hidden pocket of her jumpsuit. She pressed a button on her bracelet, and her appearance changed. She had a gray sweatshirt and turquoise pants with pink cats on them.

"*New-Ashemore Bulldogs'*?" Lachlan said, reading her sweatshirt.

"I am trying to appear typical to the time," she replied. "This was a local college."

"That doesn't excuse the pants," he said, stifling a laugh.

"I *like* them!" Peaches said, stamping her foot dramatically. She let out a short giggle.

"Are you ready?" he said, a smile still lingering in the corners of his mouth.

She gave a curt nod, her round blue eyes locking with his. They shimmered with anticipation.

"Let's do it then," Lachlan said, clearing his throat. He took his place behind the dais.

Peaches walked a few steps and stood in front of the Gate, swiping her wrist over the panel on the wall next to it. The energy shifted, and the presence she had been feeling in the Gate lessened. Slowly, the appearance of a dark room with debris and rubble appeared on the other side of the portal. Peaches recognized every piece of detritus. This was the Gate Aldric had used for their previous missions. Only she had always stood where Lachlan was now.

Peaches turned to look at Lachlan one last time.

"See you when I get back?" she said breathlessly, her blue eyes vibrant. Her heart shuddered in her chest.

Lachlan nodded, his eyes drinking her in. "Aye, Peaches," he replied. "I will see you very soon, lass. It's a promise."

Suddenly, the ship shuddered, throwing Peaches to the floor. She sat up, grasped the ledge of the Gateway, and stood—bracing against it. An alarm sounded, the emergency lights casting a red hue across the Time Lab. A robotic voice sounded, warning of an airlock breach.

"Go!" Lachlan shouted. "The portal is open, just go!"

Peaches nodded, grasping the sides of the Gateway. The ship's alarm sounded again as she stepped into the portal and vanished.

AEOR-ETERNA, AMARANTHINE LOOP

Renata and Vincent walked hand in hand through the barrier of fog surrounding the Henge of Time. Inside the fog, it felt like they were falling—but at the same time weightless and flowing— jettisoning in every direction, yet also completely still.

When Renata opened her eyes to see the standing stones and the Henge, she audibly gasped.

"Vincent, are you seeing this?"

She turned, and only then noticed her hand was empty. Her mouth open in shock, she scanned the Henge, looking for him.

The fog was banked low here. It came no higher than her knees in a circuitous route around the Henge—in the suggestion of a path. A slow, meandering funnel of fog spiraled up in the center of the Henge, obstructing what would be an otherwise clear view of all the standing stones and the horizon beyond the cliff.

The fog that banked across the ground was cool against

Renata's skin. It was bracing to the touch, and pulled like a cat draping its tail across her shins. It tumbled forward and fell past the edge of the cliff.

She observed all of this and peered down the path for Vincent. It was empty. He was gone.

"Fear not," a voice from the Henge said. "He slumbers. You will find him at the white willow. We sent him there."

The surface of the first stone flickered, like small star bursts were erupting across its surface. An image appeared. It was Vincent, covered in the undulating rainbow of light Renata had only seen once before—when they traveled to Aeor-Eterna via Vincent's white willow, the conduit of his power and his Pillar's nexus between worlds and dimensions. Renata remembered he had called it the Tree of Aimer.

"You may find him there," the voice said. "Once you take your place in the Order of Things."

In the rare gaps of fog that shrouded the ground, Renata glimpsed what appeared to be blood. Once she noticed it, the fog parted at her feet, giving her an unencumbered view.

She gasped—it *was* blood. It ran in rivulets across the ground, winding around pebbles and smaller rocks littering the ground.

The source of blood was shrouded in the center of the Henge, in an impenetrable spiral of fog. Dark puddles of it had pooled in front of each of the boulders like a silent offering.

Renata walked down the bloody path, passing the one showing Vincent sleeping in his Pillar. She paused, stopping at each stone. She frowned, sensing what the voice from the Henge said was true.

As she kept walking, hazy images flickered across each stone's surface, a wispy glimpse of another world, in another time.

The second boulder presented an image of a room of some sort, its walls were clear panes of glass with a large dais in the center. Renata stared for several moments, before moving on.

Another stone in the Henge showed what looked like Renata's former salon, her styling chair sitting vacant in the center of the portal opening. Another boulder displayed a view that was underwater, with a murky green hue and water weeds swaying visibly in the frame.

"The Pool of Verite," Renata whispered.

Something drew her attention to the farthest part of the Henge. There, a tall boulder glowed with blinding, bright light—voices emanated from beyond the portal, calling her name.

Their calls were laced with need. Combined with the pull of energy from the portal, the sound created a lulling weight. She felt it draw her forward, the bright light eclipsing all else in the Henge.

"I would avoid the Arbiters," the voice from the Henge said, interrupting her reverie.

Renata blinked and shook her head, the pull of the light from the portal lessening.

"The other side of that is the... Arbiters?" she said, rubbing her neck.

"The force compelling you is from the Breaking of the Light," the voice replied. "The gravity there is the only thing in this Universe that rivals our power. As for the Arbiters themselves, they call to you for different reasons. They only narrowly missed you in the car—"

"That was *them*?" Renata said, thinking of the car accident. "So, the Arbiters know who I am..." she paused, looking around for the source of the voice.

"The Arbiters have no answers for you," the voice replied, coming from nowhere and everywhere. "Your only value to them is your powerful lineage. The power running through your mortal veins holds the only possibility of their release."

"Do you know what my power is then? Where it came from?" Renata said, looking around.

"You are of the Dark star," the voice said, the words rolling over Renata like a tide. "You are of Aeor-Eterna."

She put her hand over her mouth, tears threatening in her eyes. "What—what happened here?" she whispered, trembling.

"The Supreme Elders, as you said to Vincent. They recognized Aeor-Eterna as one of the Seven Stars of the Forgotten Queen. They have traveled great distances, between Universes—searching, hungering for the fragments of Her power."

"Her power?" Renata said, her eyes round.

"The Dark star, the Aeor, the One of Many Names. She is the Binder of this Universe, and it is Bound to the Queen. She split herself into Seven Stars to deny them, to hide from them. Her power is why Aeor-Eterna was almost destroyed."

Renata froze, the words ringing true. She swore to herself, squinting through the fog. "Who the hell are you?"

"I am you," the voice said. "I am the Henge. I am the fog. I am the past."

"If you say so," she said, her expression feeling frozen, almost in shock. "So, what are all these stones? What am I seeing on the other side?"

"Time and space," the voice said.

"Oh, well if that's all—" Renata shrugged, crossing her arms.

"You are ignorant of your power and your past," the voice said. "You warned me this could happen."

"My past?"

The fog dispersed slightly, and she saw it. The Stone of Time in the center of the Henge. The source of blood was *her*.

"The dream. This *is* my death from the Future War—" Renata felt herself mouth the words, her throat suddenly dry. A figure resembling Renata's body lay across the Stone of Time, weeping blood onto the ground.

"Divine Death," the voice said. "The Supreme Elders are cunning predators. They sacrificed you, creating this Henge for themselves to control space and time. You, Renata-Aeor, were once the Wanderer of the Undying Lands, the dream and the prayer of Aeor-Eterna."

The fog shimmered, and the Blood Light of Elaria appeared. Inside, a woman who resembled Renata took a vaporous form.

"The Queen in the Dark," Renata whispered, unable to look away from her own body on the Stone of Time. Finally, her gaze flickered upward.

The Blood Light contained Renata's ancient power, like smoke floating inside a soap bubble. The woman's eyes stared back at her, her eyes glowed with pupils of blue flame.

This was the woman Renata had always dreamed of—chained to a rock, in the dark, looking up at a distant moon. The woman's ghostly image floated in the red orb that wavered in and out of the fog blanketing the Time Henge.

"She is the Aeor, eternal truth—our origin and our destiny. She is the spark of time in your blood. You must now understand that our blood is *of time*," the image in the Blood Light said to Renata. "To consume it gives great power. One can see the future and the past, even bend space and time to your will. On this Henge, it opened Quantum Gateways for the Supreme Elders."

Renata stared at the body—her body—on the slab, as if indicating an inevitable future. She observed symbols drawn across the stomach and chest that oozed blood, saturating the Stone and the ground beneath.

"They used us," Renata said finally, her voice shaking.

"They used all the inhabitants of Aeor-Eterna," the ancient entity in the orb said. "All suffered under their dominion."

Renata swallowed, curiosity winning over her fear. "How is it you—er we—can use the Blood Light of Elaria? Shouldn't she be with Vincent, in the Pillar?"

"At the conclusion of the Future War, her Blood Light was sheaved from her mortal body, and remained here, in Aeor-Eterna. The Blood Light of Elaria stabilized Aeor-Eterna while it fractured in Divine Death—" the woman said.

Renata swore, running her hands through her hair. She looked away from the entity in the orb.

"Can I destroy them?" she said finally, pivoting from the Stone of Time to look at the portal of bright light that contained the Arbiters.

"They will never again escape the Breaking of the Light, they are locked. Forever to remain in the time before time, in the place that was *before* this Universe."

"I want to punish them," Renata said, grinding her teeth.

"You must take your place in the Order of Things."

"Yeah, message received!" She tapped her head. "You've got that firmly in there, gracias. You forgot, however, to tell me exactly what that means?"

"You must coalesce with all that came before you and become the spark that will ensure all who come after. In the Order of Things, you will regain your ancient knowledge, and with it, your powers. You are special, Renata. Your blood is mortal *and* of time. To spill it on the Stone has been your destiny. It will heal Aeor-Eterna, cleanse it of of the Quantum corrosion that caused the Elders to flee for the Breaking of the Light."

The image in the orb light flickered, glittering lights obscuring her features for a second.

The spiral of fog above Renata's corpse on the Stone dissipated, revealing what it obscured.

There were thousands upon thousands—no, millions—of versions of herself, as if a stop motion camera had taken a photo of her after every slight movement before she lay on the Stone and had her body cut in ritualistic savagery.

There was one gap, one tiny slice of space between herself on the slab and before she finally lay upon it.

"As you said to Vincent, you are only a fragment of yourself," the image in the orb explained. "A drop of blood cast through a Quantum Gate, through space and time. You are Bound eternally to this place, to what you once were."

"That is why I have the dream. The same dream," Renata said, numb.

"You are the last. The last to return, and you brought Vincent as well. It is as he foretold in his books of Elderaen mythology. The story of your blood is undeniable—across space, time, and dimensions," the woman explained, the smoke in the orb curling in on itself. "Your return completes his oldest prophecy." She smiled a ghostly smile. "His clever poetry, attempting to remember *our* history—"

"Which is?" Renata interrupted.

"Aeor-Eterna's discovery, assault, and abuse by the Supreme Elders. Your sacrifice—creating this Time Henge, the Future War," the woman paused, her eyes glittering at Renata from the sphere of Elaria's Blood Light. "Then Aeor-Eterna's resurrection, by a mortal Anchor of Time—"

Renata hissed, crossing her arms. The wind played with her hair, and she breathed deep the salt air coming from the ocean. She remained silent, staring up at the stars. Tears threatened in her eyes but she blinked them away. "That last part isn't history."

"History, like time, is a matter of perspective. You admit you have a reoccurring dream of this place—the Henge and the sacrifice, proof that your destiny was written in the stars, long before you were the last of our name."

"Fair enough," Renata said, rolling her shoulders back and clearing her throat. "That all seems to line up, I'll give you that. But the Amaranthine—"

"Alas, Aldric was right. To breach Vincent from the Amaranthine you must attend the final Anchor Point. After that, he need only willingly leave," the image in the orb said. Her eyes seemed sad. "But to do so, he must remember he is in an illusion of time. He may have already forgotten. An Amaranthine loop preys on the mind."

"Why can I not just *break* the Amaranthine? You said I'm a mortal Anchor of Time—that has to mean something," she said, pacing in the fog.

Frustrated, Renata walked around the Henge, looking in each portal. She stared at a portal that showed a young woman with fiery locks of orange-red hair looking at a holographic display. She stood on a dais in front of a vast glass wall. Renata spied golden sand blowing strange patterns behind the glass panes that framed the room.

"It's Peaches," she said, staring at the portal. "Isn't it?"

The orb floated next to Renata. She turned, observing the blank expression of the ghostly form inside it. After a beat, she resumed her critical observation of the portal, studying the room it displayed.

"Time Lab!" Renata exclaimed, the words popping into her head. She watched the moving image displayed on the surface of the boulder. The girl in the image looked up, staring with piercing blue eyes that were round with shock, seemingly locking eyes with Renata. The holographic display from her computer illuminated her face, putting her orange-red hair in stark contrast to the sterile environment she was in.

"Centius can sense your gaze through this Gateway," the flickering image in the orb said. "As does Peaches. Sanguin-Aeor. Blood is truth eternal, and the bonds of the Sanguin-laeth cannot be denied."

"Okay," Renata said, uncertain. "You're still not answering my question. How do I escape the Amaranthine?"

"But I am. That is your grand-daughter," the woman in the orb said, fog rolling past Renata's shins in cold waves. "She has been searching for you in time."

"She looks so young," Renata said, her eyes softening and looking deeper at the young woman in the portal. Peaches was fluttering about the dais, pressing a few buttons on the collar of her jumpsuit that changed its appearance. Suddenly, she had a gray sweatshirt on and turquoise pajama pants with pink cats on them.

"She is a Quantum Manifestation and has existed onboard Lupus Obsidian for almost an entire Earth century." The orb glowed a deeper red as the ghostly woman spoke. "How she survived outside of her original timeline has everything to do with your blood."

"If she's my grand-daughter... Where is my child?" Renata said, turning to the woman in the orb. This close, Renata could see her ghostly image was comprised of vapor and small sparks of light.

"We unmade him earlier today."

Renata put a hand up to her mouth. "Then it is true. Aldric."

"You can make him again," she replied, the orb glowing

a deep red around her as if buoying her image to help drive her point. "You are of the Forgotten Queen, you are of the Seven Stars. How much history you have lost in your time beyond the veil—" The woman looked sympathetic. "You can do all of this—*and more*—once you take your place in the Order of Things."

"And when I do... take my place," Renata said, pausing to find the right words. "What will happen to Elaria? Will her Blood Light still remain in Aeor-Eterna?"

"No," the woman in the orb said. "You will absorb her Light. She will keep you conscious long enough to complete the ritual. She only asks to be transformed, as you did for Aldric."

Renata nodded, numb. She stared in silence at her corpse on the Stone of Time. "I'm scared," she whispered.

"The Quantum power in your mortal blood has been called through space and time to cleanse Aeor-Eterna. You were born to do this," the woman in the orb said, offering only clarity. "Your blood is a living Anchor, take comfort that your sacrifice may never be undone."

Renata swallowed, her throat going dry. *I guess sympathy for losing my mortality is asking a lot for a disembodied spirit,* she thought, staring wide eyed at the wispy image of the woman whom she intrinsically knew was also herself. She chuckled darkly about the casual conversation they were having with each other about one of them dying. Or would it be both of them dying? Renata squinted, biting her lip.

"I will always find Vincent in the last loop of the Amaranthine," she said, exhaling and crossing her arms. "As long as it exists. That's a positive at least."

The woman the orb nodded. "Once all of the Quantum

Gates of the Henge are closed, you will ascend and become as you once were: Renata-Aeor, Wanderer of the Undying Lands, the Dream and the Prayer of Eterna—"

"But I must give up my mortality," Renata said, trying her best to quell the shuddering in her body. "Renata Stone must lay down her life. Renata Stone must die."

"This was always her destiny—as a human," the woman in the orb replied.

Renata put her hand over her mouth, quaking.

"The full power of Aeor-Eterna is too much for a mortal, finite form to hold," the woman in the orb said, insistent. "This *must* be done."

"What about my conduit?" Renata pleaded, her dry tongue mouthing the words. "You know, my wolf?"

"No," the woman said. "Aeor-Eterna is your conduit. You are of the Seven Stars of the Forgotten Queen. You are Aeor-Eterna, Renata. Accept your destiny, the dream and the prayer of a goddess."

"I don't understand what that means!" She shouted. "Quit hiding behind poetry and tell me what I am!"

"A dream made flesh. The prayer of a goddess who was an eternal land, who wished to walk amongst her creation —to wander her Undying Lands and know herself and what it meant to be alive. *That* is the source of your power, *that* is what is in your blood."

"I am... Aeor-Eterna?" Renata said, awestruck.

The woman nodded. "This was how you met Vincent. The Elders would keep their human Sanguin-laeth here, and they became Blood Orphans—orphans of time. Here, even mortal life is everlasting," the woman in the orb said. "Here even mortals become *more*."

"Vincent was mortal," Renata said. "I knew it!"

"He was—at first. Aeor-Eterna was once inhabited by thousands of mortals like him."

"Vincent has a different story," Renata said, looking down. "He doesn't even remember being human."

"The shared histories between the oppressed and the oppressor are rarely similar."

"He said Eterna gave herself to the Elders, that the Henge was a *gift*." Renata pushed her hair behind her ears, recrossing her arms.

"The Supreme Elders learned of your love with a mortal —Vincent. His transformation to an Elder made him their pawn. He helped them subjugated Aeor-Eterna. When he realized what he'd done—"

Renata felt hot tears stream down her face as the pieces came together and she began to remember—then, an inexhaustible feeling of loss and grief overwhelmed her. She cried out. It was a keening, sad sound.

"Do you see now? Why you must lay down your human life on the Stone? Take up your mantle, Renata-Aeor. You are the last to return. The Undying Lands will be healed at last, cleansed of the Future War," the ghostly woman said.

Renata nodded, feeling the deep reservoir of her power coiling up inside her, causing her to tremble—her heart thundered in her chest.

"How do I begin?" Renata said, not believing the words coming out of her own mouth.

"You already have. You are the mortal with the reoccurring dream. You came as the wolf, you came with the warrior. Next, you must release Elaria of her guardianship," the woman said. "When you absorb her Blood Light, you will also absorb me and all that came before and become the spark for all that will come after. You will absorb all that bled on this hallowed ground and lingers at the base of the Gates. Your blood will Bind this point in time, and all of the Universe will be Bound to its events. After that, you will rest."

Renata nodded, quiet and listening. After a thoughtful moment, she turned, her face streaked with tears as she spoke. Her voice was strong and clear.

"I release you of your guardianship," Renata said, kneeling on the stone. "*Elaria*, Sanguin-Aeor,—"

The orb of Light moved, eclipsing Renata as she knelt on the slab. Renata squeezed her eyes shut, memorizing the steady refrain of her own pulse, her breath a rapid staccato of short gasps.

When she opened her eyes, they were fully alight, emitting bright red energy that penetrated the fog surrounding the portals. The image of the woman lingered in front of Renata, watching her absorb the Blood Light. After a moment, the woman nodded, evaporating into the mist.

Renata whispered incoherently, ancient words that she didn't understand but a deep, aching power inside her responded to.

Kneeling upright on the slab, her fingertips glowed a blinding bright white. In a low broad streak, from hip to hip, she drew her fingers across her flesh.

She bled, her blood searing the stone, becoming molten, golden energy before it reached the ground. The fog that blanketed the ground ignited with light. Renata's arms extended forward, in front of her, as if welcoming an energetic force into herself.

She drew her fingers up vertically, from her naval, between her breasts and above, ending at her collar bone. Light from the fog poured into her then. Her head reeled back as if she had been struck.

"I take my place," she shouted, her hair blowing in a flurry of wind. Sparking energy, vapor, and light poured into the wound Renata had drawn with glowing fingers across her body, allowing those elements to trespass her flesh.

Her skin glowed, and blood vessels became visible beneath her skin—she was illuminated from within.

With a burst of light, her blood bubbled and steamed through the wounds on her chest and abdomen. She screamed—her knees losing contact with the Stone as her back arched with a spectacular crack of lightning that burst up from the Stone. The lightning arched upwards and penetrated the fog writhing in the sky above.

Her eyes sparked—energy pouring down her face like rivulets of lava that glimmered and broke off into globules of light. Beads of the light globules floated around her head like a wreath. Her hair writhed and coiled about her face and shoulders, irreverent of gravity.

Suddenly the ground shook and white light poured from her throat and nostrils, her eyes still sparking and glowing as more energy flooded from her, renewed. Her outstretched palms turned into beams of bright light, her body levitating off the Stone—lightning cracked and sizzled across the Henge, electricity snapping like whips striking the ground. The stagnant blood retracted from every Henge, closing the Gateways in spectacular bursts of golden light.

The fog condensed then, and spun like a cyclone, touching down from the sky. Clouds shrunk and disappeared overhead, revealing a crescent moon and the glittering starlight of distant constellations.

Lightning sparked, jumping and touching down on different boulders in the Henge as Renata's power continued to crescendo. The cyclone expanded, moving the standing stones off balance, electricity striking them from within the fog. Large boulder-sized pieces began chipping away before the furious energy dissipated and funneled back into the cyclone, building once more.

Finally, balmy and electric, the fog created a spiraling funnel that touched down and met the point of a crown of bone and Quantum Glass that had solidified on Renata's head.

The energy, touching the relic, reverberated like a shockwave across Aeor-Eterna.

Her power sizzled across the cliffside, and sparked onto the seashore. Her power extended and expanded across the grasslands, causing the glowing fuchsia flowers to flatten to the ground—spurting glowing petals into the shockwave as it sped across the plains.

As Renata's blast of energy seared over the last remaining yards between grassland and the Night Forest, the trees extended their branches—welcoming the energy.

The Night Forest transformed. The dark exteriors and polluted bark of the trees and vegetation evaporated in the snap of Renata's spark—the flora and fauna shedding the toxic build up of the Future War.

The Night Forest came alive—in jewel tones of green, purple, brown, even blue. The choking foliage turned into a winding vine with fragrant white buds that perfumed the air. The understory of the Night Forest blossomed with aromatic flowers, each bud containing a memory.

Renata physically felt the moment her power touched the Night Forest. Her body convulsed, suspended by radiant light above the Stone.

In her mind, she felt overwhelmed by nostalgia, a crowd of memories flooding into her—jumbled pictures tumbling over each other. Her long journey away from Aeor-Eterna had caused her to forget—but the Night Forest had not forgotten.

Her body faltered and collapsed in a heap on the slab, her heart sputtering under the strain of all it had endured. She was still, her head hanging awkwardly to the side, blood flowing from her mouth. Her lifeless eyes upturned to the moon. Her heart shuddered, and slowed while her spirit wandered elsewhere.

Enveloped within the winding foliage of the Night Forest, Renata's mortal spark was drawn deeper into the woods. The further she traversed into the enchanted forest, the more keenly she felt the cords of her mortality straining—the bonds between what was eternal in her and her fragile, mortal body shuddering.

At the Stone of Time the oval of Light around her body dimmed and her body grew cold.

The blossoms of the Night Forest grew close in what Renata perceived as her vision. The light was warm, giving the flower petals a distinct shimmer. She became crowded with flowers, their petals caressing her aching body with reminders of who she was and distracting her from the mortal life she was letting go.

Renata spied the tree that had been Vincent's conduit when they had first traveled to Aeor-Eterna. It too had been transformed by her power.

The willow had soft white bark, its pale trunk glowing with the reflected light of the blooming flowers-of-memory dotting the forest. Magenta, turquoise and green leaves covered its unfurled branches. A small garden bloomed around the base of the trunk.

"*My hyacinth in bloom,*" the tree intoned, the leaves on its tendril-like branches brushing the flowers growing at its base tenderly. The garden contained newly sprouted hyacinths with fresh green shoots and small lavender petals. Each budded hyacinth flower contained the memories of Renata Stone's mortal life.

Renata felt herself kneel onto the soft mossy ground, then lay down completely and curl around the delicate purple blooms.

The branches of Vincent's willow caressed her face. She inhaled, laying on her back and observing the canopy. She smiled, smelling the light fragrance of the hyacinths.

Soon her eyes grew heavy, and she turned once more on her side. Sighing into the flowers, she rested, at last.

"RENATA-AEOR," someone whispered.

Renata blinked with some difficulty. Her eyes were grimy and dry. She closed her mouth, feeling her tongue was mossy as well—as if she had slept with her eyes and mouth open, her face pressed against the Stone.

Finally, she blinked in earnest, her eyes seeing what lay before her.

The world came into focus. She was laying across the Stone, hands outstretched, her head hanging to the side after she had collapsed onto the surface at the conclusion of the ceremony.

Her entire body was covered in blood. A ring of vibrant flower blooms blanketed the ground in a symmetrical radius around the Stone.

The fog was gone. Without it, the cliff offered an impressive view of the sea at night, the clear sky above glittering with starlight. A full moon hung overhead.

The ground beyond the flowers was littered with fragments of boulders and even smaller rocks and pebbles—what was left of the standing stones. The boulder that had served as the standing stone of the Arbiters was ground to dust.

"Serves you right," she whispered, attempting to move her stiff body. Her hair was bound in soft clumps, wet with blood that still dripped occasionally onto the Stone.

Sitting up, thick coagulated sludge—dark red and gelatinous with veins of black—oozed off her shoulders and into her lap.

"Ugh," she grumbled, smearing it off her shoulders and onto the stone. As it fell with a muted 'glop' onto the Stone of Time, more flowers appeared at the Stone's base, filling the empty Henge with more blooms.

Renata began to fling the substance off her, resulting in more vegetation and vibrant blooming plants appearing in the Henge. Dense moss grew over what was left of the boulders, flowering vines covered the emptiness between the larger fractured standing stones. The dusty corner of the Henge that the Arbiters' standing stone once occupied was a flourishing rose bush with different colored blossoms on each stem.

Feeling less gelatinous, Renata attempted to stand. Her foot disappeared into flower blossoms, and she waded, hip deep in the blossoms until several feet from the Stone. The petals and some whole blossoms stuck to her skin—sticky with the residue of whatever substance she had woken up in. Some kind of coagulated fluid, she guessed, looking at her hand.

Momentarily distracted by her own hand, Renata bent down, touching the ground. She felt Aeor-Eterna shiver beneath her touch.

Her eyes flared, glowing with the intensity of blue flame as she accessed her conduit's power.

"It's true," she said into the wind. "I am you, and you are me."

Just then, a shooting star streaked across the sky, a fiery streak simmering with an orange, pleading light. Renata stood, head upturned to the dramatic display of an object entering the upper atmosphere of Aeor-Eterna.

"Vincent," she said, his name a promise on her lips. She lifted her arm in the air, her hand reaching as if she meant to pluck the fiery tail of the trespassing object from the horizon. She twisted her outstretched arm, and with a flick of her wrist, she froze the object in the sky—pausing time around it.

She walked to the edge of the cliff, observing the object with a critical eye.

"Our reunion is blessed with trouble immediately, I

see." Renata stepped back from the cliff's edge and lifted both of her arms. As she did, a new standing stone rose from the cliff's rocky base. She bit her thumb, smearing golden blood over the stone. As she did, sparks erupted across its surface, and an image came into focus. Renata drew symbols with her blood, whispering to the new Time Henge as she did so.

"None but my blood may enter here," she spoke to the Henge. "And they must give their own to pass through." Thunder cracked overhead, and lightning struck the top of the boulder, baptizing everything in a pale, electric light for an instant.

A Quantum Gate had been created.

THE PILLAR, AMARANTHINE LOOP

Renata entered Vincent's Pillar from the same place she had exited.

He remained asleep, at the base of the Tree of Aimer. A rainbow crystalline structure blanketed his body with a forcefield that shimmered with light. She could feel him regaining strength, his energy almost completely renewed.

She didn't wake him. She wanted him to rest and fully recover for the last Anchor Point she knew they both still must face. She could sense him dreaming—perhaps remembering since he had some of her timeless power in him again.

With Vincent sleeping under the canopy of his conduit, Renata followed a stone staircase that had appeared next to the tree since her last visit.

She could smell the saltwater at the top of the stair, and as she came to the last step, she could see through the crystal-clear water to its farthest depths. It was a cenote.

Old limestone statues, broken and covered in bright saltwater plants, lay at the bottom of the clear water. The shores of the cenote were covered in soft seagrass. Wide-leafed green plants created a hedge around the farthest bank, and several tall moss covered boulders separated this secluded spot from the rest of the expansive forest that served as Vincent's conduit.

Renata gasped when she realized why. One statue remained above water. It was limestone, chiseled flawlessly but her angles had been worn smooth over time. It was a woman, resembling Renata, and held a pitcher in her stone hands. Her stone back was bracketing the other side of the white willow. From the pitcher, salt water poured forth, clear and cold from the Obsidian Sea of Aeor-Eterna.

"Sanguin-Aeor," Renata said, her hand covering her mouth. Their conduits were connected—she could feel the strength of this ancient grove, with its saltwater cenote and ancient buried statuary. This cenote had been forgotten in the Amaranthine, obscuring their undeniable link before she and Vincent traveled to Aeor-Eterna.

"Vincent, are you remembering me?" she whispered, her mouth open in awe at the bottom of the stair. White petals from a blooming fruit tree speckled the surface of the cenote, as if beckoning her to bathe.

She looked down at her body. She was filthy. Being reborn was not a clean process, no matter the dimension. Closing the distance between her and the cenote's edge in an eye blink, she dipped her toe into the cool saltwater.

She shivered. Suddenly, the water coming from the stone pitcher began to steam and turn hot, smooth limestone rising from the depths to create a shallow, stone pond for bathing.

"It's good to be the Queen," Renata said and smiled.

As Renata was squeezing the last of the water out of her hair she stilled, sensing a presence at her back. His.

She turned. Her green eyes bore into Vincent, her skin still slick with water. Her hair looked almost black when wet. He had not noticed before.

"Renata," he whispered, pausing at the bottom of the forgotten stair. "It was not a dream... You survived." He fell to his knees, gazing at her in the cenote.

"Renata-Aeor," she replied, shivering. The trees parted in a gentle breeze, allowing sunlight to pierce the canopy and shine directly on her. Backlit with golden honey light, her dark hair became rimmed with gold. She stood up.

She emerged from the cenote, steam wafting off her skin. Her wet hair spiraled in the humidity, drying in the sun and reflecting the deep red and golden tones he had seen before. She stood over Vincent, who remained kneeling in shock at the base of the stair.

"*Sanguin-laeth,*" Renata called to Vincent's mind.

He moved suddenly, faster than she anticipated. Her breath hitched as he stood behind her, embracing her.

With delicate fingers, he moved her hair, bending her head to expose her neck. He trailed kisses from her earlobe to the base of her throat. She exhaled, smiling. He felt the tremendous power rolling up inside her, energy coiling and begging for release.

"You are more than you were," he said between kisses. "When I am near you, I can almost—" he sighed into her neck. "You are what I *remember*." He let himself bury his nose in the crook between her neck and shoulder. He inhaled. It was her scent, it had changed. She was iron and oxygen, time... still floral, but different. She still smelled of life, but she was no longer mortal—but *alive*—in the truest sense of the word.

"My hyacinth still blooms. Your fog is gone—you smell of clear skies, sunlight, and sea salt," he said, his lips brushing her throat as he spoke.

"Your poetry is prophecy." She closed her eyes, leaning into his embrace.

Vincent's predatory senses felt Renata's power flutter as she paused, relishing his touch. He let his fingers wind into her hair as he held her neck against his lips, his other hand possessively splayed over her abdomen, threatening to go lower.

"Is this what you remember?" she said, leaning into him.

He growled and nipped her earlobe.

"Ma louloutte," he hissed. "You first came to me as a wolf." He said into her ear, reminiscing. "The wolf and the warrior..."

Renata had a pleasant smile on her face, her head tilted back, she cut her eyes at Vincent. Experimentally, she took his hand from her abdomen and moved it to her apex. She drew in a breath, making a tiny surprised sound as he moved his fingers, exploring her.

He bit her neck without preamble, letting his fingers

glide into her—drawing power and giving pleasure in one movement.

"*Renata-Aeor,*" he voice was like honey in her mind.

"*To you I Bind myself and to you I am Bound,*" she replied, repeating the words he had said to her many lifetimes ago.

"*Blood is truth eternal, Sanguin-Laeth,*" he repeated, his fingers delving further into her. She gasped, her hips bucking involuntarily against him. "*Beloved—*"

"*Sanguin-Aeor. Blood is our oldest story-teller,*" she said. "*I am ready to tell mine.*"

He moved them, apparating to a soft grassy patch next to the steaming cenote.

She looked up at him, startled. Her lips were swollen, and her cheeks flushed. Her green eyes stared at him, bright and inviting. Her hair had dried, the length spilled over the ground like a dark sunburst around her head—contrasting against the vibrant green of the moss.

Vincent, struck by her beauty, kissed her once more.

His heated kisses wandered the length of her body. He paused at her breasts, holding one nipple between his fingers while he held the other between his tongue and teeth.

Once her nipples were flushed like her cheeks, he let his mouth and tongue follow the line of her torso, enjoying the feeling of her ribcage expand in startled gasps against his lips. He paused and bent his head when he reached her apex, as if in prayer. He kissed her slowly there, licking and seducing her core. Renata writhed against his mouth, and Vincent took the opportunity to lift her legs, exposing even more of her to him.

He relished himself on her, her knees drawn around his head. He lapped at her shores and drank from her seas. Drawing life force from her there enflamed his senses. Renata cried out in pleasure, her voice carrying through the glen.

Finally, Vincent sat up, unable to resist being inside her any longer. She looked up at him with a starry-eyed expression, her complexion dewy.

"*Make me yours,*" she beckoned.

He wasted no time accepting her invitation.

She spoke his name, feeling him enter her for the first time. Her emerald gaze burned into him and he felt unable to look away. Her eyes sparked with light, evoking the passion they both felt—confirmed with every component of their being—this was *right.*

He began to thrust, his rhythm slow at first, letting her adjust to him. He lifted her legs, nipped and sucked possessively at her toes—as if to remind her there was nowhere she could go he would not find her.

"I never want to be hidden again—" she said, seizing around him, breathless. "Vincent!" she moaned.

He lingered inside her, and moved her legs, bending them at the knee to deepen his possession. It was then she broke her stare, her eyes rolling back in pleasure.

"I will *always* find you," he growled. His canines protruded past his lips, his eyes glowing gold and reflecting off her dewy skin as he ground himself into her. "You will always be *mine.*"

He blinked, and moved her astride him. Both kneeling on the soft grass—he gripped her roughly, shuddering with pleasure, his breath ragged as she contracted around him in another orgasm.

"You like being mine," he teased.

She responded by seizing again, a sound of surprise bursting past her lips. Vincent groaned and felt his body shiver, as he ached for release as well.

She turned over, and he grasped her hips against him.

"I want to feel your body against mine," she whispered. She pressed her back flush against his torso. He eagerly cupped her breasts, pinching her nipples and holding her steady against him as he entered her again. She made a startled but pleasant sound in response. Winding a hand in her hair, he kissed and bit her neck—drawing her molten blood forth, her core spark.

"Louloutte," he said, his skin glittering with the infusion of her power. He drew forth more of her spark, intending to drain her to the limit before reimbursing her.

She groaned, pushing against him with need.

"Patience," he whispered, his body clenched. He bent her over then, thrusting in and almost completely out of her in rapid strokes. He gave her all of himself, one hand possessively gripping her hip—the length of her long hair coiled in his other fist as he felt her power and pleasure rise with his.

She cried out, her breath reduced to gasps. Vincent was fully glowing, his Elder light roaming his body like a vapor, circling around hers, Binding her to him.

"I am yours," she said. *"And you are mine."*

"You are mine," he agreed. *"And I am yours."*

He swelled inside her, and it was like a dam breaking.

They were one.

He felt the warmth of his release inside her, the warmth of his Elder spark settling over her skin. The forge of their lovemaking Binding his life essence to hers once more.

He slowed his pace, stroking her back with his fingers. He bent over to kiss her shoulder, moving the hair that had clung to her face as he ravished her.

She turned her face towards his and he kissed her—his tongue claiming her mouth and pushing past her lips. A satisfied sigh echoed in the back of her throat, even though he felt her body tremble and tense with anticipation and need beneath him.

He broke their kiss, to look at her, their faces only inches apart.

"*We are one, Sanguin-laeth.*"

She groaned with pleasure, and he, still buried inside her, found his rhythm again.

VINCENT LAY with his head on Renata's belly, listening to the absent strum of her heartbeat for the first time. Renata drew her fingers gently through his hair. They had just finished swimming in the cenote and eating ripe fruit from the trees before collapsing in each other's arms again.

"*You are mortal no longer,*" he said after several moments of silence, a shadow of sadness in his tone.

"*I was given a mortal life, and a destiny,*" she replied, her hand still wound in his wet hair.

"*We are Blood Bound,*" he said into her mind. "*Sanguin-Aeor... It has been that way since...*"

"*Before the Future War,*" she said. "*You were still human Vincent, when we first met. Chosen by the Elders, stolen from your original timeline the moment before your death.*"

"Human," he said, lifting his head. His hair was still slick with water from the cenote. He leaned forward to gaze into Renata's face, letting his hands glide over the planes of her forehead and into her hair.

"I was mortal...once. Long, long ago," he said out loud, agreeing with her. "When I am near you... everything is clear."

Renata cupped his face. "Then always be near."

Vincent smiled. "That is my intention."

"They *took you* from me," she said, her voice hard. "I knew they would and that even if we resisted, they would conquer all of Aeor-Eterna, eventually. I would be too weak then to keep you from their grasp."

"Was this when you Bound me to you?" Vincent said, stroking her face with his fingers. "I don't remember it exactly, but I can *feel* it." He placed his hand on Renata's chest then, casting his emotion into her. Her eyes flashed in response, their bodies levitating a few inches off the ground. Vaporous light wound around them, bright sparks bobbing in the smoke, slowly igniting and dying out.

"Yes," she whispered. "I Bound you to me—in secret, in the ways of the Elder, in ways that even they could not undo." Her hair floated around her face as they both stared at each other, hovering above the glen.

"Our conduits confirm this," he said, as if to assure himself. "The Binder and the Bound."

"I am eternally yours." She wrapped her arms around his chest, turning her face up to kiss his mouth.

After a few feverish moments, Vincent broke away, as if distracted by something looming in the forest beyond.

THE PILLAR, AMARANTHINE LOOP

"**W**e must return to Sid at once," Vincent said, looking back at Renata, his eyes round.

"What?" Renata sputtered.

Dark clouds moved in, and the light inside the forest dimmed. Even the white willow seemed to darken as thunder rumbled in the distance. Lightning struck a high branch of a tree nearby, and it fell to the forest floor, only a few yards from the cenote.

"Trackers," Vincent said and held Renata tight against his body. She felt the wind rush past her face, the glen disappear beneath her.

They apparated back to the cottage, appearing by the front door. Renata rolled away from Vincent, feeling slightly dizzy as she sat up.

"Still not used to that," she wheezed, propping her hands on her knees.

Sid appeared next to them.

"*The Gate energy has drawn them to us,*" Sid said plainly.

"*Gate energy is not usually their foremost quarry. I fear Aldric had his hands in this*—" Vincent responded.

"*But the Aldric they know is gone*—" Renata interjected, her eyes flashing gold with the memory of absorbing his spark.

"*They will want retribution,*" Sid said, looking at her. Their eyes lingered on her, as if absorbing the tremendous change that had occurred with her in a single glance. Sid's eyes inflated, and darted over to Vincent. He gave a single, shallow nod.

"Retribution?" Renata sputtered, looking up from the ground, unaware or unconcerned with the private conversation Vincent was having with Sid, bringing the Tardigrade up to speed. Her hands were still braced against her knees. "It was a gift, what I did." She stood up finally, brushing off the seat of her jeans. They were black and tapered at the ankle. She had matching black Chuck Taylors on, with a blue and black plaid shirt. Her nails were their usual blue as well, a nod to the Renata from New-Ashemore that had caught Sid's attention in the first place.

"They will not see it that way," Sid said matter of factly, blinking. "Your presence still disrupts the balance of this entire dimension, and you absorbed the spark of their *leader.*"

She rolled her eyes. "Everyone's a critic."

"I will go and confront them," Vincent said, his stern gaze silencing her and Sid. "Ready the Pillar, we will close the branch in this dimension when I return."

"I'm going with you—" Renata said but was quickly cut off.

"No. You are an Anchor of Time," he said. "Now that

you have reconnected with your original conduit—Aeor-Eterna—you are a Quantum being of immense energy, in a super concentrated form. Your power, unchecked, could create a black hole—"

Sid nodded in agreement.

"What?" Renata said, looking between them both. "What are you saying?"

"Vincent is correct. You shouldn't leave the Pillar," Sid said. "Not until you learn how to properly channel and disperse your energy. Your power is so dense that a few minutes outside of the Pillar could cause a gravitational event that would deform spacetime."

Renata laughed, not knowing what to say.

"Besides, Aldric just sent a few of his minions," Vincent said, as thunder rumbled again in the distance, reminding them all of the Trackers attempting to penetrate the Pillar. "I can dispatch them easily. Then, we leave."

"Together," she said, her green eyes sparkling.

"Together," he replied, a smile appearing on his face.

Renata sighed, still not convinced she should stay.

"Vincent, you must ensure Aldric did not give anyone knowledge of Renata. We cannot risk her true identity being found out among the Trackers," Sid said, looking at her more critically. "I can read your timeline now—and it's not a line at all. The Forgotten Queen indeed. And you said I was superstitious!"

"I agree with those priorities." Vincent nodded, and turned to Renata before she could voice a protest. "The Undying Land's power flows through you, easily identifying you to those who know what to look for. Aeor-Eterna was used once, we cannot risk it happening again. I must go," he finished, resolute. He grasped her cheek, his gaze locking with hers. It was as if eternity stared back—his blue eyes held the truth of his unconditional love, and his grateful surrender to it. She was mesmerized, heat flowing from his fingertips. "I will return before sundown."

He let go of Renata, the heat of his touch still warming her skin. He turned to Sid. They exchanged silent but meaningful glances as the wind whipped around them, the storm increasing in violence as the Trackers persisted in penetrating the entrance of the Pillar. Vincent turned and began walking into the vines, headed for New-Ashemore.

"Wait!" Renata yelled, running after him. He turned from across the vine covered forest to look at her. "I don't like that you're already going where I can't follow. This doesn't feel right."

When she bounded up to him, leaving Sid some distance away at the cottage, she realized he had already changed.

His expression was dark, his blue eyes the deepest, and darkest she had ever seen. The briars seemed to snag and tug at her legs, keeping him out of her reach.

"What are you going to do?" She stumbled a little bit over one particularly stubborn vine.

Vincent cast his hand palm down over the vines, and they ceased interfering with her.

"You know why you cannot go." He smiled down at her, but it didn't quite reach his eyes. His eyes—where there was once only unconditional love were now clouded with pain, doubt. His gaze lost in a moment just out of reach. "This is a task for me, and me alone."

"Take Sid then," she said, pointing at Sid who stood

motionless at the edge of the clearing. "You might need help."

She shifted her weight back and forth on her feet, flexing and unflexing her hands, staring at him. She let Vincent feel her power thrumming beneath her skin, the reliable rhythm of it reminding him of her heartbeat—she gave him a small but urgent smile, knowing it would have that alluring effect.

"I am many things," Renata said, whispering. "But human is not one of them anymore. I am not fragile. You need not shield me from danger —"

"Ma louloutte," he whispered back, letting the phrase carry a drop of his deep affection. Renata shuddered, feeling the warmth of his desire heat every part of her, turning her limbs to honey.

Vincent's hand cupped her face, a gesture of familiarity that flushed her cheeks, reminding her of their fervent reunion in the glen.

Looking into his eyes, she realized she didn't know what she would do if something were to happen to Vincent —again.

"There is something—waiting for you on the other side of the vines, I can *feel* it," she sputtered, her extraordinary senses confirming her words. Tears welled in her eyes. "It's the Anchor Point, I know it. Please, Vincent. What if you forget because of the Amaranthine? *Don't go.*"

"Shhh," Vincent said absently. "Shed no tears for me. I face Trackers quite frequently, there is no need for tears. If this is the Anchor Point then you know I must face them. It's an irrevocable event, Binding space and time."

Renata shifted her gaze toward the abandoned

lamppost.

"Light that lamp, light it with your Elder-essence. Bind it to your life force. The flame will let me know that while it's still burning, you're okay. Can you do that for me?"

Vincent's eyes penetrated Renata. Scorching—that was the intensity of his gaze.

"Is that your only request, Sanguin-laeth?" Vincent said. He lifted his hand from her cheek and extended it toward the lamppost. Vines and briar receded, curling in on themselves unnaturally until they merely wound around its base.

A blinding, white light popped and sizzled inside the glass pane of the lamp. A small flame emerged, illuminating the ground. Renata turned her eyes again on Vincent.

"Kiss me," she said in a hushed whisper.

He looked at Renata, his expression frozen—as if he could still time with a single glance. She thought for a moment he would say no, he was so stoic. Then he leaned his head down, his mouth finally finding hers. She could sense his bridled desire as his tongue gently parted her lips.

Thunder rumbled again as Renata let her fingers wind into his hair. She stood on her toes to fully reach his mouth, while her other hand grasped his neck, her fingers drawing him deeper into the joining of their mouths—as if she could somehow force him to stay by means of only kissing him forever. She felt his strong arms encircle her, pressing his body against her.

They broke their fevered exchange. Vincent slowly backed away, involuntary breaths seizing his chest—the breath of desire, the breath of lovers.

Renata was flushed, not only from the kiss but from his heat—it was as if the air around them had gone up a few degrees just by proximity to their passion. She felt weak-kneed, almost forgetting the dread and anxiety she felt from the idea of him leaving the Pillar.

"*Stay—or you could forget your claim on me. We could be lost to one another again.*" The thought burst out of Renata's mind like lightning. It echoed between them like the after-glare of a bright light, quivering and shrinking into the dark. She felt her lips form the word "stay" but remained silent, waiting for his decision on whether to remain or go.

He gave her a heavy look, aching with restrained desire. His face remained ineffable and still as stone. She felt his heat retreat gradually, like the sun dipping over the horizon.

"You are *mine* and I don't want you to leave," she said. "Please."

He drew himself close to her within the blink of an eye, as if he had suddenly made a decision. His arms encircled her and he buried his face in her neck, inhaling her scent. She felt the pulsing of her power quicken with every caress of his hand.

He hoisted her against him then, pressed her into him, let his Elder-light warm her skin as he slung one of her legs up and around his hip. The wind seemed to still around them, the thunder suddenly far away.

"I am *yours*," he whispered. Renata felt Vincent's hands gripping her and she shuddered with desire. "Civilizations would rise and fall, nebulae bear stars, those stars ignite and fade as supernovae before I could perfect... loving you. You are like no other—" his voice broke, and Renata leaned forward, kissing him. He cradled the back of her head, mahogany curls spilling out between his fingers. His tongue slid into her waiting mouth, and he consumed her with a kiss that left no part of her unaffected.

She whimpered, a hushed sound in the back of her throat. A chord of longing strummed inside her. She lusted unapologetically for his touch, but somehow he stepped away.

She stood alone, flustered. Her mouth rosy and swollen from his kiss.

"Look to the lamp, beloved," Vincent said, the wind lashing his hair back from his face. He nodded, indicating the lamppost, burning bright in the twilight and trees. "You will know I am safe, as long as that burns."

Renata dared to break her gaze from Vincent and stole a glance at the lamppost. A robust flame burned clear and bright inside its singed glass walls. She smiled weakly and turned back to him.

But he was gone. A wall of briar and thorn obscured the clearing where he had stood as thunder finally gave way to rain.

Renata sank to her knees, the steady downpour soaking her hair. Her shoulders shook as a moan tumbled out of her throat. She could not tell if she was crying, her tears impossible to distinguish in the rain.

Something is about to happen that I can't stop, she realized, shuddering. Renata covered her face with her hands and caged her breath, squelching the racking sob that was swelling in her lungs.

She wept, illuminated by the abandoned lamppost at the edge of the Pillar. But she was not alone. The vines of the Pillar surrounded her, and in the hush of the evening, they too felt her sorrow.

NEW-ASHEMORE, AMARANTHINE LOOP

Vincent felt the drift of time like a warm breeze on his face.

Thorn, stalk, and leaf—a shimmering illusion —swirled around him like smoke as he finished exiting his Pillar and stood in real-time.

His eyes refocused. Colors outside the Pillar were bright and immediate. A memory of the sun, however complete, was merely a memory. Here, colors were alive. There was active light—light only eight minutes old— reflecting and refracting on all the surfaces in this dimension, in time ever-moving.

Four Trackers greeted him as he emerged from the bramble.

Vincent looked through their bodies. He gazed intently, focusing on the Tracker spark that swelled in the deep recesses of their cells. In this way, he never saw their physical bodies and avoided the reminder that they were once human. Once perhaps as human as he, Vincent realized.

Now, they were merely undead puppets—the Trackers wore the shells of once-humans, forever counting the intangible total of all things in the Universe.

"*Sanguin-laeth*," the Trackers snarled the word like a cursed epithet. He winced at their twisting of the Elderaen word for endearment, one that he had only recently won back from shame and grief. They spat at his feet, sullying the phrase with their repetition.

Vincent rolled his shoulders back, his palms open and crackling with blue energy. He faced the four Trackers, looking through them to confirm their spark.

"You have committed no crimes and may leave," Vincent said with authority, his eyes alight with Elder energy. "If you continue interfering with my Pillar—"

"We don't care, Elder," the smallest Tracker spoke up. "We are here for balance." This Tracker had taken on the body of a pimply faced boy, just after he had crossed the cusp of puberty. Sensing the body's youth, Vincent felt a shadow of passing sadness that the human had died so young.

"I am here as well for balance. My Pillar has been in this dimension a longer span than your spark gave the last breath to that body." Vincent replied.

"Aldric sent us," a large Tracker spoke up. This one tall but hunched with age slowly looked Vincent up and down, anticipating his reaction.

Vincent's eyes flared a blue-white energy that also sizzled and crackled from his fingertips.

"Aldric is not here," Vincent said. "Leave now, while you have the chance."

"Aldric says you have a human, who traveled by

Quantum Glass. The human brings imbalance and should be destroyed," the smaller Tracker said.

Vincent's hand flashed, and the blue-white energy circled around all the Trackers and himself, creating a perimeter of Elder-energy around them. They were impeded from any escape and also disguised from any outside interference.

"Your parlor tricks don't scare us, *blood-slave*," the third Tracker said, her voice musty and bitter. This Tracker appeared to be a middle-aged woman with bleached yellow hair and smoked a cigarette through an open hole in her neck.

"There is no mortal, not any longer—"

"And that is your crime," the small Tracker interrupted Vincent. "You break your oath, your penance from the Future War. Your are commanded to destroy your Pillar. And you are hereby banished from this dimension."

Vincent raised an eyebrow. "I actually have no problem with this gracious offer—"

"It is not an offer! It is punishment!" the haggard, yellow haired Tracker said.

"I refute the judgment," Vincent said slowly. His hands, palms-out, were cringing with bridled blue-white energy. "Let it be known, I never broke my oath."

"Then you are a *liar* as well, blood-slave!" The smallest Tracker released his spark into Vincent like a flash flood, hoping to overload him with his core energy. The small Tracker's strategy hinged on the immense surge of Tracker spark causing the Elder to lose cellular cohesion for a small span of time—he intended for Vincent to scatter like sand.

All the hair on the small Tracker's head stood up, and

his hands burned, as his power arched like lightning and plummeted into Vincent's chest.

Vincent closed his eyes and let the atoms of his physical body absorb the Tracker spark. His hunger vibrated, greedily absorbing the energy being harpooned into his chest. Vincent realized an Elder who gluttoned on mortals regularly would have been gravely affected by this blow.

Finally, Vincent's abstention was an advantage.

When Vincent opened his eyes, they were dark red—the color of submission to his intrinsic malice, his insatiable need to consume. His face was still, but a low growling sound caused pebbles and detritus to rise off the pavement.

Eventually, the hungry must eat.

Within an eye-blink, he had the small Tracker in his grasp. With nimble savagery, Vincent lifted the Tracker off the ground, bringing his small body up to his eye level.

Vincent glared at the small Tracker's face—as he snapped his neck. He did it easily, like a bird wing in cat's claws. He tightened his grip further. Out of his other hand, he manifested a blue-white knife of Elder energy. With a swift stroke, he divided the Tracker's head from his shoulders. The head rolled slightly on the uneven pavement.

Blood splashed liberally over Vincent's hands, arms, and face—his crimson eyes never wavering from the rest of his prey.

The tall Tracker, his old eyes gleaming with the heat of the fight, put his hands up in defeat.

Vincent directed his blue-white Elder force at the tall Tracker—with a turn of his fist bringing the Tracker to his knees.

Vincent looked down at him, his face a mask of calculated rage, splattered with fresh blood.

"Watch while I kill your Tracker siblings."

The cigarette-smoking Tracker ran toward the outer most limits of the perimeter of Elder energy. Her skin seared and sizzled at the wall of Vincent's power. The Tracker turned in desperation, but like a nightmare Vincent was already there. With nowhere to go she yanked her soiled collar away from her throat, offering him her neck.

"I know what Elders want most," she wheezed. "Take this, with my request of mercy." Vincent's crimson eyes muted with dark smoke—an Elder spark of dark energy—anger and rage broke through his hunger. It was all the time the yellow haired Tracker needed to summon a surge of her own spark. She imagined it as a blade and swiped delicately, like a surgeon with a scalpel, across Vincent's torso.

He gripped his midsection, molten Elder blood flowing and coating the ground like lava. The Tracker cackled and seemed to grow taller—only it was Vincent plummeting to the ground, in shock. In a fraction of a second, on his way to the pavement, he grasped her lower jaw and pried it away from her neck. Her cackle was suddenly muffled by wet gasps and then silence.

This left two Trackers.

Vincent turned his crimson gaze—the Tracker's jaw remained intact in his hand, her lower bicuspids pressing into his palm. He stood up, numb.

He concentrated on his abdomen, blue-white energy

healing his body. His tissue fused as if there had never been a wound, his Elder energy healing him.

He directed his attention to the tall Tracker on his knees. This Tracker had a blank and harrowed expression, the blind fear of an immortal suddenly realizing that their time had run out. He walked over to the tall Tracker, dropping the mutilated jaw on the ground before him.

"There were four, where is your fourth? After that it is your turn—"

The tall Tracker smiled, raising his chin and pointed over Vincent's shoulder.

A girl stood there. Gone were her plaits of dark hair, instead, her hair had been cut awkwardly, in torn chunks all over her head, in some places grazing the scalp and the skin beyond. Slender hands attached to nimble arms, covered in bruises.

What stared back at Vincent had once been human, but no more.

He knew she once had gray-green eyes, but now they were clouded and white—rotten and blind with the Count of the Ledger. Despite this, he would have recognized them anywhere. Those were her eyes.

"No," Vincent muttered. Was he laughing? Or was it the Tall Tracker behind him? Were they having a good laugh at the absurdity of it all? Trackers could not use the body of a Blood Orphan. This couldn't be *her*.

"The last service I must perform." She broke her long silence, her voice cobwebbed and broken.

"Your Blood Light was in Aeor-Eterna," Vincent heard himself say. He willed himself to look into her, to only see her Tracker spark. Instead, he felt the heat of his eyes bear the image of her, how she had been used, the heaviness of her physical presence choking him.

"The Amaranthine exacts a heavy price. You probably no longer even know that you are in one, trapped in your own illusion of time," she said.

"It is not possible for a Tracker—" Vincent managed to say. He kept talking, his words desperate to disprove what stood before him. "Elaria died in the Future War. Her Blood Light remained in Aeor-Eterna."

"Vincent," she said. "Do what you've come here to do. I am why you came, I am why you stayed. I was all that ever kept you here—starving, alone, and repeating this grim discovery every thousand years. End my suffering, leave this place. Break free of the Amaranthine!"

She enunciated every word, every syllable an epoch as it resounded in his ears, so terrible was it to hear.

"Do not speak her *name*," Vincent snarled in warning, his Elder canines bared. The name, the last thing that was his, he clung to with a ferocity. He would defy the Universe to keep at least the sanctity of her name.

Blue-white energy swirled like a blizzard around his hands, crackling and arching back into his body.

"Elaria," she whispered, defying him. "I am what is left of her."

Vincent's eyes widened. It was more than he could bear.

"NO," he shouted. The tall Tracker behind him stirred, attempting to break free while Vincent was distracted. His bridled energy, encircling his hands, sprang forth with his fury, his sorrow. The seething blue-white energy snarled and hissed as it arched like lightning through the air and into the face of the tall Tracker. The flame on the Tracker's flesh was white-hot and incinerating—

Without realizing it, Vincent had turned the tall Tracker to dust.

The ground burned beneath Vincent's feet, his rage so profound. A thousand years of emotions crashed over him, sweeping all of his coherent thoughts away. The knowledge of his sister in servitude to Aldric for a repeating millennia inside an Amaranthine burned his mind, his eyes crackling with light. His body became transparent, like glass glowing incandescent, singeing the air. He floated above the ground, buoyed by his heat.

He floated toward her. Her eyes were wide, but not with fear.

"Aldric served as an obscure prison guard in your time loop. You followed him into this mirror dimension because of me. You forgot your Sanguin-laeth, your beloved, and all they did to you in the Future War because of me... Perhaps the latter is a blessing."

He didn't respond. He approached her slowly and caressed her cheek. Her skin blistered beneath his touch.

"Blood is the raw consumption of truth, Sanguin-Aeor," she said quietly.

"Blood is our oldest story-teller," he whispered back. He felt his heart breaking, despair attempting to douse his anger. Her white eyes closed, and she turned her head, exposing her neck. His nostrils flared, the predator within him stirred.

"Now you will always carry my story brother," Elaria spoke. "And you will remember your own."

He enveloped her in his arms then. He was like the sun,

his heat the combustion of grief, rage and unchecked Elder power. His hands were hot brands on her skin but she did not flinch or cry out. She surrendered into his embrace, her skin becoming flame and ash as he buried his teeth in her neck—devouring her until she was nothing. Nothing at all.

THE PILLAR, AMARANTHINE LOOP

It felt empty in the cottage without Vincent. Even though his library—with its multitude of books and overcrowded shelves—still smiled cozily at Renata and Sid as they walked through the front door.

Renata froze, looking at the library in a different light since her return from Aeor-Eterna. The library was Vincent's only remaining attachment to his memories. The Amaranthine had obliterated the rest. She stared, turning over the thought that Vincent did not even recall that he kept a library as a defense against the Amaranthine anymore.

"I will make tea," Sid said, and vanished without waiting for Renata's response. She had been silent since Sid had collected her, prostrate and crying alone in the woods.

Clanging the old metal teapot against the sink, Sid filled it with fresh water and placed it on the stove. Then they began scurrying around the kitchen for mugs, sugar, and cream. Renata stood numbly in the doorway to the kitchen for a few moments before exiting. She didn't have the strength to remind Sid that she wasn't human anymore and tea wouldn't work to soothe what conflicted her now.

Bright ribbons of twilight were beginning to recede from the trees. Renata sat in Vincent's wingback armchair and stared out the window at the fading light of the evening. The chair had been Vincent's favorite when he took a break from the old tomes and star charts.

Her eyes unfocused, as if hypnotized by the lamppost staring at her from the darkening forest. The lamp light reassured her Vincent was okay. Still, the weight of time and distance grew heavier as the sun set. Renata felt the tugging thread of—*What? Nostalgia? Fear? Longing? Like a memory. Yes... Anchor Points are like time's memories. He must be in the Anchor Point now.*

She felt their connection tremble, siphoning some of their conduit's power.

Sid was still clanging around in the kitchen. An unexpected tear rolled down Renata's cheek. She smeared it across her face and pushed her hair back from her shoulders in one fluid gesture.

"He's in pain," she whispered to herself, realizing it was Vincent's emotions she was experiencing. "One thousand years of..." She shuddered to herself. Something was wrong.

She sat forward as the last rays of sunlight disappeared through the trees. *He said he would be back by sundown*, she thought to herself, her anxiety blossoming. *How long can an Anchor Point be?*

Torn from her thoughts, she swore out loud as the lamp flickered and died out, the light only a smoldering ember behind the glass.

Renata stood up, banging her hands against the bay window, her eyes squinting into the twilight.

"Sid!" Renata shouted. "Vincent is in trouble!"

She heard a ceramic mug shatter on the tile floor in the kitchen. It was a violent, clattering noise followed by an uneasy silence.

In an eye-blink, Renata left the bay window and apparated to the kitchen. The kettle on the stove was whistling, the water finally boiling for tea. A broken teacup lay on the floor, but Sid was nowhere to be seen. She shook her head and both the kettle and broken tea cup vanished.

"Sid?" Renata turned, scanning the kitchen. The Tardigrade's shared psychic link was cut. She could sense its absence. Sid could no longer project and manipulate the physical world without the link to Vincent.

Renata bit her lip. "The hearth," she said, recalling that Vincent had transferred Sid's physical body to a glass ornament on the hearth before they left for Aeor-Eterna.

She had not been able to re-establish her connection with Sid—they were likely attempting to assist Vincent. Left with no other choice, Renata apparated to the hearth, grasping the hearth stone for balance. She looked up, spying the glass.

"Gotcha," she said, turning it over in her hands. She looked across the open room to Vincent's desk. The satchel was on it, as well as various other sundries from the tent they had shared during their travels to Aeor-Eterna.

Apparating to Vincent's desk, she picked up the bag, thumbing through its contents. Her book, with the golden hieroglyphics and the red cover, was still inside. She placed the glass orb against her forehead, attempting to reconnect with Sid.

"*I need your help,*" she thought urgently, reaching out. "*I need you to help me channel some of this energy so I don't beat up space-time too much. I can help Vincent, but you gotta help me get to him—*"

The orb glittered in confirmation, but Sid made no audible reply.

"*Good enough,*" she replied.

Renata burst out of the cottage door, the vines receding from her as she stepped onto the grass of the front yard. She looked back at the cottage, feeling something final about leaving the Pillar this time.

Then she pressed on, into the forest, the winding vine and vegetation parting so that she could easily walk through. She vanished into the woods, bound for New-Ashemore.

43

NEW-ASHEMORE, AMARANTHINE LOOP

"**B**lood is the raw consumption of truth," Vincent remembered.

It was daybreak, and the sleeping streets of New-Ashemore were empty. The crisp morning air still had the night's chill clinging to it, despite the arrival of the early morning sun.

Vincent walked naked but for a bright and ethereal light, his raw Elder spark flowing and cascading off his back like wisps of golden smoke. The store fronts and boutiques framing the street reflected his glowing body in their darkened shop windows, indifferent to the raw, ancient energy smoldering before them.

"*So much of a life story can be read in blood. Now you will always carry my story, and remember your own.*" Her voice needled Vincent. He squeezed his eyes shut, muttering her words to himself. He opened his eyes, hands shaking. His Elder body quaked with power, surging and testing his limits. Vincent held his trembling palms to his face. It was then he noticed the stain of blood on them.

Suddenly, a figure appeared before Vincent on the street, literally occurring out of thin air. A beat passed, and the two figures surveyed each other. The other figure was only discernible by its silhouette, the sun pinking the sky behind it.

"So, this is what an Amaranthine looks like," the backlit figure said finally, its features non-distinguishable.

"This is not an Amaranthine," Vincent growled.

"You're right, of course." The figure replied and took a few steps forward. The light slowly illuminating her pale features and vibrant hair. "It is so much more."

She was young. She had red-orange hair that was pulled back in a braid that fell almost to her waist. He could hear the gentle contraction of her heart as it pumped blood through her body. She wore turquoise pajama pants with pink cats on them along with a grey sweat-shirt that said 'UNC-Ashemore Bulldogs'. Her feet had pink slippers with a sequined 'P' on each foot.

The young woman glanced at Vincent's bloody hands. She moved a strand of hair behind her ear, swallowing and licking her lips. She reached inside her sweatshirt, producing a slim metallic case.

"I don't know if you remember—" she began nervously.

Vincent's expression soured. "Elders cannot forget."

"He explains this to you every time you both meet." The strange girl frowned, clearing her throat. "It is the effect of the Amaranthine. Elders normally have excellent memory because they experience time in the 8th dimension and..." Her expression changed, she paused, biting her lip in thought before continuing. "I thought the final loop would be different. I thought you would actually escape the Amaranthine on your own. You even went back to the Cerulean dimension!"

Vincent saw the woman's face clearly in the ashy light of the early morning. He hadn't deduced immediately that she was more than just human—her heartbeat, her pulse was a steady buzz in his ear. He stared past the edifice of her body and looked within, to the recesses of her cells, searching for a clue to who or what she could be.

His eyes widened. She held some of Aldric's spark. The energy in her blood was unmistakable.

And yet it couldn't be.

Renata had consumed the Tracker's spark, and yet here was the Tracker's spark, in a different body. A *living* body.

"Renata destroyed him —" Vincent sputtered. He held his hand to his head, the memories coming and going in his mind like debris in a rushing river. "Aldric!"

"No," she replied, the words penetrating Vincent's disbelief. "Aldric is your son. You and Renata—he is your son!"

"That is not possible—" Vincent trembled, his hands holding his head. "He used Elaria... to trap me..."

"Aldric is my father," the strange woman interrupted Vincent. "He and Renata started the Time Lab. They searched many Amaranthine Loops to find you—"

Vincent snorted, his raw spark causing the air to grow stuffy. "An Amaranthine cannot hold an Elder."

"Yes," she said. "You are not trapped here. You could break free of this loop. It is within your power, and yet you never leave." She smiled stiffly, eyes softening.

"Why would I stay? What could ever keep me here long enough to forget," Vincent snapped.

"I don't think you meant to stay *here*," she said. "But in Aeor-Eterna. But then Aldric abducted Elaria. Her Power couldn't leave Aeor-Eterna, but her body could..."

Vincent felt the words ring true. He felt his power hush and grow cold, the realization that his wait was over. Vincent remembered, falling to his knees.

"Elaria," he whispered. "I have released her."

"Yes," the woman said, her blue eyes glowing with sympathy and cutting away in shame.

"And I am the last part," Vincent whispered. His eyes shedding a golden tear.

The woman remained silent, her expression stone and unreadable.

"Are you ready to go?" she said at last.

Vincent was about to answer when he turned to see Renata, hands braced against her knees, satchel draped across her shoulders.

"*STILL* NOT USED TO THAT," Renata sputtered. "I mean I feel like I'm going to vomit, I seriously might—" She looked up from the ground, hands still braced.

"Renata..." Peaches whispered in awe, her blue eyes round like marbles.

Vincent began to glow, his body giving off heat like a forge as he absorbed some of Renata's density and power so that she wouldn't break the current dimension apart.

"Thanks," Renata said, blinking. Confident that her

presence wouldn't destroy the dimension, she stood upright, squinting at the backlit figure of the woman. Her eyes widened with recognition.

"Peaches," Renata said, her voice hushed. "Aldric told me... you'd be here."

"Yes," Peaches said, her words careful. "I came for Vincent. To take him from the Amaranthine."

"Were you always a Tracker?" Vincent asked, his voice shifting, brow pinched in thought. "Renata, the energy coming off her is *unmistakable*." He growled the last word as his anger sparked anew.

"No," Peaches said simply. "I have never been a Tracker."

Vincent's brows furrowed, confused. Renata could feel his thoughts, distraught and blurry.

"It is a human before me now, and yet, it is not a human. It is also a *Tracker*," he replied, power gathering in his open palms.

"Vincent..." Renata said, clearing her throat. She stood behind him still, observing the effect of her energy. Her eyebrows were drawn in concern. His thoughts were erratic, and though he was successful in channeling her energy, his mind was deteriorating—becoming unstable. "Vincent," she repeated, but he wouldn't look at her.

"I always calculated that you could survive to this point in the Amaranthine," Peaches blurted out, cutting through the awkward silence. She held up a device. It was thin and metallic, like a cigarette case.

"Amaranthine?" He scoffed, shaking his head. "This is not an Amaranthine."

"Vincent," Renata said. She tried to touch him, but he shrank away.

"I need you to trust me," Peaches said, making eye contact with Renata.

"You say that as if we have a reason not to," Vincent snarled, his eyes thinning in suspicion. He began to manifest his Elder power. It blossomed from his palms and spread like a sphere of golden energy that sparked and writhed around him.

"I don't have time to explain. But trust me, it's the only way," Peaches said.

Renata ignored Peaches, her eyes drawn to Vincent. Her hand was only inches from the golden smoke and light emanating like a bank of fog over his shoulders, she grasped his hand through the fog. The golden vapor whispered over her arm, burning and crackling as her own power answered the conflicted, aching energy of the Elder. Her *Sanguin-laeth*. Her beloved.

Inside the churning ball of glowing Elder light, she felt as Vincent's arm became molten, drawing on the power of their combined blood. She felt the firm grip of the knife handle form in his hand, the cool tip of the blade press against her leg.

It happened in an instant. Vincent turned, faster than Renata knew he could, aiming true; he plunged the knife into Peaches' abdomen. She made a startled sound, raspy and animalistic, dropping the metal case onto the sidewalk.

"No!" Renata screamed.

Vincent looked into Peaches' eyes.

"I need to see them!" Vincent shouted, and then more

personally into Peaches' face. "The light go out—the Tracker spark drain away..."

He shuddered. Renata felt his horror, the macabre give of Peaches' abdomen as the blade sank into her gut.

"*Renata*," Peaches spoke in Renata's mind, as blood dribbled out of her mouth. "*Grand-mére. Use the case I brought, it will make him viable for transport. You must leave before...*"

Vincent twisted the handle. Peaches' mouth twitched involuntarily. Renata heard herself crying, a jarring sound from far away.

"You used her to get to me," Vincent said, his voice shaking. His light had dimmed, and he looked like a human man—his skin ashen and covered in a cold sweat, his eyes glassy and confused. He held Peaches in a clammy grip, her body spasming in his arms. Vincent screamed into her face, delirious. "Trackers only inhabit corpses. *Let her go!*"

"Vincent," Renata said, grasping his shoulder. "She isn't a Tracker."

Vincent let go of the knife and held Peaches' slack body. Peaches, weakened by Vincent's attack, was helpless in his arms.

Renata's face felt flushed, her hands shaking—white light crackling and sparking from her fingertips. She stood, stumbling away from Vincent and the broken body of her granddaughter. Numbly, she examined her tingling hands.

"*Use the case,*" Peaches said telepathically. "*You can take him from the Amaranthine with it... Complete... the mission...*"

Vincent kept his arms around Peaches' limp form, holding her until her gasping breaths became shallow and quiet, her body still. He looked at Renata in confusion.

Dimly, behind Renata's enormous sense of grief, were the inklings of terror and disbelief at Vincent's calculated actions. She scanned the pavement, looking for what Peaches had described. She spotted it on the sidewalk, discarded like a piece of trash by a parking meter. She picked it up, examining it. She ran her fingers across the edge of it until she heard something click.

Suddenly a shrill sound emanated from it. It was so grating it made her eyes water. She doubled over in pain, dropping it back onto the sidewalk as she cupped her palms over her ears.

"*Y*OU NEED TO LEAVE *NOW*," Sid intoned loudly in Renata's mind.

Renata was wincing. Her eyes squeezed shut while the piercing note reverberated in her mind, chattering her teeth and making her mouth water.

"*Not without Vincent*," she managed to think through the noise to Sid.

The sound stopped.

Renata slowly opened her eyes.

A gritty, fine dust was covering her face. She smeared it from her cheek, examining it between her thumb and forefinger.

It was then Renata saw that her hand was covered in blood. She removed her other palm from her ear and found it too had a slick coating of blood. Her ears felt wet as blood dribbled down the sides of her neck.

She wiped her hands on her jeans and stood up, groggy and disoriented.

"*Renata. Take Peaches and the case and GO NOW,*" Sid exclaimed. Renata shook her head, in confusion.

"I can't leave now, I have to get Vincent," she muttered. Her voice was gravel.

"Vincent is... with you," Peaches managed to whisper from the ground.

Renata squinted through the fine dust clouding her vision.

"Vincent will always be... with you... Sanguin-Aeor," Peaches said, choking on the words

"*Renata, take Peaches and the case, flee! To your Gate,*" Sid implored. "*That is what your survival depends on. GO!*"

Renata stumbled, Sid was shouting into her mind, the Tardigrade's voice clanging in her head. She tried to fully open her eyes, but the gold grit kept getting stuck in the corners like dirt. It floated up her nose, making her sneeze. She coughed, rubbing her eyes.

"Vincent," Renata sputtered, still confused. Her tongue felt thick in her mouth, her thoughts syrupy and dull in her mind.

"*He is there,*" Peaches said telepathically.

"What did you do to Vincent?" Renata snarled, her skin blossoming with a radiant heat. She glowed with warning, the world coming into focus at last.

Peaches said nothing, her eyes distant. Renata looked down, the metallic case was on the ground again. She picked it up, examining it and finding another button on the side to open it.

All of the gold grit levitated off the pavement, Renata's

skin, and clothes. The golden dust swirled like a funnel and rotated furiously until every last speck was sucked into the case.

"*It was your idea,*" Peaches said telepathically, holding onto consciousness by a thread.

Renata gasped, finally comprehending—the gold grit. *That* was Vincent.

"*Go. Now.*" Sid repeated.

Renata screamed instead.

All of the shop windows lining the city street shattered and exploded onto the sidewalk. Waterfalls of glass cascaded onto the pavement. Streetlights and stoplights shattered too, the bulbs fizzing and sparking. The small saplings planted along the sidewalk shook violently until they shredded themselves into a confetti that blew across the pavement.

"*None of this pageantry matters, Renata,*" Sid said. "*Aldric has been absconding with him, piece by piece at the moment of his destruction in every subsequent loop of the Amaranthine. Can't you see? This is a rescue!*"

"*How can you know that?*" Renata said.

"*Aldric has been here before,*" Sid said. "*I see the evidence of his energy all over this Anchor Point. There is memory here.*" Renata looked down at the body of Peaches. Her face was slack, her eyes were hooded, and her breathing shallow.

Renata realized then Sid was right. Aldric sent Peaches to finish the rescue that he could not.

"He knew he would not survive to the final Anchor Point," Renata said out loud.

"*He sent his only child,*" Sid said. "*To finish what he started. For Vincent. For you.*"

Renata shook her head in denial, but a cord of power within her thrummed, echoing and agreeing with the Tardigrade's words.

"But why must he be destroyed?" Renata said, finally able to speak.

"*Anchor Points*," Peaches replied. "*Cannot be changed...unmade...*"

"That's unimaginative," Renata replied, her gaze turning dark. "I look at you and know the ways in which I can change and unmake you."

Peaches shuddered as Renata let a shred of her fury roll over the psychic link they shared.

"*This moment, Vincent's immolation, is an Anchor Point*," Peaches protested in Renata's mind, her breaths audibly wet and strained. Stiff, Peaches checked a holographic clock that projected from a shimmering bracelet at her wrist. "*We have six minutes before your presence in this dimension goes critical. Renata—*"

"*He has not been destroyed*," Sid said. "*Get the case and take it with Peaches to your Gate, Renata-Aeor. Or lose all that you are Bound to.*"

Renata bent down, touching the cool metal of the case with her fingertips. She picked it up, examining it in her hands. She pressed it to her forehead as if to confirm the wild possibility it was Vincent.

"*Ma louloutte,*" he said, his voice the sound of ash and regret. Renata's eyes flung open.

"Vincent," she said, her voice aching. She placed the metallic case containing his remains in the satchel with her book and Sid's Tardigrade orb.

Renata helped Peaches to her feet. With a shaking

hand, Peaches pointed to an abandoned, crumbling building at the end of the street. The second floor was completely gone, only broken cement and exposed iron beams.

Renata turned to look, shouldering Peaches against her.

"It's your Gate," Peaches whispered. Blood colored her teeth and leaked down her chin. "Do you remember... how to use it?"

"Yes," Renata exhaled, hoisting Peaches against her side. Peaches stifled a yelp, clutching her side.

Renata looked over at Peaches. Her granddaughter was resilient. Renata was sure that Vincent had fatally stabbed her—she had barely been breathing earlier. Peaches looked at Renata, discovering she was observing her.

"Do you know... what I am?" she asked, wincing and clutching her side.

"You are my granddaughter," Renata said slowly.

"Yes," Peaches nodded, her eyes glistening. Her skin was drenched in a cold sweat.

"You're going into shock," Renata said. Her eyes flashed as she took in her granddaughter. Vincent's knife had not been ordinary. It was made of a dark Elder power —blood magic—and it was festering. "Did you know your mother named you?" she asked, attempting to distract her.

Peaches gasped in surprise, and then inhaled sharply in pain, her eyes watered.

"Aldric never told you," Renata said, continuing to talk. "That's a shame. Your mother Eva—what a beauty."

"Maman," Peaches whispered. "No... He never said..."

"Your name was her last word," Renata continued talking. "Ganymeade brought his first harvest of peaches over, to celebrate your birth—"

"*Go... Hurry... to the Gate*," Sid admonished weakly. Sid was only just a whisper in her mind, becoming obscured by the radiation leaking out of the Quantum Gate that was near.

Renata paused, looking down the street to a row of abandoned buildings. *The Gate was in the salon. I worked in a salon.* Renata shook her head, her mortal life seemed like pieces of a jigsaw puzzle, moments and sentiments now only scattered scraps of a prologue compared to all that she knew now.

"The Gate... is just over there," she said out loud. Peaches nodded drowsily. Her complexion while already pale was beginning to turn sallow.

Renata apparated with Peaches to the front of the abandoned building. Peaches fell limp and unconscious against Renata as a surge of power reverberated through the dimension, originating from the Gate.

"*The Anchor Point... is shifting*," Sid said. "*Your Gate and your power are about to turn this dimension... atomic.*"

Renata blinked, realizing she had only seconds. She levitated before the Mirror. Shards of Quantum Glass suspended like puzzle pieces merged into one pane before her. Renata shifted Peaches' unconscious body over her shoulder, freeing her hands. She extended her arms, palms out.

Suddenly, as if it could wait no longer, light flooded out of the Mirror and into Renata's waiting palms.

Her fingers curled, arms bracing against the onslaught of Quantum energy. Her shoulders flexed, her muscles trembling as she engaged with the Gate energy. Her expression remained calm, her gaze determined and staring beyond the Glass, beyond the Amaranthine.

Amidst the sizzle and crackle of energy surging out of the Gate, a door through time opened once more.

Renata locked eyes with her own reflection. Green eyes, haunted and electric stared back before giving way to the image of the Time Lab, a glass paned room she had built in another lifetime—anticipating a moment in this one.

She spoke into the Gate, instructing the Quantum energy as she stepped into the Glass.

"Close the Gate once I have passed to the other side—"

Adjusting Peaches on her shoulder, Renata stepped through the Mirror, the Gate glowing and yawning wide, the Time Lab still waiting beyond the threshold.

The Gate closed behind her after she stepped completely into the Quantum Mirror. The pieces of Quantum Glass that had fused to create the portal shattered into dust. That dust billowed in a sharp breeze that gusted through the exposed roof of the building. The remaining flecks scattered into the scraps of what was left of the second floor that had fallen many years ago and still lay sprawled awkwardly on top of the first.

Streaks of morning light pierced the horizon, and the hour passed into late morning.

The Amaranthine had fallen, at last.

44

LUPUS OBSIDIAN, CERULEAN DIMENSION

Renata felt as if she were falling at great speed. She readjusted Peaches and the satchel against what she assumed was her body. Her senses were on fire. She glimpsed the image of the Time Lab draw closer and closer through the brilliant display of Quantum energy. Chaotic bursts of light flew at her vision, and she began to feel disoriented.

She put her leg out, as if she were still walking forward. She felt her other leg follow her—her entire being condense into the space between Gates.

One step... more, Renata tried to think. She concentrated on her perspective before she entered the Gate. The Time Lab could only be a step away.

Suddenly, she exploded onto the other side of the Gate. The feeling of gravity and the hardness of the floor as her torso and elbows ricocheted off it were a surprise. Peaches followed, her body limp and heavy on top of Renata, landing with an audible thud.

The satchel tumbled through last. It skidded to a halt beside Renata, and the top flap fell open and Sid's glass orb rolled out—speeding across the spotless floor of the Time Lab, only stopping when it met the opposite wall. Vincent's metallic case also slid out of the satchel, moving with some speed due to its sleek metal, but stopped just short of a shoe covered foot.

Renata grunted. Every muscle ached. She could feel her energy and body adjusting to the temporal dimension she was in, as well as the gravity. She sensed something familiar about it.

"Well, well," a voice said, interrupting her thoughts. "I come for one stowaway, and a whole crew arrives."

Renata squinted, looking up for the source of the voice. Three beings dressed in ornately decorated interstellar jumpsuits bracketed her and Peaches on the ground. They held energy-blasting weapons in their hands and had other more primitive weapons strapped to their body. They all had ivory skin and ivory hair, steel gray eyes and held themselves with a predatory superiority.

"L-D2130," the voice said, it belonged to the one in the middle. She noticed then his ears were large and pointed, like an elf's. "Be a gent and get her off the floor." When he spoke, Renata saw that he had large canines, like an Elder. She arched a brow, curious. He wore several silver and crystal rings along his long ears. His hair was ornately braided with a thread that sparkled, giving him an icy glow.

Renata got to her elbows, still flat on her stomach. Her skin was steaming, Quantum energy hovered over her bare skin like sunlight glistening on water. She pushed up, letting Peaches' body roll off her.

"Better yet, Lachlan," Renata said, her face looking up from the floor. "Get Peaches to the medical suite."

Strong arms bent down and collected Peaches. Renata finally stood up, crossing her arms over her illuminated body that was nude but too bright to stare at for any length of time.

"Now," Renata said, looking up. "What's this about stowaways? I'm somewhat of an expert." She scanned the motley crew before her. They too were familiar. Golden sand illuminated a pane of glass behind them. Renata's pupils dilated, understanding and absorbing all the information Centius was relating. Her eyes rounded, looking at the intruders once more.

"Numerean pirates," she said, in awe. "I read about them in your library, Vincent, but never thought to meet any!"

"Your powers of observation," the leader began, but didn't finish. Renata looked at the Numerean and identified him as the voice ordering Lachlan earlier.

"Do you know where you are?" Renata said, her face becoming serious.

"A ship," the man said. "In space. Containing my long-lost property. Isn't that right, L–D2130?"

Lachlan appeared at the Time Lab's entrance from the medical suite. His brows were low, his mouth tight.

"Aye," Lachlan said finally. "I was once your property. But now I belong to Aldric Lemair. You left me for dead, he found me. Your ownership is forfeit."

"He's not here," the man, who was clearly the leader, interrupted. The Numerean to his left held up an instrument, scanning the Time Lab. The leader glanced over at the results of the scan, projected from the screen. "Negative. He doesn't even *exist*."

The same pirate pointed the instrument toward Renata, scanning. Several readouts came up. The leader's brow arched, and he lifted his chin, as if to defend his statement.

"Maybe we can start with names." Renata's voice boomed, echoing off the panes of the Time Lab. "And then we can discuss how living beings can be another's property?"

"He is not alive," the lead Numerean pirate said. "Look at him. He's more machine than *meat*."

"That's your standard," Renata re-crossed her arms, her light slowly dimming. She noticed her reflection on the Time Lab's many paned glass walls. Her body was covered in a fine layer of soot and dust from the abandoned building that contained her most recently used Quantum Gate. She also had a fair amount of Peaches' blood on her. Her eyes turned back to the lead pirate. "Meat or machine. That's how you identify living beings?"

"You won't distract me. LD-2130 is my property, his enhancements are proof of my investment. He is part of my *crew* and the only name you deserve to know. He was a gift from the CEO, and you have no authority to question my *ownership*—" The leader adjusted his stance, hand on the hilt of his weapon. His companions followed suit. The lead Numerean continued. "My scanners picked up on his transponder signal in the Alpha Quadrant. I followed him to this ship. He seems to think he belongs to this place—" The Numerean pirate leader put his hands up. They were stark white with long fingers. He wore a silver ring on each one and had long sleeves with ornate embroidered cuffs that looped over each thumb. "Which I accept. It means it is mine as well, by succession of ownership."

He put his hands back down, resting them on the energy-weapons in his side holsters.

Renata nodded, silent, listening. Her expression remained neutral.

"You picked up on his signal?" she said finally, when the leader fell silent. "As in, he was broadcasting to you?" Renata looked over at Lachlan. He locked eyes with her, giving a curt but slight shake of his head.

"N'auch," the space pirate swore. "Every member of my crew gets a transponder, so if they get lost, I can find them." A feral smile spread across his face, revealing his large canines that grazed his bottom lip. "I'll put one in you too, just as soon as I get you over to my—"

"That will be quite enough, thank you," Renata said, uncrossing her arms. She lifted her hand and made a quick gesture in the air. At the same time, a small bead of technology ripped out of the base of Lachlan's neck. He fell to the floor in a heap. The blood-soaked transponder came to rest in Renata's outstretched palm.

The space pirate blanched but said nothing.

"Is this the transponder that indicates your ownership?" The pirate nodded slowly, his granite eyes round, but his face tight and unrevealing. Renata squeezed her fist for a moment and slowly opened her palm. She turned her hand over, letting the dust that was once the Numerean transponder whisper onto the Time Lab's immaculate floor. "Ah, now you see? Without that transponder, he's over fifty percent *meat*. That means he doesn't qualify as property to a Numerean anymore. Now, you could ask him if he'd like to become crew but as you can see, he is unavailable right now—"

The Numerean said nothing, instead, firing his energy-weapon at point blank range. Renata ducked. She missed the electric blast by a hair's length as she swooped down. Without hesitation, she kicked out her leg, causing the lead pirate to stumble into the other two like bowling pins.

The Numerean's initial fire penetrated part of the dais and the ship's primary controls. Several alarms began to shriek, and the lights flickered in the Time Lab. The ship shuddered.

Distracted by the commotion, Renata sensed only just before the hull of Lupus Obsidian glanced the upper atmosphere of Aeor-Eterna—the gravity and friction causing a drag and pressure buildup on the already compromised hull.

The joints suspending the glass panes in the Time Lab groaned before sparks erupted at all the seams. The glass cracked where the energy blast from the Numerean had ricocheted off the dais. Golden sand began sprinkling onto the floor. Renata's eyes rounded.

"Vincent!" she swore. She dove for the case that had landed at the space pirate's feet, but the lead Numerean was closer.

"What's this then?" he said, holding the case above her in his hands. His eyes thinned to slits. They both realized he finally had her at a disadvantage. Renata did nothing to conceal the fear in her eyes as the Numerean held the only key to Vincent's resurrection.

"Mine," Renata stood, her eyes glowing. The Numerean stood back a pace, taking her in.

"You *are* a rare beauty," he said, not taking his granite eyes off her. "What planet did you originate from, hmm? I haven't seen the like of you before, mistress. I would so like to see you among the treasures of my Menagerie." His voice was butter-soft as he bent his head down to better train his eyes and gun on her. He plucked something from a hidden compartment at his wrist.

"You won't leave this ship alive," Renata whispered. "That's a rare beauty."

The pirate said nothing, firing a slender dart at Renata's neck. Meanwhile, his two crew mates opened fire on her as well. Renata froze, bracing for their impact.

After a moment's hesitation she looked up. The dart was suspended in mid-air. The laser blasts merely streaks of light, paused in flight.

Time had stopped.

"Finally," she whispered.

Acting quickly, Renata plucked the metallic case from the pirate's hand. She opened it, dumping the golden sand on the floor where the rest was streaming out of a fractured glass panel, creating a small bank of golden debris at its base.

At first, it remained only a pile of dust. Then, the energy started to spark and swirl within it. The fractured glass panel completely shattered as all the golden sand flew forth, blowing in a controlled, small spiral until a man's profile began glowing within it.

Renata sank to her knees, watching with bated breath.

The sand blew faster, coalescing more and more on the

glowing shape within. The light was brighter than a star, melting some of the glass panes next to it. Renata covered her mouth, watching as Vincent took form before her.

Finally, he stood, his skin flawless and sparkling. His chestnut hair hung well below his shoulders, his muscled arms slack at his side. His head was pointed down, his eyes closed. As the last bit of dust swirled around him, collecting and coalescing to his chiseled body, he looked up.

His eyes were blue. They glowed, seeing Renata. She remained seated, her mouth open in shock, her green eyes leaking tears.

"Renata," he said, his voice honey.

"I found you," she whispered.

Then time began again. An explosion rocked the farthest corner of the Time Lab.

"Right," Renata said, bouncing up from the floor. "Can you land the Obsidian?"

"Of course," Vincent nodded, his blue eyes flashing, and several of the alarms silenced themselves. The ship groaned, and certain panels began to spark and chirp as the dais started to repair itself.

An energy blast glanced off Renata's shoulder. She turned, her shoulder still smoking from the blast. Her skin was unmarked.

"I was curious—" she said, looking at the stunned Numerean pirate who had just fired the blaster. Their leader looked particularly horrified. "—If your weapons could affect me. Seems I have my answer now." White light glittered over her skin, sparks of energy forming large glowing orbs at her wrists. She began to levitate, speaking an ancient language that caused the air in the Lab to grow humid and thick with heat.

The second in command spoke into a comm unit on his lapel, and suddenly the trio glowed and disappeared, ion-transporting back to their ship.

Renata dimmed, and jumped to the ground. The writhing white electricity that encircled her entire form only moments ago disappeared with an audible pop and flash of light.

She blew a few wild strands of hair out of her face, scanning the ship before another explosion rocked the Time Lab. Renata and Vincent both shifted on their feet as the hull groaned and buckled under the strain. She looked, wide eyed at him.

"It will be a controlled crash landing," he said, his blue eyes glowing. Glowing blue strands of electricity surrounded some of the more badly damaged panels, allowing Vincent to steer their heading.

"Just get us home, *Sanguin-Aeor*," Renata said, her eyes sparking with desire. She let some of her power unfurl, merging with Vincent's, assisting him energetically to land the Obsidian.

Satisfied Vincent had the Obsidian under control, Renata leaned over and picked up Sid's glass orb from a pile of debris from the fire fight. She held it to her forehead, closing her eyes.

Lachlan! Sid practically shouted.

Her eyes sprang open.

"Right, I should be attending to Lachlan—of course!"

Sid's orb still in hand, Renata apparated to Lachlan—who remained unconscious at the Time Lab's entrance.

He was surrounded by a dark pool of blood and nanite fluid.

Renata knelt, feeling the warmth of the liquid coming from Lachlan as her knees touched the floor. Realizing she would need both hands, she flung Sid's orb at Vincent. It defied gravity as it floated across the Time Lab to his outstretched palm. Never taking his eyes off the dais, he deftly injected Sid's orb into the panes where his golden sand used to reside. The panes re-fused, filling with water that emitted a pearly, opalescent sheen. Renata smiled, happy that Sid was more secure.

She looked down at Lachlan then, and grasped his neck —searching for the wound. His A.I. protocols chirped, a hologram projected from his empty eyes indicating he was in medical stasis. Renata gripped the back of his neck, slick with blood and nanite fluid—where the transponder had been inelegantly ripped from him.

"I'm sorry," Renata said through clenched teeth. Golden light glowed from her palms and whispered like vapor into Lachlan's wound. Soon his eyes opened.

"Renata-Aeor," he said, correctly. His eyes glowed green as he oriented himself, the quantum computer in his brain assisting.

"Status report?" Renata smiled, relieved. The golden light from her hands glimmered down his torso and enveloped his body. The warmth of her energy caused beads of sweat to appear on his forehead.

"Peaches remains in stable condition," Lachlan began, his voice cracking with relief. He gasped for breath on the floor, a wave of emotion overtaking him. Renata nodded, closing her eyes and extending her energy out. She felt

Peaches regaining strength only a few yards away in the medical suite.

"The wound she suffered from Vincent at the unraveling of the Amaranthine requires its own complex energetic healing," Renata said after a moment, opening her eyes. She looked at Lachlan. "Rest and our return to Aeor-Eterna will revive her."

Renata cocked her head to the side, squinting. She moved her hand from the back of Lachlan's neck, his wound already closed by her energetic healing. She placed instead her hand over his right eye, where his nanotechnology had been surgically implanted.

"I am sorry," Renata said, feeling the coldness of the technology. It grated against her power like iron against stone. Removing her hand, she looked over his body with pity. "I didn't know how cunning an enemy the CEO was. I thought you and Vlad would maintain the truce while I was... away." She paused. Her most recent mortal life felt like a grain of sand on a beach, along with all the other lives that came before. And yet it was a precious lifetime—they all were—but she felt keenly those who suffered because of her absence, her dalliance with time. Renata caught Lachlan's eyes with her penetrating gaze. "What were you even doing on a Numerean ship—"

"Peaches died," Lachlan whispered, distraught. "So I turned myself in, as a war price. Too late I realized Vlad had been compromised. He watched as the CEO sold me as meat to the Numereans. Eventually Aldric intercepted me, the Vellinor had left me for dead —"

"What?" Renata's eyes thinned to slits. "But you're not a Quantum Manifestation."

"No," Lachlan said. "Aldric was piloting the Obsidian. Centius had not yet taken control of those duties..."

"Lachlan," she shook her head. "I'm so sorry. How long were you on the Numerean ship?"

He stared at her. "Long enough."

She nodded, looking down.

"Before I went into cryptobiosis Aldric said the truce held, and that Charing Cross survives."

Renata inhaled, her eyes rounding with hope.

"How can Peaches be here?" he barked, his voice sharp. "How was she here all this time?" He sobbed, putting his hand over his face.

Renata shook her head, relaxing from her kneeling position to sit on the floor completely next to Lachlan. Her shoulders slumped, and she put her hand on his forehead.

"Aldric knew his time was finite," she began softly. "He knew he would be giving up the mortal life I gave him by saving his father from the Amaranthine. He suffered much loss in his one human life..." Renata paused, thinking. "Alas, mortals pass their mortality onto their offspring. Perhaps his daughter's fate was one that he couldn't bear." Renata paused again, turning her head in the direction of the medical suite, her eyes distant. Finally, she continued. "She is a living Quantum Manifestation, plucked from her moment of death like the Blood Orphans of old. Aldric effectively gave her immortality. Certainly you can sense that, without your nano-bot's help."

"Yes," Lachlan said, smearing tears from his eyes. Renata placed her hand on his shoulder.

"She's no longer the woman you married, Lachlan-Aeor.

She's a dream of her, that has traveled through the veil of dimensions, through time. Yes, the kernel of her is Peaches Lemair, but she has been long dead in Charing Cross. She doesn't know her past because she didn't live it," Renata said, standing up and offering her hand to Lachlan. "Not in this dimension. You and Chloe don't exist in this dimension, so she has no memory of you. Do you understand?"

"But she left the ship," Lachlan said, batting Renata's hand away. He stretched and sat up on his own. "She traveled to the Amaranthine. She is *real.*"

"Of course she's real!" Renata laughed, chuckling at the idea that real and not real were different. "And as far as the Amaranthine, Peaches left one incubated, pocket dimension for another—the Time Lab to a time loop. As well, her lineage is of the Amaranthine so you might say she was, in fact, Aldric's back up plan." Renata put her finger on her chin, thinking out loud. "A beloved Quantum dream, to keep him sane as he completed his life's work. *Aldric — mon destin, mon étoile. Dormez bien, mon fil.*" She turned, looking across the Time Lab at Vincent.

"Doesn't matter, Renata-Aeor," Lachlan said, interrupting her reverie.

She broke her stare and turned, nodding at Lachlan. He got to his feet, she followed his lead. He looked down. Renata was almost a head shorter than him.

"I forgot how short you are. That's why I have to stoop so much around here." Lachlan growled. He looked across the Time Lab at Vincent as well, pausing. Finally he looked back at Renata. "I still love *her,* and I would no matter what those Numerean pirates did to me, in any dimension, in any time. As far as I'm concerned, she's *my wife* and the mother of my only child."

"As a Quantum Manifestation, her entire life was this vessel, and her father Aldric," Renata said. "Her entire being has been uprooted and changed already. To tell her she lived another life before this one—*has a daughter*—and her husband has been in cryptobiosis her entire tenure aboard the Obsidian... Aldric kept all of his from her for a reason. Manage your expectations."

Lachlan swallowed hard, his eyes glittering. The muscles in his neck flexed with the effort of his words. "Then, I am ready to serve aboard Lupus Obsidian, as her guardian, just as Aldric requested."

"*If we leave the Cerulean dimension and return to the third she may regain her memory,*" Vincent thought to Lachlan and Renata. "*And Lachlan is correct. Vlad is compromised. With all haste, we must go to Charing Cross.*"

Lachlan gave Renata a piercing look.

"Aldric sacrificed everything to bring Vincent and I back. You and Peaches are both his legacy. Come," she said, leading Lachlan to the broken dais where Vincent stood.

"A new mission," Lachlan said, observing Vincent steer the ship, despite the controls being damaged by the Numeraen firefight earlier.

Renata smiled up at Lachlan, grasping his shoulder and Vincent's.

"Where to, ma louloutte?" Vincent said, turning his head. He smiled. His arms were raised in the air, ripples of blue light sparking from them to the navigation unit that steered Lupus Obsidian.

"Aeor-Eterna, *Sanguin-Laeth,*" Renata said emphatically,

looking deeply at Vincent for a long moment. Desire crackled in the air between them. "We can use my Henge to get to the third dimension—to Charing Cross. To Chloe." She paused, looking at Lachlan and then back to Vincent. "Our adventures are only just beginning... "

AFTERWORDS

Thank you for reading! Please consider leaving a review. Reviews help indie authors find new readers and get advertising. If you enjoyed this book, please tell your friends!

Sign up for the author's newsletter! Check out tinacapricorn.com and sign up for Bella's Cosmic Newsletter to stay in the time loop for Book 2 in the Forgotten Queen Series, coming in 2021.

Want to be even more involved? Find Tina on Instagram.com/tinacapricornwrites where she posts daily updates on all things writing, progress on Book 2 in the

Forgotten Queen Series, her Discord book club with virtual meetings, and more!

Feeling like a super fan? Consider supporting the author on Patreon.com/tinacapricorn

ACKNOWLEDGMENTS

Once again, please consider leaving a review wherever you purchased this book, it is so incredibly helpful to indie authors!

This book was written over six long years. Nothing is created in a vacuum and I am so grateful for all the assistance, advice, beta reads, recommendations of my family and friends.

First thanks go to Adam, my moon and stars, the love of my life, for always telling me like it is and that I'm loved and that I can do it. This book was made possible by your love. I made the right decision.

Special thanks to my mother, Mary, who helped me get a new computer back in 2014, as well as my cousin Jim who advises me on all technical devices.

Thank you to all the Kates and Katie's specifically: Kate Mulderig, and Katie Anne Towner for reading my first-first-first draft and being enthusiastic and encouraging enough for me to continue.

Thanks Mom and Liz for reading that early draft too. It was not good but it was something! Thank you to all my beta readers! Thank you Leah from those early days. Thank you Susan and Veda! Special thanks to my ARC Team: Shannon Krenek, Katie Anne Towner, Nichole Esmon, Kristin Wagner, Jenn Berlin, Kimberly Myers, Marisa Blake, Blue Hughes, Amanda Reid, S. Sabuchi. Thank you ARC and Launch Team!

Thank you clients, who became friends, for always supporting this. Special thanks to Katie and Sara, your support over the years has had lasting impact on me—in big and small ways.

Thank you to all my 'shop-wives' at the salon who watched me write, and edit, and rewrite and edit—a special shout out to those of you who read chapters in the break room I left for feedback. Your sisterhood got me here, and I love you all for it. Thank you Amanda, Blue, Jenn, Marcy, Tiziana, Kitzi, Jill, Ginger—for being a part of my chapter before this one.

Thank you #writingcommunity on Instagram and Twitter. Special thanks to Elicia Hyder, who inspired to me to pursue this crazy dream. Special shout out to @Falafelpita, Sam thanks so much for the suggestion of 'Elaria'.

Sign up for my newsletter to stay in the time loop on all things Aeor-Eterna.

Tinacapricorn.com

CPSIA information can be obtained
at www.ICGtesting.com
Printed in the USA
LVHW021535011220
673138LV00016B/1816

9 781735 799704